BLACKTHORN WINTER

BLACKTHORN WINTER

Liz Williams

NewCon Press
England

First published in March 2021 by NewCon Press,
41 Wheatsheaf Road, Alconbury Weston, Cambs, PE28 4LF

NCP253 (limited edition hardback)
NCP254 (softback)

10 9 8 7 6 5 4 3 2 1

ISBN:

978-1-912950-78-2 (hardback)
978-1-912950-79-9 (softback)

Cover by Ian Whates

Text edited and laid out by Ian Whates

PART ONE:
A PTERODACTYL ON
THE MANTELPIECE

SERENA

Serena woke and did not know where she was. She should have been in her bedroom in her London house – not with Ward by her side tonight as he was in Berlin, in meetings for a film. But this was not that calm, airy room. A moment later, she realised that it was her own old childhood bedroom at Mooncote, the one that had remained hers and which she always occupied on her visits home. She could see the birdcage that hung above the window, and the old posters (a map of Narnia, for instance, now properly framed rather than bluetacked to the wall), and rows of bookshelves with her childhood favourites: Anne and Emily and Tolly and Will, and many more. Children who had seemed as real as Serena's three sisters, growing up, as real as her friends at school. They still did, Serena thought, blinking into candlelight. She could not tell where the light was coming from, either. There was no candle in evidence by the side of the bed, but the soft gentle glow was unmistakable.

The door to the room stood open and this was not right. Serena, liking privacy, kept the door closed whenever she was in bed at Mooncote. Now, however, she could see through into the hall and then, quite slowly, she saw that three women were standing in the doorway. She recognised them at once. They were not her sisters, Bee and Luna and Stella, but the spirits of the stars, the fixed stars which are always overhead in the night sky. They had haunted Mooncote, if that was the right word, for generations, since Elizabethan times, and Serena had known them ever since she was born, although they remained enigmatic, not childhood friends like the people in her books, but apart. She had seen them a handful of times in other places, but they seemed tied to the old Somerset house, rarely venturing beyond, save into whatever realm they occupied when they were not at Mooncote.

One of the stars was Capella, who had rocked Serena in her cradle and who seemed to take a particular interest in her. Sapphires gleamed in her hair and she held a sprig of thyme to her lips. Her pale green gown waterfalled to the floor. The second woman was, Serena thought, one of the Pleiades: her gown a crystal glitter and she carried a frond of fennel. The third was not one with whom Serena was very familiar: she

7

had only seen her a few times and it took her a moment to work out which spirit this must be. Aldebaran: the Eye of the Bull in the constellation of Taurus. She wore crimson, high necked and long sleeved. A string of garnets adorned her hair and she carried a thistle. She was staring directly at Serena, her dark-eyed face sombre. None of the stars were smiling.

"Hello," Serena said, uncertainly. She swung her legs onto the faded rug which lay beside the bed; her mother, Alys, had brought this home from Iran during some hippy trail trip back in the day. The star spirits said nothing, but Aldebaran strode forwards. Serena, startled, stood to meet her and the spirit clasped her hands. Aldebaran's hands were cool and rather hard, not like human skin.

"Ware the bull," Aldebaran said. As was often the case with the star spirits, the movement of her lips did not quite match her words.

"What?"

"Be careful," said the star, and the room began to move, spinning slowly at first and then faster and faster until Serena blinked with dizziness. She felt her hands released and sank back onto the bed. She was in the London house, back in her own four poster bed with the smell of lavender and roses still drifting from the unlit candles in the fireplace. Serena went to the window and opened the curtains, but clouds blotted out the London skies and not even the usual faint tracery of stars was visible.

STELLA

Stella was walking up Peckham High Street when she saw the angel sitting in the tree. Mid-December, speeding towards Christmas, and Stella's mind was on clearing the decks before going back down to Somerset for what her sister's boyfriend Ward had described as 'the festering season.' She had, therefore, been to see several people that morning, at Club 90, at the Hussey Building and Rye Street Rhythm, to set up some DJ-ing work for the New Year.

"Peckham's the new Dalston," her friend and agent Dejone Brown had said earlier that morning. "So they say."

"No, Dej, they were saying that four years ago. Then it was the new Hoxton. Now it's back to being the old Peckham."

"Maybe, maybe. Still bringing the punters in, though." He had swivelled in his chair and looked out of the window onto the grey roofscape. "Anyway, so yeah, you've got gigs at Club 90 in mid-January, and Rye Street a bit later on – nice money, too. Now before that, though, you've got a gig on New Year's Eve itself and they were very particular, asked for you specially."

"Where's that then, Dej?"

"This is the thing – I don't know. Around London somewhere, the client says, but not actually in town. The location's to be announced on the night."

"Exciting!"

"Are you happy with that? They'll send a driver. The woman sounded all right on the phone and she's a friend of an old mate of mine, but…"

Stella said, "Yeah, I'll do it. A bit old school rave style. I don't mind an element of mystery."

"I'll let her know, then." Dejone made a careful note. "Not long till Christmas, now. You going home?"

"Yes. My sister and I are driving back in a couple of weeks."

"'My sister and I.'" He rolled the words on his tongue. "Sounds like the Queen, ma'am."

"We don't live in a castle, Dej."

"Big house, though? You showed me a photo once."

"Bigg-ish. And I suppose it's quite old, but not like Norman castle style old. When are you going to come down? I keep asking you."

"I will come, one day. But it's tough getting out of London, finding the time. I'm like a clam in its shell."

Stella laughed. "You need to be winkled. With a pin."

Now, remembering this exchange, she smiled and zipped her parka up further against the winter chill. Today, however, was bright, with a high, cold blue sky that might betoken an overnight frost. Fingers crossed: December so far had been rather grey and wet. Stella, admiring the sky and navigating Peckham High Street with its litter and graffiti and people, was not expecting to see an angel, or indeed anything untoward. But then, dodging an abandoned cardboard box, she looked up and saw a tree.

It was full of lights. Globes of subtle mist drifted through its bare branches and it glowed as if it had swallowed a little sun. Stella, who knew her trees, could not identify this one and that alerted her to the fact that something was amiss. She was not, in fact, certain that the tree was even there: it seemed a bit out of place, too close to a wall rather than standing on the edge of the pavement in a neat rectangle of soil.

And then she saw the angel.

She assumed it was an angel because of the wings, which were black and white and folded. The angel sat with her legs crossed at the ankle, frowning at her fingernails, and she, like her wings, was monochrome. Her skin was night-black and her hair, which was braided, was moon-white. The braid seemed to have a life of its own, for the end was twitching like a cat's tail.

"Hey," Stella said in greeting. The angel looked up. Her eyes were black, also, without whites. They widened.

"Oh! You can see me. Bollocks."

"Sorry," said Stella. "I can pretend I haven't, if you like."

If anyone was startled to see a young woman talking to a tree, or perhaps to the wall, they did not show it. This was, after all, London.

"No, it's cool. I'll come down. I'll walk with you for a bit, if that's okay. I'll get my shit together first, though."

She slipped down out of the tree and descended, floating slowly, to the pavement.

"Right. Would you mind turning your back, please? I don't like changing in front of other people."

"Sure." Stella did so and contemplated passing taxis, blowing crisp packets and a random cat for a moment. Behind her, there was a flickering flash.

"You can look now. I'm decent."

When Stella turned she found a young woman in a hoodie standing in front of her, hands in the pocket of her jeans, which were ripped at the knee. Her feet were shod in Skechers. Her eyes were now human.

"So who are you?" she asked.

"My name's Stella Fallow."

"Cool. Mine is Mags."

"Mags?"

"Yes. Mags, that's me." She gave a little hop. "Ooh, twenty pee." She bent down and snatched something small and bright from the pavement.

"Don't spend it all at once," Stella said.

"Nah. It'll go in my stash. My mag swag bag. Where are you going?"

"Back to the Tube. You're welcome to walk with me."

They set off. If passers-by could see Mags, there was no sign of it. No one so much as glanced at Stella, bundled up in her coat. She preferred it that way. Probably Mags did, too.

"So what were you doing in the tree?" Stella asked.

"Oh, it's where I live. I've been there a long time. I remember when this neighbourhood was nothing but fields and trees. It was really pretty."

"Must have changed a lot, then!"

"Oh yes. But this is nice too." With a sweep of her hand she indicated the sooty Victorian frontages and the shoddy modern hoardings: *Kek Supermarket, Vijay's, RJ's Betting. We do Afro Hair. Peckham Goes Plastic Free. Prepaid Phone Cards for South East Asia.* Stella agreed. She liked Peckham.

"Lots going on here," said Stella.

"Yeah, all the time. Lots to look at, you know? I like looking at stuff. I like to see all the people. You know, the countryside is great but it can get a bit boring."

"I know what you mean. Cows."

"Cows, totally. So I think you must be the person I've been waiting for," Mags said. "I've been sitting up there all morning and no one has so much as batted an eyelid, so it's probably you."

"Okay," said Stella, nonplussed.

"In which case, I've got a message for you."

"Who from?"

"Yeah, I don't know, exactly. These things, you know, they kind of filter down the chain and it's not always clear where they start. It might be from – well, anyway. But I think this came via one of the geese, so it'll be reliable. Anyway, if it is you, you're to go to Southwark, on Friday night. To the boneyard."

"That's this evening. The boneyard! This does not sound good, Miss Mags!"

"No, it'll be fine. The geese are gathering. They'll look after you."

"Geese? Sounds like A Christmas Carol. What is this boneyard, then?"

"Behind the market. You know the market in Southwark?" The girl put her head on one side.

"Do you mean Borough?"

"Yes, the big market. With all the stalls. When the clock strikes six."

"I'll see how I feel."

"No, you've got to go," Mags said. "It's important, apparently. Top priority."

Stella felt a surge of irritation. This was not the first time this sort of thing had happened. It was a bit like being a spy. But she didn't want to take it out on Mags; it probably wasn't her fault. They were now at the entrance to the Tube.

"Give them this," Mags said. "Safe passage." She handed Stella a long blue-black feather, shining, oiled in the winter sun. Stella opened her mouth to thank the angel, but Mags was gone. Holding the feather, Stella looked about her. Apart from the stream of commuters there was no one there, only a magpie hopping about in the overspill from some rubbish bins. Stella put the feather carefully in her bag and went down into the underground.

BEE

Bee made more lists at Christmas than at any other time of the year, even cider season and summer holidays. They were pinned to the fridge with magnets, they littered the kitchen table, and occasionally their remnants were amalgamated into one big list and the originals thrown into the fireplace. Now, with two weeks to go, Bee sat chewing a biro and staring at one of these big lists.

Serena, fellow list-maker, had once asked her why she didn't just put them on a tablet or her phone, but Bee preferred paper and pen. It made it easier for her to keep track. She tried not to list things that she had already done, to make the list look more accomplished, but often failed. Now, she took the pen and drew a firm line through *church meeting*. Because that was about to happen and soon Bee would be on her way out into the wet cold of the night and down the lane and into the meeting room which joined onto Hornmoon church. It was a meeting about the Christmas flowers because Bee, in an unguarded moment, had offered to become a church warden.

"It's a bit hypocritical, seriously," she said to the vicar, who was new. "Since I'm not a Christian. Sorry."

The vicar waved this aside.

"I don't actually care. You believe in God, you told me. You go to church. Occasionally. I have *seen* you in the congregation." Kate flicked a swatch of turquoise hair back from her forehead and sighed. "More than I can say for most of this village."

"It's as much about the old building as anything else," Bee said, still apologetic. "I know that's not very – well, religious. I suppose you might say it was spiritual. I do believe in an afterlife, for example."

Difficult not to, when you're going out with a ghost. And when you can go and have a chat with your grandfather's spirit in the graveyard. And when your mum has once again buggered off into a parallel dimension. Bee did not, naturally, say any of this out loud. The vicar had already scandalised the more elderly part of the congregation by going to Harry Potter conventions, but there were limits to disclosure.

"That's still more than most people," Kate said. "Here's the key. I'll WhatsApp you the rota."

So Bee was now a guardian of the village's little arts and crafts church, and, as such, responsible for things like the flowers.

Before putting her coat on, she went into the long dining room and made sure the French windows were locked. The tree shimmered in the corner of the room, its familiar baubles and ornaments catching the light of the standard lamp and glowing against the pale gold wallpaper.

"It is a lovely thing," Dark had said when they decorated it. His face was a little awestruck, the black eyes wide. The pearl that hung from one earlobe shimmered dimly in the light from the tree.

"But you must have seen such marvels, when you were alive," Bee told him. She forbore to say, "Queen Elizabeth must have looked like a Christmas tree," fearing that he might take this the wrong way.

"Not such as this, at Christmas. Garlands and greenery only; rosemary and bay. Candles. Maybe ribbons in the houses of the gentry. And a tree, in the house! Such a thing, with its crown of stars." He shook his head in slight wonder.

"They became popular a couple of hundred years after your day, I think. Another Queen. With a husband from Germany."

Dark nodded vaguely. She knew that he was aware of the intervening years, but sometimes his memory seemed as ghostly as he himself, running from his mind like rainwater down a window pane. Bee accepted this. As long as he remembered who *she* was.

She hoped the cats would leave it alone. She had, one year, come home from the pub to find the new kittens swinging, like Tarzan, across the room on tinsel chains. The chains had not survived; the kittens, barely. But now both cats, Tut and Sable, were too staid and elderly to get up to such kittenish nonsense. She hoped.

Bee went back into the kitchen and put her coat on.

The lane was very dark, this moonless night. Bee carried a torch, which made the frost glitter. The thorn hedges had a look of iron. When she approached the part of the road opposite the lych gate, she paused for a moment, just in case her mother might step out of the air from the lych path, the corpse road that could take you into those darkly shining, chancy realms that lie alongside our own. But Alys did not reappear and, second time around, Bee refused to worry about her. Her mother was old enough to know what she was doing and she'd disappeared before. That first time, they had not known where she had gone and what she was doing. Bee remembered, with an internal shudder, the police enquiry, the articles in the newspapers, all the stress and worry and fuss. When Alys came back, they had been about to face the necessity of explaining her return to the authorities: memory loss and time in a women's refuge had been the favourite candidates. But then Alys had once more skipped, almost as soon as she had returned, leaving a note.

I'll be back for Christmas.

Don't hold your breath, thought Bee. She missed her mother; they all did. Yet Alys had also royally pissed her off: it wasn't the fact that she'd left her daughters twice – Luna, the youngest at twenty five, was expecting a baby of her own, everyone was grown up now – but that she hadn't told them where she was going, and where she was going was very dangerous. Bee, standing with her mittened hand on the latch of the lych gate, took a deep cold breath and tried to think of Christmas. It had to be said that she was not really feeling the festive spirit.

Inside, the church was, as usual, chilly. Bee kept her hat and coat on, but removed the mittens. She went into the small meeting room and found that the new vicar had installed an electric fire, but the stuffiness was welcome after the winter night. Kate looked up as she came in, wearing jeans and a sweater rather than her dog collar.

"Hi! Great, you've made it. Even if it's just us, I'm sure we can sort something out…"

But other people soon filtered in and Bee forgot her irritation with Alys and allowed her head to be filled with white chrysanthemums versus crimson, lilies and hellebore, ivy and bay.

An hour and a half later, she walked back out into the night. Her companions, including the vicar, were a little way ahead down the path. Bee's attention, however, was caught by a small blue light, azure-flickering among the tombstones.

"Sorry, Kate!" Bee called. "Forgot my scarf. I'll lock up. 'Night!"

She waited until they had gone through the lych gate, but she did not go back into the church. Instead, she followed the dance of the light to a tomb in the shape of a pyramid, overlooking the silent fields.

"Hello, Grandfather," Bee said. But to her surprise, the small star of her grandfather's spirit did speak and did not stop at his tomb, but fluttered on. "Okay," Bee said aloud. "I'm coming."

15

The light led her along the wall of the churchyard and down, following the slope towards the stream that ran along the other side of the wall. Bee frowned, because there was nothing down there of interest – no family graves or monuments – but then she saw that she was wrong. There was something there, huddled against the wall itself. Bee took her torch out of her pocket and shone it. Someone was lying on the frosty ground, bundled up in a mass of garments and unmoving.

"Oh God," said Bee. Thoughts of bodies and *Midsomer Murders* came, unwelcome, into her mind. More interactions with the police. She would need to call an ambulance… But then the figure moved.

With the little light dancing above her head, Bee cautiously knelt down and touched the person on the shoulder. The body jerked, then half rolled over and sat up. Bee found herself looking into the face of a girl, considerably younger than her sister Luna. It was a dirty face, with huge grey eyes blinking in the sudden torchlight, and an untidy crown of hair that made the girl look rather like a dandelion. Her cheeks were hollow. She whispered something that Bee did not catch.

"It's okay," Bee said quickly. "I'm a friend. Are you hurt?"

The girl grabbed her garment – a woolly shawl – and pulled it up to her face. She reached out and seized Bee's hand. Her fingers were thin and strong, but Bee had no sense of threat. The girl said something but it made no sense. It certainly wasn't English. Was it Welsh, perhaps? Bee didn't speak Welsh but she sometimes listened to folk groups from the Principality and it didn't sound much like that. Or maybe it might be Gaelic?

"She wants to go with you, I think," her grandfather's voice said.

"Abraham, do you understand what she just said?"

"No, I don't recognise the language. I don't know who she is. She's not a spirit."

"I wonder if I should take her into A&E?"

"I think you might find that she would just run away again. Look at her clothes."

They were definitely homespun and rough. Under the shawl she wore a kind of linen smock and leggings, made of strips like bandages. Her feet were bare and blue-white with cold.

"Well, I could take her home…" Bee didn't much care for the idea of having a stranger in the house, but then Dark would be there, and he might be able to shed some light on who the girl was. She might not be a ghost, but she didn't look very contemporary either.

"It might be best," her grandfather said. The girl wouldn't let go of her hand, although Bee did manage to make her relax her painful grip a little. Bee led her out of the churchyard, grateful that the rest of the flower arranging team had by now gone home, or to the pub. She said goodnight to her grandfather's spirit and as quickly as she could, marched the young woman up the lane and into the house. The girl pattered alongside, saying nothing, head down.

When they reached Mooncote, Bee put the kitchen light on and the girl gasped to see it. She looked around, wide eyed, then began to wander about. Occasionally she made a tentative move to touch something: a piece of paper, the oven knobs, the butter dish. When Bee opened the door to the hall and the spaniels, Nelson and Hardy, who had been illicitly asleep upstairs, rushed in, the girl gave a small squeak of fright, but then, seeing the wagging tails, embraced them. She sank down into the dog basket that stood by the Aga and put her dirty cheek next to Nelson's.

"You need food," said Bee. She thought for a moment, then poured a mug of milk and spread the heel of a recently-made loaf with butter and honey. The girl drank the milk in one go and wolfed the bread, gnawing it messily. Watching her, and looking at those sucked-in cheeks, Bee reached the conclusion that this was due less to primitive table manners, and more to do with missing teeth. Some of the front ones were visibly not there and Bee guessed that not all of her back molars were present, either.

She sighed. "Want some more?" The girl stared at her, clearly uncomprehending. Bee buttered more bread and handed it over and the girl ate it, but more slowly. One arm remained around Nelson, who appeared delighted. Always an affectionate, anxious spaniel, the sudden manifestation of a person who was prepared to hug him at length and who might moreover give him something to eat was a gift.

"All right," Bee said. She wondered whether she should run a bath for the girl, whose face was now noticeably cleaner after the washing she had just received from Nelson (Bee thought the honey rather than devotion was to blame for that).

But now that the dirt was removed, Bee could see that her skin was a faint, leafy green.

"Oh!" Bee said. An alien? Well, who knew, around here, but apart from this anomaly, the girl looked human enough. Bee frowned. Was it just a trick of the light? Somehow, she did not think so.

The prospect of wrestling the girl out of her clothes was obviously not on the cards. She did not actually stink, but she did smell: of woodsmoke and earth rather than body odour. Then the girl herself settled matters by curling up in the dog basket and going to sleep, instantly, like an animal.

Bee nodded, slowly. She stood at the kitchen door for a moment, looking for Dark, but there was no sign of her lover. Making arrangements with a ghost was always a bit hit and miss, time not running the same for Dark as it did for the mortal world. Bee had learned to accept this. She might wake to find him beside her in the bed or she might not. After some internal debate, she left the kitchen door unbolted, but did lock the door between kitchen and hall, just in case. She did not think the girl was dangerous, but she was a stranger in the house, and if she woke up with theft on her mind, there was nothing to steal in the kitchen except food and she was welcome to that. Bee left the bread and butter on the table and went, wondering, to bed.

SERENA

The alarm was going off again. Cursing, Serena swung her legs out of bed and flung on jeans and jumper over her nightdress, then pulled on her boots. This was the third time in a week and there had to be a fault with the mechanism. Why did these things always happen right before Christmas? Hopefully she could coax an electrician out of hibernation and get this fixed; she couldn't leave it shrieking away to itself all over the holidays and enrage the neighbours. Nightmare thoughts of having to drive back from Somerset to fix the alarm beset her. No one had complained so far but it was only a matter of time... Serena made sure she had all her keys and went next door to the studio.

This building, its plain whitewashed walls emblazoned with an enormous coat-of-arms mural, had once been a coachman's house. The mural was a relic from the previous occupants, a band and friends of her ex-boyfriend Ben, but it picked up on some piece of neighbourhood heraldry; the local pub was also called the Lion and Unicorn. Converted in the sixties, the studio, too, was owned by Serena's current landlady, Eleanor. Its skylight roof was ideal for a design studio and since expanding into it, Serena's fashion business had taken off enough to justify the admittedly astronomical rent.

The lion and the unicorn on the side of the building made Serena feel safer, but she was still nervous of going inside, just in case the place actually was being burgled. If Ward had been there, she might have been braver, but Ward, now returned from Berlin, had started learning his lines for a production of *Midsummer Night's Dream* next year and was back at his own house further down in Ladbroke Grove. Serena flipped the alarm panel open and punched in the code; after a nail-biting moment, the shrieking stopped. Serena let out a breath and trudged back to bed.

Once safely ensconced in the bedroom again, she found herself unable to sleep. She lay in the dark room, thinking over recent events. The split with Ben still lay heavily upon her mind. Serena and her sisters had initially been convinced that Ben had left her because of magic, a shadowy, murky magic practiced by a girl who was now dead. But her death had not shattered the spell. When Serena had returned to London after her last visit to Somerset, with Ward Garner, Ben's cousin and now her lover once more, in tow, she had tried to speak to Ben. But he seemed not to want to discuss it, clung to the story that it had been mutual, that they'd both 'found other people', that they had 'drifted apart'.

That had not at first been true but now, of course, Serena had made that a self-fulfilling prophecy by sleeping with Ward, and she had stopped being in love with Ward after their first time round, years before. He was a great friend, though. With benefits. She loved him, but she was squirming around the question as to whether Ward was in love with her; she rather thought he might be. Difficult to tell with a professional actor: if she tried to raise the subject, Ward just started hamming it up. If Ben no longer wanted to be with her, though – you couldn't do anything about that. Serena had learned the hard way that trying to persuade people into emotions just didn't work. Including herself. She had to respect Ben's decision, hard though it was. She still missed him, their connection, the understanding, brought so abruptly to a halt over a matter of days. Missing him irritated Serena; she wished it would stop.

All this went around and around in Serena's head until, sick of herself, she got up and made some tea. She would go into the studio as soon as it got light, and sort everything out then.

But that, as it turned out, wasn't going to be an option.

LUNA

Luna loved driving over the bridge. It was like flying and this was such a beautiful winter's day. Below, the Severn estuary: the vast river mouth meeting the sea, meeting the sky, with the shadowed blue hills of Somerset and Monmouthshire rising on either side out of the water and the humps of the two little islands – once hills, long ago before the sea came in – visible in silhouette. The white arches of the suspension bridge towered above them and, looking upriver, Luna could see the span of the second, older bridge and the blocky building that she liked to think of as a castle, even though she knew that it was actually Berkeley power station. She was always a little sorry when the towers had gone by and the road started to gently slope down towards the Welsh shore. Until recently, they would have had to slow down for the toll gate, but the tolls had finally been removed (long after the date originally planned, which was when the tolls had paid for the bridge) and now they were able to speed on through, past the *Croeso I Gymri* sign at the border and up to Lydney, following the curve and sweep of the river.

"Not far now," Sam said, at the wheel. "You still okay?"

Luna rolled her eyes. "I'll need to pee. Again."

He laughed. "I'll find a garage. Or a layby."

"We are literally, what, ten miles from Rowan's place? And I can't hold out."

"I'll find a suitable hedge."

He did so and Luna hopped out, unravelling her clothes behind the bulk of the borrowed Land Rover. She'd be glad when this stopped – but perhaps it never would? She wasn't supposed to be weeing this much this early into the pregnancy, according to friends who were mothers. It must be psychosomatic. Gloomy thoughts of pelvic floor collapse occupied her mind as she squatted in the verge, and that action would be harder to achieve later on than it was now with the growing baby and an expanding waistline. Luna had always been sturdy, never slight, but she suspected that the baby might be rather large. Sam was a big lad, after all. She rearranged her skirts, enjoying the contrast between the sunlit chill of the day and the warmth of the Land Rover as she climbed back into it.

21

"Okay?"

"Yes, cheers." It was a fast road up the estuary towards Gloucester. They swung back into England after Chepstow and its castle, and before long they came into the wooded outskirts of the little town of Lydney. Luna's friend Rowan had sent directions, since Sam didn't believe in Sat Navs, said it made you too dependent on technology. And the directions seemed clear enough. They drove down a bumpy track, very slowly because of Luna's condition, with an honour guard of oaks. The wheels of the Land Rover crunched over the fallen leaves, themselves the colour of pale wood, and acorns. Moth the dog sat alert between his humans, ears pricked and watching.

"They need to get a pig," Sam said.

"I think they might have one."

"Was it these people who found a random pig in their shed one Solstice?"

"Yes. When they were living on the Gower. It was a very cold night and they heard something moving about in the shed, and when they went out to see what it was, there was a big white sow."

"Was she oracular?"

Luna did not need an explanation for this remark: Lloyd Alexander's books had been a childhood favourite. "I don't think so."

"Maybe she just wasn't letting on."

"Yes. Maybe she didn't feel like speaking."

"Maybe she was on the run from Welsh pig rustlers."

"Do they do that?"

"Not these days, I wouldn't think. But they used to. Welsh legends are all about nicking other people's animals."

"There's a horse," Luna said, rather missing their own horses, left behind at Mooncote with the van. It was similar: not a piebald, but large and hairy at the heel. Ahead, the hills rose up, heavily wooded, behind the low roof of a cottage.

"That's the Forest," Luna said.

"I thought it must be. I don't know the Borders so well. It's lovely country. Aren't they supposed to be a bit – unfriendly, in the Forest of Dean? Mind you, people say that about me and mine."

"Yes. Don't mention the Bear. Talking of other people's animals."

"The what?"

So Luna told him the story of the man with the dancing bear, whom the foresters had thought to be a spy of the French during the Napoleonic wars, and put to death.

"And they've been sensitive about it ever since. Rowan knows a man who got punched in the face for raising the subject in a forest pub."

"Nice. Though I'm always careful what I say in places I don't know. Not wanting a thump in the nose. How have your mates been getting on here, then? Hippies and all that."

"I think people have been okay with them so far because Rowan's got family in Coledean. They keep a bit quiet about being pagans, though. People can be funny."

"That's wise."

He pulled the Land Rover into a wide, grassy yard. Part of the cottage was not-quite tumbledown, low and grey with a slate roof, and an oak tree loomed over it, branches bending a little as if in protection. A pile of new stones lay beside it, ready to renovate the unfinished half: the cottage was a work in progress. When Luna got out and looked back, she could see the shining bend of the river and the red banks of the opposite shore: it was higher up than she had expected.

"And you've not been here before?"

"No, not here. I've known Rowan ever since we were kids, though – I told you we were in junior school together. I went to see her a lot when they lived in Wales."

Sam nodded and then Rowan was there, flying out of the door with her long dark hair flying also, holding up her long skirts with one hand like a Victorian tomboy.

"Hey, you're here! You're early! That's great. I'm making soup." She hugged Luna carefully and shook Sam's hand. "Come in."

On the way, she snatched up a toddler who was just about to put something in his mouth, set him in a ragged armchair, and took a look at a baby in a cradle.

"You've got all the joy of this to come. I need lots of arms like an Indian goddess and eyes in the back of my head."

"You look great, though," Luna said sincerely, for Rowan did, in her layered purple skirts and a lurex jumper and her glittery eyeshadow. She liked the room, too: long and low with a wood burning stove at its heart and a garland of rowan berries hanging on the wall. It felt like a home.

"If I put make up on, there's no one to see me, right, except sometimes the postman, and the kids. Moss doesn't give a shit about that sort of thing, but I like it. I feel pretty."

"How is Moss?"

"Fine. Working. He got some part time stuff with a tree surgeon but then, hey, we live on the edge of a forest, so part time turned into all the time. We don't pay a lot of rent. We can afford to – don't be shocked now – eat out in the pub once a week. Life's good. So how are you?"

Luna grimaced. "I'm fine. However, where is your toilet, please?"

Moss, immensely tall, smiling vaguely, came back from work early in the evening and they ate vegetable curry around the kitchen table. Luna had brought a flagon of cider up with them and though she herself was not drinking right now, it went down well with everyone else. It was a night for hunkering down and staying in, with a strong westerly blowing upriver and booming in the branches of the oaks.

"So you're staying for, what, just tonight and tomorrow?" Moss asked.

"Yes. Not long. We're planning to get back on the road once the baby's born. Give Luna a month or so to get her head round being a mum and then get out of Bee's hair."

"She's been great, though, my sister. All of them have."

"And you said in your text that your mum had – come back?" Rowan's face was worried. "I didn't really like to ask. I hope it's okay to talk about it."

"Yeah, it's cool. She turned up about a month ago but she's gone travelling again. She was in a – bit of a situation and she couldn't get in touch with us safely."

Rowan looked even more concerned. "That happened to a friend of mine – domestic violence, she had to go into a women's shelter and she couldn't tell anyone where she was in case the bastard bloke found out. Total nightmare."

"Yeah, it was a bit like that," Sam said, before Luna could explain further. "But she's okay now. She'll be home at Christmas time."

"I'm really glad. I was so worried about you. And you said the baby's due around May?"

"Yes. I want to have it at home but I don't know if that's going to be possible…"

The conversation turned to childbirth and that was, Luna thought, what your friends were for: solidarity. She went up to bed early all the same, leaving Moss and Sam and Rowan to talk. The sound of their voices, audible in the confines of the little house, was comforting, like being in bed when you were a child, half aware of the grown-ups talking downstairs. Luna semi-listened for a while, huddled under the blankets in the room under the eaves. In new places – and there had been a lot of those, in their journey up and down the length of the country – she had formed the habit of thinking about where she was before she went to sleep. Locking herself into the land, feeling its sweep and swing. Now, in the old cottage on the hills that tumbled down to join the river, Luna found that she was very conscious of the Severn, of the great bend that lay below them in the light of the moon. Wintercold and chancy, with its quicksand banks and saltmarsh shores. Tidal as far as Gloucester: the big ships still ploughed up the channel to Portishead near Bristol.

Half-dreaming, Luna pictured the river and the wooded ridge behind her. She was intrigued, but not entirely surprised, to find herself slipping from her body, leaving it warm and sleeping, enfolding the child within her womb. She could still feel her physical self, a cocoon, a husk of flesh, as she herself slid free. It would, she thought, be safe.

Outside, incorporeal, she was protected from the cold. Luna's spirit ran lightly through the wind-tossed, roaring oaks and down a slope that shone faintly in the moonlight. She felt the tug and pull of something away to her right, as if it were a magnet and Luna's soul a sliver of iron. Deciding not to struggle against it, she let it reel her in. She could see low buildings now, a collection of domed roofs, the flame of a candle flickering in a window. Luna landed at a doorway, just as the door swung open.

A woman stood there. She was dressed in a long robe and her head was covered in a kind of hooded cowl, but Luna did not think she was a nun.

"Oh," she said. "You're here. At last! I was beginning to worry. The priest says there's a storm coming."

"You knew I was on my way?" Luna heard herself say. There was a faint, insect buzz behind the words, as though she was speaking in a different tongue, but hearing English.

"Yes, yes, we had a message from your father. One of his doves. I don't know what this is all about but of course you're very welcome. Come in, out of the chill."

Luna followed her into a long tiled hallway. Braziers lit it, casting shadows on the walls, which were the colour of honey, and the floor tiles were russet. Luna was shown into a side room. Here, mosaic hounds capered over the floor and she smiled, thinking of Moth.

"Sit here for a moment," the woman said. "I'll fetch the augur."

Looking down at herself, Luna could see only a faint outline in the air. She moved her hand. A stirring, nothing more. But reflected in a big bronze pot that stood on a small table she could see a boy – more a young man, perhaps – with short dark hair, wearing brown. This must be what the woman saw. But Luna felt entirely herself. And the room was surely Roman: Luna had been on enough school trips to Cirencester and Chedworth, to the local museums of south Gloucestershire and Bath, to recognise the general vibe. She was excited. She'd always wanted to see these times…

Soon, a man came in. He looked completely ordinary, like a local builder, apart from the toga.

"Felix! You're here. Cassia was starting to fret."

"I'm sorry if I'm late," Luna heard herself say. "It wasn't an easy journey."

"Did you come upon any trouble on the way?"

Luna heard herself laugh. "Only if you count the mud."

"Yes, winter in this land is always so – well, it's these northern climes, isn't it? Anyway, you're here now. And ready for your dreaming."

Luna did not want to say that she didn't know what he was talking about. At this point the woman, Cassia, came in.

"Victorinus, do you need oil for the shrine?"

"Thank you, yes, very helpful." He stood. "Come with me, young man."

Obediently, Luna followed. They went out into a misty courtyard and a dog gave a sudden sharp bark, almost questioning. Victorinus laughed.

"No work for you tonight, Woundlicker."

"That's his name?" Luna said, taken aback.

"Well, his job, really. As I'm sure you're aware, the spit of a dog is a good remedy for minor wounds."

"I'll remember that," said Luna, remembering also some of the things that Moth was prone to sampling and thinking, *No way*. The courtyard seemed warmer than it should and after a few moments, Luna realised that this was because the mist was in fact steam, emanating from vents along the courtyard wall.

"The bathhouse," said Victorinus, unnecessarily.

Luna followed him into a long, rectangular building, evidently the shrine. She could see the stone statue of a young man at one end.

"I will leave you to pay your devotions," Victorinus said, and left.

Luna walked hesitantly forwards. She took this sort of thing seriously but was slightly hampered because she didn't know who the god might be. She knelt down anyway, and bowed her head. She prayed for all the people and things she could think of and when she raised her head again, the god had moved. Alive and smiling, he said, "It's Nodens. And I know you're not attached here. You're a spirit, aren't you?"

His eyes were golden and kind. His hair reminded her of fire, flaming out over his shoulders. He had perhaps been a sun god, she dimly recalled.

"I'm a woman, actually," Luna said. "From the future."

"Just visiting? Well, that's all right, too. I don't mind."

"Victorinus mentioned something about dreaming?"

"Yes. They have a dreaming place here, an incunabulum. I expect you're supposed to use it."

"Am I dreaming now?"

"I don't think so. Just travelling. Oh, he's coming back. I mustn't startle him." He froze back into stone and Luna clambered to her feet.

Once within the little chamber of the incunabulum, Victorinus gave Luna brief instructions.

"Don't worry if you don't dream. I know your father thinks it's important, but don't make something up if it doesn't happen."

"He wants an answer," Luna said, but she did not know where the words had come from.

"I know – these are troubled times, and he must do what he thinks right. All the same, it's best to be honest."

Luna nodded and the augur left her alone, shutting the door gently behind her. She was supposed to lie down, in the little linen-clad bed, and sleep, and see what her dreams might be. But Luna was already in bed, far ahead in time, her real body dreaming all on its own. Still she thought she had better give it a go. She lay down, and blew out the lamp.

STELLA

There were hordes of people pouring out of London Bridge station. Stella glanced up at the dizzying spire of the Shard: from up there, they really all must look like ants, she thought. Rush hour in the capital didn't get any less hectic and it had taken her some time to make her way south of the river from Serena's place. But now she was here, crossing the road towards the illuminated tower of Southwark Cathedral, with a tang of the river and the cold in the air. Behind the tower, the sky glowed green and Stella, who loved these chilly winter nights when it was icy clear, smiled to herself. Then she made her way down the steps and into Borough Market, which was starting to shut down for the day. She liked that, too, all the hustle and bustle which had nothing to do with her.

The cathedral clock was accurate. It was still a little early, quarter past five, so Stella dodged into a pub and ordered a coffee, feeling lucky to get a seat at the side of the bar. Southwark's workers were starting to filter in and pack the place out: Friday night, which meant week's end, which meant drinking.

"Scuse me," said Stella to the barman. "Do you know a place round here called the 'boneyard'?"

He shook his head. "No idea. A club, is it? There's no pubs by that name round here."

Stella was about to plead ignorance when a voice said,

"D'you mean Crossbones?"

Stella turned. The man was sitting nearby in a dark corner at a small table, with a pint in front of him. He was not prepossessing. He wore a flasher's mac, thought Stella, and his curly grey hair was too long and rather greasy. He had not shaved for some time. He noticed her expression.

"'Sall right," he said, gloomily. "I get it."

Somewhat against her better judgment, Stella picked up her coffee and sat down opposite.

"I don't know if I mean Crossbones or not, to be honest."

"It's where the geese gather," the man said.

Aha.

"Yeah, someone told me that."

He raised an eyebrow. "And who might that someone have been?"

"It's a bit complicated. Actually, it's a bit weird. Look, someone gave me this." The magpie's feather lay on the table in front of them, glossy and blue, but as Stella watched, it gradually faded away into nothing.

The man's mouth twitched. His brown eyes were bloodshot, Stella saw, but there was an old beauty in his face, just the traces, fading fast. He must have been handsome as a young man, a bit Benedict Cumberbatch. She could smell him: booze and fags, and a trace of sweat.

He said, "I do weird, girl."

"Do you now," said Stella, because this could have meant anything and some of it really not very good.

"So who was it who spoke to you? A tree? A cat? A bird?"

"Sort of the last one."

"Okay. That's very interesting. Now. I can either take you round there, if you trust going off into a back alley south of the river with a dodgy old geezer like me – or I can draw you a map on a beermat."

Stella hesitated. "Don't take this the wrong way –" but then she heard the angel's voice in her head, *The geese will look after you.*

"All right," Stella said. "I'll take a risk. Show me."

"I will, then. And no risk, not from me, anyway. My name's Ace, by the way."

Stella grinned. "Ace of bass?"

"Whatever that means."

"I'm Stella. Stella Fallow, like the deer."

Ace reached beneath the table and lugged out a large, weighty carrier bag with a Tesco logo that had worn almost to invisibility.

"You want a hand with that?" Stella asked hesitantly.

"Nah. It's catfood. I get it every day. If I can afford to."

"Do you have a lot of cats?"

"Yeah, loads."

With some reluctance, she followed him out of the bright, noisy haven of the pub and into the street. Without looking back to see if she was following, Ace set off, at a long stride and a pace that had even the fit Stella scurrying to keep up. When he turned into a small, quiet street that led back towards the market, Stella swallowed hard but then she saw that it wasn't so quiet after all.

30

In fact, the street was full of people, milling about in front of a pair of industrial steel gates. Stella, now that it appeared that Mad Cat Man had not led her into some lonely alleyway, was intrigued. The crowd parted, briefly, to display a woman in a Peruvian hat tying a length of ribbon onto the gates. She was having problems finding a space: the gates were covered with ribbon and wool, resembling a piece of textile art.

"What are they doing?" Stella whispered to Ace.

"You'll see. It'll kick off in a minute."

There was a man, dressed in black and soot like a sweep's rags but with a pale face. A Morris dancer, thought Stella at first, but he had no team with him. He wore a top hat with crow's feathers in it and he smiled when he saw Ace.

"Bill sends his regards," he shouted. "I see you've found her." He raised a walking stick in the air and the end of it was a pine cone, ridged and whorled. Stella saw a shower of sparks stream out of it. She blinked.

And then the geese came.

SERENA

Serena woke, blinking at the light, and groped for the clock. The alarm was just about to go off: it shrilled in her hand. She flicked it silent and rose, yawning, then padded downstairs to make tea. On the table, her phone flickered and she picked it up to find a text from Ward: *Shall I see you later? Do you want to go for breakfast?* Ward, raised on Shakespeare as on mother's milk, refused to use text-speak and his enragement at the vagaries of spellcheck was a daily occurrence.

"But didn't Shakespeare write his own name in several different ways? Because they didn't have standardised spelling then?" Serena had said once, to wind him up.

"That is an entirely different thing," Ward replied, sternly, but then changed the subject before being asked to explain how.

Once she replied to Ward – *yes, pls, come over* – and had made a cup of tea, Serena remembered the alarm. She had groped round the door and reset it last night, before trudging back to bed. Better go and check that everything was all right before she and Ward headed to the local café – then the doorbell rang. Ward actually had a key, but felt that it was more polite to ring rather than just march in.

"Hi!"

"Good morning." Ward looked mildly hungover. Handsomely ravaged, though. He stepped inside.

"How was last night?"

"Yes." Ward said. "It was good, actually, although one can tell one had a drink last night, I must say. We went to the Wolseley, where we talked a lot of movie bollocks. He wants me to do something next year but it's more Jane Austen. Bonnets pay bills, though."

'He' was apparently Miles Lochlane, a director of whom Serena had never heard, but who was apparently more of an auteur. She wasn't entirely sure what this meant.

"Well, that's great," Serena said. "And you won't have to wear a bonnet."

"Who knows? There was a – thing, though."

"Right?"

"When we were coming out of the Wolseley, we ran into Miranda. Who is back in town, apparently."

"Oh." Serena sat down hard on a nearby kitchen chair. "And... what are you going to do about that?"

From behind, Ward put his arms around her and said into her ear. "Nothing. I'm not going to do anything about it because as far as I am concerned, I am now with you. I wasn't pleased to see her – actually, I was bloody horrified, because after what that woman has put me through, I don't particularly want to see her again and I have said to my agent that I certainly don't want to take any jobs which involve her. She's a nightmare on set, anyway. Absolute diva."

"Thank you," Serena whispered. She was startled at how relieved she felt.

"But, I thought I should give you the heads-up that she is back in the country."

"What happened to her Californian director, then? The one she was having an affair with?"

"I don't know. Miles said last night that he'd heard it was over and the wife had put her foot down, said she'd refuse to let him – whatshisname – see the kids if he ran off with Miranda. We weren't sure that she could actually do that but apparently it had him scampering back home with his tail between his legs, but then when we were chatting with Anthony van Gersden in the Groucho Club later, he said that he'd seen them in the Soho House last week, so..." Ward paused, then added, "And they say men don't gossip."

"Ha!"

"Anyway, breakfast."

"Yes, good plan. I just need to put my nose round the door of the studio – the alarm went off last night and I just ought to check..."

"Whatever you need to do," Ward said.

So he and Serena walked the few yards to the studio, where she opened the door and turned off the alarm. And screamed.

BEE

Next morning, the green-skinned girl was still in the dog basket. After Bee had pottered around the kitchen for a bit, letting her sleep, she woke. Bee watched a range of expressions flit across her face, primarily confusion and dismay. But then she sat up, faithless Nelson having gone in search of his breakfast, and crept across the room to sit at the table. Bee, in silence, gave her more honey and bread, and boiled eggs and a glass of milk, all of which the girl wolfed down. Then she pointed to the door, so Bee let her out, as though she were one of the dogs herself.

Bee did not, in fact, expect to see the girl again, but a few minutes later she was back, rearranging her garments and shivering. She stood uncertainly in the doorway, so Bee beckoned her inside. Bee presumed that she had gone out to piss. The girl skirted the Aga, glancing at it with a profound suspicion but drawn to its warmth. She took the chair closest to it. Then, as if she had reached some decision, she said,

"Aln." She flicked a hand towards herself.

"Aln?" Bee repeated. "That's your name? I am Bee."

The girl frowned so Bee, mimicking the gesture, said it again.

"Bee," said the girl – Aln – pointing. She smiled, only a little bit, but it was good to see and Bee grinned back at her.

"Aln and Bee," she said. "Like the alphabet." But Aln just looked blank at this.

Bee managed, by degrees, to get the girl to climb the stairs and showed her a bed. Sign language had to fill in the rest but Aln's grey eyes were wide. She seemed to think that the bed would not do, however, as she bolted back down the stairs with finality and Bee found her once more firmly ensconced in the dog basket. She was a strange creature, Bee thought, with her prematurely white hair and her green skin. Bee had seen people with a non-standard range of colouration before: one of the star spirits that frequented the household of Mooncote was blue. But Aln did not feel like a spirit.

Now Aln was eyeing a sheet of paper that sat on the table, about to be turned into one of Bee's everlasting lists.

"You want that?" Bee said. "Want to write something?" But she did not think Aln would be able to write, somehow. She rummaged in a drawer and took out a pack of coloured pens, used for freezer bags and list making. Aln looked baffled, so Bee showed her how to use one of the pens, taking the cap off and scribbling, and Aln began to draw, with a look of furious concentration. She was still drawing when there was a knock on the back door and Bee's neighbour, Caro Amberley, came in.

"Oh, sorry – I didn't realise you had a visitor." Then Aln raised an enquiring head and Caro's mouth fell open in shock. "Oh my God."

"I know," Bee said. "No, I have no idea. I found her in the churchyard last night. I was afraid she'd freeze to death so Gr – someone suggested I take her home."

Caro stared at the girl, who had gone back to drawing.

"I don't know what to say. Why is she so green? Is there something wrong with her? Is it her liver function or something?"

"I don't know."

"Well, has she seen a doctor?"

"Not yet. I'm going to take her in later" Bee said, lying through her teeth. "I managed to make an appointment."

"Oh," Caro said in relief. "Good thing you were able to get one so quickly. I should think she ought to go to casualty, though, shouldn't she?"

"I phoned 111 and they didn't think so," Bee said, hating herself. When had she gained the ability to lie so glibly?

Well, this was awkward. Bee was, however, pleased that Caro had showed up. Since events earlier in the autumn, she had the impression that Caro had been avoiding conversations. She and Alys had been old friends and Bee had always got on well with Caro; recently, she had been undertaking some book cataloguing for her. But the cataloguing was now complete and every time Bee had seen her neighbour, Caro seemed to have found some excuse to rush off. Now, Bee said firmly, "Caro, we need to talk. I know this is weird. I know *things* have been weird lately. I don't want to freak you out but we do need to have a conversation."

Caro said, abruptly, "Ward said he knew someone who'd changed into an animal." She sank down into one of the kitchen chairs.

"Yes." Bee did not want to say *Oh, yeah, that might have been my sister Serena.* Instead, not looking at Aln, she said, "A lot of odd stuff has been happening."

"Alys came to see me," Caro said. This was news to Bee.

35

"Oh, did she?"

"She did. Very late one night, a while ago. I nearly dropped dead of a heart attack when I answered the door and there was your mother standing on the step. She said she was on her way out and she didn't want to say where she was going. Or where she'd bloody been for all that time! She was really matter of fact about it. I could have killed her."

"I know," Bee said, with feeling. "I was a bit cross as well."

"She told me not to tell you that she'd visited. She said she'd just come from here, that you knew she was back. She made me promise. You know, I always thought Alys was a bit – wafty. Vague. I love her to bits but she always rather drifted through life. But this time she seemed really quite steely. Where had she been all that time she was missing, Bee? Do you know?"

"Not really. But it wasn't…" Bee took a deep breath and plunged, "It wasn't the world we know."

Caro gave a curt nod as though this was not in fact news. Bee expected questions, disbelief, bewilderment, maybe even confirmation, but instead, Caro burst into tears. Bee was so surprised at this that she just stared at the other woman. Caro: always capable, competent, well put together. Even in jeans and wellingtons she managed to look somehow elegant. This red faced, sobbing woman was a stranger; Bee had known her for years and never seen her cry. On the other side of the table, Aln stopped drawing and stared too, owlish but expressionless. Caro groped for Bee's hand.

"Oh God, sorry… I'm so sorry."

"Would you like a tissue?" Bee asked, but of course there were none to hand. Instead, she passed Caro the kitchen roll. Caro blew her nose into a section of it.

"*Christ.*"

"Caro, what's wrong? This isn't about Alys, is it?"

"No," Caro choked. "It's about Ben. He's disappeared and I don't know where he is. I'm really sorry to bring this up now, after your mum going missing as well and since he split up with your sister, but –"

Bee did not know what to say. She had thought that the end of Ben and Serena's relationship might also be why Caro had been avoiding her.

"I know this probably isn't the right thing to say, but he is a grown up." *Theoretically.* "Has he gone off with the band, perhaps?"

"No." Caro blew her nose again and took a breath. "His bandmates haven't seen him for over three weeks. He usually texts or calls once a week or so, and when I hadn't heard from him for a bit, I didn't think much of it. As you say, he's an adult. But then Seelie – his bandmate – got in touch and asked if I knew where he was. And I did not. So she started asking around and, seriously, Bee, it's like he's dropped off the face of the Earth. I wondered if you'd heard anything from your sister and I was going to ask you if you could ask Serena if…"

"I'll ask her. Don't worry."

"I know he's been going through a rough time – " Caro said – *and putting everyone else through one*, thought Bee, *just like Mum* – "With that girl, Dana. I haven't seen hide nor hair of her, either, or her brother. Tam. Not for some time now." She gave Bee a sharp, teary look. "I don't suppose you've seen them?"

Bee returned the sharp look. "I don't think I'll be seeing them again, somehow."

"I thought, quite frankly, the police might have come looking for them."

"No, they haven't," said Bee, with perfect truth.

"Then they must have skipped town," Caro said, "As it were. I wondered if Ben had gone off with them. They were really shady."

"I don't think so," said Bee, hating the whole conversation. "But I'll ask Serena if she's heard anything from Ben. I know how awful this must be."

"Of course, with Alys having gone missing before, I thought you might know what to do…"

"I'll do what I can," Bee told her, and she meant it. "Can I ask if you've spoken to the police?"

"Not yet – I thought about it, obviously, but Richard said we ought to wait a bit, because we remembered what it was like when Alys went missing and I think he's afraid the papers might dredge up some stuff, not that he thinks there is anything, but you know, the press often don't like Bohemian musicians… But if this goes on, I will have to call them."

When Caro, a little more cheerful, had finally gone, Bee went to look over Aln's shoulder. The girl was still drawing, laboriously, with small, careful strokes, but it was still a child's sketch. She had only used three pens: light green, dark green, and a bright sharp emerald. There were trees, Bee thought, a lot of them, and a hill with a tower on it, a bit like nearby Glastonbury Tor from certain angles, and a round green sun.

"Where is this, Aln? Can you tell me?" She did not really expect an answer, and Aln merely stared at her, pale eyed, then returned to her sketch.

LUNA

Luna didn't remember falling asleep. She was standing on the riverbank and the Severn looked much wider than it should have done, the great expanse of the river striding out under the full moon. Luna stood on a narrow spit of land, quite low, running from the salt marsh. The shore smelled of mud and the sea. When she turned, the forested line of the hills rose up against the western sky and she could see the familiar shape of the Plough wheeling overhead. The North Star pointed upriver. Someone was singing.

Luna looked downstream. The people came out of a grove of scrub at the edge of the marsh and Luna, with her good night sight and the light of the moon, thought at first that they were children, for they were not very tall. Then she realised that two of them were adults, a small man with a bushy beard and a little woman with a baby at the breast, held in a doeskin sling. The other two were children, a boy and a girl. The woman was singing softly to the baby. The man carried a spear. They were making no attempt to be quiet. The kids were chattering and laughing and the man was talking back, a teasing note. Luna wondered what they were all doing, walking along the midnight shore, but then there was a rift, a blink in the moon's eye and for a second she saw the bank as they were seeing it: bright sunlight bouncing off the water, the shore and the river and the sky all silvery, winter-bleached, and the man speared something in a pool and tossed it wriggling into the bag over his shoulder.

A prehistoric family, out for the day's hunting. Luna watched them as they came onwards, still laughing. They looked human, but primitive: these were not modern faces, and their skin was bronze-dark, their hair reddish. She saw something else, too: the river, changing.

Oh God, Luna thought. The scene was altering too fast, clouds scudding over the landscape, the visible currents of the Severn running in a different direction, and a wall down the estuary, coming on. It looked wrong and for a moment she did not understand, but then she realised: the wall was the Bore, the great wave which ripples up the funnel of the Severn on certain rising tides. Luna had seen it once, standing on a bridge quite a long way upstream and watching the wave rush up, breaking against the supports of the bridge and spattering the faces of the excited spectators.

This wave was more like a tsunami. Moonlight sparkled at its summit and the air felt prickly and charged.

Luna shouted but her voice was a spindly, reedy thing and the family did not hear her. They walked on, the children running ahead.

"The wave!" Luna shouted. "Get back!"

And she ought to be doing the same, because the spit of land on which she stood was low. She turned to run but it was too late. The huge wave broke over the little family and carried them away and then it broke over Luna, too, in a soundless explosion of water and light. Cold and weightless, Luna was carried towards the spiralling depths of the river. But as she fell, she felt a curious click inside her mind, as though the last piece of a jigsaw had fallen into place.

She was changing. Without pain, she felt her clothes melt away, her legs and arms shrinking. She felt compacted, not unpleasantly, but with an oddly cosy sensation as though she was being tucked up in bed. It came as no surprise when she flapped her hands and found herself soaring upwards out of the roar of the wave and the spray. She shot like an arrow to the bank: she could see *dark/safe/above water* there. It was a blackthorn brake and Luna, now, was tiny enough to avoid the long sharp spines and seek refuge within. But she was not alone. She could hear the shouts.

"Danger! Danger! Danger!" – the word was very clear and yet, deep within the corner of Luna that was still human, she recognised the angry chatter of a wren. More than one. There were two wrens with her, and two young. The family of the shore were all safe, transformed. Luna raised her voice and cried with them: *"Danger! Danger! Danger!"*

The chattering cry rose until it filled the air like the beat of a little drum, louder and louder, until Luna woke, for a fleeting moment, in the dreaming chamber at the shrine, glimpsing a dog sitting by the side of her bed, and then woke properly, heart thumping but not drowned after all, nor bird, in Rowan's spare bedroom near Lydney.

SERENA

Serena was sitting in a nest. It was colossal, filling most of the corner of the studio. It was made of velvet, silk, cotton and lace, in ribbons and tatters and scraps: all that was left of Serena's last collection. The clothes had been shredded, violently and completely; Serena could see bits hanging from the long light fittings and dangling from the skylights. If she hadn't felt so utterly shocked, it might have been impressive.

Her assistant, Charlie, was making coffee next door. They were on their third cafetiere. They might need some for the police, Serena and Charlie thought.

"Are you sure you don't want some brandy in it?" Ward said.

"No. I've had enough. It's not even ten o'clock." He had made her have a shot (*good for the nerves*) already but Serena didn't think she'd better have any more booze. Charlie, usually a composed young woman, had been struck speechless when she had first seen the devastation. She had stood at the entrance to the studio, gaping at Ward, frozen with shock, and at Serena, picking up a confetti armful of scraps and throwing them into the air. They had showered down around her, glints of gold and silver thread catching the sun, with Serena standing in their midst like a ragged princess in a fairytale.

"What in the world happened?" Charlie whispered.

"We don't know." Serena had sunk down onto the floor. "Someone got in. And did this."

"Serena said the alarm was going off last night," Ward told Charlie. "She turned it off but she didn't look inside."

"No, it's been playing up," Charlie said. She picked up a piece of silk and fingered it, absently.

"I didn't look," Serena said, "But I did listen. Only for a moment. But once the alarm had been turned off, it was all silent. I couldn't hear anything."

"Do you know how they got in?"

"There's no sign of a break-in that I can see," Ward said. "The skylights are all intact. The kitchenette window is shut. No sign of forced entry. No bootprints on the lino."

41

Serena gave a very wavery smile. "You sound like a police detective."

"I have in fact played one on TV."

"I know, DI Holyrood, I've seen you. Get detecting, is what I say."

"You've no clue who it might have been?" asked Charlie.

"If it had been vandals," Serena said, "surely they'd have just broken in. Joolz, that's the woman who was here before, friend of – of Ben's, said kids broke in once through the skylight and there was glass everywhere." She looked at Ward. "Look – you said you had to see your director this morning, you're going to be late for your meeting."

"I don't think I can just –"

Serena rose from her nest and put her arms round his neck. "Go to the theatre. You can't do anything here. Sweep me up later. Bring wine."

"Bring lots," Charlie said.

"We'll wait for the police."

At last, reluctantly, Ward was persuaded to go to work, leaving Serena and Charlie amid the chaos. Shortly after he had left the police arrived and the endless questions, and then the post mortem of the questions, lasted until lunchtime.

"He asked me who might have done this," Serena said, for the hundredth time, "But I can't think of anyone who hates me that much."

No one, at least, who was still alive.

"You said," Charlie had collected a lapful of bits of cloth, like some avant garde jigsaw, and she was still playing with it now, "Just before the police came, that Ward had said something about his ex-girlfriend coming back to London?"

"I didn't tell that to the police. Maybe I should have done? But I don't even know her. I don't know if she's the sort of person who's capable of something like this."

"I bet she is," said Charlie.

But Ward, when he returned later with a carrier bag full of wine bottles (having taken Charlie's instructions seriously) said that he thought it unlikely.

"Not because she isn't a demented, vindictive trollop, you understand. She's totally capable of something like this. She once threw one of my Loakes out of a railway carriage window."

"What!"

"I took my shoes off because it was more comfortable and we had a row in first class over something and she picked up a shoe and threw it off the Ribble viaduct. I watched it falling about three hundred feet before network rail sped on. I had to take the orphan back to the shop and ask them to match it."

"And did they?"

"Oh yes. Didn't bat an eyelid. You'd think this sort of thing happened all the time. Maybe it does. I told them what had befallen the shoe because for some reason it seemed better to have a crazy brogue-murdering girlfriend than be considered careless."

"I can actually see that."

"So your suggestion that she might have trashed your entire collection is not unreasonable, in my view. Miranda has form. However, on the minus side, she is also spectacularly lazy. The only times that she is not lazy is when she is acting and plotting, and, trust me, as someone who has played her leading man, she puts a lot more effort into the latter than the former. She might fantasise about doing something like this but it's too much like hard work. My shoe, unfortunately, was in reach on the occasion I mentioned."

"That is sort of reassuring."

"You know, she has taken revenge on people – the shoe, throwing a pornstar martini over Demi Mangonelli, and someone told me she flushed a boyfriend's goldfish down the loo but I don't know if that's true – but she goes off the boil. She essentially has the attention span of a gnat and she loses interest. Also, how would she have got in? I can't see Miranda risking her Guccis by clambering over a rooftop and she once locked herself out of her own flat and had a meltdown. I was the one who managed to shin up a drainpipe and open the back window." Ward opened another bottle of wine.

"Well," Serena said. She was now somewhat insulated from recent events by alcohol and rationalisation. "At least no one's died." She took a deep breath. "It's only clothes."

"You don't really mean that. It's hard work and dreams and investment."

"I'm insured. I hate the thought of all that destruction. It makes me feel sick. Clothes are – they're not like my kids; that would be really precious and stupid. Bella means more to me than any garment. But they are my creative projects and it makes me feel physically ill to have them trashed like that. And it's put me back – there's no way we'll make fashion week, now." She felt herself welling up and dabbed her eyes with a paper napkin. Ward gripped her free hand.

"Shit. I'm so sorry."

"I'm just going to have to wait for the police to report back. They did start making enquiries and maybe they have some ideas. I've told Eleanor. She's horrified, of course. She said that this sort of thing does happen, though it's only happened to the studio once before and that was just kids, they broke the window, I was telling Charlie. I've seen clothes destroyed before, razored, when I worked for Elada, but only once and it was an ex staff member bent on revenge. I did wonder, though, if Madam –" Her eyes met Ward's.

"If you mean our recent acquaintance, she's definitely dead."

"But she wasn't quite –"

"I know. Still dead, though, and her brother is – where Stella left him. And this seems different, somehow."

Serena ate another forkful of pasta. She wasn't going to waste food, no matter how terrible she felt. And it was sensible to eat. She hadn't felt up to eating lunch.

"You're right. It does feel different. But who could have *done* such a thing?"

When they next went into the studio, however, Serena found out.

STELLA

Stella was trying to find Ace. Not helped by the fact that Crossbones was much bigger inside than out, TARDIS-like. Perhaps Ace was in fact a Time Lord? By this point, nothing would have surprised Stella. If she could just find the gate – but it seemed that this, too, was elusive. Beyond the high wall, the lights of the city had gone out.

Stella made herself stop and think. No point in running about like a headless chicken. Part of the problem was that she wasn't very clear as to what had actually happened: she'd been watching the woman in the hippy hat tie a ribbon on the gate, but then the geese had come... Stella's memories of this were vague. After the man in black had waved his pine cone staff, the air had become a sparkling mist, with ragged women walking out of it. Barefoot and bareheaded, their skirts trailing, their hair matted and their eyes kind. Stella did not know who they were, only that they had called the geese and that they were there to help her, somehow, there to help everyone. Then the gate, with its ribbons and tatters, had swung wide and let them all in. Stella had lost sight of Ace almost immediately. Behind, a shout went up.

"The geese have come! The geese have come!"

Everyone had poured in, to a wide enclosure shaded by trees. There were a great many gravestones: it was a cemetery, but there were no names on the graves. Stella collared an older woman and asked about this.

"Oh," the woman said. "You're new, aren't you? Well, it's because the geese have taken them back."

"Taken them back? You mean their names?"

The woman nodded approvingly, as if speaking to a bright pupil. Perhaps she actually was a teacher: she looked like one, somehow.

"Yes, that's right. This is Crossbones. This is the cemetery of the outcast dead, and of the unborn. Excuse me – my friend's calling me." And off she went.

Stella wandered around. It should have felt creepy but it didn't: maybe that was just Stella, who liked graveyards and spent quite a lot of time in the churchyard in Hornmoon, talking to her grandfather's spirit. She must remember to tell him about the geese...

Someone plucked at her sleeve. Stella turned and saw a girl, perhaps twelve or so, dressed in classic Dickensian urchin style. Her hair was lank and she was wrapped in a grubby shawl. But she was smiling as she held out a skein of red wool, cat's cradle, inviting Stella to play. Stella let the girl wind the wool around her fingers. Alys had taught them this, and her grandmother, too, but it had been a long time ago and Stella couldn't remember. She fumbled it and the cradle fell apart and the girl threw her head back, laughing. Then – somehow much later – Stella was walking along the bank of the Thames, though the cemetery was at least half a mile away, and the city across the ship-crowded expanse of the river was not the London she knew, with this low huddle of buildings and smoky lights. There was someone by her side and she knew them, but it was like a dream, even with the woodsmoke reek in the air and the slap of the river against its bulwarks.

"Look," her companion said. "The hour has come but not yet the man. Or woman, perhaps?"

"I don't understand," said Stella.

"There's the ship." Her companion pointed and all at once Stella recognised one of the star spirits. She wore a long pale gown and her hair was piled and powdered. A beauty spot in the shape of a small black heart rode high on her cheekbone. Instead of the herbs that the stars usually bore, she carried a twisted stick, perhaps a foot long, like the horn of a small unicorn, perhaps a wand. It glowed amber in the dim lights. Was she Aldebaran? Stella could not quite place her.

Stella looked down river. There was a black-sailed boat coming in, sailing fast up the Thames. She saw faces lining the deck and men hauling on the sails, trimming into the wind.

"How did it get past the bridges?" Stella asked and then saw for herself as the ship did not stop, coming up to a big bridge just behind them, a bridge lined with tall houses that no longer existed in today's city.

"Oh God," said Stella. "It's going to hit the bridge."

"No," the star – Stella did not know her name – said calmly.

And indeed the black-sailed vessel glided through, no more than a shadow. For a second the candles in the windows dimmed but then the boat was sailing on, Stella could glimpse it through the great barrels of stone which supported the bridge. She turned to speak to the star but the river was gone and the city too, and she was once more standing outside the gates of Crossbones. Ace was peering at her nervously.

"You okay, kiddo?"

"What?" Stella blinked. The air was cold and full of petrol fumes. "Yeah, I think so. That was – odd."

He smiled. He was still clutching the bag of cat food.

"You're not wrong. I'll see you around, Stella Fallow. I've got to go and feed the mogs."

"I – "Stella started to say. But the world was darkening, narrowing, She looked down a black tunnel, towards a tiny light. She did not remember going into the Tube, was her last thought – but that was that.

She woke to the sound of rain, hammering against the windows and bringing with it a pale grey light. She was swaddled in wrappings which, on investigation, turned out to be a bulky, old-fashioned eiderdown in a shade of dirty pink. Or perhaps it was just pink and dirty... Stella thrust it away and fought free.

She was lying on a sofa. This, like the eiderdown, was ancient. The springs had long since gone, resulting in sagging: this accounted for a degree of soreness in Stella's normally limber spine. The place was full of towering piles of newspaper and books, overflowing from the high shelves that lined the walls. Plates of cat food stood on several of these piles and the food had dried to smears on the dishes. The room smelled terrible and Stella suspected that cat food was only one of the culprits. In between the bookshelves, someone had hung paintings which made Stella feel peculiar: she had to look at them obliquely, then away. Most were of women's faces, attenuated and not modern, and at an odd angle. Stella softly tried the handle of the door and it opened into a dark hallway: more paintings, more long-faced women, and one of a ferociously beautiful cat. But by the open door of the kitchen, she saw a familiar face: Ace himself, a lot younger. A self-portrait? It was incredibly good. And Ace had been seriously good looking when younger, too, as Stella had previously thought. She studied it for a long time before going into the kitchen.

This was filthy as well. Stella's standards were not unrealistically high. She was not one of the world's greatest devotees of housework, but if she lived in a place, at least she cleaned the oven. And the sink.

And the floor, usually. Her host appeared not to find these things necessary. Even the ceiling was greasy.

A sudden bang behind her made Stella jump, but it was only the cat flap, swinging on its hinges. However, there was no sign of an actual cat: it must have gone out. Probably she had startled it. As if in response, a second loud thud came from down the hall. Stella peeped out.

"Ace?"

No reply. God, maybe he'd fallen over or out of bed. There were an awful lot of empty whisky bottles standing around the kitchen. She trotted down the hall and knocked tentatively on the door beyond the room in which she had woken up.

"Ace! Are you in there? Are you all right?"

The door was flung open.

"He's gone out," a woman said. A London accent, crow-harsh. She wore a silk dressing gown, much the worse for wear, and her hair, which was jet black, looked strangely askew. A wig? Her eyes were bright blue, summer sky colour, and to Stella's secret delight she had delivered her sentence around the edge of a cigarette holder, clamped in crimson lips. Something pungent and not main-brand was smouldering away at the end of the holder: not marijuana, to Stella's experienced nose, but perhaps some foreign cigarette.

"And you would be?"

"I'm the cleaner."

Stella's expression must have given her away because the woman said, "What?"

"Er, well…"

"I know what you're thinking, love," said the woman. "So there's no need to say it. I'm not that sort of cleaner, all right?"

How many sorts could there be? Stella's mind went to some very strange places before the woman said, "You'd better come in."

To Stella's surprise, it was not a bedroom. It looked more like a parlour, with a black-polished grate and sconce lighting. More bookshelves and a brazier standing in front of the grate, from which a faint warmth emanated. This room was actually relatively clean although there was an odd, underlying odour, rather sweet, which reminded Stella of incense.

"What's that smell?" she asked.

"That? Oh, it's kyphi. He likes it." She pottered over to the brazier and poked its contents with a toasting fork. A thread of smoke wove upwards.

"Oh," said Stella. The word did not mean anything to her. "So where is Ace?"

"I told you, he's gone out. Just down the road, for some fags, but he's probably in the pub by now, knowing him. It's gone eleven. Said I was to wait in until you woke up, just in case."

"What happened? Did I pass out?"

"Yeah, I think so. He said you were dead to the world so he picked you up and brought you back here, stuck you on the sofa. I know he looks a bit rough – he's seen better days, poor bloke, but then haven't we all? – but heart of gold, really. I expect he sees you as a sort of cat."

"I saw some plates of cat food. Well, ex cat food."

"He does sketches down the boozer, flogs them to tourists, uses the money to buy Whiskas. Not drink. Well, some drink. Actually he's not very keen on Whiskas: says they put those additives in it and there's stuff that's better." She sat down on a nearby chaise longue and rearranged the dressing gown, which was becoming hazardous: Stella did not think she was wearing anything beneath it. Early sixties? But though most charitably described as blowsy, she was not in terrible shape. Her nails were lacquered the same vivid red as her lips.

"And do you like cats?" Stella asked, feeling that the conversation was now becoming surreal.

"I like some cats," the woman said. She scowled, suddenly and alarmingly, but Stella did not feel that it was aimed at her. "He said your name's Stella. Is that right?"

"Yes. What's yours?"

"Anione."

"Unusual name."

"Yes, people always ask me about it, if it's Greek and that, but the fact is, I haven't a bleeding clue *where* it comes from. I think my mum made it up. Some people just call me Annie but I think that's a bit naff, actually."

"I won't call you Annie, then. You said he sells sketches to tourists. Those paintings," Stella said, "the ones in the hallway. Did Ace do those?"

"Yes, he did." The woman – Anione – looked slightly complacent.

"They're very good."

"I know they are. He went to the Royal College of Art, long time ago. Could have been another Augustus John or Lucian Freud but said it was too much pressure. So he packed it in and moved to Southwark – that's where we are, by the way. Been here ever since."

She took another drag of the cigarette and its lingering smoke mingled with the fumes from the brazier. Stella, reminded that she had not eaten, began to feel slightly light-headed. At this point, however, the door opened and Ace stood there, dressed exactly as he had been the night before. Stella wondered whether he had just gone to bed in his clothes.

"Oh, you're up. And gasbagging. Nice." He sounded as though he meant it.

"Now you're back you can stick the kettle on," Anione said. "This young lady hasn't had any breakfast, have you, duck?"

"Actually no. And I wouldn't mind some." If only the kitchen was cleaner.

"I'll stick some bacon on." Then he gave Stella a sharp look. "Let me guess. Vegetarian?"

"Actually, yes."

"Thought you were. I'm like Sherlock Holmes, me. I made a series of intensely logical deductions."

"Really?"

"No, I just guessed. Lot of people are these days. Do you eat eggs?"

"I love eggs."

"I'll do eggs, then," said her host.

"I'll stick the kettle on and make you some tea," said Anione. "Because I don't hold out much hope of him being able to do two things at once in the kitchen, really."

She left Stella in the room – the study? – to look around. A lot of the books were old and untitled, leather bound and stamped with gold. The plaster fireplace had Egyptian supports: a man and a woman, perhaps goddess and god. Thick carpet, so dark a burgundy red that it was almost black, like good wine, muffled Stella's prowling feet. The window was covered with a thick layer of lace curtain, with long velvet companions in dark green on either side. Stella drew the net curtain aside and recoiled. Outside was darkness, with a snarling, toothed maw on the other side of the glass. It thumped heavily against the window, which shuddered. There was the fiery golden glitter of an eye.

"Ace!" Stella shouted, leaping back. "Ace! Help!"

Her hosts came running. Anione was first into the room and on seeing the drawn-aside curtain, her first comment was, "Fucking hell, not again. Get out of my way, Stella."

Stella was only too pleased to do so. Anione stepped forwards and suddenly she was not dressed in a grubby dressing gown, but in a sheen of silk, and her hair flowed down her back beneath her lotus crown and her dancing feet were bare. She raised her hands, spoke a word composed of many syllables, and the brazier flared up into an eye-searing starry brightness and the thing at the window was gone. Everything was quiet and still. The lace curtain prickled with winter light.

"I'd better get back to me eggs," Ace said.

The eggs had been eaten in silence, punctuated with desultory comments from Stella's hosts about the whereabouts of various cats, and then Ace had made more tea. No one had volunteered any information about the thing at the window, though Stella had finally asked.

"Oh, that." Ace frowned as though he barely remembered the episode. "Yeah, it happens sometimes."

"If that was madam I'm going to be really pissed off," Anione said. "I've told her before."

"Who else could it be? Don't answer that." He looked at Stella. "I'm off down the pub again in a bit and Anione's got a couple of things to do."

Stella took the hint. She had been a little afraid that they might try to persuade her to stay, so she'd rather they wanted rid of her.

"Sure. I ought to get back to my sister's, anyway. She'll be wondering where I've got to." This probably wasn't true, since it wouldn't be the first time that Stella had been gone all night, but it sounded convincing.

"If you need to find me again," Ace said, "You know where I am."

"Do you have a mobile number?"

"No. Nor email, or fax, or a normal telephone. Complete Luddite, me."

"How do you *manage?*"

"I don't go out much. People write me letters if they really want to get in touch. But at a pinch you could phone the Southwark Tavern. Or just pitch up."

When Stella left, a little nervously given what might be lurking outside the house, she found herself in a perfectly ordinary old-school Victorian street, not very long, and with some disastrous 1970s low-rise flats looming over the end of it. Ace's tiny front garden was overgrown with privet and filled with dustbins. A cat shot out from behind one of these as Stella went through the gate, causing her to start and swear. Once out onto the pavement, she took a good look around before heading onto the main street, where there was a sign for the Tube. As soon as she was out of Ace's road, however, her phone, which Stella had thought to be out of juice, pinged and kept pinging. A string of texts scrolled down the screen, all from Serena.

Where are you? I have to talk 2 u.
There's been an emergency.
Stella, pls call me. Really important.

Shit, Stella thought. Had something happened to one of the family? Bella? Oh no, Luna's baby? She fumbled for Serena's number, feeling guilty.

"Oh, thank God," Serena's voice said.

"Look, I'm sorry I've been gone for so long. It's a bit hard to explain – I'll tell you when I see you."

"I don't care about that!" Serena retorted. "Someone's trashed my entire collection."

"*What?*"

But Serena was crying, snuffling into the phone.

"Hold on," Stella told her. "I'm on my way."

When she turned the corner of Serena's road, almost running and a bit out of breath, she saw that Serena's front door was open. Ward Garner stood on the step.

"Oh, good. She's been trying to get in touch with you."

"I've been out all night," panted Stella. He raised an eyebrow, an accomplishment which Stella always envied. Perhaps it was a special actorly trick and could be taught?

"Dirty stop out, eh?"

Stella snorted. "Not dirty enough. Unless you count a really filthy kitchen. What the hell's happened here?"

"Serena's studio was burgled – well, invaded, might be a better word. Someone has torn all her dresses to shreds. We're going back round there now – she's just gone upstairs, she forgot the key to the cupboards in the studio kitchen."

"Jesus! Has she called the police?"

"Yes, they've been and gone. Oh, there you are."

Serena looked pale and wan and more than somewhat tear-stained, but her cheeks had spots of pink, like a Dutch doll, and Stella knew that this meant anger. Good! Serena clutched at her sister.

"Stella! Come and look at this." Seizing Stella by the arm she dragged her sister into the studio which, Stella was disappointed to note, bore no crime scene tape.

"They only do that for murders, apparently," Ward said, reading Stella's mind.

"That's a bit shit, isn't it?" Then Stella saw the devastation. "What the *fuck*?"

"Impressive, eh?"

"It's like a tornado ripped through it. God, Serena, I'm so sorry!"

"I'm really quite cross," said Serena. Stella stared at her.

"Understatement of the century! Do you have to be so British about it?"

"At first I was just numb. Then I cried. Buckets. And now – I'm really *quite* cross."

"Do you know who it was?"

"No. The police asked me about disgruntled ex-employees but I haven't got any. There's only Charlie and the two cutters and Ginny who's been doing that marketing and they're all still on board."

"A rival couturier, perhaps?"

"I'm personally in favour of this idea," Ward said.

"Yes, but who? I don't think I've got any rivals, not really. We're all doing different stuff."

"All the same," Stella said, "it might be worth asking around and seeing if anyone else has had similar problems."

"It would have been in the papers if they had, surely," Ward said.

At this point, a small man in a puffy jacket and a camera around his neck, who had been hovering about outside the pub at the end of the mews, approached.

"Good afternoon. Ms Fallow, my name's Ed Russell and I'm from the Daily Mail – I wonder if –"

"As if by magic!" Ward snapped, and banged the studio door shut.

"That's all we bloody need," Stella said.

"All the same," said Serena, unhappily, "I'd better say something to him, you know. Or they'll just make stuff up."

Ward sighed. "Do you need me to loom over him?"

"No, I'll deal with it and oh God, all they'll write anyway is a headline that starts *Ward Garner's Girlfriend In...*" She rushed outside, leaving Stella and Ward in the wreckage of the collection.

"This really is a vile thing to do," Stella said. "I can't get over it."

Ward was not looking at Stella. He said, sharply, "What was that?"

"What was what?"

"I thought I saw something. By the chimney."

Stella looked. Her sister's studio was a long room, converted, but whoever had done the original architectural work had left an older fireplace intact, right at the far end of the room. It was a large, plaster construction. Serena sometimes lit scented candles in the grate.

"A bird? Down the chimney?"

"Can't be. The chimney's blocked off."

"Oh yeah, you're right. She did tell me that."

There was a scuffling sound.

"This is weird," Ward said. "It's coming from the fireplace but I can't see anything."

"It must be a bird. Or a rat."

Stella lifted her foot and wrenched off a Converse.

"What are you doing?" Ward asked.

"Giving it something to think about." She aimed the shoe for a moment, then flung it into the fireplace. There was a squawk and something shot out, circled the room, making Ward and Stella cry out and duck, then settled on the mantelpiece.

There was a short silence as all three of them stared at one another. Then,

"What in the name of fuck is *that?*" said Ward Garner.

BEE

Bee had not yet spoken to Serena about Ben and her promise to Caro Amberley. Normally entertaining a degree of confidence in her communications with her sisters, particularly sensible Serena, she found herself at a loss. A text would not do. Email was perhaps better but Bee felt that this would be an act of cowardice, somehow: she needed to speak to Serena directly but every time she tried to pick up the phone, she found her mouth going dry.

"What would *you* do?" she said to Aln, but the green-hued girl simply stared at her, uncomprehending. Luna was still in Gloucestershire, visiting her friends, and Bee thought it might be a good idea to sound things out with her younger sister, when Luna got back. Or Stella, but when she rang the latter, there was no reply.

So Bee got on with things. Did accounts, cleaned the house, fed Aln. The girl ate everything except meat and fish. She showed no disgust, but simply ignored it. All else she consumed voraciously, and from what Bee could see of her under all that hempen sackcloth, she was starting to fill out. She had been starving, Bee realised. Austerity Britain? But she was convinced that wherever Aln came from, it was not here.

However, there was a limit to how much energy Bee could put into wondering. Christmas was coming and the goose – well, the geese, plural – had already been ordered. It would have been extremely expensive except that Bee had managed to do a trade-off with the farm for apples. Besides, everyone would contribute: they were not a family who free-loaded on one another, although prior to the advent of the dishwasher Stella had sometimes had to be prevailed upon to do her share of the washing up. Bee now had one list for the church, one for the house, one for food, one for presents and a spare list for anything else. Today, the church must take priority because the flowers were arriving.

She trudged down to Hornmoon in the wet. December rain, rather mild. The beech branches dripped into the road and Bee had to dodge the puddles. The church felt damp, which was worrying given all the old plasterwork, but someone had lit the Gurney stove and it was warming up. Bee looked with satisfaction at the big blowsy heads of cream-coloured chrysanthemums, the berried holly, the improbable Kelly green of bay. All very traditional but it was what people wanted at this time of year. It was what Bee herself wanted: that sense of timelessness even though all these traditions must have started somewhere and she realised that many of them were relatively new. Kate's helpers filed in, one by one, and they began arranging the foliage in the tall white Victorian vases that, remarkably, had survived both wars.

Towards the end of the afternoon Bee felt in need of daylight, but she could tell from the muted patter on the church tiles that the rain was still hammering down outside. She went across to one of the leaded windows and, being short, stood on a kneeler to look out. In this window, the old glass had formed a knot, a dimpled eye in the plain pane. Beyond, the churchyard was misted in rain, the soft greys of the day rendering the graves almost invisible. On a whim, Bee looked through the glass eye, expecting to see the graveyard through its fisheye lens.

She looked out into thick woodland, the ground covered with snow and the bare branches of oak and ash black against it. Through the lacework of the trees a red sun was going down in winter fire.

Bee jerked back and nearly fell off the kneeler. She glanced around, but Kate's helpers had their heads down over the floral altarpiece – a discussion about holly or bay, from the sound of it – and no one had noticed her reaction. She steadied her footing on the kneeler and looked once more through the window.

A veil of rain, drifting. But through the eye Bee saw that the sun had gone and it was growing dark. A figure stumbled through the snow, one arm flung up over its forehead as though to shield its eyes. Bee frowned: what on earth was it wearing? A fur coat? But then she saw that the long matted hair belonged to the creature itself, not clothes at all. It left carpet-slipper footprints in the snow. It came quite close to the window and she saw its face, which was not human. Sad dark eyes like an otter, in a countenance that was half-muzzle, half man. Its nose was broad and in its panting mouth she glimpsed sharp teeth, a thick pale tongue.

Alarmed at the creature's proximity, Bee stepped back from the window, picked up the kneeler and clutched it to her chest as if in self-defence. But as she did so, it occurred to her that the expression on the creature's face had been equally terrified, that it was running as though something was after it. She also found herself possessed of the conviction that this was the world from which Aln had come.

She got home to find Aln herself asleep in the dog basket and a text from Luna to say that they were on their way back. Bee was relieved at this information; she felt rather burdened by having to cope with Aln even though Dark was there, and maybe Luna and Sam might have some thoughts on the matter, or even information. Sam knew all sorts of things. Bee had spoken to Dark the previous evening, but he was as puzzled as she was. She had taken him to meet Aln, but the girl, gasping, screwed herself up in a ball in the basket, head stuffed under the dog blanket, and Bee and Dark, not wanting to distress her further, had gone outside.

"You actually look pretty solid to me, right now," Bee said. "I can't see the light through you or anything."

"She knew, though. She could see that I am a spirit. It frightened her."

"Where do you think she comes from?"

"I have seen people like her, from very long ago." Dark laughed. "But you know, a peasant is a peasant. Many would have worn what she is wearing, from many ages. And you know, too, that there are many worlds."

"Yes," Bee had said, for she did know this. The Secret Commonwealth, she thought of it, after the writer Robert Kirk: patchwork Britain.

"I'll tell you this," Dark said. "In my opinion, she is running from something."

As if Luna's message had opened the family floodgates, Serena was the next to ring.

"How are you?" Bee said into the phone. "How're things going?" She was horrified to hear her sister burst into tears.

"My collection – it's gone – something tore it to pieces and now we've got this, this *thing* in the studio."

"Serena, slow down. What 'thing?'"

"I can't talk on the phone," Serena said, evidently getting hold of herself. Bee heard a deep breath. "Sorry. I just want you to know that

I'm still coming down with Ward. I wanted to confirm that. I am *determined,* Bee, whatever happens."

"Serena, that's great. It will be lovely to see you both, whatever the circumstances. But —"

Tell her about Ben, Caro's voice said in Bee's head, but the last thing Bee was going to raise was the issue of Serena's missing ex when her sister was in such a state. *Ben will just have to manage, whatever has happened to him.* She felt guilty all the same, as though she was withholding information. It wasn't information she wanted to have anyway. Caro had foisted it on her — but Bee knew this wasn't fair. It must be awful for Caro and they knew what it was like, to have someone you loved go missing. There might be a way round it, though, and she should have thought of this before.

Bee took a deep breath of her own and said, "Do you think I could have a quick little word with Ward?"

"Yes, what about?"

"Oh, just a couple of Christmas surprises," Bee said.

"I've taken this into another room," Ward said. "I'm assuming that what you want to discuss isn't about the festive season? Also I don't want that *thing* overhearing me."

"What 'thing'?" Bee said. Serena had mentioned a 'thing.' She had thought vaguely that her sister meant some kind of object. "What do you mean, overhearing?"

"Never mind."

"Anyway, it's not about Christmas. God, Ward, this is really difficult. Sorry. Has Caro spoken to you?"

"My cousin? No, why?"

"Okay," Bee said. "I'll tell you why."

When she had finished there was a short silence.

"Well," Ward said. "This is a shit sandwich and no mistake. I don't think now is a good time to tell Serena — she's got enough going on and it's not actually her problem."

"I'm really sorry. I know he's, well, her ex but he's also your cousin, and —"

"Not to worry about all that. I am basically civilised: I'm not going to thump him if I see him in the street. Which, from the sound of it, does not seem likely. I am a bit concerned, though, Bee. He's never been prone to vanishing acts. Never replies to his bloody messages but that's not the same thing."

"I was wondering…"

"If I could go round to his flat? Yes, I suppose I'd better. I'll run it past Stella – she's just got back. We could go together."

"Ward, I really would be grateful. Caro's very upset and what with Christmas coming up…"

"Yes, it tends to put the icing on the disaster cake, doesn't it, at this time of year. Why do these things always happen at Christmas? All right. Leave it with me and I'll do what I can."

"Thank you so much. Ward?"

"Yes?"

"What *did* you mean by a 'thing'?"

"Exactly what I said. Speak soon," Ward said and hung up just as Bee, disconcerted, heard the Land Rover pulling into the drive. Luna and Sam were back. Thank God.

STELLA

Serena, Stella and Ward stared at the thing perched on the mantelpiece.

"Do *you* know what that is?" Ward said to Stella.

"Mate, I haven't seen anything like that in the whole of my life. It looks like a baby pterodactyl." She turned to her sister. "And you thought you had problems with the Daily Mail."

The thing grinned. It was perhaps the size of a cat, and indeed, it had the characteristic diamond-shaped body of the flying dinosaur. But its curving head did not seem to end in a beak, being all of one piece. There was a small half moon of sharp teeth in the lower part of its face, and its triangular tongue occasionally flickered between them, vibrating like a tuning fork. The tongue was sharp, too, a dark old-meat red like the rest of its body. It had stubby claws, which were black. It flapped leathery wings and gave a sharp caw.

"*What is it?*" Serena whispered.

"I'll tell you what, though," Ward said, "Those teeth are sharp. So are those claws. Want to bet we now know what shredded your clothes?"

"It was not I!" the thing said, in a shrill, sweet, inhuman voice.

"Jesus!" Ward stepped back.

Stella was regarding it narrowly. "What's your name?"

"Oh no," the thing said. "I shall not say. I know these tricks."

"I think it's some sort of spirit," said Stella. "What are you?"

"Oh no," it replied. "I shall not say this, either."

It shut its beady, quicksilver eyes, shuffled its wings, and tucked its long head into its stubby body.

"Well, that's helpful," Ward said.

"What can we do?" Serena's voice sounded, to her sister's ears, almost as shrill as the creature's own. "We can't leave it in here."

"I think we might have to," Stella told her. "It can't do any more damage than has been done already and I don't fancy trying to budge it off its perch."

"That's a good point," Serena admitted, after a pause.

Ward slowly took out his phone, presumably to take a picture.

"No!" Stella spoke quietly, holding out a hand to forestall him.

He looked at her, eyebrow raised.

"We don't want to antagonise it," she explained.

"So what do we do?" Serena asked.

"Leave it in here, on its own. I expect if it wants to talk, it will. Or maybe it'll just go of its own accord. Like we probably should."

So they did.

Back in Serena's kitchen, Stella said, "And I haven't even told you about my adventures. Which were epic."

"Yes, where were you last night? I didn't like to ask."

"I met these people," said Stella. "And I think they might be able to help with the current problem."

"Can you give them a call?" Ward asked.

"Actually, no. Not on the phone."

"What, not at all? Not even a landline?"

"I don't think so. But I can go down there."

Serena said. "I need to call Bee." She did so, and then Ward took the phone into the kitchen. When he returned, Serena had gone upstairs to the bathroom. Ward hissed at Stella, "I need to talk to you! Bee told me Caro says Ben's gone missing."

"What? Oh shit!"

"She asked me to go round to his flat and I said I would, but I'd prefer it if you came with me. I feel the need for some back-up, as they say on police procedurals. I haven't told Serena and I can hardly ask her to go."

"Come with me down to Southwark," Stella said. "We'll cut across to Camden first, check Ben's flat, and take the Northern Line or a bus over the river."

"What's in Southwark?" Ward asked.

"These people," Stella said.

Ward insisted on taking a taxi to Camden, although Stella thought the Tube was just as quick.

"As long as you pay for it," she said. But Ward did tend to get accosted by people: actors were public property. She remembered this when the black-cab driver turned round at a red light and said,

"Are you that bloke? You know, on that cop show. That noir thing." He pronounced it *noyre*.

"Er, yes, probably," said Ward.

"My wife really likes you."

"How kind!"

"She'll be that made up when I tell her I've had you in the back! DI Holyrood his own self! Tell you what, why don't I phone her…"

And so that took up most of the ride, with Stella trying not to smile and Ward being furiously charming into the cabbie's mobile phone. He also handed over a big tip when they got out.

"Don't you find this exhausting?" she asked him.

"Depends what sort of mood I'm in. They don't always do that. One can't complain too much. It pays the bills. Although one chap once shouted at me in a Dublin park "I saw you in *Oscar Wilde* last night. You were shite!""

"Oh dear. But it must be a bit of a liability even if they like something. What if you're in a foul mood or pissed? Do you feel you can't get ratty because if you do they'll be writing to the Daily Mail?"

Ward sighed. "It's a bit of a thing, yes. *Star Hurt My Feelings*. God, Camden always changes and yet somehow it never changes, does it? It's been tacky since as long as I can remember."

"I liked the Lock, as it was. Bit of cybergothery."

"I'm not even sure what that means."

"Girls with pink dreads and stack boots and dayglo bras."

"It sounds fascinating."

They turned the corner of Ben's street. The last time Stella had been here Ben himself had opened the door, but now no one replied to Ward's knock. It was not far off dusk and the drizzle was cold. Ward knocked again.

"I thought this might happen," Stella said. "If he is indeed missing, you wouldn't expect him to answer the door."

"Which is why I brought this," Ward said, producing a key from the pocket of his expensive and voluminous overcoat.

"Get you! Where did you get that from?"

"I've had it for ages. Ben gave it to me in case he got locked out – he had several keys cut, distributed them around the neighbours and his mates. I think he'd forgotten he'd given it to me and I'd forgotten he had as well, until this blew up and I suddenly thought: *key*. I keep it on my fob with my own. Serena had one, too, but she posted it back to him."

"Yes, she would do something like that. I bet she didn't have a copy made. No guile, my sister."

"Which is why we love her," said Ward, smiling gently.

"Oh yes. So, want to see if he's changed the locks?"

But the door swung open easily enough. Ward went first, and Stella followed him up the stairs. When she had last been in this flat, some time before, it had been aspiring rock star shabby-chic, with framed vinyl and posters on the dark walls, and some quite good furniture. Now, the flat looked as though it had been abandoned for a century, locked in Haversham aspic. Everything was encased in a thick layer of dust.

"Shit," Stella said. "Why are all the pictures facing the wall?"

"I don't know. Bit creepy, if you ask me. And Ben had a cleaner. This is like the *Marie Celeste*."

Stella could smell something and it wasn't good. With the sleeve of her sweatshirt welded to her face she said, "You don't suppose he's –"

"People always talk of the 'odour of death' but I'm never quite sure what that means. We used to get dead rats under the floorboards sometimes when I was a kid, back in Gormenghast, as I like to think of it, and they stank but it wasn't quite like this. I think it's coming from the kitchen." He hesitated. "Do you want me to go first?"

"No, that would be cowardly. We'll both do it."

Once within, the source of the smell was revealed: a burgeoning cluster of mould that embraced the entire fridge and was climbing the walls.

"God Almighty," said Ward, swallowing hard. "It's like something out of *The Exorcist*."

"I've never seen mould like that before. Impressive," said Stella through her sleeve.

"That's got to be more than the milk gone off."

They looked at one another.

"You don't suppose…" Stella said, and the words trailed away.

"Suppose what?"

"That he's… *in* there?"

"Christ, I hadn't even thought of that. You do have a dark imagination, Stella."

"You say that like it's a bad thing. Do you think we should call the police?"

"I don't think I can cope with the Plod twice in one day, frankly. Hand me that –" Ward looked around him. "That pole thing."

"I think it's for opening tall windows," Stella said. But it was a good idea. It had a sizable hook on the end. Ward seized and – rather bravely, Stella thought – plunged it into the cloudy grey-green mass. A puff of rancid dust swelled out.

"This is disgusting. I'm trying to remember how his fridge opens – ah!" He had found the ridged handle and, after some tugging, the door swung outwards. Inside, the fridge was also filled with mould. Ward poked at it, rather frantically, but managed only to disturb a bottle, which fell to the floor and broke.

"I hope that wasn't wine," Stella said.

"I think it's mineral water. Talking of wine, though, I am definitely buying you a drink after we get out of here. Or you can buy me one."

"I'll buy," said Stella. "You paid for the taxi. Christ, I'm so glad he's not in there."

"What's causing it, though? A rogue cheese?"

"I've never seen anything like it," Stella repeated. "I hate to ask, but can you see a freezer?"

"No, he didn't have one – I do know that, because I had a conversation with him once about eating at home and he said he didn't need one, because there's a freezer compartment in that fridge and all he ever used it for was ice cubes and peas, like most people. And it's not nearly big enough for a body."

"Thank God for that," said Stella. "Ward – for various reasons, I think it's a good idea to look upstairs."

"All right. I shall take my pole with me. Who knows what we might find lurking in the bathroom? After pterodactyls and mould monsters, anything could happen."

"Yeah, I haven't even told you properly about *my* day, yet."

They took the winding stairs up to Ben's bedroom. The rain had started to come down in earnest now, spattering against the window.

Stella said, "I'm going to say this now. Ben's little friend Dana, of late unlamented memory, left something nasty up here once, like some kind of voodoo crap. Except not real voodoo, something of her own, made out of twigs. It was hanging in the window."

"You say *was*? I can't see anything now."

"No, neither can I. It's gone. Maybe she took it. Or it took itself." Better not tell him that they thought it had made its way into Serena's bedroom and been beaten into dust.

"It's not looking good up here, though. Where did all this dust *come* from? It might be worth getting hold of Ben's cleaner and finding out when she – or he, can't remember who it was – last came in here."

"But it would take years for this amount of crud to build up, surely," Stella said.

"Yes, it would. The bed's not made, either, as far as I can tell under all that. Let's take a look in the bathroom. Words I might regret."

But they found no more mould. The fittings looked ancient, however, the bath and sink stained green. This was the second really nasty lavatory that Stella had encountered in one day and she said so.

"The thing is," Ward said. "I have been here before. Quite a bit. Popped in for drinks occasionally, before we went out. Crashed here a couple of times after parties. And I don't remember anything untoward in here – trust me, I would have done. I'm fussy about stuff like this. It was perfectly clean."

"I honestly can't see Ben living like this. This is like a really rough squat. Mind you, if you're that picky, you'd better go to the loo in a pub before we hit my new mate's place. That's not very special, either."

"I can't wait."

"Seriously, don't hold your breath."

"I may have to." Ward went back into the bedroom and looked around. "What's that?"

In the dust on the bedside table, stood a photograph, propped up against the lamp. Ward picked it up: the picture was dust free. Stella peered over his shoulder as he studied it. A black and white snapshot, with that indefinable look of age – curling, a little yellowed. It showed a large and imposing house, not quite a stately home, but not far off. In one of the upstairs windows, a figure was very faintly visible, dressed in white.

"How Daphne du Maurier," said Ward.

"It is a bit Gothic, isn't it? Turn it over and see if there's anything on the back."

Ward did so. There was a date, 1943, and a name: *Hex Heath*, then *D.*

"A clue!" said Stella.

"I think you've been reading too much Nancy Drew, young lady."

"Famous Five. I'm not American. Or maybe the Secret Seven? We had all of those. They were my gran's. I read them like sweets when I was about eight, one after the other."

"Whatever your childhood predilections towards detective work, I think you're right. D stands for 'Dana'? We'll take it with us." He turned to face her. "Stella. I didn't like to say this, but quite apart from all the other weirdness, there is one big question outstanding."

"I know. Where are the cats? God. I hope nothing's happened to them. They were Siamese. Bit standoffish, but lovely. I did wonder if we might, well, find them in the fridge but I didn't like to say at the time."

"So you were okay with finding Ben in the fridge, but not the cats?"

"Well… you know. Beautiful cats versus beloved sister's ex-boyfriend who dumped her…"

Ward sighed. "There's no sign they've been shut in, though."

Steeling themselves, they made a thorough search of the rooms, but no little feline skeletons greeted them. At last Ward said, "Your fortitude is amazing but I don't think I can actually handle this much longer. Would you mind if we left?"

"Yeah, let's get out of here. I've been looking for an address book or something but I suppose he kept it all on his phone. Which is nowhere in evidence but you'd expect him to have taken that with him. Wherever he's gone. But it's hard to tell with all this shit in the place."

They went rather shakily out into the street. Stella lifted her face to the rain, letting it cleanse her. Even the smoky London wet was acceptable, after that. But as Ward was closing the door, a woman bustled up.

"Excuse me. You're Mr Amberley's cousin, aren't you?"

"Yes." Ward turned to her.

"I've seen you on that police show. Very good, I thought."

"Thank you!"

"Although I didn't like that woman."

"Oh dear."

As others had before her, the woman seemed to decide that since Ward had played a policeman on television, he was a kind of surrogate for the law in real life and could thus be confided in.

"You see, he let me go."

"He –?"

"I'm his cleaner. Mrs Clements. I'm local, not that there's many of us left these days. Three weeks ago, he said he was going off for a bit, he had a gig somewhere but he needed to get his head together whatever that means, and not to bother to go in and do the place. And I said, what about the cats, then? And he asked me if I would look after them, so I did. I fed them for a few days but when he didn't come back, quite honestly, I popped them in a basket and took them round to mine. I hope that was all right." She looked anxious, as if about to be accused of cat stealing.

"Oh, thank God for that! We were a bit worried, you see."

"We didn't know what had happened to them," Stella said.

"Well, I'm ever so fond of them."

"This is terribly kind of you," Ward said, scribbling on the back of a receipt. "This is my number. If you need – well, if you would like me to subsidise the moggies while my cousin is away, then don't hesitate to get in touch."

"That's really lovely of you," Mrs Clements said. "I could tell you were a gentleman from seeing you on TV. Do you know where Mr Amberley is, then, or when he's coming back?"

"We don't," Ward said. "I've been in the States, you see."

With a second round of mutual approbation, they parted.

"I took your lead," Stella was marching along now, head down against the wet. "I got the impression you didn't want to tell her he was actually missing."

"I was a bit concerned about it getting into the papers, to be honest. I mean, it may have to. But I don't want that to happen without consulting Ben's parents first. I don't think, from what Bee implied, that they've spoken to the police. I suspect Caro might be thinking that they'd want to know about Dana, and her brother."

"Fair enough. Oh look, there's a pub."

"We're going in it," said Ward, grimly.

The pub, rather oddly called the Bull and Bishop, looked wonderful to Stella. It was an old school London boozer, with etched glass, red leather stools and a stamped crimson ceiling. It gleamed with mirrors and light. The wooden boards were scuffed, but it was devoid of dust and mould. After Ben's flat, it was a haven.

"This is all right," said Ward. "What are you drinking?"

"I'll get 'em. A medium house red, please. No, make that a large. Ward?"

"I'll have the same," Ward said. It was still quiet enough for them to slip into a corner booth although the young barman did give Ward quite a sharp glance.

"This is weird, being out with you," Stella said. "Last time I went in a pub that wasn't the Hornmoon Arms or the Lion and Unicorn with you must have been before you were famous."

"Happy days."

"Oh c'mon. You like being famous!"

"It does have its drawbacks."

"At Christmas we'll go to the Arms and no one will affect to notice you unless they're tourists."

"Right now, that is an appealing prospect." He took a large sip of wine. "Better. Okay, let's have a look at this photograph."

But the mansion was no longer there.

Luna

It had been a good trip. She had talked a lot to Rowan, about childbirth, about having a baby. Rowan was honest and she did not mince her words.

"I love being a mum. But it's not easy. I worry a lot, if I'm doing it right. But my own mum's been great and so has Moss' ma. Lots of advice and they help when they can. You need family around you."

Luna smiled. "They say it takes a village to raise a child."

"I don't think that's true, actually. I think it takes the entire population of somewhere the size of Birmingham to raise a child properly but we haven't got that sort of society right now so we have to make do."

"Mum used to say it took a vineyard," said Luna.

Rowan, laughing, got up, quickly, and snatched a toddler away from the fireplace. "See? Eyes in the back of your head, like I said... But you've got a good family, Luna."

Luna nodded. "Yes. My sisters. Sam."

"And your mum." Rowan paused, jogging the toddler on her hip. "Where's your mum now? After all that."

Luna had given her friends an edited version of events. "She's gone off again. Travelling."

"Lucky her."

"Yeah. I always thought she was a homebody but she's not. Midlife crisis, maybe. Old age crisis. I don't mean that in a nasty way."

"Perhaps she thought *now or never.*"

"I think you're right. She said she was coming back for Christmas."

"Then I'm sure she will," Rowan said.

And now they were bouncing back over the bridge. Luna looked down at the silvery churn of the Severn and thought about tides and the Bore. She had not spoken about her dream to Rowan or even to Sam; she wanted to think about it first. But Moss, seemingly telepathic, had said that morning at breakfast, "Did you know, Luna, that people have been here for thousands of years, on this river shore?"

Luna had jumped as though he'd accused her of something. "No. I suppose if I'd thought about it..."

"They found footprints, human ones, embedded in fossilised clay."

"Really?"

"We went to see them," Rowan said. "At Goldcliff. It was weird, looking at them. It was very moving. Some of them were kids' footprints, tiny, like those impressions in plaster some people make of their babies' feet."

"Wow!"

"Imagine," Sam said. "Thousands and thousands of years ago, more than you can get your head around, and they're still there."

But Luna said nothing, thinking of that family, long ago, who were both human and wren. And the people at the temple. Had they been real? Or had her dreaming mind conjured them up, out of something read long ago? Perhaps it didn't matter.

They had got on the road at mid-morning, reached the bridge a half hour later. It was like driving through the sky: the winter light fracturing all around them and sending sparks across the river. Luna looked downstream to the humps of the islands and her own shore, past Avonmouth and the cranes, where a big container ship was trudging up the channel, to where Brean Down thrust its long nose out into the estuary. She liked this sense of weightlessness, of being between two worlds, just before they came down to earth and were dumped immediately into the traffic hell of the southbound M5. Sam would get off the motorway as soon as he could, she knew.

"Llogres," said Sam.

"Sorry?"

"The Land of Logres. Like in King Arthur."

"What —"

He nodded towards the big sign welcoming them back to England. "Lloegr. It's the Welsh word for 'England.' That's where Llogres comes from."

"I never knew that."

"I'd like to say it's an old piece of knowledge passed down by my people from ages past but actually I only realised it three weeks ago when I came back over here after that run to Monmouth and saw the sign."

Luna laughed. She repeated it. "Lloegr. Logres. It's a nice word."

"It's a good name."

And then they were past the sign and speeding up the long slope that led onto the main carriageway. Nearly home.

STELLA

"What the hell happened there, then?" Stella asked. They were still peering at the photograph.

"I definitely, definitely saw a big house."

"So did I. And it's the same name and date on the back."

But now the house had gone. The photograph showed an old cottage, tumbledown with a sagging roof. A ragged privet hedge partly obscured it.

"Not so much Daphne du Maurier now. More like Roddy Doyle."

"I think I preferred the mansion," Stella said. "What do you bet that 'D' stands for Dana, though?"

"In 1943? But we know she was around in Elizabethan times, so why not, although the thought of Dana as a landgirl tending to wounded soldiers makes my blood run cold."

"When Sam made enquiries," Stella said, "A while ago, back in the autumn, didn't he say something about talking to some bloke who had been to Tam and Dana's place, and said it was a whopping big house, but then he spoke to someone else and they said it was a bit of a hovel?"

"Yes, that rings a very faint bell."

"I'm going to ask him about it again, when we go down. Can you google Hex Heath?"

"I can try." Ward produced his smartphone and began tapping in queries, while Stella sipped her wine.

"Any luck?"

"Amazingly, yes. It's in Norfolk. It's out near Lowestoft."

"Norfolk! That was where the Stares were supposed to be from."

"But it says here it burned down during the war. Doesn't say why, or who owned it."

"Well, I think we know that," Stella said.

Having finished their drinks, they ventured out into Camden once more. It was now quite dark, the rain lashing down. The city had become a monochrome landscape: silver and steel, waterblack.

"Taxi or Tube?" Ward shouted above the downpour.

"Up to you!"

"Taxi, then." He hailed a cab, and they jumped in. "South of the river. Sorry!"

"S'all right, mate." The driver was Sikh and if he recognised Ward, he did not say so. He concentrated on driving: St Pancras, Holborn, and the Embankment. They went over Southwark Bridge, the skyscrapers gleaming through the rainy night. Stella squirmed back in her seat to glimpse the bald dome of St Paul's, rising like a skull amid the modern towers. To their left, the floodlit turrets of London Bridge reared up, a river cathedral, and ahead lay the tooth of the Shard.

"Where to?" yelled the driver.

"Back of the market, please," said Stella, fumbling in her bag for a ten pound note. "Southwark Tavern." But Ward had already given the driver the fare. He bundled her out into the sopping chill of the night.

"I've been here before, after stints at the Globe. Decent old pub."

"Yeah." She held the door for him. "I don't know if my – contact – will be here, mind you."

Ward rolled his eyes. "A bit hush-hush, eh?"

"I don't think that's who he works for, somehow, but yeah, I thought the same – oh, Ace! You *are* here." For he was standing at the bar.

"Stella. Didn't think we'd see you back quite so soon." He eyed Ward. "You're that bloke, aren't you?"

"I expect so."

"Look, Ace, I'm really sorry – we've got a bit of a problem and I thought you might be the one to give me some advice. If I buy you a pint…"

"Not Fullers, cheers all the same. They've got Directors on."

"Should I just get a bottle of red?" Ward asked.

"Do that."

They sat in the same seat in which Stella and Ace had their previous conversation. Perhaps he had it permanently reserved, in some mystical way. She launched in to her story, with occasional additions from Ward, and Ace listened, frowning. Sometimes he grunted.

"So that's what's happened," Stella finished up.

Ace was staring up at the ceiling.

"Lincrusta," he said, at length.

"Sorry?"

"That dark red stuff, which covers the ceiling. It's Victorian. You find it a lot in these old pubs in the Smoke. They called it 'lincrusta.' Sometimes it's green."

"I'm not quite following…"

"Nah, it's got nothing to do with your problem. I just remembered its name, that's all."

"Right."

"Things occur to me. This is a very old city, but I'm sure you know that."

"Roman," said Ward.

"Bit before that, actually. A tribal village, so they say. Then the Romans. Then Boudicea burned it down – I suppose you call her 'Boudicca,' now. When I was a kid, it was 'Boudicea.'"

"My dad always said 'Boudicea,'" said Ward.

"I prefer it. My point is that things remain, the memory of things, but they get changed. People who come in here regularly see that ceiling every day, but how many people know what that stuff's called? Not many, I should think."

"Are you trying to tell us something really obliquely?" Ward did not look irritated. Instead, he was frowning, as though, Stella suddenly realised, he was listening to one of his theatrical directors. Perhaps he would ask about his motivation?

"I think I'm just rambling, actually. Sorry. I've got a lot of unconnected thoughts about all this and I'm trying to fit them together. Basically, what you've got back at the gaff is a demon."

"A –!"

"That's what it sounds like."

"I thought demons were large and fiery and had horns and stuff?"

"Well, you're not wrong. They come in all shapes and sizes, really. And the size of the demon doesn't relate to its power: you can get quite little ones which really pack a wallop and then great big ones who're fundamentally rather gormless. Hard to tell without seeing this one which kind it is."

"I would have taken a photo on my phone," Ward said, "But I didn't want to piss it off."

"No, very wise. Because you never know what's going to annoy them. Unless you're really experienced in dealing with them and that's not a common phenomenon these days. They've gone a bit shy. Also, they don't always show up on film."

"That reminds me – but it can wait for a bit. Without knowing anything about demonic powers," said Ward, "I would have thought there was plenty about the modern world to capture their interest. Money. Porn. Wars. That sort of thing."

"You definitely have a point. However, people actually conjuring them – in this country – isn't that common nowadays. So they're still around, and they're interested in the kind of things you mention, but without directly interacting with humans. The situation in which you've found yourselves is not typical."

"How so?"

"It sounds like it trashed your sister's work. But that's not what demons usually do unless they're actually contracted to do so. And it's not very easy to put them under contract because, as I say, few people in this country have any expertise in demonic conjuration. Does she have any enemies who might be into this kind of thing?"

"I don't know. I don't think so. We did have a run-in with some people back in the autumn." Ward gave a brief recapitulation of events. Ace was silent for a few minutes.

"I see. I'd be surprised if the two events were linked, to be honest, but I could well be wrong."

"Can I show you something? You said sometimes stuff doesn't show up on film," Stella asked. She fished the photograph out of her bag. It once more showed the country house. Ace looked at it without expression.

"Nice pad."

"Last time we looked at this photo, about forty five minutes ago, it was a run-down hovel. But when we first saw it, it looked like this."

"Oh, it's one of *those*. Okay. Unfortunately, this bears out my theory that this is not connected to your earlier altercation. The sort of people you had the trouble with, and the sort of people who work with demons, generally don't have a lot to do with one another."

"Why is that?" Ward said.

"Different sorts of magic. Chalk and cheese. Neither is necessarily very pleasant, but they're qualitatively not the same."

"Not connected," Stella said. She took the photo, intending to put it back into her bag, but it crumpled, until it was no more than a film of dust on the table, like the ash from a cigarette. She snatched her hand away. Ace watched this without expression. Then he said,

"That's right. But that doesn't mean they *aren't* connected in this particular instance. I wouldn't rule it out."

"So what do we do now? We did speak to the – the demon but it didn't seem very co-operative."

"No. They're usually not." Ace sighed and swigged the remainder of his drink. "With my astonishing psychic powers, I sense that you're about to ask me to come up and have a word with it."

"*Would* you?"

"I suppose so. Means going north of the river, mind you."

"I don't know how you operate," Ward said, "But we can, well, pay you. Do you have an hourly rate?" He spoke tentatively, but Ace did not appear offended.

"Nah, I don't charge for this sort of thing. It's a hobby. You can buy me a pint. Or some cat food."

"Now?"

"No. When I've actually done something. I may have to get rid of this thing for you, but we'll see. Let's go, before it starts pissing down even more."

SERENA

Left alone, Serena felt drained and flat. Batteries run down. Maybe that was a good thing? She wandered about the house, cleaning random items: the sink in the downstairs loo, the skirting board along the landing. Cleaning was good, made her feel more in control, if only a little. At some point during the afternoon, she had faced the wreckage: not the ripped piles of fabric, but the collapse of any hope of getting something together for London Fashion Week. It would put her back, just as she was getting more established on the fashion map, but it was not terminal. She told herself this, firmly. No one had died; there would be other opportunities. Perhaps she would make pieces that were even better than before. It might prove to be one of those watershed moments. She had seen this happen – a catastrophe, followed by revitalisation, new doors opening, as if the collapse of one thing had created a hole in the universe for something else to fill.

In the major arcana of the Tarot, Serena remembered, the falling Tower is followed by the oceanic peace of the Star.

But first you had to fall all the way.

Ward and Stella had not yet returned. She ought to eat. She had sent Bella to her dad's for the night, though Bella had been warmly sympathetic, practical. Her daughter was growing up and though Serena had dreaded the difficult teens, perhaps it wouldn't be so bad. Bella was not quite there yet, still a little girl in ways and unlike some of her classmates, seemingly in no hurry. Her mother thanked her stars for that.

Serena opened the fridge and took out a carton of soup. Soup was good. Healthy and nourishing, warming on a cold night when you'd just had a shock. She told herself this as though she was her own mother, although Alys didn't always advise something so conventional. In fact, these days, who knew what Alys might advise? And she was, once again, God knew where. So Serena would have to be her own parent: adulting, self-care, big girl pants and all that. She carried the soup to the stove and put it into a pan, preferring to warm it through gently rather than risk the burn of the microwave. It was while she was waiting for the soup to heat up that the landline rang.

Serena stared at it in momentary stupefaction, as though it had never done such an outlandish thing before. Then she shook herself and picked it up.

"Serena Fallow."

"Good evening. I'm so sorry to ring you rather late in the day." The voice was male, well-spoken, unfamiliar.

"Who is this, please?"

"My name's Caspar Pharoah. My friends call me Cas, but I'm on LinkedIn under my full name."

"Okay," said Serena, calming down slightly. This was not sounding creepy or stalkerish. Caspar Pharoah was brisk, businesslike, and there was something reassuring in his voice.

"I'm phoning because I'm a venture capitalist, basically, and a backer. I mainly do start-ups, but I'm branching out."

"Okay," said Serena again.

"On a more personal note, I used to go out with Sydney Hannon."

"Oh, right! I've known Sydney for years." Also, this was ringing faint but still distinct bells. "Weren't you based in San Francisco at some point? I think I remember her talking about you."

"San Jose, actually, but I do love San Francisco. Fabulous city. Anyway, when Sydney was working in LA we used to meet up there sometimes, because we both liked the Bay Area so much. Then I had to come back to London and Sydney had other irons in the fire, so she stayed out there and we split up. All very amicable. You can check that with her, if you like."

"If you don't mind," Serena said politely. "I was going to write to her at Christmas. I suppose I've missed the international post – I always do."

"You still send cards?"

"Yeah, I know it's bad for the planet but I draw my own."

"That's really lovely. But I imagine you're very organic when it comes to that sort of thing. Anyway. Sydney loved your stuff, really loved it, and she looked great in your dresses. I don't know if you're aware of this, and I don't want to clothesplain to you, or whatever, but fashion is the next big thing for us financial angels, has been for a while."

"You're not mansplaining," Serena said. She turned the soup down. "Actually, though, I do know this. I read a piece on it recently, which said it was a great combination of market size and global demand."

"That's absolutely right. In hideous marketing-speak, fashion is held to be an industry that has yet to be fully disrupted."

"Urgh!" said Serena.

"I know, awful; what does that actually mean, right? Basically it makes little venture capitalists' eyes light up like a fruit machine. We're beginning to look at start-ups in fashion and I know you're way ahead of that stage, but – well, I won't beat about the bush. I'd be seriously interested in investing. In you."

"Oh. Wow."

"How does that sound?" Pharoah's voice was – not anxious, exactly, but concerned. Fake sincerity? Maybe.

"It would sound great but I've just had a massive disaster with the latest collection. I've lost everything."

"Oh my God! What, literally? What happened? Was it a fire?"

"No, it was vandalism. The police are looking into it." Much good that may do, given later developments.

"Serena, I don't know what to say."

"If this is putting you off, I'll totally –"

"No, not at all. Shit happens. Look, if this isn't a good time, I can send you some details and we can talk a bit later. I'm also conscious that Christmas's coming up and everyone's starting to wind down until the New Year."

"No, it's okay. Are you in London now?"

"I am. I'm based here, now. I have an office just off Cannon Street but I'm running about all over the place at the moment. Could we meet up, maybe? Cup of coffee? In the New Year if not now."

"I think I'd like to meet up before Christmas," Serena said firmly. "Given what's happened. This is a lot more positive, whatever comes of it."

"That's a good attitude. All right. What's your mobile number?"
Serena gave it to him.

"I'll leave you in peace now – sounds like you've got quite enough on your plate."

"Thank you so much for being interested in my work!"

"You make beautiful clothes, Serena. You deserve a bigger platform. Sorry, was that more marketing bollocks?"

"It's fine. Thank you."

"We'll talk soon." And he hung up, leaving Serena with a tiny glimmer of something that was not exactly hope – she'd had too many things fall through for that to be the case – but was, as she had just said, more positive.

LUNA

The M5 was congested all the way down through Portishead. From the high vantage point of the Land Rover, Luna looked longingly across the estuary: past the span of the bridge over which they had so recently driven, to the long silver sleeve of water and the vanishing point of the Welsh coast. They crawled towards the slope which led towards Weston-super-Mare.

"I've had enough of this toss," Sam said.

"It's awful, isn't it? You can smell the fumes." She didn't want to say *it can't be doing the baby much good.*

"I'm going to turn off." He swung the vehicle onto the next exit road and cut across country, heading for the Bristol ring road and the Mendip hills. "I don't like the motorway at the best of times. But it beats driving through Bristol."

Once they were free of the traffic, Luna started to relax again. She had still not told Sam about the dream, if dream it had been. It had felt too real. But it was hard to know, because she was no longer one being, but two. Did a child dream, in the womb? It would depend on cognitive development, probably, but then Luna told herself that maybe cognitive development had little to do with the human soul.

The road rose up and down, rolling towards the line of hills. Soon they had left the main road and were crossing the Mendip plateau, lined with fir and still bearing the hummocks of early barrows. Ancient country, Luna thought, rarely mentioned although it was on the edge of the supposed Arthurian lands: once they were down past Ebor Gorge, they would be able to see the hump of Glastonbury Tor, a candidate for Arthur's Avalon, rising out of the low plain. It felt old, up here, windswept and forgotten, though the land was intensively farmed and there were several villages. They were driving in the direction of Priddy, where a folk festival was held every year. Beneath the fields, Luna knew, the hills were riddled with caves, limestone hollowed and witch-marked.

It was winter-light, the sky becoming overcast and heavy. It did not have the yellow tinge of snow, and did not to Luna beckon rain either. Just grey. And soon, this close to the solstice, the sun would start its descent to a red twilight smear. Remembering the dreaming place, Luna was half asleep when there was a bang and the Land Rover braked and skewed, rumbling up over the edge of the verge and grazing the thorn hedge.

"Shit! Sorry!"

But Luna had seen the thing that had run across the road, hunched and low, a gold owl's eye flash before it went under the wheels.

"Sam! Oh, Sam! Did you hit it?" But she knew he had. Sam was already out of the driver's side and running back down the empty road. Luna struggled out of the passenger door. The Land Rover had not gone over, but it was leaning up, tilted at a sharp angle, and she dropped down into the grass. A hawthorn branch snagged her coat and pulled, tugging her towards the hedge.

Don't be sad, the hawthorn said, thin and spiky-voiced. Luna shot it a puzzled glance and went down to where Sam was standing in the middle of the road.

"What happened to it?"

"I don't know. I know I hit it – you heard the bang. I *felt* it."

Luna stepped onto the verge and looked down. There was a narrow ditch, a trickle of brown water in the bottom of it, but it was too narrow, too shallow, to conceal the thing that had run in front of them. She looked into the high green field: the slope was untroubled and empty except for a lone rook, pecking among the stones.

"I can't see anything," said Luna.

"No. There's nothing here." Sam returned to the Land Rover and began examining the front wheels and the bumper. "And there's no blood."

"Well, this is good, right? That we didn't hit anything?"

"That wasn't an animal. It was on two legs. It was wearing some sort of furry cloak. I don't think it was human, though. So what *was* it?"

But Luna did not know.

STELLA

Ace refused to get in a taxi and wouldn't explain why.

"Sorry to be precious. I realise it's a shitty night. But I only ever take the bus." And once ensconced upon the upper level of a rumbling double decker, he insisted on occupying the two front seats, which fortunately were free. Stella bounced down beside him.

"This is my favourite place on a bus."

Ward rolled his eyes. "God, you really are a big kid, aren't you?"

"Says the man who pretends to be other people for a living."

This shut Ward up for the moment, allowing Stella to admire the cityscape. Back over the bridge, with the bus shuddering and jolting, threatening to plunge them excitingly down into the light-sparkled dark water. The fairytale of Tower Bridge was again glimpsed and gone. Monument, dwarfed by tower blocks, dazzled with gold. Then they were into the city, the proper City of London, heralded by dragons. Ace had sunk into the collar of his coat, brooding and silent. Ward, she could tell, was noting the landmarks of theatres as they trundled through the West End, his own personal geographical rosary. Piccadilly swung by, a glimmer in the hammering rain. Then down the Cromwell Road and the imposing façade of the Natural History Museum. After this the embassies, but the route had started to become more residential. Stella, craning her neck, could see into upper rooms: lit and unlit.

"Ooh, there's a man in his underpants!"

"I think you need to get out more, Stella."

She nudged Ace. "This is our stop."

And they were back out into the downpour. The bus stop was some distance from Serena's mews; Stella led Ace through the intervening maze, zigzagging along passages. Ward followed. No one spoke until they reached Serena's front door.

"We can lend you a towel," Ward said to Ace.

"I'm going to frigging need one."

Serena opened the door so quickly that she might have been standing behind it. She ushered them inside, with a curious glance at Ace.

"Brought a friend over," Stella said. "Says he can help." She hoped this was true. Serena had enough to put up with, without Stella producing a literal ace from her sleeve.

"Would you like a cup of tea?" Serena said to Ace, remembering her manners. Stella expected him to refuse but instead he said,

"That would be lovely. Cheers."

"I'll put the kettle on," said Serena.

"So it's not in here, then, this demon?"

"Next door, in her studio."

"Okay. Cup of tea first, then I'll take a deck at it." He was looking around Serena's long living room. "Nice place. Without being crass, your sister must be earning a decent crust."

"Yes, she does. But she's renting. The house and the studio, from a goldsmith. A lady named Eleanor."

"So this – incursion. This hasn't happened before?"

"Not like this. The studio doesn't seem to have anything – attached – to it."

Ace gave her a narrow look. "You'd notice if it had?"

"I think one of us would have noticed."

"Okay. Thanks," he said to Serena, who had brought in the tea. "All right if I take this next door?"

Serena gave a rather strained laugh. "You couldn't possibly do much more damage, could you?"

"Also, I hate to put you to the trouble, but do you have any oil, and some honey? It's not for going in my tea, don't worry."

"I – yes. Is olive oil all right? And Manuka?"

"That will be just lovely, my darling, thank you," said Ace, sounding suddenly plummier. "Could you mix them together for me in a small glass bowl."

Serena disappeared and returned in due course, bearing a sticky mixture in a little dish, which Ace took charge of.

"Marvellous. Let's go."

Serena came with them, but Stella thought she was reluctant to do so. Couldn't blame her. Serena unlocked the door to the studio and switched the alarm off. Then she turned on the lights.

All of the shredded material had been piled in one enormous pyramid in a corner of the room. It was suspiciously regular and symmetrical: torn cloth, thought Stella, should not behave like that. The demon squatted on top, wings folded, eyes closed.

"Oh, right," said Ace. "Okay."

Ward looked at him. "That's all you have to say?"

"So. Yeah. This is indeed a demon. A spirit, to use a less loaded term, and we like 'less loaded' terms around here, don't we, because they allow things like the de-escalation of situations, and not panicking, and remaining calm."

Ward's mouth twitched. "You do seem pretty calm, actually."

"I generally do remain reasonably chill in these situations, because a more agitated range of reactions have pretty much been burned out of me. Let's say I'm more at the 'Oh. Yeah. One of those,' end of the panic/calm spectrum rather than the 'What the holy fuck is that?' end. Make sense?"

"I think so. It *is* a demon, then? Or a spirit, if you prefer?"

"Yes, it is. It's also not asleep. It's just pretending." He held up the bowl in both hands. To Stella's alarm, the bowl began instantly to smoke, and Ace cried in a ringing voice,

I adjure you, O Spirit, Ram-bearer, who dwells among the graves upon the bones of the dead, that you will accept from my hand this offering, and do my will by bringing me you who are bornless. Raise yourself up so that you will speak to me without fear, and tell me the truth without deception. Let me not be afraid of you, and let you answer whatever questions I ask you.'

A shadow, man-shaped but smaller, began to form in the corner of the studio.

"Cheers," said Ace. The demon's eyes snapped open. It observed the proceedings with beady interest. "For the record," Ace said, over his shoulder to his audience, "If you ever want to do this again, it's from the grimoire of the Sefer Ha-Razim. Handy."

The form, Stella saw, was taking shape. It manifested as a naked child, fair haired and with the dissipated, grumpy face that you see on some middle-aged men. It reminded her slightly, but horribly, of a miniature Boris Johnson. It wore a tilted golden crown, of the sort that is reminiscent of paper hats found in Christmas crackers. It radiated a rosy heat and this made Stella step back and tremble.

"What, now?" it said, querulously.

"Yeah, sorry about this but I need some information and I don't have time to muck about. Who conjured the imp?"

"No one conjured me!" the pterodactyl said, rattling its wings like an outraged bird. "And I am no imp!"

"No, come on, don't bullshit me. You're not a free agent."

The child sighed, a hot gusty breath. It all but rolled its eyes. "One who opposes the priest of the bull."

Ace regarded it for a moment with his mouth open. "So – does this mean anything to you, Serena?"

"No, I don't know what he's talking about!"

"Anyone else?"

A small chorus of denial came from Stella and Ward.

"Who is the priest of the bull?" Ace demanded.

"One who is long lost."

"See," Ace said, turning to his audience. "This is what you have to put up with. He's actually being straight with me. He won't be able to give me the name, if he's contracted, so he's doing his best and there's no point in getting cross with him."

"How annoying," Stella said.

"Welcome to the wacky world of demonic conjuration."

The pterodactyl opened its beak and gave a high, sweet cry. The child shimmered and was gone. Ace dropped the glass dish with a curse and it broke upon the floor.

"Bollocks. Time to try something else," Ace said.

LUNA

Luna and Sam arrived at Mooncote in the late afternoon, still shaken. They had searched the area around the van, but there was nothing to be found. At last, they had driven away, more slowly than before, but no one sprang from the empty air in front of them. Luna kept a close eye on the barrows of the dead, but the landscape felt blank and flat, grey beneath the darkening sky. By the time they reached the house, the sun had gone down in a brief flare and the evening star trembled above the fields, visible between a gap in the clouds.

Bee came out to meet them, looking worried.

"Luna, Sam! I'm so glad you're back. How was your trip?"

"Mainly good," Luna said. "Are you all right?"

"I'm fine, but we have a – visitor."

"Oh, has Stella come down? Or Serena? I thought they weren't coming till closer to Christmas."

"No, not yet. This is someone else." She knitted her fingers together and gave a tight smile. "You'd better come in. Shall I help you with your bag?"

Luna smiled in return. "You sound as though we're checking into a hotel."

"Sorry!" Bee picked up the rucksack and hauled it over to the kitchen door. Then she paused.

"This visitor – I'd really like Sam to meet her, without me giving any impressions first."

"All a bit mysterious," Luna said. But then she saw why.

The girl was fast asleep, curled around Nelson. But the green tinge of her skin was quite evident.

"Where did she come from?" Luna asked, squatting on her heels to study the visitor more closely.

"Originally? God knows. After what happened in the autumn… could be anywhere. I found her in the churchyard. I was worried she might freeze to death. She's been here ever since."

"She looks half starved," Sam said.

"Yes. But she's been eating normally enough. She won't touch meat. A veggie, like you, Luna! Bread and honey, butter – I found her finishing off the contents of the butter dish yesterday – and milk. And porridge. And apples and cheese. She seems to like dairy."

"I remember my nan talking about green people," Sam said. "Only the once, when I was a kid, after we watched something on the box about aliens. She said she'd met a woman with green skin but she wasn't from another planet. So I asked her where she was from, then, and Gran said she didn't know. She met her in a wood and the woman was gathering woodruff."

"Did your nan say if she spoke English?" Bee said.

"No, but then again, Gran speaks quite a few languages and some of them are some funny ones. She can just about get by in French, for instance, but I've heard her speaking stuff I don't understand to people."

"What sort of people?" said Luna.

"People who came to the van when I was tucked up in bed so I didn't see them. I tried to listen once but the van was too small and the floor creaked. I got a swat near the ear and told to mind my own business."

"Might be worth getting hold of your nan," said Bee.

"Yeah, I was going to try to pop up at some point over Christmas anyway. So I could ask her then."

In the dog basket, the green girl stirred and whimpered like an animal.

"She's waking up," Sam said.

"Her name is Aln," Bee told him.

"Aln." And at the repetition of her name the girl sat up and gasped. She looked hard at Sam and Luna, but harder at Sam, and more warily.

"She's nervy of men, looks like," Sam said. "I don't want to freak her out. I've got to go down to the horses, anyway."

Bee took a piece of paper from the table and handed it to Luna.

"She drew this. All green, even the sun."

"It's like a child's drawing," Luna said, looking at the round emerald sun, the green knoll, the small round building that resembled a fort. "Is that the sea?"

"I think so. Look, she's used the lighter green pen on the sky, too."

"There was a story," Luna said, "of some green children who were found. Medieval times?"

"Yes, in Woolpit in Norfolk. I remembered that in the middle of the night, after I'd found her. I got up and went through some of Abraham's folklore books – it's quite a well-known story. Two kids, a boy and a girl. The boy died but the girl survived and went into service. She would only eat beans. But eventually the green in her skin faded. I think she might have got married, even."

"Do they know where the kids came from?"

"No, but it sounds like that drawing."

As they were talking, Aln watched them closely, her pale gaze sliding from face to face.

"It was a green land, they said. Not like the world we know."

"Well, we know all about those," Luna said.

That night, Luna woke. Sam lay sleeping beside her in a mound of blankets. She got out of bed and went to the door. Moth the lurcher raised his narrow head in enquiry as she passed and Luna let him come with her. She was not sure what had woken her but she could hear someone moving about in the kitchen: a distant scraping. As quietly as she could, Luna went down the stairs with the dog at her heels.

In the kitchen, Aln was trying to drag the kitchen table across the floor.

"What are you doing?" Luna said. The girl jumped, gave a cry, and collapsed across the table. Luna patted her gently on the shoulder.

"It's okay. I'm not going to hurt you." She did not think that Aln could understand but she hoped her tone would be reassuring. Aln, however, was not looking at Luna. Instead, she was staring out of the window.

"Nothing's there," Luna said, in the same trying-to-reassure voice. Only twigs, rattling against the glass.

Except the kitchen window opened out onto the courtyard, where there were no trees.

Luna held a finger to her lips, hoping Aln would understand. She seemed to, for the girl froze, standing trembling by the table. Swiftly, Luna went to the kitchen door and checked that it was bolted fast. Then she sidled along to the window and risked a glance.

Something was shuffling about in the courtyard. The spaniels could hear it: their wide-eyed, unmoving stance was identical to Aln's own. Why were they not barking? But Luna thought that they might not bark if they were afraid. Then Moth growled, low and deep. She could not see what the thing was: only that it was man sized, but stooped. It was close, on the other side of the window. Inside the kitchen, Aln sank down, very slowly, as if sudden motion might attract attention. She slid under the kitchen table and crouched there, still. Something scratched against the lowest pane of glass. Luna looked quickly about her. The only thing to hand was a heavy cast iron frying pan. Her fingers curled around the handle. The window pane cascaded inwards in flying shards of glass. A finger followed it: long and white and corrugated as bark, tipped with a pointed claw. It groped along the sill and Luna brought the iron pan down upon it, slamming it against the wooden sill. The finger broke off and fell to the floor, where it became a gnarled twig ending in a small black hoof. She heard its owner withdraw and pad off into the darkness.

Aln darted from beneath the kitchen table and seized the ash twig in a fold of her shawl, taking evident care not to touch it with her bare hand. She scurried to the Aga, wrenched open the door, and thrust the twig into the heart of the stove. There was a flash of green fire. Luna heard footsteps running down the stairs and Sam and Bee hurtled into the kitchen.

"What happened? I heard a noise." Bee stared at the broken window in dismay. "Luna, did you knock it with that pan?"

"No, something was trying to get in. It broke the window."

"Shit."

"What was it?" asked Sam.

"I don't know. It was a finger, with a claw. It broke off when I smacked it and Aln shoved it in the stove."

Sam was peering through the window. "I can't see anything. I can patch this up."

"I'd rather you didn't go out to the woodshed, until it's light," said Bee. "There's some plasterboard behind that cupboard."

"I'll tape it up. And I'll bring a quilt downstairs, sleep in the kitchen till sunrise. Oh, wait –" He nodded in the direction of Aln.

"I'll stay with you," said Luna. "In case she's nervous around men, like you thought."

"Why is the table there?" Bee asked. "Did someone move it?"

"I think Aln was trying to barricade the door," Luna said. "The dogs were scared."

"The dogs are useless!" said Bee. "Aren't you?" But Nelson and Hardy, now that the humans had come to their rescue, just wagged their tails, and Moth stared grimly at the window.

SERENA

Stella's new friend looked a little rough around the edges, but Serena liked him, somehow. This surprised her. Normally, although she was a little ashamed of it, she would have felt nervous of someone who looked so down at heel, with a definite vibe of the alcoholic. But as soon as Ace came through the door she felt her spirits rise. And she did what he told her.

"Could you, my love," he said to her now, "pop back home and bring me some stuff?"

"What sort of stuff?"

"I'll need some salt, in a dish. Do you have a chimney?"

"Yes. Smokeless fuel, though."

"Hmmm. Well, I only need a little pinch, so if you could put your hand up it and see if you can scrape off some soot, that would be fantastic. And could you make me some toast? Make sure you burn it."

"Anything on it? Jam? Marmite?"

"It's not for me," Ace said.

Wondering, Serena ran back to the house and did as he asked, keeping a stern eye on the toast in case it set the smoke alarm off. When she had what he wanted, she took it back to the studio, where Ace, Ward and Stella were chatting.

"…just don't find them terribly helpful but it's mainly because I get freaked out in all the traffic," Stella was saying.

"You won't catch me cycling," Ace said.

After a moment, Serena realised that they were talking about Boris Bikes. She handed the plate of toast to Ace.

"Here you go."

"Marvellous."

The pterodactyl was perched on the mantel, eyes firmly shut.

"So," Ace said. "I'm not totally sure about the results of this one, but let's give it a go, shall we?" He put the plate of toast on the floor and scattered the sooty salt around the room. The demon opened one eye at this point, but shut it again when it saw that it was being observed.

"I'm a bit worried about all that crap over there," said Ace, pointing to the mound of fabric. "Sorry, love, I know it's all your work, but it's crap now, isn't it?"

Serena sighed. "Yeah, it is."

"However, I don't actually want to fucking set fire to it."

Ward shot him a nervous look.

"What exactly are you planning to do?"

"This," said Ace, and raised his hand. Around the room, the circle of sooty salt flared into fire: burning blue-green like driftwood.

Stella gasped. Serena should have been horrified – her parquet floor! – but all she could think was that it was beautiful. It was like watching the sea turn to flame: fire and water as one and the stuffy air of the studio was blown away on the shore wind. On the mantel, the demon flapped its leathery wings and cried out in despair. Serena suddenly pitied the thing. The green-blue flames rose higher, the demon's wings beat hummingbird fast and now Serena could see the ripples they made in the shimmering air, a Doppler migraine zig-zag. The walls of her studio were melting: unmaking in layers from the ceiling. For a moment she and her companions and the demon stood on emptiness with the walls of the city shining up around them and then they were travelling down.

BEE

With Sam, Bee made a thorough search of the courtyard once it became light enough to see, but there was no trace of anything untoward.

"Things have started happening again," Bee said. She looked at Sam, grateful for his presence. A calm young man who knew things. She was glad he was there.

"Yes. The season's on the move. Embertide."

"I've heard that word before, from the vicar. What does it mean, Sam?"

"Well, I'm not a Christian. You'll have noticed that." He smiled. "But my nan still goes to church sometimes. Says it can't hurt. Although what she actually believes in is anyone's guess. I think she takes some of their words and uses them in a different way – it's hard to tell, sometimes. She's a bit of a magpie, I suppose. But I know that, according to the church, there are four tides of the year and we're past one of them now – St Lucy's Day."

"Oh! Yes, that's right. Wasn't it the start of advent? Honestly, Kate shouldn't let me through the door of that church – I'm so ignorant about a lot of this. I know in Sweden, is it, it's the feast of St Lucia and girls wear a crown made of candles."

"That's right. Although I wouldn't fancy that much. Chances of setting your hair on fire... Anyway, stuff often happens around the embertides. Things change. We saw something on the way home..."

Bee's interest was quickened. "What sort of something?"

"It ran out in front of the van. I was sure I'd hit it. Luna saw it. The size of a person, but she doesn't think it was human."

Bee laughed. "A very tall badger or a very small nun?"

"Ha! Yeah, I like that. It had big eyes, she said. We stopped, obviously. But there was nothing on the road."

"I saw something out of the church window. But I'm not sure what I saw, either. Another land... I wonder if Mum's going to show up soon?"

"Well, Christmas is coming and the goose is getting fat. We'd best keep an eye out. Talking of which, Bee, your young Martian – how confident are you about her?"

"I don't know. I don't feel that she's bad, somehow. But I might be wrong."

"That's often the way of it."

When things seemed to be flying apart, chaos in the air, Bee liked to run a tight ship at home. Something hearty on or in the stove. Bread in the Aga. Floors hoovered, sinks scrubbed. If she'd been one for nail polish, she'd have got her nails done, but gardeners and housewives were high risk for any manicure even with this new gel stuff that Serena had told her about. Maybe for Christmas she'd do something different… She filed them anyway, feeling that this small piece of self-care was all part of the process. Luna, she noticed, had tidied the van and got the local vet over to see to the horses' teeth for their annual check and file. But Bee still felt like King Canute, shouting vainly at the rising tide.

At least she had spoken to Ward about Ben. This was a distinct relief: an obligation discharged. Stella, in a separate and later phone call, had also said she would look into it, and although Stella was not always completely reliable in small matters, she could be trusted with important things. And Ward, whatever his relationship with Serena, would not want to have a missing cousin. So when she ran into Caro Amberley in the village post office, Bee was at least able to say that she had done as she had been asked and Ward and Stella had been to Ben's flat and found nothing. Although that wasn't entirely true, apparently, but no need to worry Caro.

"Thank you. I'm truly grateful."

"Have you – heard anything?"

Caro shook her head. She was looking more drawn, Bee thought. Sometimes people whom you saw nearly every day underwent what the French call a *coup d'age*, ageing overnight. This blow of age had not yet befallen Caro, but Bee wondered whether it might. Honestly, Ben was thoughtless – assuming he was actually all right. At the very least, it would blow a hole in the Amberley's Christmas if he didn't turn up soon.

"Stella has done this, by the way. When she's been abroad and working – she can be a bit thoughtless. Sometimes creative people can be like that."

And Mum did it, thought Bee — but she didn't feel able to bring that up, because look what had happened to Alys. She did not want to remind Caro that her son might be trapped in some other dimension, beset by horrors. Bee herself had had quite a good time in the otherworld, if one could call it that, but Luna and Stella had told her different stories. It didn't seem fair, somehow…

"Yes." Caro was clearly trying to sound firm and resolute. "I'm sure that's what it is and I'm just being stupid. Richard still doesn't think we should call the police: he says Ben would be cross. But he's been contacting Ben's friends. I'm sure he'll turn up in time for Christmas."

Bee reached out and gripped the other woman's arm. "Hang in there."

Caro managed a smile. "Nothing else to be done, is there?"

SERENA

Serena was wandering. She couldn't see the others and ordinarily this would have sent her straight into heart-in-the-mouth panic, but it just didn't seem to matter. The place in which she found herself was calm and cool and so was Serena – just like her name, for once. It was a respite from the alarms and distress of the day and distantly she welcomed it.

It was also very blue. Serena looked through cerulean glimmer, glimpsing indigo shadows. Once, she thought she saw a star, but when she looked more closely it winked and vanished. Beneath her feet, the track was silvery. She was not sure if she was outside; this world felt enclosed. It began to resolve, the blue shimmer starting to coalesce into marble pillars and fade to pale. There was stone beneath her feet and scrolls on the walls, bearing inscriptions: she could not make out the names or the dates, but saw a little carved ship, scudding across a stone sea.

She stood before a huge stained glass window, arched and made of sea-coloured shards and fragments. Between Serena and the window was an altar, and on the altar stood a cross that looked as though it had been made out of driftwood, studded with copper nails that caught the light. On the altar cloth, embroidered, was another ship in full sail. This time the waves over which it raced were silken. For a second, it seemed so real that Serena's hair was stirred by the salt-filled wind.

"Leave an offering. That's my advice."

Serena looked up to see a magpie perched on a windowsill, high above her head. The bird see-sawed forwards and back, rocking as if on a bough.

"What? What kind of offering?"

"Up to you." The magpie might have shrugged.

Serena was wearing a bangle: not gold, just gilt and pink plastic, very cheap. She'd found it in the mews that day and slipped it on her wrist, not liking to let it lie in the road. Would that count? She had no other jewellery: she'd had no time to put any on.

"It's so you can come back," said the magpie, bouncing. "Like a fish-hook."

Serena slid the bangle from her wrist and laid it on the altar, in front of the cross. Maybe it was the wrong thing to do – a link with this unknown place – but it felt right, to be here. The magpie watched her with a beady, approving eye. Once Serena had done as the bird suggested, it flew up right through the stained glass: she gasped, but bird and window were unscathed. Through a patch of green glass she saw the magpie whirl up into the sky.

Beyond the chapel – she would call it a chapel, it felt like one – where the bird had flown, she could see a garden. Very formal, laid out in an Elizabethan key pattern, regulated by box hedges. A knot garden. A not-garden, Serena thought suddenly, and shook her head at the wordplay. She searched for a segment of clear glass and peered through. It was not winter here: there were roses in full bloom, crimson and apricot and cream, and beyond stood a bank of tall trees in full summer leaf.

But it was as though the bird's transgression through the window had broken something, after all, for the chapel began to dissolve, shattering around Serena in jigsaw strangeness. She stood still, fists clenched, feeling unsafe. Then the chapel was gone.

"There you are! God, I've been worried." Ward grabbed her by the shoulders. Serena fell forwards into a hug. "Where have you been?"

"I don't know." She disengaged a little to look around her. "Where am I now, then?"

"We think it might be under the studio." Stella was very grubby. Her hands were black with dust or soot and a long cobweb trailed from her hair, giving the light brown a premature grey streak. "But we don't know for sure. Did your place have a cellar?"

"Yes, I think so, but Eleanor told me it wasn't safe. There's a trap door in the floor. I did poke my head through once but it looked empty. Eleanor thought if we could afford an architect to come and have a look, we could convert it to a basement: maybe get some slanting windows put in. Or just lights. But we haven't got round to it yet."

"Anyway, I think we're in it. Your cellar."

"What happened? Did you fall?"

"No, we were just suddenly here and then we realised that you weren't with us. Cue massive panic. Well, apart from him." Ward nodded towards Ace, who was studying the wall. "Not that we've been here long. Ten minutes?"

She had been absent for longer than that, surely, in the chapel which overlooked the knot garden. Serena decided not to mention this just yet.

"What's he doing?" she asked.

"He's looking at the bloody wall," Ace said, without turning round. "There's something wrong with it."

"Looks solid enough to me," said Ward.

"Yeah, really?" Ace stretched out his hand. It passed effortlessly through the bricks, as through a hologram. "C'mon. I want to see what's behind this."

Serena and Stella exchanged glances. But Serena could tell that her sister was intrigued – and indeed so was she. As Ace disappeared through the wall, they fell in line behind him.

As soon as they did so, Serena felt that she had travelled downwards again. There was a slight jolt, as with a lift. She took a breath of cold damp air. It felt as though they were near a river – the Thames, or one of the city's many buried streams? But as her eyes adjusted to the darkness, Serena saw that they were in another long, enclosed room. At the end of it stood a stone table, stout and roughly carved, and on it rested a head. Serena's hand flew to her mouth, but the head was also made of stone: a pale honey colour. Male, blank eyed, with a curling beard.

"Oh," Ace said. "It's one of those." He walked forward, circumnavigating the table, and Serena, curious, followed. The head had no back. Instead, a second face gazed tranquilly at the wall. Ace stared at it, clearly lost in thought.

"Can you speak, then?" he said at last.

The eyes belonging to the backward-looking face remained tightly shut, but in the countenance that looked outwards to the room, they flew open. They were molten gold, without pupils. Somewhere a fire raged.

"Who asks?" said the head, in a voice like a bell.

"A practitioner of magic. You know me. We've met before. Or one of your kind has. You're all connected, I know that."

The head was silent for a moment, as if contemplating this. Then it said, "Yes, we remember you. To what purpose have you come here now?"

"I need information. Things are happening. The city is stirring. There are a lot of rumours, and quite a bit of collateral damage. What's afoot?"

The stone head smiled.

"Change." Then the gold fire faded from its eyes and it stood silent for a second, before its mouth opened and exhaled a breath, vast and water-laden. Serena's hair was stirred with salt air, weedwater rivers roared around her, rain pattered down. She had a fleeting glimpse of the blue place, a flame the colour of seaside sky. She heard a great bell toll once, then they were standing in her ravaged studio once more, quite dry. Serena's ears were ringing. Of the pterodactyl upon the mantelpiece, or the head upon the table, there was no sign.

"Caspar Pharoah? I know him."

"You do?" Serena rolled over onto her stomach and looked at Ward. He frowned into the shadows of the bedroom.

"Well, when I say "know," I mean "met." Actually, when I say "met" – I'm lying. I've seen him."

"Ah."

"Not the same thing."

"No."

"I saw him at some gala. He went out with Sydney Hannon, didn't he? For a bit, anyway, because she does tend to burn through them – she's like Miranda. Nicer person, though."

"She's lovely. She's just bad at *staying* with men."

"Anyway, I remember because it wasn't that long ago – it was before I came back from the States, obviously. Maybe it was at the Met? Well, whatever. And I remember because Sydney was in one of your frocks."

"I'm surprised you recognised one of my frocks! Was it a sort of oceanic blue thing with frondy seaweed bits? That's the last thing she bought from me and she had it fitted."

"I think so. Yes. Anyway, to be brutally honest, I only knew it was one of yours because Miranda screwed up her eyes in a ferrety sort of way and said, 'That's one of your ex's dresses. It makes Syd look fat'."

"Typical!"

"Alas, Miranda was always saying that things made other women look fat. And they never did. Or if they did, so what?"

"So, about Caspar Pharoah."

"Yes. Sorry. He was with her, sort of hovering, and Miranda said, 'What's HE doing with *her*?' and I said I supposed they were an item and she rolled her eyes and said, 'His name's Caspar Pharoah and *he's* supposed to be stinking rich. East End barrow boy made good. Recently arrived in town from the gutter.' Then she sniffed."

"Oh dear."

"Anyway, in the interests of full disclosure, I would like to say that I definitely would have gone there myself, gutter or no gutter, because he is really rather good looking. Pale gilt hair and dark brown eyes. Like a spaniel."

"You're not totally selling me here, Ward!"

"What? I like spaniels. Although perhaps not quite that much. However, his manner was not spaniel-like: rather upright. A bit stiff upper lippy. Very English – you know the type, sort of Norman: narrow head, long nose, high brow, could be stoat faced and weaselly in some public school products but this all fitted together nicely and his eyes weren't too close together. Definitely the countenance of the oppressor, though."

"Your way of describing people…" Serena said faintly. "I'd love to know how you describe *me* when I'm not around."

He kissed her hand. "A sylph, a nymph, a creature of moonlight…"

"You terrible ham!"

They stared at each other.

"Anyway, he's posh."

"Yes, Miranda was just being a cow. He's certainly not from the gutter, unless it's a gold plated one. I'd describe him as a bit posher than me."

"You are quite posh, actually, Ward."

"Indeed. It has lost me many roles on film as a son of the soil. However, I think our Cas is a bit more than upper middle, somehow, from the way he was speaking. What did you think?"

"Yes, he sounded as though he was dumbing down his accent slightly, now you mention it. Not in a condescending way. Although maybe it's always condescending when someone does that? I got the impression he wanted to put me at ease." She took a sip of water from the bedside glass, frowning. "'Caspar' is quite posh. It's an odd surname, though, 'Pharoah'. He can't be Egyptian."

"I don't actually think it's an Egyptian name. I used to know a woman called Pharoah. And she was upper class, too. She was something to do with the National Theatre admin and I sat next to her at a dinner bash once. I asked her about her name and she said it was Medieval English – maybe Middle English, not sure if I'm remembering this correctly – and it was originally Farrar."

Serena had retrieved her tablet and was googling.

"Oh, yes, it is. You're partly right, if Wikipedia is. Medieval English and Old French, coming from 'ferour,' meaning 'iron worker'."

"So he probably is Norman, then."

"Looks like it."

"Well," Ward said, leaning back onto the pillow, "Let's hope he's inherited enough from centuries of looting to bail *you* out, then."

By the time Serena left the house, on the day of her meeting with Caspar Pharoah, it was not far from darkness. The sun had already set invisibly behind the buildings, but in the west the sky was a shining green, shading down into gold. She had taken a long time to dress, feeling that it was important, and a number of outfits lay rejected on the bed. Serena, in high collared shirt, a velvet skirt of so rich a blue that it was almost black, and riding boots, would have been cold except for the jacket she wore. It was expensive, sculpted like a redingote, and its tails fell into the lines of the skirt and swished. Neither business nor eveningwear, but hopefully somewhere between both. She had confidence in her clothes and she had piled her hair on top of her head.

Before meeting Caspar Pharoah, she had promised to see a visiting friend, last-chance-before-Christmas, in Villiers Street. Niamh was living in Yorkshire now, but they had been close all through school and Serena welcomed the opportunity to catch up, a bit of grounding before the business meeting.

The chill nipped her skin as she made her way to the Tube. It was almost a relief to get down into the underground, an oven in summer, but now simply warm and stuffy. It was crowded, as usual, coming up to rush hour. She had to wait out two trains but squeezed onto the third, with no hope of finding a seat. The train rattled away and Serena, nose in a businessman's armpit, sank into the unhappy transport trance familiar to most Londoners. At Victoria, however, the carriage thinned out and Serena was able to collar a seat and read a discarded copy of the Evening Standard. When she got out, at Embankment, the river still held the light, silver-gleaming. That gave Serena an idea.

The wine bar was called Champagne Charlies, and Serena had been there several times before. Old school London, a bit seventies still, but she liked its dark vaults. Niamh sat in solitary state, surrounded by carrier bags but looking as regal and raven haired as ever. She leaped up when she saw Serena and flung her arms around her.

"I'm so glad you could make it! It's so good to see you? What are you drinking?"

Serena wrinkled her nose. "I've got a business meeting after this near Tower Bridge. With a business angel, so it's quite important. It had better be coffee…"

One eye on the clock. But it was good to see her friend all the same, a lot to tell her, a lot to hear. She left plenty of time to get downriver, though, and when she and Niamh left the bar it was fully dark. Serena waved her friend off towards the Tube and Kings Cross for the north, then turned and trotted down towards the river. She paused, as she always did, to say hello to the twin sphinxes who guarded the spike of Cleopatra's Needle, but despite a floodlight on the Needle itself, their wide, calm faces had their eyes tightly shut. They reminded her of the Janus-head in the cellar.

Down on the river, the clipper was waiting. Serena loved the word: it sounded like a swift ship, white sails unfurled, the blue sea waiting. But this boat was more like a small catamaran, rocking on two long parallel hulls. She tapped her Oystercard to the pad and stepped on board. The river bus ran frequently and it soon pulled out, heading into the dark water of the Thames. It was much colder on the river. Serena watched the bulk of the Tate pass by on the opposite bank, then the clipper pulled into Blackfriars in a flurry of water. The Globe Theatre and then floodlit tower of Southwark Cathedral appeared, visible in a gap between the big riverside buildings as the boat crossed the river to the south bank. A little while later, the illuminated turrets of Tower Bridge hove into view and Serena was at her destination, stepping off beneath the wall of the raven-haunted Tower.

She was not very familiar with this part of the city and took a moment to get her bearings. But Cas Pharoah had not lied. The Merchant Prince, the bar he had suggested for their initial meeting, was indeed opposite the entrance to the station. She could see the sprinkle of Christmas lights down one side of the bar.

She walked past the Tower, flinching at the bite of cold air. The building trapped the river wind, sending it in eddies around the base of the Tower and down the road which lay beyond. She was glad to reach the bar, shove the heavy glass door open and enter the opulent bronze and chocolate brown interior, filled with a smell of coffee and the murmur of conversation.

Caspar Pharoah did not have a photo on his LinkedIn profile, but she recognised him at once from Ward's description. He was very conservatively dressed, in double breasted navy blue three piece, and his hair was shorter than men usually wore it these days. Early forties, perhaps? His smile was polite rather than warm, perhaps a little anxious.

"Serena?"

"Hello." She had to tilt her head to look up to him. Ward had been right: he was very good looking. "Thanks so much for finding time before Christmas to see me."

"That's quite all right. I didn't order because I wasn't sure what you might like to drink – or whether you do, in fact. Drink alcohol, I mean. It's probably wise to stick to mineral water in a business meeting but I am not wise and Christmas is coming like an oncoming train, so…"

"I do drink. And wine is fine, although I sometimes drink gin and tonic."

"Impossible not to these days. Gin is the thing. I quite like it but I'm happy to order a decent bottle of wine." He gestured to a seat. "Is this all right? We could move if you prefer."

"No, this is fine, too." It was by the window, looking out onto the darkness and the reflection of the lights in the water. No one was sitting nearby.

"I have an hour and a bit," Caspar said, "And then I am meeting another business contact – an older one this time – for dinner. I'm sure you have plans, too."

"That's absolutely fine," Serena said again and wondered if raiding the thesaurus when she got back for an adjective other than 'fine' would be a good plan for future reference. "I do in fact have plans." Loose ones, anyway. But she was relieved that the meeting had a finite end point, with no risk of it extending into something more personal. Although he seemed a little too diffident for that. Perhaps he might be shy? All at once Serena was filled with mistrust.

She gave a polite smile of her own and said, "I don't want to hold you up."

"No, no, that's – really, it's okay. I suggested we meet, after all. Serena." He leaned forwards, clasping his hands on the table, brow a little furrowed. Serena had seen Ward do this, when he wanted to appear sincere, on television. She assumed an expression that, she hoped, conveyed bright enquiry.

"I'll come straight to the point. I'd like to fund you. I like your designs."

Serena gave a hollow laugh. "What's left of them."

"I know you've had some sort of a setback. I saw something in the Mail – not that I pay much attention to what the press writes. Something about 'vandalism'?"

"Well, the collection was completely destroyed," Serena said, eliding. Ed Russell had, in fact, demonstrated some basic standards of journalism and had not amended the quote that she provided him. However, a photo of Serena, looking frail in front of the heraldic mural, had also appeared and she had been obliged to switch off her phone that day to avoid long fashion industry commiserations: everyone loved a drama. And of course the paper had brought up her mother's past disappearance, all over again, in addition to a long and irrelevant section about Ward. Thinking about this now, Serena gritted her teeth.

"That's terrible. I'm so sorry. I assume you're insured?"

"Yes, and they should pay out, too." *We hope.* But in fact the loss adjuster had been very helpful so far, even though they had not quite told him the truth.

"Well, that's something. But so much work... I recall Syd raving about your clothes. She loved them. She took me to one of your collections – Paris, I remember. I think you were backstage and we had to run, so she didn't introduce us, but it blew me away."

"Unusual reaction, for a man," Serena said. "In my experience they're usually bored to death at fashion shows, unless they're gay." She took a sip of her wine.

"I like beautiful things," Caspar Pharoah said. "All sorts of beautiful things."

For a horrible moment Serena feared that this might be the point where he looked deeply into her eyes and said something really cheesy, but instead he looked out to the blackness of the dock. Serena looked, as well, and saw them both reflected in the glass, against the night and the lights. In the window, Pharoah's aquiline face resembled a sudden skull, the eyes hollow and colourless. But Serena, too, was as pale as a ghost, with the lights of the Merchant Prince washing the gold from her hair.

Then Pharoah turned back and became very businesslike, talking briskly about projections, alternatives to stock market investing, capital gains tax deferral and enterprise schemes. He talked about risk spreading and the Financial Conduct Authority; about the top 20% yielding 40% returns. He had, it seemed, looked at this seriously and moreover he had done it before.

"I'm not," he told her, looking a little pained, "what they refer to rather unfortunately as a virgin."

Eventually, just as the inevitable question was trembling on the edge of Serena's tongue, he mentioned a price.

"£100,000. That's quite high, compared to a £25K average investment, but it's not at all outrageous considering how much some of my partners are putting into other people's schemes."

"It's still a lot," Serena said, feeling close to hypnotised by Pharoah's quiet voice and the concentration with which he was speaking.

"Venture capital investment would be a lot higher, but I'm not sure that's the right option at this point."

"If you are sure," Serena said, and despised herself. Why couldn't she be more American about these things?

But Pharoah said, "One of my business mentors once said to me: there is no more compelling reason to invest in a company than faith in the people who run it." Then he did look into her eyes, but it was a sharp, quick, foxlike look, warning her not to say more.

Serena raised her glass and gently chinked it against his, making the remaining wine slide up in a small wave. "To business, then."

"To business."

After this, Pharoah's impersonality returned. He ushered Serena through the doors of the Merchant Prince, into the biting black night.

"Do you need me to call you a cab?"

"No, I'll walk to the Tube. I like walking. It helps me think."

He smiled. "I know what you mean. Have a great Christmas, Serena."

"You too."

They shook hands. His were cold, even though they had been sitting in the warmth of the bar for over an hour. He did not make any of the mistakes that Serena feared he might: keeping hold of her hand for a fraction too long, or pecking her on the cheek. She could not help feeling reassured, but perhaps it was going out with an actor that made her a little wary… She did not quite trust this exemplary performance of Pharoah's, all the same.

But a hundred thousand pounds is a lot of money.

Serena crossed the road towards the Tube, but discovered as she did so that she had not lied to Pharoah: she really did feel like a walk. She headed down the road, following the path of the river. It was still early evening and there were a lot of people about, heading no doubt for office Christmas parties and other celebrations. Serena slid through the crowds, feeling invisible. There was a sudden spatter of rain, cold on her face. Her phone buzzed in her pocket and she took it out to see a text from Ward: *how did it go?*

Good. I think. Want to meet me in the Lion&Unicorn?

With a plan in place, Serena felt even better about things, in spite of the weather. That earlier green sky, full of cold promise, had lied. The clouds had built up and it had now begun to rain quite hard, blurring the city lights. Serena headed quickly onto Byward Street and as she turned left towards the Tube, she saw a now-familiar figure up ahead. Cas Pharoah, striding fast. His long coat flicked about his knees. Serena was immediately seized in the grip of a squirming embarrassment. What if he turned his head? What if, oh God, he saw her, and thought she was following him? She resolved to cross the road and wait, stare into a shop window until he was safely gone, but then Pharoah himself resolved her dilemma. Abruptly he turned left and disappeared.

This time, Serena was seized by curiosity. Maybe there was some classy restaurant hidden close by? She could see a place between the trees, a block which looked like another bar, dimly lit. Beside it, stood a long oblong building with a small frivolous turret: a church. It looked

Georgian, she thought, but there was a modern neon cross visible through the plain window at its end.

She knew she shouldn't. She was now stalking her backer. Yet all the same, Serena slipped from the main road, following.

On reaching the door, she saw that the church had a name. All Hallows. The door was firmly closed. Serena turned away and bumped into a man right behind her. She gasped, but it was not Pharoah.

"Oh! I'm so sorry. I didn't see you there," he said.

The man was bald and there was a flick of white at his throat: a dog collar. He was holding a large box, the reason for his inattention.

"It's all right," Serena said, quickly. "I moved a bit fast, I suppose."

"Do you think – would you mind very much unlocking the door for me?" The vicar was clutching a set of keys, along with the box.

"Of course," said Serena, wondering where Pharoah had gone. She inserted the key, which was large and old, carefully into the keyhole, and turned it. The door swung open.

"Thank you so much!"

"Would it be all right for me to come in for a moment?" Serena said. It was now pouring. And she did not think Cas Pharoah could be inside, if the church had been locked.

"Of course. Isn't it wet? We'll be having a carol concert later – you're most welcome to stay. Or just look around." The vicar vanished into a side office, leaving Serena alone in the church. She slid her hands into her pockets for warmth and did as he had invited.

It was high and columned. Most unusually, model vessels hung from the rafters; she had never seen such a thing inside a church before. Her gaze lingered over a great black ship with crow-dark sails. The ships drifted a little, moved by the tides of the winter air. Serena walked around the church, finding more ships depicted in the stained glass, a calligraphic reminder of the London Port Authority. A memorial commemorated those lost to the Thames: it was glassy, like ice, and it bore a quote from Isiah: *When you pass through the waters, I will be with you.*

Below it was a table with some leaflets. Serena picked one up and read the section belonging to the memorial, seeing that it partly commemorated the Marchioness disaster, when a dredger had run down a Thames pleasure cruiser and drowned the people partying on it. Serena remembered her grandfather talking about that, although she

107

was too young to remember the incident. It had happened in the year of her birth. Fifty one people died. Serena shivered, thinking of the little boat and the great dredger bearing down, silent in the darkness, the pleasure cruiser crumpling under its bow... She stepped back from the memorial and nearly cannoned into the vicar again.

"Oh! Sorry. I seem to be making a habit of this."

"I just wanted to mention that the vaults are still open, if you'd like to see those, too."

"The vaults?"

The vicar, proud of his church, was happy to explain. "This, you see, is the oldest church in London. I know it doesn't look it; one would think it was Georgian. But it's built on Roman foundations. We have a Saxon cross downstairs. Samuel Pepys watched London burn from the tower which was here then, and if you do go down there you'll find a funny looking piece of metal, like a stalactite, which is when the roof melted during the Blitz. You might say that this place encapsulates London's history."

"Like a microcosm of the city," Serena said. The vicar beamed.

"Exactly."

After all that, she felt she had to go downstairs and found herself in an underworld of small stone vaults, arched like a wine cellar. One was filled with seats, some kind of chapel, but then beneath another arch she found a roped-off area. The floor was covered with a tessellated pattern of tiny tiles and, reading the informative plaque on the wall, Serena discovered that the big red tiles on which she was standing were the original Roman ones.

"It's coming," a voice said. Serena turned, expecting to see the vicar, but all she could see were the shadows of two men, dark against the red tiles and cast by a flickering light that lay out of sight.

"When? Now?" The shadow moved and Serena thought, *he is wearing a dress*. A kilt? His shadow was skirted, the long drapes visible in outline.

"Now. I have been up on the steps. The boat is coming up the river."

"It has made it across the seas, at least." He did not sound pleased.

"Yes. But now? Come. We'd better see the damnable vessel in."

The shadows withdrew. Curious, Serena went to look and as she turned the corner she could see the men retreating down the passage.

The first wore a toga, not a dress. The other wore a tunic under a metal breastplate. Their sandalled feet slapped softly on the tiles. The passage was lit by torches, not electric light. Serena, herself now a ghost, followed.

The maze of corridors was long, twisting and winding. Serena did not know if the men could even see her but she did not want to take the chance. She kept out of sight as best she could. She could hear the murmur of their voices still, but not the words. Then she smelled the air of the river, damp and weedy and sweet in the stuffy atmosphere of the vaults.

"Caeso!"

"Yes?"

"Wait a moment. Hold."

There was a pause and then the torch at the end of the passage abruptly went out. Serena stopped dead before she realised that she could still see. Moonlight fell silver on the river and there was another torch, beyond the end of the passage. She could see its warm flicker.

"Can you see it?"

"Not yet."

The voices were receding and Serena followed them out onto the river bank. London, the city she knew, had disappeared. A building with tall columns lay behind her and along the bank she saw other structures, low compared to the monstrosities of the twenty first century, and torchlit. The river itself looked wider than it was in her day and it breathed out cold. She wondered how the Romans fared, so far from their own warm country and so relatively lightly clad: were those togas woollen? Her professional fashion designer's mind became engaged. Caeso and the other man were standing on a low stone shelf, before the wall that separated the city from the river. Both were staring downstream, to where, in modern London, Tower Bridge reared its twin turrets. Now, the river ran black under the moon as it sailed through the rainclouds.

Serena could make out nothing but the man called Caeso hissed, "There! Do you see?"

The moon soared up. Coming west upriver was a great ship, not Roman, maybe later. Serena did not know much about ships but she thought it was a clipper, a proper one, not the fibreglass catamaran on which she had made her own journey down the Thames. That model which hung in the church… its sails billowed dark in the river wind. A lantern hung at its prow.

"At last," she heard Caeso say. "Damn them. It won't be long now."

Close by, the soldier accompanying Caeso stirred. Serena saw his hand go to the short sword at his side.

"Wait!" Caeso said. "There's nothing you can do. Not yet."

The man sighed. "Very well. You're right, of course." His hand fell away from the weapon.

"We need to send the message, all the same. Victorinus will be waiting for word." He jerked his head back towards the building from which they had come and as he did so a bell began to toll. Serena felt it strike her deep within, a physical blow, each toll matching the beat of her heart. The river world grew dim. The ship began to break up, a series of angles and fragments, spinning into lamplight and darkness as the light at its prow swung wildly, the ship turning on the tide. As its prow swung around Serena saw faces, white in the lamplight, looking down at her from the deck. One of them was Ben's.

"Ben!" Serena cried, breaking cover and running out onto the wharf. The two Romans did not seem to see her, or hear. "Ben!" She teetered on the edge. His face was reflected in the river, a slice of captive moonlight, but then the water eddied as the boat moved and the face disappeared. She looked up and Ben was staring down at her directly, with a terrible sadness in his eyes. His lips moved and she thought he said her name. She reached out but the ship was too high, and too far away, caught on the tide.

"No!" Serena shouted.

But time slipped and slid, she was whirled around like a child's top and when, breathless, she came to a stop, the ship was docking. She could hear the shouts of the deckhands, the footsteps of a man running down the dock to throw a rope, then the black ship was nudging in. The men were crying out to one another:

"Get it off the ship! Quickly, quickly!"

Serena looked up and saw a black square descending.

"Get out of the way!"

She scurried backwards as the men lowered an enormous crate onto the dock: it shuddered and shook as if alive and Serena felt a wash of sorrow and fear. She put her hand to her mouth and reeled back, lost her footing on the wet stone and sat down hard. The water roared up black below and then she was sitting in the church, collapsed into a pew, with the model ship crow-twisting over her head. Her breath was coming fast, as though she had been running. She put a hand to her chest; her heart jumped and pounded within. The bells began to ring, the church's own bells in the tower, and Serena began to breathe more steadily. She counted before the bells fell silent.

It was time to go. She ran out into the street, where the rain had stopped and the traffic was pouring by, and flagged down a black cab.

PART TWO
WATERS RISING

BEE

She would be happy once everyone was home, Bee thought, late on the eve of the solstice. Safe, within the walls of Mooncote, under her watchful eye. It wasn't as if they couldn't cope without her, only that Bee worried so. *Stop being such a mother hen.* She couldn't help it, however. For snow had begun to fall that morning; a few uncertain flakes and then, as if the weather had made up its mind and become resolute, a steady drift. At first, the snowflakes had not settled, but then more and more lingered, forming an icy white lace across the lawn and the courtyard. Serena, Ward and Stella would be driving from London today and Ward had asked to be dropped off at Caro's first, before coming to Mooncote. He needed to talk to his cousin and her husband, he'd said on the phone, and Bee was too cowardly to ask exactly what it was about, though she thought she could guess. Because Stella had said, some days before, that there was 'weird shit happening', and Bee knew that there were things they weren't telling her.

"It's just going to be easier if we explain once we're there," Stella had said. "A lot's been going on."

Bee had not felt like arguing. She had enough on her plate at the country end, what with Aln and Christmas, and glimpses of other lands, and Luna's baby. Not that these things were all impossible in themselves, just that they all added up to become one big lump of stress.

She would cope with it, she told herself firmly. She was down to one final list. They were all set: Christmas was a go, greenlit. The church had already held two carol services, one for advent and one for the local school. No one had been sick in the nave. No one had cried. Bee was aware that, like every other church in the country, the congregation would swell over the next few days as everyone got into the Christmas spirit, and then it would dwindle again, perhaps with a little jump at Easter and a smaller one yet at Harvest festival. She mentioned this to Kate, who had smiled and said that this was just how things were nowadays and perhaps the church needed to work a little harder at generating that same Christmas spirit throughout the year.

"But then people would really need to be Christian, wouldn't they?" Bee had said. "To feel the same about Easter and Michaelmas as they do about Christmas?"

She did not like to say that the thing that drew people to the church at Christmas was surely that pagan feeling: that sudden presence of magic. She did not know Kate well enough to embark on that kind of discussion and, besides, they had secrets to keep.

So now, teetering on the edge of the year's shortest day and dark already fallen, Bee sat at the kitchen table, waiting. She kept checking her phone. Nothing from Serena. Nothing from Stella. She looked up sharply as the back door opened but it was Luna, stamping snow off her boots like a child.

"It's coming down faster now," Bee said, unnecessarily.

"I hoped we'd have a white Christmas. You know, I don't remember *ever* having one, not properly."

"I do," said Bee, "but I'm older than you and it was when I was very little. Mum took Serena and me out onto the lawn and we built a snow thing."

Luna smiled. "Not a snowman? Gender fluid?"

"No, it wasn't even a person. It was a dragon, I think. We've got some polaroid photos somewhere: Mum had a new camera. The sort that fades and makes everything look a funny colour. Anyway, Serena and I wanted to be different. Of course we did. So we made a long snow dragon with a proper tail and some chunky spines."

"We could make another one if it does snow properly," Luna said. She took off her woolly hat, freeing her mass of dark red hair. Her cheeks were spots of crimson.

"You look like something out of a fairytale," Bee said.

"Not a dragon slayer, though. I don't like St G. As a vegetarian."

"Besides, they're an endangered species."

"Yes. St George would be prosecuted today and his face splashed all over Facebook with snarky titles like those awful big game hunters who pose with their prey."

"Down with St George!" said Bee.

"Down with St George!" they cried together, as Aln watched wide-eyed from the dog basket and Serena and Stella and Bella came through the door together.

"Oh!" Bee stood up. "You're here!"

"What's up with St George?" Stella asked.

"We've decided he's evil."

"Yeah, down with that sort of thing. I'm sorry we're a bit late. It's been snowing all the way since Andover but one of Bella's mates sent her a text saying it was also coming down in London, quite heavily. So we thought we did well to leave when we did."

Then Bella spotted Aln.

"Who's that girl? Why is she sitting in the dog basket? And why is she *green*?"

Aln, defensive, drew Nelson closer and buried her face in his feathery fur.

"I see things have been happening at this end, as well," Serena said. Bee looked at her in alarm.

"God, what else?"

Serena sighed. "As I said, there's a lot to tell you. Is it okay, to talk in front of your guest?"

"We don't think she speaks English," Luna said.

"But where is she from?" asked Stella. "Mars?"

Very firmly, Bee said, "I'm going to open a bottle of wine and make sure the dinner is underway. It should be, it's stew."

Later that night, Bee sat with Serena in the living room. They had dimmed the lights and the tree shimmered and sparkled. Dark had not yet appeared and Ward had sent an apologetic text to Serena, saying that he was staying at Amberley because there was a problem with Richard's car and Caro's had had to go into the garage for repair. Serena was not to come and fetch him; she had done enough driving, and it was raining hard.

"But," Bee said, "You'll see him tomorrow."

"Yes. And we're all caught up."

Bee fingered the stem of her wine glass. The others had gone up to bed, but Bee felt wide awake. "I'm so sorry about your collection."

"I know. Thank you."

"And you still don't know what – did it?"

"No. This friend of Stella's – Ace, I like him, I think you would too – has been making enquiries, he says, but apparently everything stops for Christmas. Truce time, he called it. Said it's a time when everyone comes out of their trenches and plays football in No Man's Land. I assume he's talking about the war. Metaphorically."

"But we don't know who the enemy is?"

"No. Demons, maybe. Although I've only met the one and I felt a bit sorry for it, to be honest. Mind you, it was a bit creepy and the spirit Ace called up to question was even creepier. Think I'll stick with the star spirits."

"So where did this demon come from in the first place?"

"I don't know. I asked Ace about Hell, because I've never really believed in that, and he said it was another dimension and thinking of everything as a spirit rather than demons was probably easier and more accurate. I told him about the Behenian stars – how we'd always seen them around this house and that we thought they were star spirits – and he said he knew about them but he'd only seen one once. He didn't know which one. He was impressed, though, I think." Serena laughed. "That made me feel quite cool, actually. Like we're in some kind of secret club."

"I get the impression there are all sorts of worlds."

"Maybe Aln is from one of them."

Bee nodded. "She must be. Have *you* heard of the Green Children of Woolpit?"

"I'm not sure. Isn't it a fairytale? Or a folk story?"

Bee recounted it, briefly. "I don't know if it's the same. But she's not from round here, that's for sure, and she *is* green. Though maybe not quite as green as she was. Sometimes I think she's fading and sometimes I think it's just a trick of the light."

"What are you going to *do* with her, though? She can't live in the dog basket forever."

"No. But she's all right for the moment. It's going to be difficult if anyone drops in, mind you. I'm going to get Christmas out of the way and then see if we can find out more about her. She behaves as though she's human enough. She eats, she pees outside. I haven't dared try and find out about what else she might do."

"Maybe she goes in the ditch. Does she wash?"

"I don't know. I think she might scrub down in the horse trough. But she doesn't smell, either. Well, not much."

"She smelled of smoke to me," Serena said. "Woodfires, like camping." She took a sip of her wine. "And talking of people dropping in, has there been any sign of Mum?"

"Not yet."

"She did say, though…"

"She did."

That night, the long night before the shortest day, Bee woke up. There was someone sitting on the side of the bed.

"Dark?" she said, fumbling for the lamp. But as the room flooded with light, she saw that it was one of the Behenian stars. The spirit's skin was also very faintly tinged with green and her white hair was intricately braided and looped. Her eyes were like spring leaves, no whites and a pupil of gold. A necklace of silver hung around her long neck and she held a sprig of winter savory, mirrored in the embroidery of her white and green gown. The savory's strong, herbal scent filled the room.

"You are Vega, aren't you?" Bee said.

The star spirit smiled. As with all of them, human expressions did not quite fit. *Trying the smile on for size,* thought Bee. And when she spoke, her lips did not quite fit the words, either.

"So you see," Vega said. She bent her head and unfastened the clasp of her necklace, holding it up. From the chain hung a sphere of chrysolite, green as grass and confined by two thick silver bands. An armillary sphere, thought Bee. The sphere caught the lamplight as it turned and spun, sending emerald sparks flashing about the room. Bee blinked. The sparks had not gone: they were spring leaves in dappled sunlight, or perhaps the flashes of light on a fast-running stream. She stood in a glade, moss soft beneath her bare feet. When Bee glanced down, her toes, too, were green, not the faint jade of Aln's skin but deep sage, almost invisible against the moss. Bee held up a hand, the nails almost black. Across the glade was a chapel, small and stone with an open door, flanked by immense oaks. The trees made the chapel look as tiny as a doll's house. The moss was studded with acorns, dry and brown now, faded with the coming of the spring.

Bee stepped forwards. No mirror, no pool: she could not see her face. She was not certain that she wanted to, afraid that it would not be her own face that she saw, but someone else's. She did not think that this was Aln's body: the girl was slighter, less sturdy. Perhaps a past Aln, before whatever famine had dwindled her? But Bee felt in her bones that this was not the case. She did, however, want to see what might be in the chapel.

The door was oak and it looked old, having the silver-silk patina of ancient wood. Its frame was carved with leaves, intertwining fronds of vine. The faint trace of grapes, almost worn away, was visible still and Bee touched the smooth wood with her green fingers, feeling them glide as if the carved vine were pulling them in. She withdrew her hand and stepped through the door.

Inside, the chapel was cool and had that characteristic old church smell. Smoke and damp and stone. It reminded Bee for a moment of Hornmoon and she smiled. There were pews, from newer oak than the door, and their ends were carved into the familiar trefoil shape, which the old vicar had once told Bee were called poppy heads. They did not look much like poppies to Bee. In the middle of each carving was a small wooden face, staring blandly outwards, and there were green men at the end of every roof beam. This was familiar, too. Hornmoon did not have them – built too late – but Medieval churches often did. The flags of the floor were covered in rushes and at the end of the aisle stood a small altar. No cross, though. Bee did not think that this was a Christian chapel. There was a figure on it, made of black oak, and squat. Curious, Bee went up for a closer look but it was shapeless, vaguely human but indeterminate of sex, and it had no face. There was what might have been braiding around its head, rather like the pattern on the head of the Venus of Willendorf. In front of it was a small wooden pot filled with ferns. Maybe on the back? Bee reached out to touch the figure but as she did so the chapel filled with rushing shards of emerald light and with a soft jolt she was back in her body, in bed. She had a glimpse of Vega's serene face, lit by green fire, and then the star winked out.

LUNA

Winter solstice. Luna's favourite day. It felt filled with meaning, from the cold red line that heralded the dawn to the enveloping darkness. She liked the cosiness of the van, stove lit, lamp lit, to drive away the things that might cluster out of the night, but she also loved the hard-ringing frost cold and the nearness of the stars. Not tonight, though, with all this rain – for the snow had been brief, replaced overnight by sleet and then simple wet. Now, on the eve of the Solstice, already feeling gravid and house-bound, Luna felt the year turn and she began to do small things to mark it. She dusted the table that she and Sam had set up as an altar in their room and lit a red candle and a white, greeting the dawn of the day. The altar was ringed with oak leaves and with holly, for solstice is the time when the Oak King battles the Holly King, sends him underground for a sixmonth until summer's height when the days start to grow shorter once more and the nights lengthen.

"It's a Druid story," she had said once, to Sam.

He smiled. "Modern Druids, though. Comes from the writer Robert Graves, or someone like that."

"Oh, does it? I thought it was old." She was disappointed, but Sam knew these things.

"No, it's modern. There's something like it in the Welsh stories but my nan says the old boy tidied it. Gussied it up. A lot of old stories – aren't."

"Well," Luna said hopefully, "maybe there are some old stories which haven't been told yet. Because they haven't been found."

"I bet there are loads of those." But he made no objection to Luna's modern paganism. She made it up as she went along, she told him, from books. She'd never belonged to a group. That wasn't her. "Although I do know quite a few pagans. Rowan and Moss. Dave and Charlotte. Manda."

"Making it up is fine," Sam had said. "Better that way. Keeps everyone on their toes."

But she had not been quite sure what he had meant by that.

Now, Luna sat on a cushion in front of her altar and shut her eyes, praying to the goddess. Whichever one might be listening. Within, she thought she felt a stir and it wouldn't be that long before she was too pregnant to sit on a cushion on the floor. But she would bear it, Luna told herself. Literally. She prayed for everyone she could think of and then she clambered to her feet and went downstairs. Bee's strange visitor still slept, green cheek resting on a small green hand. Aln wasn't very green, Luna thought: the colour was like a wash over her pale skin. She felt protective of Aln, who seemed to like spending time around her. *You're part of an old story, I bet,* thought Luna. She hoped they would find out which one. If it was a good one, anyway, with a happy ending. She had the sense of things unfolding, half excited, half alarmed. She fed the dogs, including Moth, and went outside.

She knew the sun had risen, but the sky remained grey and overcast, the rain blowing over. Luna didn't mind, though. It was the time that counted and she could feel the day begin to stir. In the hedge that bordered the lawn, a black bird was singing, water-clear, the notes ringing out across the garden. Then it gave its urgent alarm-cry and was off, shooting in a black arrow towards the barn. The reason for its fright soon became apparent: a cat slinking along the hedge. Not one of theirs. *You'll be popular,* Luna thought. If Tut saw him (the cat had a tom's round face and belligerent swagger), he'd be in for it: Tut was the neighbourhood warrior and had been known to take on foxes. Surely some old Celtic warlord in a previous life, said Bee. Luna walked on, down towards the horses. She'd had adventures in this field but now the morning was quiet, except for the beasts and birds going about their business. She liked feeling part of it.

The horses greeted her mildly. She had carrots in her pockets and a couple of windfall apples and they knew this. They nudged and bumped until Luna produced the loot. Then, having sucked it up, they ambled on. It was now considerably lighter, with a strong westerly blowing off the Bristol Channel. Luna fancied she could smell salt on the wind. She liked the thought of the great funnel of water, the Severn opening out into the sea and then the Atlantic swinging beyond. At night, she would think of it, especially when the moon was full and Luna could almost feel the pull of the tide, remembering the dream. She walked back up the hill, noting that there were already tiny buds on the blackthorn hedge which followed the field boundary, and clambered over the stile which led to the lane.

And there was a footprint. It was small and bare, silvery on the wet tarmac. Luna stared at it. When she looked up, she saw another one, and another, heading down the lane towards Hornmoon church as though someone were running. Luna strained to see but could glimpse no child's ghost, there in the lane. She followed, all the same.

Just as she reached the lychgate, the sun came out from behind a bank of cloud and suddenly the world was sparkling, the light catching on the raindrops. Luna, dazzled, blinked and ducked her head. The lychgate towered above her, blinding black with the light all around it and high in the eaves of the arched roof she saw a skull, bone-white, fire-eyed. Luna cried out. The sunlight splintered and the path beneath her feet turned bright and silver. She took a step and the path bore her away.

SERENA

Serena was thankful to be back at Mooncote. She knew that it wasn't entirely safe – nowhere was – but it had more good memories than bad and she had never lost faith in the Behenian stars, confident that they would not let her down. Protective spirits. And her grandfather was still around, over by Hornmoon, and her sisters were there. Ward, too, of course. Perhaps her mother might even put in an appearance. She felt that it might, very cautiously and carefully, be possible to breathe out.

Pottering about the kitchen, she made toast and took it up to Bella's room. Her daughter was still asleep, curled under a counterpane like a child in a fairytale: Bee preferred them to duvets.

"Here you are. Breakfast in bed. Bee made the jam; it's strawberry. Don't say I never do anything for you."

Bella struggled into wakefulness. "Oh, cheers, Mum!"

"I'm going to have mine downstairs. Take your time. It's the holidays."

Leaving Bella to it, Serena went back down to the kitchen and stood for a moment contemplating Aln, asleep in the dog basket. She felt a sudden maternal pang, though Aln was too old to be her own child. Perhaps only just, though. She sat down at the table and studied her phone. Several messages, including one from Cas Pharoah. They had agreed to meet again in the New Year, but then Cas had wanted to change the date from the second of January. Something had come up, he'd said.

"That's fine," said Serena. No! There was that *fine* again.

"It really has, though. I don't want you thinking, *oh, he's putting me off.* Firm date for January 4th?"

"Absolutely." The day before Twelfth Night, she thought, though it depended on how you counted the days from Christmas. Maybe it would prove lucky.

"I'll email you in the New Year just to keep in touch. You have a lovely Christmas, now – I'm assuming you celebrate?"

"We do, yes. And you?"

"I've got plans," said the voice on the other end of the phone. Then he laughed. "Best made plans, though, eh?"

"Oh," Serena said. "I hope nothing goes wrong."

"So do I. Families… See you soon."

His text now was simply to hope she was having a good trip.

In a way, the festive delay came as a relief. Plunged into limbo, Serena could only wait – and perhaps there would be no deal after all. Enjoy Christmas, she thought, with everyone, just as it's always been, and then take a deep breath and plunge into the New Year. Not much happened in the working world at Christmas, after all, unless you were in retail or the health service or something.

She opened the back door and looked out. Dim and damp and grey. The door was unbolted so someone had been out, perhaps Bee or Luna, who usually rose early to feed the horses. It was very still and she could hear singing, from down the valley. After a moment, she realised that it was coming from Hornmoon church. A Christmas choir, perhaps, and then the bells rang out.

LUNA

The world whirled around Luna and the breath was ripped out of her throat. She fell to her knees, realising that the movement had stopped. There were dried leaves beneath her palms, oak and beech, dry and rustling and somehow a comfort. She looked up. The trees towered around her and through the gaps in their branches she saw that the sky was grey, laden with snow. She could smell it on the windless air and there were traces of it among the roots.

At home, in Somerset, perhaps there would be no more snow this year. They had been lucky to have the little they did on Solstice Eve. Time didn't run smoothly, Luna knew that, and this felt like White Horse Country, one of the patchwork places that lie alongside our world. She had been here before and it had frightened her. Slowly, she hauled herself to her feet, hoping that the baby was all right. She felt winded and put her hands in the small of her back, taking a deep cold breath. This was a dangerous place and she did not know the way home. She must not panic. Luna looked about her, seeking clues, but the wood was thick and impenetrable, with clearings rather than tracks, fenced in by thick masses of bramble. Any blackberries had shrivelled to tiny warts in between the thorns, which looked longer than bramble thorns should. Luna threaded her way around the trunks of the trees, clambering from root to clearing to root. She startled something: a partridge, which rocketed into the distance, low flying as if hurled. In search of a pear tree, maybe? Luna found herself smiling.

She was heading downhill, hoping to find water at the bottom of it. A stream could be followed. But halfway down the slope she saw the building. It was small and low, its tiled roof covered in snow. It had no windows and only an opening for a door. Luna looked at it. Above the door, very faint in the old stone, was a carving.

She knew that the otherworlds had chapels. Stella had found one, on a Channel shore, but there had been something in it, something awful, and Stella had fled. Yet it had also been the place where Stella had found and freed a Behenian star. Light and dark, thought Luna, and you couldn't have one without the other. She stumbled over the rough, frozen ground to the building and stood there, listening. She could not hear anything moving within.

But the wood was a different story. Something was running fast, crashing through the brambles. Luna heard its breath, rhythmic and hoarse. She ducked into the opening of the chapel before it saw her. She thought of wolves, running through the snow, but surely a wolf would not make so much noise? There were distant shouts. Luna pressed up against the stone wall and tried to keep quiet. Something was snuffling about outside the chapel. She could hear long, deep sniffs, like a dog blowing under a door, and it seemed to her that she could hear her heart, too, a black-red beat behind her eyes. She had to fight to keep her eyes open, not squeeze them shut in fright, but she could not see very much in the single room itself, only a table, dim in the chinks of light that fell between the tiles. There was something on the table and Luna thought that it might be a skull.

Then, suddenly, the thing that had been snuffing about outside was in the room. It was taller than Luna, standing upright. She knew at once that it was not a man. It was covered in a ragged hairy cloak, the hair long and dark, and its mouth, which resembled an otter's muzzle, fell open when it saw Luna. Its teeth were like an otter's, too: triangular and jagged, with long, sharp canines. Its eyes were goldenblack. She realised that it was not a cloak, but its pelt. It was like the thing that had run out in front of the Land Rover. It hissed at her.

"Do not speak. Do not breathe." It put a clawed finger to its lipless mouth in emphasis.

Dumbly, Luna nodded. The thing stank of bones, that rank, damp smell. The charnel odour filled the chapel. The creature shrank back against the wall, opposite Luna. She kept as still as she could. She could hear, once more, someone moving about outside and then a voice spoke, but it wasn't in a language she recognised. It was harsh and staccato, as if issuing orders. And she could hear dogs, the high goose-like cry of hounds. It was a sound with which Luna, former hunt saboteur, was familiar. She looked across at the creature and the dark gleaming eyes were frozen with fear. They were trapped in the chapel; there was nowhere else to go. Then a figure stepped into the doorway, blocking out what little light there was. Luna and the creature did not move, did not breathe. But the chapel filled with a shimmering grey, a soft no-colour that reminded Luna of the light at dawn, and dusk, in spring. It blotted out everything, like fog, and it took her fear away with it. She could breathe again, and the tight constriction in her chest eased.

The voice spoke again. She did not know the language but it sounded disgusted. The sounds of the hunting pack faded, footsteps tramping away. Luna could see the chapel once more and the creature cowering on the other side of the room paused for a moment, then bolted outside. Luna ran to the door and looked out. She couldn't see it anywhere, but the sounds of the huntsmen going away through the wood were still faintly audible, further down the slope. She could not stay here, she had to find a path. Ver March, Sam's nan, had once showed her a way to do so: you needed a berry or a nut on a red thread. There were no berries here, but there was beech mast... She picked up a small brown husk, prickly with the chill, and after a moment's thought plucked a hair from her hennaed head. She tied the hair, with some difficulty given her frozen fingers, to the husk, and swung it. The husk twitched, rose to a horizontal point and sat suspended in the air. Luna looked eagerly in the direction that it pointed and saw the ground shimmer. But as she stepped forwards, there came a triumphant shout from behind her.

Luna turned and nearly fell. A figure strode down the slope. It was not the otter-faced being. It was tall and dressed in leather and skins, and it had a deer's skull instead of a face. She could see the velvet still trailing from the horns. The body, in a leather jerkin and trousers, looked human: two hands held the leashes of a brace of straining hounds. The dogs were big and moon-white and as soon as they saw Luna, they began to bay.

Luna did not hesitate further. She spun around and ran, as fast as she could through the snow, to where the path was waiting. Once more it snatched her up. She saw the beech branches flying by, a single star in the greening sky above. Snowfall whirled around her, pricking cold against her skin, painful as briars. But the figure was not left behind. She glimpsed the skull-face, once far away, tiny in the growing dark against the trees, then looming over her so closely that Luna screamed, then distant once more. Luna thought of the lychgate, the entryway.

"Grandfather!" she cried. "Grand-dad! Help me!"

...and she was falling out into the roadway opposite the church. Luna again found herself on her hands and knees. But the road was tarmacked, and opposite the opening in the hedge stood the lychgate. Through it, she could see the church and the ball of evergreens and red apples, the kissing ring that hung in the doorway for Christmas.

"Oh thank fuck," breathed Luna. Then she looked up. The horned figure reared over her.

Luna scrambled to her feet. It was taller than her. The skull was green with moss, ancient despite the velvet rags. The dogs had disappeared. From behind the bony carapace, a voice said, "Luna! Are you all right? Didn't you hear me calling?"

Luna stared for a frozen moment. Then she whispered, "*Mum?*"

BEE

Was this how it was going to be from now on? Bee wondered. She was so cross that she could barely speak. She had to go upstairs, pretending to need a wee, and lock herself in the bathroom. She gripped the edges of the sink and stared at herself in the bathroom mirror. Her face was unbecomingly red, from the heat of the Aga, over which she had been bending when Luna and Alys walked in. Wisps of hair had come undone from her braid and she looked, Bee thought, as though she had actually been dragged through a hedge.

"That bloody woman!"

She was conscious that this was a bit unreasonable. Alys had said she would be home for Christmas and indeed, here she was. She had kept her promise, strolling in, draped in deerskins and leather like – like something out of *One Million Years BC* or whatever that film was called, Bee thought, searching for similes, though Alys was rangier and more angular than Raquel Welch and certainly wearing a lot more clothing. Home as if nothing had happened, but Luna, who had been gone all day, still wore the unmistakable aura of fright. Bee had not got to the bottom of that, yet, but she intended to. Luna had said firmly that she was 'all right.' Bee did not believe her.

Then the handle of the bathroom door turned.

"Oh, sorry!" It was her mother's voice. "Didn't know anyone was in there."

Bee took a very deep breath. Then she released the sink from her grip, unlocked the bolt, and opened the bathroom door.

"It's only me," she said. "I've finished in here. Did you want the bath?"

Alys grimaced. "I need one, I think. Don't you?"

Bee nodded. "Maybe. You smell of woodsmoke." And blood.

"Could be worse. Am I being very inconvenient, Bee? Were you planning supper?"

"Yes, but it's a casserole and baked potatoes. There's plenty to go round. At this time of year – well, you know what it's like. You never know who might turn up. I think Ward's coming over tonight as well, so…" She tried hard to keep accusation out of her voice and did not think she had wholly succeeded.

"I won't be too long," Alys said.

"Take your time, have a good soak. There's plenty of hot water; the immersion is on," Bee said, and fled down the stairs.

She found her sisters in the kitchen. Aln had gone outside, on some errand of her own: maybe to pee, maybe not. Alys had thus not seen her yet and for this, Bee was obscurely grateful. Serena was bending over the crock pot.

"Your casserole is looking great. And thanks for going veggie tonight."

"No one minds," Bee said. "Although Ward might, if he comes over."

"He'll grumble but he'll eat it. Well, he might not grumble. He is basically polite."

"Mum's having a bath." Bee went to peer into the casserole as well. "Says she won't be too long."

"Is that door shut?" Stella asked, rather sharply. She went to the door between the kitchen and the hall and gave it a push.

"Why?"

"Because I'm not sure I want Mum overhearing this," Luna said. Behind the curly dark red curtain of her hair, her face looked pinched and pale.

"We waited till you came back," said Stella. "Luna has a story."

She did, and she told it, faltering a little towards the end. "...and you didn't see this thing, this creature, but – Bee, it sounded like that thing you said you saw, through the church window."

"What thing?" asked Serena.

"I haven't had time to tell you. I'll do it later. I don't want to interrupt Luna's story."

"It was afraid," Luna said. "There was some sort of hunt – they were chasing it. It was like fox hunts, it felt awful. Like the thing was a fox, but it was aware. It *spoke* to me. Anyway, even if it had been an animal the whole thing would still have been horrible." She curled her fingers around her mug of tea, as if they were too cold to warm. "And Mum was with them."

"Oh my God," said Serena. "What, you mean she was part of this hunt?"

"Yes." Luna was whispering. "She was wearing that leather thing and she had a deer's skull over her face. I didn't recognise her. She said she'd been calling my name but I didn't hear it. She had dogs with her – big ones, a lot bigger than the ones they use for foxes. They didn't come with her." She forced a laugh. "After all, there's no room in the dog basket."

"I thought they trail hunted these days?" Serena said. "Now hunting foxes is banned. Although you went sabbing, didn't you?" She looked at Stella and Luna.

"Drag hunting, not trail – that's the Lake District," Bee told her. "But yes, you're right, more or less. They lay a scent and the hounds follow it."

"They *say* they do," muttered Luna. "But there's plenty of footage of kills even after the ban."

"That's why we went sabbing," Stella said. "They don't all stick to the law."

"I remember," Bee told her.

"Anyway, as we were coming down the lane I asked Mum why she hadn't just taken the skull off so I could see who she was in the wood and she said, 'I thought you knew it was me'."

"Are we actually sure she's Alys?" Stella said. "And not something wearing her face?"

Serena stared at her. "God, way to go with creeping us out, Stels."

"Well, sorry, but yeah, I did wonder that when she went missing first time round."

"We can hardly throw her out of the house," Bee said. "Especially since it actually is her house still."

"Not if she's something else, it's not."

"How could we tell, though?"

"We'll just have to keep an eye on her," Stella said. "I might make a couple of phone calls."

"Oh," Serena said, "Do you mean to Ace? Because I bet he'll know what to do."

"Because when she came back, the first time," Luna said, still pale, "She wasn't quite like Mum."

"No, but she had been through a massive amount of shit." Stella got up and went over to the window. "People change. I'm interested in what she's going to say when she sees Green Girl."

"Yes, where is Aln?"

Bee put up her hands. "I don't know, Luna. She went out a while ago – maybe an hour? I can't let myself worry. She's essentially feral and we don't even know what she is, let alone who." She did not want to say: *I'd rather Mum didn't see her.*

But she was not to be given a choice. There was a knock on the hallway door and Alys stepped through, just as the kitchen door opened to Aln.

"Oh!" Alys said, taken aback. Bee was relieved to see this, but did not quite know why. Aln scuttled to the dog basket and pulled a blanket over her head.

"Mum, this is our house guest. Her name –" Bee hesitated. "Her name is 'Aln'. We don't know where she comes from. I found her in the churchyard. She was almost dead."

"Oh no, poor child." Alys looked concerned, just as she had throughout Bee's own childhood, when she heard of someone in trouble. Vague though she might have been, Alys sharpened up into focus if there was a problem, and was often surprisingly practical. "She's obviously not from round here."

"No. We thought: the Woolpit children. Do you remember that story?"

Alys nodded. She pulled out a chair and sat down at the kitchen table. She had dispensed with the skins and was wearing a loose pair of her own linen trousers, woolly socks, an Arran sweater. Her fair hair was still a little damp but it fell in slight and elegant waves. She looked like an eccentric Bohemian mum, a picture in a magazine, not some eldritch huntsman. But was she? Bee wondered. "Yes, I do remember. The girl became a maid and would only eat beans. They lived in a place with a green sun."

"Have you come across such a place, Mum?" Stella asked. "On your travels?"

"Not like that, no. But I've heard of something similar. There are a lot of places. As you're aware by now. Thank you." She took the glass of Rioja that Bee passed to her and took an appreciative sniff. "Oh, I haven't had wine in such a long time. There's nothing like that – there. Where I was." She looked around at her four daughters. "So, my lovelies. What's been happening here?"

Bee was in the middle of serving up the casserole when there came a knock at the door. She opened it to find Ward, his hair starred with rain.

"It's set in for the night, I think. Oh, hello Alys, good to see you." His face betrayed nothing. He took off his gloves. "Hark at me, old Farmer Garner. Like I knew anything about the weather."

"Old Farmer Garner knows when to show up, though. Do you want some casserole?"

"I would love some." He kissed Serena. "I've been running Caro all over the county today while her car is being fixed. It's still in the garage but she'll be lucky if anything gets done this close to Christmas. We had a repulsive sandwich each from Podimore services and that was hours ago."

"This is vegetables: sweet potato, butternut squash, other stuff, and then there are baked spuds and peas. No meat. Eat it or starve."

"Bee, my darling, I don't currently care if it is a thin gruel. I am wasting away after my toxic sandwich experience."

"Ha!" Serena said.

"What's *that* supposed to mean?"

"You are not very wasting. Not that you're fat," she added hastily.

"I should hope not after all the time I spend pounding the pavements of Portobello and sweating away in the gym. More of that will be needed, by the way," he added, gloomily. "This is a very *physical* Oberon, the director informs me."

"Oh yes," Alys said, "You're doing *Midsummer Night's Dream* next year, aren't you? Always one of my favourites."

"I'll bet it is," said Ward. She arched an amused eyebrow. "After the events of the last couple of months, Alys, I have to say that I am rather over the whole fairyland thing, but never mind. It's a run at the Pelican, always one of my favourite theatres. Some really good pubs near the Pelican."

"We shall come and hang around the stage door," Bee said, handing him a plate. "We shall be your groupies. I hope we're going to get tickets?"

"Of course. Excuse me if I don't speak for a bit. I shall be stuffing my face."

They had given Alys an edited version of events: the damage to Serena's collection had been mentioned, but not the demon, nor Ace, nor any drifts into parallel realities. Aln had been partially explained earlier, but not the thing Bee had glimpsed through the eye in the church window. Bee was reminded of when they had been children, or teenagers: *don't tell the parent everything, they'll only worry*. But now they had a different reason for reticence.

Sam was, Luna said, down the pub having a drink with a mate and would not be joining them. Ward, who had not been in the loop, was savvy enough to pick up the undercurrents, and, when not steadily eating, kept his conversation to earthly things like the traffic and the theatre. Helpfully, he rose to take his plate to the dishwasher and dropped it back onto the table with a clatter.

"Jesus fuck!"

"What? What's the matter?" Serena said.

"There's a face in the dog basket! A human face! Looking up at me!"

"Oh God, we didn't tell you," Bee said. "I'm so sorry. She's our house guest."

"So I was actually planning on staying tonight, hopefully with Serena? And not, say, in the cat bed? Or the coal hole?"

"I really am sorry. She likes the dog basket. I'd actually forgotten she was there."

"You are very green," Ward said to Aln, accusingly.

"She doesn't speak English."

"What does she speak, then?"

"We don't know."

"I see." He sighed. "Whatever. I'm sure all of this is taking years off my life, by the way."

Alys snorted. "Try living in my world."

By mutual and tacit consent, no one asked her what she meant.

Later that night, the house was still. Everyone had gone to bed, including Alys, who looked suddenly wiped out, older than she had seemed earlier in the day. Despite her lingering irritation, Bee regarded her with concern.

"Sleep well, Mum."

"Thank you, my darling. You, too."

Sam had returned from the Hornmoon Arms before closing time, cheerful but not much the worse for drink, and he and Luna had retired together. Now, Bee pottered about the kitchen, trying not to disturb the sleeping Aln, and decided to leave unloading the dishwasher till the morning. She turned off the kitchen light and went into the dining room to gaze for a moment at the shining tree.

"Your mother is home, I see."

Bee did not turn. She smiled. "Yes. Earlier. We've been rich with stories."

Dark laughed. "I should think so."

"It's the longest day today."

"A good day to come home, then. Away from the powers of darkness."

"Then let's go away from them ourselves. Even if we turn out the light."

Bee was expecting more trouble in the night. But it did not come. She went to sleep in Dark's arms, dreamless. She woke before the dawn, found her lover gone with the growing day, and went downstairs. All was quiet. Aln was still fast asleep. Bee let the dogs out and put the kettle on, humming *The Holly and the Ivy* under her breath.

Behind her, a voice intoned, *"I pray thee, gentle mortal, sing again.*
Mine ear is much enamoured of thy note.
So is mine eye enthrallèd to thy shape.
And thy fair virtue's force perforce doth move me
On the first view to say, to swear, I love thee."

Bee burst out laughing. "I must say, Ward, you do get the day off to a classy start."

"I've been up since six. Serena's still in bed. I actually do have to learn my lines and it's nice and quiet in the sitting room."

"So which is that bit?"

"Me falling in love with Bottom."

"Hang on," said Bee. "Isn't that Titania?"

"In this production, the director has objected to portraying a powerful woman drugged to have sex with a donkey, basically, and so he has swapped Oberon and Titania's lines."

"Oh! Wow, so now, it's *you* who –"

"Bottom is played by an enormous, gormless young man rather like a Labrador. It's not his first part, it's his third. He's quite good, mind you."

"And do you fancy him?"

"I'm going to have to, aren't I? He's not really my type but then, unmagicked, donkeys and labourers are presumably not Titania's in the ordinary run of things. So that's sort of the point. At least as long as the spell doth last, anyway. Is there any tea? I made some but it's gone cold. I can do it myself."

"I'm making tea," Bee said.

"I'm also Theseus."

"How does that work? Oh, wait – are Oberon and Theseus ever on stage together? I can't remember."

"No, they're not. Shakespeare structured it that way, probably to save on actor's wages. Theseus and Hippolyta originally doubled up with the fairy King and Queen. Now, of course, we can weave in all sorts of subtext about their ordinary selves and their night-time selves, darkest desires only coming out when the sun's gone down and so forth."

"I must ask Dark if he's seen it," Bee said. "Or you can ask him yourself, when he next appears."

"Would he have – oh Christ!" Ward said. "Shit, he might have seen the original. He might have *actually seen Shakespeare*." Bee had never seen him look awed before. The studied actor's manner fell away, making him look round-eyed and younger.

"I know. I've never got used to it. He saw Queen Elizabeth once."

"Oh my God. I'm rarely impressed, but really… I didn't even think. Stupid of me."

"You're not so used to ghosts," Bee said.

"Well, not from that period."

"How is Caro, by the way?"

"Bearing up. But not good, really. Looking a lot older. She's trying to be determinedly cheerful: Christmas and all that. She hasn't actually had bad news, like a body being found, although I understand she has now contacted the police and they are looking into it. What they'll think when they go into his place, I don't know. Richard didn't want the police involved – I think he thinks it might raise some awkward questions – but he had to agree eventually. The press haven't got hold of it yet but they did do that piece on Serena's collection and they'll have a bloody field day when they find out about Ben."

"Stella told me about the state of Ben's place."

"Put it this way, if the cops do go in there, we couldn't have left any fingerprints."

"So that you know, there's a limit to what we've told my mother," Bee said.

"Because?"

"Reasons."

"Right. That was said darkly. I'll steer clear of anything even vaguely supernatural, in that case. However, now that she's home, I should think she'll want to go and see Caro and if she does I don't think you'll be able to control what Caro tells her or vice versa, since they are very old friends."

"No, I know. I'm not expecting to."

"Also, she might even be able to shed light on where Ben's gone. How much did Stella tell you?"

"About the photo, and the house? And her new friend, Ace, isn't it?"

"Quite a bit, then."

Bee sat down. "Ward, I just want – as Serena's sister, thanks for being here. She said you'd been a pillar of strength through all this."

He looked uncomfortable. "What else could one do?"

"Run away screaming?"

"But I am part of this myself, whatever *this* is. My family. You know that."

"Even so." She reached out and briefly gripped his hand. "Thanks, anyway."

"I am very fond of her, you know."

Bee grinned at him. "How terribly British."

"Give me a month back in LA and I'll be sobbing my emotions all over the kitchen table. 'I just wanna thank my agent...'" He put his head on his arms and emitted a muffled cry.

"Are you all right?" Bella was there, in her nightie.

"He's just being an actor," Bee said.

"God, so *embarrassing*. I'm going to take Mum some tea." She gave Ward a disgusted look and left, bearing two mugs.

"I may not be so great at the whole step-parent thing, though. If it comes to that." Ward re-emerged.

"Who ever is?"

"Dark didn't have offspring, did he? You don't find you're stepmum to a lot of little ghostlets?"

"Thankfully, no. Neither trick *nor* treat."

SERENA

It was almost like being normal, as though one was a person who did not have concourse with living stars, or visit supernatural chapels, or speak to demons above the fireplace. She would miss these things if they were not there, Serena thought. Well, some of them. She could do without having an entire collection trashed or a missing ex-boyfriend. And the adrenalin level was sure to do awful things to your blood pressure. Serena felt, however, that in these liminal days, suspended by one twirling foot like the Hanged Man in the Tarot, between Solstice and Christmas, there was a magic in being ordinary.

Ward had taken her out to dinner, just by themselves, to a country house restaurant on the evening after Solstice, and they had stayed the night. It had been luxurious and Serena, mermaid-like, had spent most of the time before dinner in a silky warm pool with a glass of champagne. The glass had been a plastic flute, just in case one was an idiot and dropped it on the expensive Italian tiles, but that didn't matter. They had woken to more rain, a garden in runny silhouette beyond the tall French windows of the old house, but Serena had not minded.

Then Alys had driven her into Glastonbury, with Bella, and they had done all the charity shops and most of the esoteric ones, and found treasures and done the last of the Christmas shopping, finishing with fish and chips brought home for everyone, in a box in the back of the Land Rover, with Alys putting her foot down on the narrow country lanes in case the takeaway got cold. Serena had almost forgotten that this might not be her mother, had been indeed a woman who had travelled unimaginable pathways between realms. For this time, Alys was once again her mum and Bella's grandmother and nothing more. Except weren't all women more, always?

Then Serena and Bee had run away one lunchtime and gone to the Hornmoon Arms, and drunk a lot of white wine and talked a lot about all sorts of things, sometimes in low voices in case someone overheard and summoned a doctor.

And then, all of a sudden, it was Christmas Eve.

Serena had been enjoying a few mornings of lying in, not a luxury she usually experienced. Normally, at least during term time, Bella needed getting ready for school, and even though she was now old enough to do much of this herself, the studio and work needed attention, and so Serena was generally up around six. In winter, this meant the day was greeted with the dark and the damp and the cold and Serena did what she could to fend it back, lighting scented candles and flicking switches and keeping the curtains closed. But here at Mooncote there was no need: she could sleep past the sun's rising, and had done so.

This morning, however, was Christmas Eve and she wanted to have the whole long day, only a few minutes longer than the Solstice itself. She sat up in bed and put the bedside light on. There was a mumble from the blankets beside her: this morning, apparently, Ward had also decided to sleep late.

"What're you doing?"

"Sorry! But it's Christmas *Eve*."

"Bah humbug," said a voice. She poked the blankets.

"Is that Shakespeare?"

"Dickens, as you know full well, you horrible girl."

She leaned over. "Ha! I won't give you my Christmas Eve present, then, if you're not in a seasonal mood."

"Present?"

Some time later, the sky behind the curtains was significantly lighter and Ward stretched and said, "I was going to have a lie in but that was better."

"You still can have a lie in."

"No, I'll get up. I can hear movement from downstairs. Don't want to put Bee to the trouble of cooking individual breakfasts – she'll be busy enough as it is. So will you, I expect."

"You could cook your own breakfast, Squire Garner, rather than making the serving wenches do it."

"I could. I could cook cornflakes."

Downstairs, Serena and Ward found the kitchen in full swing. It was, in fact, Stella who presided over a promising full English, including bacon; Bee had nipped down to the church. At the table, Alys was rolling a cigarette in a black licorice paper.

"I had stopped smoking. Perforce. But now I think I shall take it up again over Christmas. Don't worry, Luna, I'll go outside." She gestured to the pack of Golden Virginia. "Do you want one, Ward? I'll make you one."

"Don't encourage him," Serena said. "On the other hand, it is Christmas."

"Go on," said Ward. "I'll come out with you." He accepted her roll-up and they disappeared into the yard.

"So," Stella said, "I'm doing beans, mushrooms, eggs and veggie sausages for the vegetarians and the same with bacon for everyone else. Who wants fried bread? Everyone doing carbs?"

Everyone was.

"What about Aln?" asked Serena. She peeped into the dog basket but it was empty.

"She's gone out. She's in the orchard. Or was. Picking up some windfalls."

"There can't be many left."

"The deer have had most of them," Bee said. "We took a lot to the cider farm but I'll be doing our own next year. And the redstarts and fieldfares will finish them off in January. No waste."

"Natural recycling," Sam murmured.

"I think wasting food is wicked, honestly. But if it goes to the wild things, it's not wasted, is it?"

Serena thought about it. Apple to bird, to shit to compost, back to apple again. She liked the idea of being part of a cycle. She would mention it to Ace, when she next saw him. She thought he would understand, although he seemed so urban. She had found herself thinking about Ace a lot in the past days: not in any romantic way, or fuelled by attraction, just as an anchor, somehow, in the shifting strange world of which she had become a part.

She tuned back in. Bee was saying, "...so, big lunch but all cold stuff like Gala Pie and soup and then I'm doing game stew for the carnivores and vegetarian pasta for the others tonight..."

"What's happening tonight?" Ward had come back in, smelling of smoke and cold.

"We're going to the pub, and then some us might actually be going carol singing, collecting for the church roof fund, and then there's church itself, not in that order. Whoever wants to."

"Is that at midnight? The church?"

"No, it's at six. Carols. Fancy it, Ward?"

"I might, actually. I used to go when we were children. So it's the carol service and then to the pub?"

"We go to church first – even though it's early, Kate wants to do a service for the kids, and then we can go carol singing and then the pub and then, assuming we're not all shitfaced by that point, we come back here and have a late-ish supper," Stella said.

"Sounds good to me."

Bee said, "And this morning, I want to clean the house, from which no one is exempt."

"Fine."

"Fair enough."

"Can we also go and get more greenery? For the mantelpiece? Or are you worried about the fire?" *Holly and ivy would look better than a demon*, Serena thought.

"No, as long as no one actually falls over and knocks stuff into the grate."

So Serena and Bella and Ward went down the end of the garden and through into the field with a pair of secateurs and cut branches of holly from the hedge, and ivy with its round balls of flowers. There was still a bee, even in this chilly weather, moving sleepily around the ivy and Serena hoped it would survive. She gave the elder that stood at the end of the field a wide berth, but it seemed silent and dead; reassuring after the events of the autumn, for the elder was not what it seemed. The day was misty but not wet, with a copper sun sailing through the veiled air. They took the greenery back to the house and Serena arranged it, as artfully as possible, around the fireplace, while Ward hoovered. She tucked in a spare string of fairy lights and switched them on so that they fired white and emerald behind the leaves.

"So pretty! Definitely a good idea, having a professional designer around at Christmas," said Bee, coming in. "Anyone want a mince pie?"

"Yes."

"Yes."

"When we were kids," said Stella, "Christmas was basically all about eating. I don't know why we're not all the size of truckles of cheese."

"Speak for yourself," said Bee. She grimaced. "I'll start worrying about my weight in the New Year. If I can be bothered."

"Bee, you're going out with someone who is sometimes transparent. I don't suppose he gives a shit about your weight. Have another mince pie. Cheers for doing the vacuuming, Ward. If your public could see you now…"

"I really need a pinny."

"Slightly reminiscent of a 1970s porn film," said Stella. Ward gave her a look.

"I don't know what *you* might have been watching in the 1970s, missy."

"Not a lot, on account of not having been born. And you would have been, what, one?"

"A gentleman never reveals his age."

Bee made everyone stop for lunch and Serena was grateful. It felt like Christmas now, a sense of being able to sit down calmly, with the house sparkling around them and festive food on the table. The sun, no longer a brass penny through the morning mist, had vanished at noon into cloud but the day was not yet dark. Stripes of pale blue, the colour of a blackbird's egg, painted the sky above the southern hills and caught the last yellow flags of the willow in the garden.

"Did you say you wanted to go for a walk, Serena?"

Serena swallowed a mouthful of soup. "Yes. Love to. Fresh air. And then we could go straight to the church and meet you there."

"I won't come," Bella said. "I want to wrap my presents. Have you done yours, Aunty Stella?"

"'Wrap'? Any present I give looks like I wrapped it in the dark."

Serena felt a little smug and then guilty about feeling smug. Her own presents had been wrapped in London and brought down in a box in the car. They sat, delicate and beautiful in their paper and ribbons and tags, beneath the tree.

So after lunch it was down the lane, past the churchyard. The tower clock showed the hour; the weathercock was still in the windless winter air. There was no sign of anything untoward, though Serena looked for the small blue star of her grandfather's presence and did not see it. Ward was uncharacteristically quiet and she wondered if he, too, was remembering how she had changed, ended up sprawled against a gravestone, human to animal and back again and back. Now, all of it seemed like a dream. But perhaps it was being supplanted by other dreams. The knot-garden chapel showed fleetingly against her mind's eye, tiny as a stained glass window, seen at night from far away.

They hurried past, down the road that led into the village. Hornmoon was settling into its Christmas Eve peace, the festive lights starlit in the windows and a dim murmur from the pub.

"We'll be lucky to get in tonight," Ward said. "Do we need tickets?"

"Not for here. New Year's Eve, yes. But there are other things to do on New Year's Eve. Might be a bit of a squash this evening, though."

"Never mind. We'll show our faces. And we have booze at the house."

They passed a girl on a horse, a big chestnut, both intent on the road, and listened to the sound of receding hooves as they left the village behind and came out onto the wilder land, the flat valley chessboarded by ditches. Serena paused for a moment to take stock. The lane took them past a tump, National Trust owned, with a few stones from some ancient church remaining at the summit.

"Want to climb it?" Ward asked.

"Yes, let's do that." Serena hopped over the stile and set off up the path. It did not take long to reach the top, spotted with patches of nettles. The stones were bramble-bound and crumbling, limestone gold and grey. Glastonbury Tor, also crowned with a tower, was visible from here and, faintly against the hills, Serena could see Burrow Mump, another little hill with a ruined church of its own.

"There are a lot of these in this county," said Ward, very slightly out of breath.

"Yes. Are they glacial deposits? I can't remember much about geography from school. Beacon hills, maybe. For alerting the nation in times of emergency."

Further away, she could see the rise of Brent Knoll, and then the long whale-shaped headland of Brean Down. A hump of island showed in the Bristol Channel and beyond lay Wales, misty as a dream. From up here, the land was winter-coloured: after all the rain, there was a lot of standing water in the fields, reflecting the sky in mirrored steel, and the remnants of harvested sweetcorn, used for animal feed, protruded from the dark earth of the fields like the spines of beasts, buried below the soil. Away to the west rose the ridge of Cadbury Camp, perhaps the

145

original Camelot if the more fanciful amateur archaeologists were correct, but certainly the site of a Dark Age hillfort.

"Don't ask me to stay up here for long – that wind is bloody cold. I suppose that's because it's from the north," Ward said. "I only know that, mind you, because of the direction your hair is blowing. Still, it makes me feel like a wise old countryman."

Serena stuffed her hair under her hat. "You're not old enough. And you ought to have a crimson countenance like a wrinkled apple."

"I have met old crimson faced countrymen who, on investigation, turned out to be about thirty two. I should take to saying things like "Where's she to, then?" relating to my tractor." He paused. "There was a reason I moved to the capital."

Serena smiled at him. "You like it here really."

"I like it at certain times when it conforms to all my mental clichés about the picturesque nature of the West Country."

"Like Christmas Eve."

"Yeah, like that." He leaned against one of the fallen blocks of masonry and pulled her back against him. "You look very festive, by the way, in your woolly hat and your mittens. Like Little Red Riding Hood."

"No big bad wolves, though. Don't want that."

"No, no wolves today. Are you happy, madam?"

Serena pondered this. "I think so. I'm usually happy on Christmas Eve, no matter what's happened in the run up. It's been a bit shit, but that's not your fault. You've been great."

"I don't think I could have done otherwise. What an odd life we seem to have. At least," he gave a manifest and exaggerated shudder, "we are not like *other people.*"

"You can tell it's close to the Solstice," Serena said. "The light's going down already." There was a sudden golden blaze of sun, away to the west. It caught the willows and the rhynes, turning the land to a vivid, unexpected green. Then the clouds were rolling in up the channel, blotting out the light.

"I'm going round the back of the ruin," Ward said. "I seem to remember an inscription."

"Okay."

She stayed, standing on the lip of the slope and watching the big clouds build over the sea, their summits icy-white. Snow, maybe. A white Christmas after all. It was surely cold enough. Serena blinked. The light that caught the clouds was gone, too. A shadow raced over the land. There was a touch on her face like wintry fingertips and she shivered. Then something pale and low blundered out from between the stones. Serena gave a faint shriek but it was only a sheep, an old ewe. Burrs were caught askew in the woolly mop between her ears, like a fascinator. She gave Serena a panicky glance from the oblong pupil of her eye and bundled away down the slope. Serena swallowed, feeling stupid. The close-cropped grass and little balls of dung should have told their own story.

Suddenly she did not want to be on her own. Dusk was coming down fast, the distant clouds blackening, and Serena scrambled around the stones to find Ward.

But Ward was not there.

"Ward?" Serena called. "Where are you?" At the end of the ruin were the remains of a wall, high enough to conceal a man. Must be round there, then. She went to see but there was no sign of Ward. She looked out over the valley and for the first time realised that although twilight was now quite advanced, there were no visible lights. But the village was only a quarter of a mile below and there were a lot of individual houses: Mooncote, Amberley, not to mention the one with skeins of blue Christmas lights which Bee always said reminded her of a road accident. She could not even see the church. And the land looked more wooded than it ought, the trees forming ridges of shadow. Then she looked properly at the ruin and it was a ruin no longer but a chapel, standing on the summit of the hill with a dim light shining within.

Serena thought, *"Not again."* Aloud she shouted, "Ward!"

"Yes? What?"

Serena felt her knees give way. She sat down hard on a block of stone.

"Are you all right?"

"Yes." She blinked. The valley was starred with lights, Christmas and welcoming. "For a moment – I think something weird happened. Dislocation."

"Time to go," Ward said, firmly. They stumbled down the slope, disturbing more sheep, and reached the lane without incident, just as the church bells chimed out. High on the hill, the woolly mass of sheep was a pale blur against the ruins, and then they were gone over the crest. A faint bleating echoed back.

The rest of the family were standing at the lychgate as they came down the lane.

"*There* you are," said Bee. "We thought you might have got lost."

"Easily done round here," Alys murmured.

"We went up the tump," Ward told them. Serena did not want to tell anyone what had happened. Let it still be Christmas Eve. And most of all, she wanted to conceal it from her mother.

BEE

Christmas Eve was one of Bee's favourite days of the calendar, but she never took its smooth running for granted. One year, a pipe in Mooncote's attics had burst, flooding the bedroom below while the family had been, as now, at church. Another year, a dog – let out for a wee in the orchard – had hurtled off into the distance and not been found until dark. Everyone had spent the day scouring the lanes. Bee had been young, then, too young to join in the bottle of Scotch that her infuriated grandfather and mother had consumed between them. One by one the girls had crept off to bed, leaving their relatives singing bawdy songs in the sitting room.

This year, nothing had gone wrong so far, but Bee remained vigilant and alert, just in case. After all, Aln was back at the house and things had been happening…

"Merry Christmas!" That was Kate the vicar, clad in surplice and dog collar. Her hair had returned to a sober dark brown. She looked clerical and professional.

"Thanks! You, too! How's it going? Dare I ask?"

"The birth of our Lord is always a time of gladness and celebration," said the vicar, "And I tell myself that in a couple of days it will all be over and I can put my feet up and catch up on Strictly Come Dancing over the turkey sarnies and the Christmas gin that the old people's home have just sent me. Don't tell anyone I said that. It's good to see you all. Is this your mum? I don't think we've –"

"You must be the vicar," Alys said. "Well, obviously you are, what a silly thing to say. I'm Alys. Back from my travels." She made it sound as though she'd been to the Riviera. "How lovely to meet you."

She extended a graceful gloved hand. Today Alys wore a red coat with black velvet trim, rather military, rather foxhunting, and black velvet boots, brave against the inevitability of mud, Bee thought with a trace of envy. With her silvery hair swept up and garnet earrings dangling, discreet and age-appropriate make up, Alys looked exactly like an upper middle class parent, sliding gently into older age. Not like a traveller in realms beyond the haunts of men. For a blinding moment, Bee nearly hated her. But Kate was evidently charmed.

"Oh!" Alys said. "Caro."

Bee turned and was horrified. Caro Amberley, leaning on her husband's arm, in contrast looked twice her age. Her chestnut hair was almost white and her oval face had become haggard. Her usual air of calm confidence was gone.

"Alys," she whispered. "You've come back."

"Caro's not been very well," Richard Amberley said, smoothly. "Touch of the flu." But to Bee, who knew him, there was a shadow behind his dark eyes, so like his cousin Ward's.

"Oh no! Sorry to hear that," the vicar replied. "So much going around at this time of year. Members of the diocese have been dropping like flies. I have to cover a couple of churches."

"Nightmare," said Alys, firmly. "Come on, Caro, you can take my arm." She linked arms with her friend, at the other side, and together Richard and Alys bore Caro away. Bee, staring after them, felt a touch on her shoulder and looked round to see Ward, who mouthed, "What the fuck?"

"Well," said Bee.

"I know, I know. Ben. But it's not like his corpse has showed up in a ditch. For all we know, he's rocking round Amsterdam or somewhere. I only saw her a couple of days ago and she wasn't like that then, though she didn't look herself, I must say."

"You don't believe that, though. About Amsterdam. Not after what you and Stella said."

"No, I don't. The French call it a *coup d'age*," Ward said. "You sometimes see it in elderly actresses."

"It's stress and shock in Caro's case. She's not that old. Look at Mum."

"I have been. From a distance," Ward said, "your mother could be in her early thirties. I'd like some of what she's having, I must say."

Bee looked at him. "I don't think you would, actually."

Inside, the little plastered church was almost full. Alys had left Caro's side and was standing with Stella and Serena. Bee joined them and noticed that either Kate or the verger had lit two long wan candles on the altar. The little flames picked up the shining leaves of ivy and the white-winged amaryllis which Bee had, at great expense, bought in Wells market for the church decorations ("they last for weeks"). They glowed in the candlelight, eclipsing the rather sterile illumination from the sconce lights along the wall. Kate, by some magic of the switchboard, dimmed the sconces and the church was in semi-darkness except for the little reading lights along the pews ("all very well to have atmosphere," the vicar had said, "but not if no one can read their bloody hymnbook").

The choir's rising star, a young woman named Jodie, began to sing, starting with *Once in Royal David's City as they did in* the King's College Chapel service, and everyone settled quickly. Then the vicar, striding into the pulpit, said a few brisk words and broke the spell and the service properly began.

Bee had exercised a fleeting churchwarden's prerogative and asked if they could do *The Holly and the Ivy*. Then she extended her power even further and asked for *Emanuel* for Serena, even though it was a bastard to sing and would doubtless be mangled by a congregation of limited musical prowess, in which Bee included herself.

"Jodie can hack it, though," Kate had said. And when it came to it Jodie did, hitting the high piercing notes with effortless ease while everyone else mimed and mouthed. Bee felt Serena's hand steal into hers and give it a squeeze.

Then Jodie sang the Coventry Carol, which Bee always considered a tough one even with music. Jodie sang unaccompanied, her voice soaring pure to the rafters, and when Bee glanced down the pew in the direction of her mother, she was startled and touched to see tears in Alys' silver-blue eyes. Touched and somehow reassured. If something other than her mother stood along the pew, would Lullay, lullay have brought tears to its eyes? Well, maybe, thought Bee, mentally paraphrasing the carol. "*Oh sisters three, what may we do, thus to preserve this day?*"

Bee blinked. Alys wasn't the only one with damp eyes. The church blurred, its cream plaster walls and the grey stone turning to the colours of rain. For a moment Bee stood in birch woodland, monochrome, with a leaden sky where the church rafters should have been. She kept very still. It seemed a mistake to let the world know where she was. She looked down at a long spire of bramble, sharp-thorned and with only a single dark red leaf clinging to it, old blood against the snow. Someone was singing still, but it wasn't Jodie: it was a small, raw voice, not very tuneful, and then another voice joined it.

Very slowly, Bee turned. She found herself looking down a long slope into a valley, where a grey river snaked through the snow. Two little figures struggled along, clad in ragged cloaks and singing bravely. One bore a staff and pulled the other along: were they boy and girl? The one with the staff was taller.

Something burst out of the woods behind Bee, nearly frightening her to death. She gasped and staggered in the snow. A doe leaped over the bramble patch and prinked down the slope, skidding as she did so. Bee caught a glimpse of the panicking dark eyes, the delicate antlers, then the doe's spotted hide vanishing down the slope. Behind her, a horn blew, sweet and unrelenting. The two little figures heard it, too. Bee saw their heads go up and the one with the staff began to run, stumbling along with the other's wrist held tightly in his hand. Bee was now sure that they were boy and girl; she could see the smaller person's pale hair flying across its shoulders like a flag. And the boy's hand bore a faint tinge of green.

Bee did not want to be there when the hunt appeared. But a flurry of snow whirled up, choking her with sudden cold. A hand grasped her own. Bee was back in church, with the last notes of the carol fading away. She looked up into her mother's warning eyes. Then Jodie began to sing again, a carol that Bee did not know. It was in a language that she did not recognise, either, and the girl's pure, high voice soared up, the song almost visible, crystals in the air. Then the person standing in front of Bee moved and Bee saw that it was not Jodie who sang, not any more. The village choir member had returned to her pew and was standing by her beaming mother. The girl who was singing was Aln.

STELLA

This was definitely the way to do religion, Stella decided. First carols, then the pub. Her sisters had accompanied her, but not her mother.

"Caro's asked me back to Amberley," Alys had said, coming over to her daughters outside the church. "For a sherry. I'll catch up with you later."

"Like Hell," Bee said, when her mother and Caro Amberley had been bundled into Richard's Range Rover. "She's never drunk sherry in her life."

"Caro looks awful," said Bella. "Is she ill?"

"I don't know, darling," Serena answered.

"Is it – you know." Bella knew about Ben. Her young voice faltered a little. She had not wanted to talk to Serena about it, she had confided in Stella, feeling that her mother might still be too raw.

"I'm sure your grandmother will find out what's wrong." Stella saw her sister's gaze meet Ward's, and lock for a moment.

Then they had spent an hour singing carols around the village, with Kate and others in the congregation, and Stella had joined in with gusto, delivering *Good King Wenceslas* and *Silent Night* and other old half-remembered songs. It got everyone in the mood, said Kate, and Stella agreed: not just the singing, but the glimpses into other people's Christmas, the lights and laughter coming from the opened cottage doorways, driving back the night and the drizzle.

"All we need is a candle in a lantern and some fur muffs."

"Or a sou'wester," the vicar said. "The BBC said it would get wetter later on. It must make a change for you, singing rather than playing music? Or do you sing, too?"

Stella admitted to feeling a little hypocritical, since she was not a church-goer. "And I can't sing very well. I wanted to be a singer, when I was young. But I didn't have the voice."

"I don't agree, by the way," Bee said. "I think she's rather good."

"Well, DJ-ing is probably less hassle," said Stella. "Any idea how much we raised this evening?"

"The box feels quite heavy and I know several people put notes in."

Once they had done a circuit of Hornmoon and reconvened at the lychgate, Stella expected Bee to decline and return to the house to start the Christmas dinner preparations, the peeling and parboiling, the stirring and baking. Instead, Bee said,

"Oh sod it. I'm coming to the pub. I didn't want to mention this in front of the vicar but did you see where Aln went?"

"No. Was she there, then?"

"Yes – in the church, not with us with the carols. She sang the last carol in the service. Then she slipped into the back somewhere – I didn't see her again – before Kate did the blessing."

"Oh, God, I didn't realise it was her! I thought it was whatshername. Jodie. There was a really tall man in front of me and I couldn't see."

"To the pub," Ward interrupted, rather firmly.

As they walked along, footsteps ringing on the hard damp road, Stella nudged Bee and said, "I'll help with the dinner prep, if you like."

"No, it's all right. I did a lot of it this afternoon. And supper tonight is in the Aga. I had – a bit of an episode, there in the church."

"Oh Christ!"

"I'll tell you later. Mum pulled me out of it. But I want to tell you before she gets back tonight."

"Okay," said Stella. She held the door of the Mooncote Arms open for her sister. "What are you drinking?"

"Alcohol," said Bee.

"God, look at it, it's rammed. Christmas Eve, of course. We'll be lucky to find a seat."

"No," Bee said, "I reserved the big table in the back and I told George we'd be in directly after carol singing." Stella stared at her.

"You are actually awesome."

"I've had a lot of disappointments. *Always* make a reservation."

Stella followed her through the throng, ducking to avoid dangling Christmas decorations, which George the landlord had strewn across the rafters with more enthusiasm than taste. They found the table at the back, with a reserved sign upon it, and secured it.

"Prepare to repel boarders," said Bee.

"Which reminds me. Where *is* your boyfriend?"

Bee grinned at her. "He's not a pirate. Well, not really. And he's over there."

Ned Dark stood by the inglenook fireplace, talking to someone indistinct. Stella tried to see the person's face, but could not. No one seemed to be paying any attention to Dark, or to his companion, but no one was trying to occupy the warm space by the flames, either.

Stella, Luna and Serena listened while Bee briefly caught them up with events. Ward had taken Bella over to the bar, and was waiting to be served, along with Sam.

"Okay," Stella said, nodding. "Okay. So it's like the walls between the world are getting thinner."

"They talk about the veil being thin," Serena said, "at times like Hallowe'en."

"And May Eve," said Luna. "Beltane."

"I always thought that Christmas Eve was one of the magical times of the year." Bee looked down at her hands. "So it doesn't surprise me."

"But what does it mean? And what's happening with Mum?"

There was a short silence.

"I don't know," Bee said. "I don't feel that I know who she is any more."

"Maybe she doesn't know. Oh, cheers, Ward." Stella relieved him of the drinks.

"It's a madhouse at the bar. Are we eating here? We're not, are we?"

"No, I've got food back at the house. If it's too much of a scrum, we'll have one and go back."

"We've got booze back at the house as well," Stella said. "Obviously. It is quite Christmassy in here, though. Good vibe."

Leaving her sisters at the table, she rose and went over to the fireplace. The person Dark had been talking to had disappeared.

"Who was that?"

"He's sometimes here," said Dark. Stella could, very faintly, see the mantelpiece through his collar.

"Did you see where our houseguest went to? The greenish girl?"

"No. But I heard her sing."

"Do you know what language that was in?"

Dark shook his head. "I did not know it. And I have travelled. It was not French, nor Dutch nor the language of Spain. Also I watched the faces of the congregation, and none seemed surprised at the hue of her skin. I wonder if she looked to them as she looks to us."

"I wish we knew who she was," said Stella. She was not afraid of Aln; in fact, she had rather taken to the girl, a classic waif and stray and

155

Stella always had a soft spot for those, but she could not help feeling that Aln was key, somehow, to whatever was going on.

"I think she has come here for a reason," she said now to Dark.

"So do I," he replied. "But I do not know what that reason might be."

As they walked home, it began to rain more steadily. Stella was warmed by firelight and wine; she didn't really mind the wet drops on her face after the stuffiness of the pub. Pity it wasn't cold enough for snow... she was glad when they reached the house and she was able to duck into the kitchen out of the wet.

"Oh," said Luna. She pulled off her woollen hat and shook her curly hair like a dog. "I hope Mum gets a lift. It's hammering down now."

"Where's Aln?" Bella asked.

"Not here." The dog basket was empty.

Bee opened the back door and called. "Aln? Aln!" There was no reply.

"Well," said Bee. "She knows where to come."

"Perhaps she's gone home." Stella went over to the stove and peered into a pot. "Wherever home is. Is this the veggie one? Oh, it is."

"Help yourself. If you want to warm up some bread, stick it in the Aga."

Stella did so. Privately, she thought it quite likely that Aln had gone back to wherever she came from. It was Christmas Eve, after all, as Bee had said, a magical time, and Bee said, too, that she had found Aln in the churchyard... Perhaps the music had permitted her to slip back, slide through time and worlds. Stella hoped the girl was all right but maybe it was better this way, less trouble for Bee. She could not have a house guest in the dog basket forever.

After supper, Luna went up to bed, pleading tiredness, Sam with her, and Serena went up too, for a bath. With Bella on some interminable teenage phone errand of her own, this left Stella, Bee and Ward downstairs.

"We could toast chestnuts," said Bee. "The fire's roaring away, look at it."

"We could. Although I was actually going to watch something. I don't know what's on. We could do Netflix."

Ward was buried in a paper copy of the Radio Times. "This is like being a kid again. I used to spend days reading the Radio Times Christmas bumper edition. We made our own fun in those days. We don't need Netflix. I'll find something. Trust me."

The something turned out to be an older version of *Dracula* on BBC 1.

"Very festive," said Bee. "Well done, Ward."

"I love a bit of Gothic at this time of year. Christmas seems to call for it, more than Hallowe'en. Bit of M R James, for instance."

Just as the Count's narrative drew to a close, Ward sat up from his slouch on the sofa, nearly spilling his wine, and said,

"What was that?"

"What?"

"I can hear music."

"Someone's probably playing something upstairs."

"No, it was outside."

Bee was already on her feet. "You're right. I can hear it, too."

The front door of the house was rarely opened and Bee had to wrench it hard.

"Don't invite them in!" Stella said, recently reminded of vampires.

But instead, it was another round of carol singers. Stella heard the same sweet, high music that Aln had sung in church, although it was a different song. When it came to an end, Bee called,

"That was lovely – thank you! Would you like a contribution?"

Stella expected a child to step forward with a tin, but no one did so.

"Is anyone there?" Bee said, sharply. Stella squeezed past her, out onto the drive. The rain had stopped and the polar stars prickled overhead, the Bear wheeling up, Arcturus yellow as a daffodil in the western sky. Stella listened, half-expecting to hear children laughing as they fled down the drive, a Christmas trick or treat, but the garden and the orchard beyond were silent. She looked up again and the sky seemed to ring; the stars shivered in her sight. She thought: *there is a story about animals who kneel on Christmas Eve,* and wondered why the memory had come. She went back inside and Bee closed the door.

"It's Thomas Hardy," Bee said, when Stella mentioned her thought. "It's a poem."

"Perhaps they do." Ward paused at the bottom of the stairs. "Perhaps we should go and look."

"Perhaps not! You're the one who mentioned M R James."

Later, as Stella lay in bed, she thought she heard the music again. Snatched from sleep, she kept as still as she could, listening. Maybe it had been the stars... but then she was asleep.

In the morning, the rain had stopped, but it soon began again. Stella woke to a sliver of greengold sky, deep behind the bare branches of the chestnut trees which stood at the end of the lane. But even as she was staring at it through the bedroom window, there came a sudden spatter on the glass and the green gleam was gone. *Never mind!* thought Stella. It was Christmas Day. She found a dressing gown and went downstairs.

Bee was already up and there were signs that she had been out of bed for some time. She wore cords and a sweater, with a nod to the season in the colour of her clothes (dark green skirt, crimson jumper). Stella herself had found a novelty sweater with a sour-faced cat and the words 'Bah Humbug' on it and she intended to wear this when she eventually got dressed.

"Those," her sister said, pointing to a tray of sausage rolls, "are the vegetarian ones. It's Quorn. But they won't be cooked for a bit because I can't fit them in the oven."

"Fine. I can wait. Is there any tea?"

And she ate a chocolate biscuit, too, just because.

"Right." Bee stepped back from the Aga and surveyed her empire. "The geese will go in at ten. They're not as big as a turkey, although I always think they're bigger, for some reason. They're like ducks – all ribcage. So I'm doing a lot of extra stuff as well and the vegetarians will be having a mushroom Wellington."

"Fab!"

"And fruit salad as usual instead of Christmas pudding because who can eat all that food?"

"Probably Ward and Sam. Just to be sexist. But I know what you mean. Anyway, we've always done pudding on Boxing Day."

These were all ritual conversations, Stella thought. Christmas did not change, or had not in all the years that she had come back to Mooncote. Sometimes her Christmas had been spent on a beach, and once in a ski lodge, but it was best to be home.

"Did Dark show up last night?"

"Yes. But Aln didn't."

"Oh. Oh dear."

"I am worried about her, Stella, all the same. She might have been an uninvited guest but she seems so fragile, somehow. Lost."

Stella nearly said that Aln could look after herself but she was by no means convinced that this was so. Aln had given a good impression of someone who was hiding from something. Until she had crept out of the dog basket and sung so beautifully in church. Why had she done that? Stella could not help feeling that it was a message. But to whom?

"What about Mum?"

Bee glanced at her. "I don't know."

"Want me to take her a goodwill Christmas morning cuppa?"

"Yes." The words *to see if she's actually in her bed* hung unspoken between them both.

"She still takes it with lemon."

"Whatever." Stella took the cup and saucer from her sister and carried it carefully up the stairs, passing Serena on the way.

"Oh, you're up!"

"Don't sound so surprised. The tea's for Mum."

"That's a nice thing to do."

"Bee and I want to see if she made it home," Stella hissed.

Serena looked doubtful. "She might have stayed with the Amberleys. I didn't hear her come in last night."

"Well, who the hell knows?"

But when she knocked on Alys' door, her mother called, "Come in."

"Merry Christmas! Brought you some tea."

"Oh, darling, how kind." Swathed in Japanese silk, cream and blue, Ays looked ethereal and much younger than her years. She sat up in bed. "I was so late getting home... Richard drove me back, probably shouldn't have done given that he'd had a drink, but we were all talking, you know how it is... Did you have a nice Christmas Eve?"

"Yes. We watched Dracula and ate all the mince pies. So Bee is making some more. But we didn't drink all the wine. We nearly did but the Christmas spirit prevailed and we have left some for other people."

Alys laughed. "Glad to hear it."

"How is Caro?"

Her mother pulled a face. "She's not good. Because of Ben, obviously. Richard's told me but Caro didn't mention it. Talk about the elephant in the room."

"They all must be worried sick. I know Ward is. Whatever his issue with Ben about Serena – even if he's got one, I'm not sure that he does, actually – it's pretty vile, having someone going –"

Their eyes met.

"I know," Alys said, and Stella was glad to see a trace of shame. Then her mother looked away, staring out of the rainwashed window. "I – I have been making enquiries, Stella. You know what I mean, I think."

Stella had to laugh. "Chief Inspector Alys Fallow, CSI Fairyland."

Her mother laughed, too, rather gruffly as though it had been forced out of her. "Yeah, fair point." She groped for Stella's hand and clasped it. "I asked the – the people I trust, and there aren't very many of those. But something's happening."

"Well, that sounds fucking ominous! What sort of 'something'?"

"No one knows. Things are stirring, it's out of sequence. Like seeing daffodils in August."

"A sort of supernatural global warming?"

"In a way. I suppose. No one really seems to know but there are things abroad."

Alys let go of Stella's hand and rubbed her face. "God, I sound like *I* ought to be Dracula. I don't even know what kind of things. I saw – something, once, not long ago, moving through the woods. But it was dark and the thing was a shadow and the person I was with said, it shouldn't be happening, someone's doing something they oughtn't."

Stella's neck prickled. "Are you going to go back?"

At that Alys looked her full in the face. "I think I'm going to have to."

Later, Stella was peeling potatoes when she heard the horn. Bee had opened one of the windows slightly, to let out the steam ("Close it if it gets too cold in here") and gone up to dress for champagne before lunch. Stella, now clad in her novelty sweater and leggings, did not think she would bother. But Bee spent so much of her time in scruffs that she liked to dress up, when there was an occasion to do so. The kitchen remained steamy and Stella left the window open. The sound of the horn rang out inside the room as though the hunt were at the door.

It took her a moment to recognise it. Years had passed since her sabbing days, and she hadn't encountered a hunt for some time, though the Wickley rode out around Hornmoon. It was always an eerie sound and Stella treacherously liked it, although she knew full well that it had once betokened death for some poor old dog fox or terrified vixen and sometimes still did. She went to the kitchen door and peered out. Nothing was visible. They'd better not come over the hedge – but it was unlikely.

"Getting some air?" Bee asked. She had exchanged the sweater and cords for an amber velvet dress and a string of garnets.

"You look great! No, I opened the door because I thought I heard the hunt."

Bee frowned. "What, on Christmas Day? They won't be riding out till tomorrow. I actually saw Nick Wratchall-Haynes – that's the new master, you don't know him – in the pub last night and he mentioned it then. Nice man. I know you don't approve."

"I don't mind the hunt – it's the *hunting.*"

"They are supposed to keep within the law, these days, as we were saying the other night. I don't know how many actually do."

"Yeah, right."

"I think Nick does, though. I had a conversation with him. He said they don't go looking for foxes. And he grew up in Cumbria, apparently, and they've always done trail hunting, so he's used to it."

"I've no objection to trail hunting, or drag hunting, come to that. Anyway, I thought I heard a horn but maybe I was wrong."

"It's pretty unmistakable, though. Here, give me those spuds and I'll stick them in the oven. Then we'll open the Moet."

"Oooh, Moet. There's posh."

"It is, actually, since Ward brought a case. Very, very kind of him. Of you!" For the champagne donor had just walked in.

"There are eight of us. Only one bottle would mean a thimble for everyone. Actually there are nine. I'm assuming Dark doesn't drink?"

"He kind of does, in fact."

"Oh. Right. Well. Anyway, Luna might not be drinking. Although I doubt a tiny amount of booze will hurt."

Luna was not drinking, but everyone else had champagne, standing around the long dining room with glasses while the rain streamed down the French windows. Beyond, the land was a blur of grey and green and water. Ned Dark, Stella was delighted to see, had actually brought a spectral drink. It looked like a very dark red wine. Perhaps it was sack, whatever that was. Or blood? – Stella thought, remembering last night's Dracula. But Dark was a ghost, not a vampire. Too nice to be a vampire. He looked very solid, today; you would not necessarily know. Perhaps some special dispensation was made for ghosts for Christmas, like the kneeling beasts and the ringing stars. Alys was curled in an armchair, dressed in a vintage trouser suit of heavy cream silk with a lot of ethnic jewellery. Stella had often seen her sit like that at Christmas, cat-like, with a flute of champagne. Despite Alys' recent strangeness, she was glad that her mother was there, all the same, that Alys had kept her promise.

"Well," said Bee. "Merry Christmas!"

Then it was time for presents. Stella was always more excited to give than to receive: peripatetic as she was, storing stuff was a problem. No one had gone overboard – the presents were mainly books and booze – but Ward had given Serena a pair of earrings in some winking pale blue stone, which hung in her earlobes like fragments of sky and which elicited gasps of admiration from her sisters.

"Thank you," Luna said quietly. Stella had given her a massive woolly wrap and a little tiger's eye goddess from Glastonbury, on a thong.

"I didn't want to give you baby stuff. Not yet. You're not just a mum."

"Thank you," Luna whispered again.

"What did Serena give you?"

"Oh," Luna said, beaming. "Look!" It was a tiny bronze wren, also on a leather thong. "We swapped," Luna said. Serena turned and smiled.

"We did." She held out a pendant on a long chain around her neck: a little silver hare, running.

Alys said that she had not had an opportunity to do any proper Christmas shopping despite the run into Glastonbury and had given everyone wine or chocolates.

"A relief, frankly," Bee confided to Stella, back in the kitchen. "Who knows what we might have got."

"With what strings attached, as well."

"Exactly. It'll all turn to leaves in the morning."

Bee smiled. "I hope that book on orchards you got me is still here tomorrow. I'd like to read it."

"Hopefully I am not yet contaminated by fairy impermanence."

"Okay, these potatoes are done. What else? Stuffing, carrots, parsnips, gravy, bread sauce, peas, pigs in blankets, mushroom thing, goose – we're there."

She organised a kind of human chain to the dining room.

"This is like a military operation," Ward remarked, with a bowl of stuffing.

"Too right. I haven't organised Christmas dinner lo these umpteen years without getting it down to a fine art."

"It's much smoother than when I used to do it," Alys said, sitting down. "I always forgot something or put it all in too late. You never do."

"Lists, Mum. It's all in the lists. Cheers. Merry Christmas, everyone."

The Queen's Christmas speech went unwatched although Ward did invite Stella to have a look, for the sake of irony. She declined.

"The only person who wants to watch it, he told me this morning, is Dark! Bit of a shock!"

"I think it's because they didn't have TV in his day," Bee said, apologetically.

"They had Queens, though. Imagine seeing Elizabeth the First on the box. She'd never be off it. She'd be like a Kardashian."

But Stella accepted Serena's invitation to go for an afternoon walk.

"Just down to the church, before it gets dark."

There was a break in the rain, but they both wore Wellingtons. The road was awash with puddles and they had to step into the verge to avoid being splashed by the occasional passing car.

"You can really tell where's old round here and where's not," Serena said. "I don't mean the architecture. But where's wet and where isn't."

"Yeah, it's like a spine. All the old buildings are a bit higher and the church is highest of all, but it doesn't look like it when you're there. Mooncote and Amberley next."

"The church must have been an island sometimes," Serena said. "Did you know we had a tsunami here?"

"What? No, when? Not recently."

"No, hundreds of years ago. Early 1600s, I think. There was an article about it in an old copy of *Somerset Life* I picked up a night or two ago. Churches have a marker – I think that's what that black mark in

Hornmoon must be. I ought to ask Bee. Or the vicar. It's the height of the water mark."

"Is that the black line up the wall? That's taller than me."

"It was either a massive storm surge or an earthquake off the coast of Ireland. It swept over Somerset, Monmouthshire, Gloucestershire… It killed thousands of people, the article said."

"Jesus. That's a sobering thought. What if it happened again? What about Hinckley? They didn't have nuclear power stations bang slap on the coast in those days."

"Yes. Think of that thing in Japan."

"Worrying."

They had now reached the churchyard and the sky was still overcast, darkening down into dusk.

"I wanted to wish Grandfather a happy Christmas," Serena said.

"Will he need it? Isn't he technically reposing in the bosom of the Lord and all that?"

"I don't know. I don't know where he goes when he's not here. I don't think he's allowed to say."

"Dark is mainly here and sometimes back in his own day, apparently."

"The afterlife seems to be a thing, but not a very fixed thing."

"I did ask Abraham once and he just laughed."

"Not very helpful," Serena said, severely.

"I'm not sure we can expect him to divulge the secrets of the universe. He might not even know."

But the blue light that was Abraham's spirit was not to be seen in the graveyard. They lingered for a moment, reading the familiar names. Fallows and Darks, Amberleys and Coldlines, Merrows and Sparkens.

"Most of these people must have been related," Stella said. "It's a wonder we haven't all got birth defects."

"Maybe someone purchased a bicycle. That was supposed to add to the threat of immorality and seduction, you know. As well as barges."

"You wouldn't seduce very fast, on a barge."

"No, but people claimed at the time that it caused promiscuity. Maybe rather slow promiscuity."

Stella said, "Who can blame the Fallow women, then, for looking outside the box? No more slut shaming for us. Good old school genetic diversification."

"Are you going to say that to Mum?"

"I've already said it to Mum. Ages ago."

Serena gaped at her. "And how did she react?"

"She agreed. Although she said it wasn't actually the first thing to come to her mind when counting our various fathers. She stopped there."

"Well," said Serena, "I suppose that was good old fashioned sex."

"Quite right too. Although not the first thing on my mind right now – God, it's cold."

"And it's getting dark," said Serena. "Look at that cloud."

It was coming up from the west, fast and dark, a great wedge of stormfront. Moments later, the first drops hit: forming huge spots on the lichen-encrusted gravestones and making Stella wish she had worn a hat.

"Into the porch!" Serena said. "It might go over in a minute."

They took shelter in Hornmoon's small porch, beneath the ball of rosemary and bay tied with red ribbons and tiny scarlet crab apples.

"Is the church open?" Stella asked.

"I don't know. Try the door."

Stella turned the iron ring that formed the handle and the door swung open.

"I'm going in. If anyone's there…"

Serena followed her, but the little church was empty. Their footsteps echoed on the stone flags, the occasional hollowness of a gravestone set into the floor. The stove was not lit and the church smelled of cold.

"Bee said she saw a place, through a knot in the glass," Stella said. "I was looking at it when we were at the carol service. I thought it was worth checking out."

"All right. I'll keep a look out. Where is it?"

"Up here. You can see it. Like a sort of a bulge in the glass."

She found a kneeler and put it under the window.

"Mind your boots," her sister said. "Mud."

"Fair point." Stella kicked her boots off and stood up on the kneeler. She had no difficulty looking through the knot, taller than Bee as she was.

"Can you see anything?"

"Yeah, the churchyard. But apart from the fact that it's a bit distorted by the glass, it actually looks perfectly normal. No otherworld or anything. Disappointing."

"Oh well," said Serena, sounding somewhat relieved. "I'm glad it doesn't happen every time, to be honest."

"I know what you mean." She got down and replaced the kneeler.

"What's that?" Serena said.

"What?" She turned. The rainclouds were lifting and there was a sudden shaft of sun, striking the knot in the pane of glass and illuminating something on the other side of the church. "It's just sunlight. Maybe we can walk home without getting wetter."

"The window's in the north. So where's the light coming from?"

"Oh!" Stella said. "You're right." She did not want to look through the knot again. The light was strong, hard and cold and bright. Serena walked across the church, following the beam. Together, they stared at the point where it landed, partway up the wall. Here, there was a memorial set into the plaster: a marble plaque with carved calligraphy proclaiming it to be the memorial of one Sarah Sparken (b.1715; d. 1756, beloved wife of Hugh and mother of Elizabeth and Jonathan). Stone scrolls surrounded this information, capped with a marble seraph, eyes tightly closed and lips parted.

"I've no idea who she was," Serena said. "I always meant to look her up but I haven't."

"Neither have I."

"It tells you," the seraph said. Stella stepped back.

"Shit!"

"Did I startle you? I'm sorry. I don't usually speak to people, it's true. But you look as though you might be able to hear me."

It had a small clear voice, very sweet, which reminded Stella uncomfortably of the demon.

"I'll talk to anyone," Stella said. "How do you know what we look like? You've got your eyes shut."

"Oh! But of course I can see anyway. Both ways." The seraph's marble lids slipped up, revealing blank stone eyes with a film of gold. Now it reminded Stella of the stone head.

"Both ways?"

"Forwards *and* back," said the seraph, with a trace of pride. "This world and that world."

166

"Which world is that world?"

"The one that lies behind me," the seraph said.

"Like Janus," said Serena. "Remember the head?"

"I was just thinking that. I expect so."

"I want to ask you a question," Stella said. "My sister saw another world through that knothole across the aisle, the one in the window. Is that the world you're talking about? She said it was snowing there."

"Oh no, I cannot see that world. The world I see is golden and a god is there. It's very beautiful. All the trees are aflower with lights."

"Sounds lovely. But you do know the place I am talking about?"

"I am glad I cannot see it," said the seraph. "It is cold, and there are terrible things there. I should not look too closely into it if I were you."

"The problem is," Serena said, "that it might be looking closely into us."

There was a creak from the door. The seraph's eyes quickly closed again. Stella and Serena straightened up.

Caro Amberley came into the church. She was bundled in a waterproof and she moved falteringly, not like the brisk woman whom Stella had known all her life.

"Oh!" she said, when she saw them. "I'm sorry. I didn't think anyone was in here."

"We were out for a walk," Serena said. "But it started raining and so we came in here. We were reading the gravestones."

Caro nodded. "I came in to – well. I light a candle, every day." She pointed to the iron rack with its small holders for tea lights. "You can probably guess why."

Serena said, "I didn't get the chance to talk to you yesterday. I know Mum went back with you but I haven't really caught up with her, either." Stella saw her take a deep breath. "I just want to say that I'm so sorry about Ben."

"Oh, Serena. I know. Please don't think I didn't know how much you loved him, or how – unfair – he was to you. Because he was unfair. He ran around behind your back with that awful woman and I didn't realise what was going on until it was too late. I couldn't have done anything, anyway – I doubt he'd have listened to his mother, and he probably shouldn't, anyway. He's not a child; he can make his own decisions. Alys told me what happened in the autumn. And Ward. I probably freaked him out – we had a really odd conversation. I want *you* to know that I don't blame you one bit for taking Ward back after all that. I know Alys said there was some kind of, well, dark magic thing going on. I don't know about all that. But even so…" She sagged into a nearby pew. "Ben's my son and I want to know what's happened to him, where he is, and I feel so *feeble*. I feel tired all the time, so drained. It's not like me. I've been to the doctor and he just said it was stress."

"Do you think it's just stress?" Serena said, gently.

"No. I think something's *getting* at me. When I close my eyes to go to sleep at night, I see things. Images."

Serena, with Stella close behind, crossed the church and took a seat in a pew.

"What sort of things, Caro?"

"Red. Everything's red. And there's this huge shape, with its back to me. Like a man, upright, but I can't see it properly because its head is lowered. I can smell it, sometimes. It smells like – like blood and manure. Like mucking out the stables. I asked Richard if he could smell anything once and he gave me a funny look and said it was probably the dog." She smiled, but there were tears in her eyes. "It wasn't the dog, obviously. I'm sure he thinks I'm cracking up."

"When you do go to sleep," Stella asked, "do you have dreams?"

"Sometimes. I have a new dream – I never had it before Ben went missing. But it's quite pleasant, actually. At first. I'm on a boat and it's going up and down – I suppose some people would say that was a nightmare, but you know us, we both love sailing – and the sun is very strong and hot, and the sea is a very dark blue. There's something just under the waves, like dolphins."

"Well, that sounds good!"

"But then I look up and the ship has this great black sail. And I can hear something under the deck, something moving about and I know it's awful. I know if it breaks out of where it's kept, we're all going to die. Stella? Will you help me? Serena, I can't expect you to –" She turned. "What was that?"

But it was only the vicar, looking cheerful and pink in the face. "Oh, Merry Christmas! I wondered if someone was in here! All those bootprints in the vestibule. I feel like Sherlock Holmes."

"The footprints of a gigantic hound!" said Stella. "Merry Christmas to you, too." It occurred to her that she had not thought to say this to

Caro Amberley. Probably just as well. "We've been out for a walk, then it started chucking it down. Is it raining now?"

"A bit. It's colder, too. I left my cardigan in here this morning, came to get it."

"We should let you get on," Serena said. Caro nodded.

"I'll just do my candle thing." She reached out and squeezed Serena's hand. "I'm glad we had a chance to talk."

Outside, it was now dark and drizzling. Serena and Stella walked back quickly, trying to avoid any further downpours.

"I'm glad she said that," Serena said, once they were nearly at the house. "About Ben."

"Yes. Bit awkward with you now going out with his cousin."

"Exactly. And anyway, he had the chance to mend things after Dana – well, after Dana. But he chose not to."

"I think you're a lot better off with Ward, frankly."

"I was so in love with Ward, all those years ago, when we first went out. Then we split up and it was awful, but I got over him. So when we – reconnected, I sort of felt, been there and done that, but it was really nice. In an old married couple sort of way."

"All passion spent?"

"Well, actually no, turns out. Not quite." It was too murky to see properly, but Stella thought her sister might be blushing. She laughed.

"Sorry. I just find it hilarious. Here is Ward, an actual heartthrob, a veritable movie star, women send him their knickers in the post, I have seen people practically swoon, and you're all, *where are my slippers and please pass the cocoa*."

"Do *you* fancy Ward?"

"Sort of, he's very good looking, but I've known him for too long and he's your boyfriend, anyway, so I don't go there. I wouldn't kick him out of bed. I don't think I'm his type, though."

"What did Caro mean, can you help her? Did she mean, find Ben?"

"Yes, I think so. But it's been an epic fail so far."

The little yellow squares of the windows came into view: homely and welcoming. Stella was glad to be back.

"I bet they've been on the sherry. I'm going to make a big cheese sandwich."

"I'm going to have some tea and read my book."

Perhaps, Stella thought uneasily, they would have the chance to do neither: who knew what might happen, on Christmas night?

But as it turned out, it was Boxing Day she had to worry about.

SERENA

They had run out of tablets for the dishwasher. Despite, Bee berated herself aloud, all those endless lists.

"Better that than running out of cat food," Alys said.

"No, we'd never hear the last of it. And it's not like I want to encourage them to catch their own grub. They bring enough mice in as it is."

"I found a kidney on the landing rug this morning," Stella said, through a mouthful of toast. "I flushed it down the loo. It's like having a really small serial killer in the house."

"Essentially that's what cats are," Bee told her.

"That's disgusting," said Bella. Bee gave her shoulders a sideways hug.

"I know. Cats are awful. And wonderful."

"So do you want someone, therefore, to go into a town and get some dishwasher tablets?"

"Ideally, yes. Unless anyone fancies doing the washing up by hand. Which is obviously an option."

"No, I'd quite like to get out of the house for a bit," Ward said. "Anyone else?"

"I'll come," said Serena, and so, it appeared, would Stella.

"If you head for Hornlake," Bee said, "the Co-op should have dishwasher stuff. It will be rammed, though. With everyone who's forgotten something and doesn't want to drive all the way to Tesco or Sainsbury's. I don't think they're open today, anyway."

"Yeah, I don't fancy Tesco, even if it's open. Mind you, I never fancy Tesco."

"Nice old English town, though, with a nice old English pub…" Stella said.

"And a nice old English supermarket."

The rain had held off so far that morning, but the sky was lowering and overcast and the air made Serena shiver, in spite of the warmth of her fur-hooded parka. Still, it was good to get some fresh air and it was good to see some of the countryside, too, with the skeins of traveller's joy furring the cropped hedgerows and occasional strings of bright bryony. Ward managed to park on the street opposite a wine

171

merchant's, but there were a lot of people heading down towards the square and the old market building, built of stone the colour of dark honey.

"It's really busy," Serena said, getting out of the Land Rover. "Look, there are dozens of people down there."

"They've probably all forgotten dishwasher tablets. They're probably all going to the Co-op."

"I hope not!"

"Oh, crap,' Stella said, suddenly. "They've come to see the hunt."

"Oh God, of course. I completely forgot. It's Boxing Day."

At the entrance to the market square, Serena was greeted by a dog. It was blunt nosed and friendly, in shades of dirty cream and fawn. Then it was joined by another one, then a third. The hunt had brought their pack of hounds with them and the dogs were milling about the pillars of the old market house, cadging treats from the general public, tails wagging.

"I hope no one recognises me," Stella said. She pulled up her hood. Ward eyed her askance.

"And why would they? Ex-boyfriend of yours?"

"No, thank you!"

"Why not? That one on the brown horse is seriously good looking."

"She used to go sabbing," Serena said. "When she was in her teens. Also I feel the need to point out that that horse is technically a chestnut, not 'brown.'"

"Yeah, country boy," Stella muttered.

Ward laughed. "Oh dear. Sabbing, eh? Wasn't that illegal? When did they ban this stuff, anyway?"

"Well, they haven't banned hunt meets. It's not legal to kill foxes, though."

"Sabbing was fun while it lasted. Although, serious purpose and all that. But I used to sneak out at night and unstop earths and things. People still do it. However! We're standing in the middle of about two hundred people who have come to see horses, hounds and huntsmen and I think I'd better shut up."

"And mulled wine."

"Ooh, is there? So there is. Alcoholic and non-alcoholic. I'll buy you one, Ward. Which? You can have one with booze if you're driving: I don't suppose it's that strong."

"I'll have a non-booze one," Serena said. She had drunk enough the day before, with the champagne and then wine at dinner. She would happily admit to being a lightweight. "Then you and Ward can have something in the pub as well and I can drive us back."

"Are you sure?"

"Yes. I really want a coffee. Why don't we do the Co-op first and then hit the pub before the meet stops and everyone piles in there?"

This was agreed to be a good plan. Stella ran down to the Co-op, while Serena and Ward sipped their mulled drinks and watched the hunt mill about. The horses were beautiful, sturdy and powerful, and Serena was amused to see that some had tinsel woven into their manes. The hunters themselves were engaging with the crowd, who were admiring the horses and asking questions.

'This is a good PR exercise," Ward said. "That old boy in the top hat looks like something out of Tobias Smollett."

"Yes. And people like it, I know. It's a bit of traditional England, I suppose. Oh, there's Stella."

As her sister, carrying a bag, made her way up the High Street, Serena saw a pink coated huntsman lean down from the big chestnut he was riding, and speak to her. She saw Stella look up at the man: he was middle aged, with a beaked nose and a patrician face. In his hunting pink and stock, ramrod-spined, he looked like a handsome local squire. How Georgette Heyer, thought Serena. He said something further to Stella and Serena saw her sister give a small nod. Then the hunter wheeled his horse around with a clatter of hooves, scattering the crowd, and the long strange call of the horn rang out: he was summoning the hounds. The back of Serena's neck prickled. Stella jerked her head at the entrance to the Red Lion and vanished through the doorway.

"What was that about?" Ward was frowning.

"I don't know. I hope it wasn't bad."

'Hope he didn't recognise her. I mean, she would have been a saboteur what, fifteen years ago? When she was a kid."

"About that."

"Maybe he fancies her? Perhaps it was an unspeakable proposition."

"What, in front of several hundred people?"

Uneasily, they returned the empty mulled wine cups to the stand and made their way into the pub. This was crowded, but not unfeasibly so: Stella was already standing at the bar and had put the bag containing the Co-op shopping on a table, thus marking her territory. A little candle guttered in a glass, sending flickering shadows across the table top. Outside, Serena could see a horse, pirouetting. Then the horn sounded again.

"What do you want, Ward? Glass of red? A pint?"

"Wine's fine. What did that chap say to you?"

"Tell you when we've sat down. I got dishwasher tablets, by the way. And more milk and cat food, because."

Once seated, Serena leaned in and her sister said, "He caught my eye when I came out of the shop. He's the MFH. He didn't give me his name but we could probably find it out."

"I think Bee told us what it was – wasn't it Nick something double-barrelled? What did he *say?*"

"He said: *it's not just a scent on a string that we hunt these days. Remember that.*"

"*What?* Did he know you were a sab? That's a threat!"

"The funny thing is," Stella said, "And remember this is me, the ex-sab, current vegetarian, speaking. I don't think it was a threat. It was the tone of voice, not what he said. I think it was an offer of alliance."

By the time they left the Red Lion, the crowd had dispersed and the dogs and hunters and horses had gone. The town was quiet, sinking into its Boxing Day afternoon stupor under a grey sky. Serena drove them home and shortly before they reached the turn off to Hornmoon, drops of rain were spattering the window.

"Oh, not again! This is turning out to be such a wet winter. I hope we get a proper cold snap in January."

She pulled into the Mooncote yard and switched the engine off. Inside the house, the kitchen was busy. Bee was dissecting the remains of roast goose and Luna was kneading bread.

"This is all very domestic," Ward said.

"It will be even more domestic if you got dishwasher tablets. I said to Luna, I bet they've gone to the pub."

"You must be psychic."

"Did you have lunch? Or do you want some? It will be goose sandwiches for the carnivores. I did chickpea pate for anyone else. And did you have a nice time?"

"Yes. Sort of. It was interesting," Serena said. Before her mother or Bella could come downstairs, she told them what had happened.

"Oh," said Bee, wiping wet hands on the tea towel. "I completely forgot about the hunt. I should have thought. But it's so easy to lose track at this time of year."

"Do you know anyone who hunts round here?"

"Yes, loads of people. The Master, Nick Wratchall-Haynes, drinks in the Hornmoon Arms sometimes. I saw him in there on Christmas Eve."

"You said that. What does he look like?"

Bee thought. "Typical English country type, tweeds, quite tall, slightly greying brown hair, upper class. Quite good looking if you like that sort of thing, which I don't mind, actually. I think he's got blue eyes? Late forties, possibly? Rides a big chestnut hunter."

"Thank you, Sergeant Fallow, that was an excellent ID," Stella said. "That's the chap."

"He's always seemed very pleasant. Nicely spoken. Top drawer, as grandfather would have said."

"He wasn't unpleasant," Stella said. "I might not approve of his hobbies but I have to be fair. He looked more worried than anything else."

"I'm sure I've heard Caro mention a Nick," Ward said.

"Oh, yes, he's good friends with the Amberleys. Because horses, I suppose. County set."

"And we know, don't we, that your family, Ward, has some – idiosyncrasies."

"Yes. I'm just not totally sure what they are."

"We saw Caro yesterday," Serena said. "In the church. I didn't have a chance to tell you. She was pretty decent about Ben."

From upstairs there came a distant shout. "Mum! Are you back?"

Serena opened the kitchen door.

"Yes!"

"I can't find my eyebrow stuff."

Serena cast her eyes to heaven. "It's in the bathroom! I moved it into your wash bag. Can't you find it?"

"Can you come…?"

Serena went into the hall. As she did so, there was a movement at the end of the passageway. She saw the hem of a skirt whisk quickly into the small room which Bee used as an office. One of the Behenian stars? Serena followed, peeping around the door frame to see her mother, standing at the window and staring out. Had she been listening at the kitchen door? Serena did not speak and Alys did not turn around.

LUNA

Just before dusk on Boxing Day, Luna went out to give some mix to the horses. Sam had offered to do it and it wasn't strictly necessary anyway.

'They're both pigs! They've got plenty of hay and no exercise."

"I know. But I'd like to get out of the house, even if it is tipping it down. I feel stuffy."

"Yeah, I know what you mean."

"This isn't good for you, is it? Being under a roof. Do you want to be back on the road?"

He laughed. "I would, but it's a real first world problem. Here am I in a lovely house being waited on hand and foot. Can't see me complaining too much."

"All right. But you're not really being waited on. You've done lots."

"Part of the courtesy of being a guest, in my view. I keep thinking of having a metaphorical belt round the ear from my nan if I don't offer to run the hoover over the carpet occasionally."

"I can't see your nan as the belting sort, really. Well, not when it comes to you. I wouldn't like to cross her, mind." She had memories of Ver March on a white horse in a dangerous wood.

"No, she's never actually hit me – she'd never do that. Occasional clip towards the ear rather than round it. She did handbag a man in a pub once, mind, but he was asking for it. If you're going to take them some mix, can you put some of that herbal prep in with it? Might as well do what we can through the winter."

"Of course."

In the barn, she measured some of the prep into the bucket of mix and carried it down the field, cradling the bucket with her arm across it so that it would not get too wet. The horses could make their way into a field shelter, under which their hay was placed, but preferred to stand out in the weather. Luna did not blame them. She loved being in with the Aga roaring away and the sitting room fire ablaze, but the central heating made the air too dry and had given her a persistent, irritating cough which went away if she was out in the fresh air for any length of time.

She paused for a moment, depositing the contents of the bucket into the hay as the horses made their slow, deliberate way up the field to see what she might have brought them. She had added apples, too: Bee had placed some of the autumn's harvest in racks in the barn. She would be popular, Luna thought. She stood beneath the field shelter, watching the rain sweep across the grey green hills and breathing deeply. They should go back on the road... but Luna was nervous about giving birth in the van. Or in the bloody hedge, come to that. Perhaps Sam's nan might be prevailed upon – but she did not want to make assumptions about Ver March. For all she knew, Sam's nan had no midwifery skills and was, say, an excellent car mechanic.

There was a long, clear call through the rain which brought her head up. A hunting horn. Luna remembered what Stella had said, about the meet in the morning. The hunt must still be out. She did not want to encounter them. A spatter of rain dashed the roof of the field shelter, hitting Luna in the face. She spluttered and wiped her eyes. Everything had gone dark. The horn sounded again and Luna thought, *oh no.*

She listened. The rain had stopped, and when Luna reached out a hand she knocked her knuckles painfully against wood. There was a door now, where there had been no door before. Tentatively, she pushed it open into a blinding white light. Luna blinked. The light was coming from reflected snow: she was back in the snowscape forest of Solstice Eve but she was not in the same place. This was not a chapel, just a field shelter, like the one she had left. A sudden shuffling movement startled her, but then Luna saw that it was only a handful of old ewes, huddled in the back of the shelter. Their homely presence was comforting. She had the impulse to shut the door and sit tight. But she needed to know where she was. She stepped to the edge of the doorway and looked around it.

A long slope, the snow broken by bushes, ran down to an icy stream. She could see the swirls of frozen water across its surface, like a damask scarf laid along the valley floor. The horn sounded again, too close. Then she saw the thing she had seen in the chapel, the otter-muzzled being, shambling through the snow along the edge of the stream. It was trying to run, she realised, but the snow was too deep and instead it was wading, stumbling, close to falling. Then she saw the hunt. They streamed out of the woods at the other end of the valley, cascading down the slope. They were not like the hunts she knew, the traditional Georgian prints you found in pubs, or the meets that her sisters had mentioned that morning. No hunting pink here, no top-hatted sidesaddle ladies. Not all of them rode horses: she saw antlers bobbing amid the throng, which numbered perhaps twenty or so. The man on the lead horse was masked like a highwayman and his cloak streamed out behind him in skeins of leather rags and tatters. He carried a long pole, with a carved oval end: a whip, Luna thought? But it did not look quite like a whip. She did not see anyone with a skull for a face. Did Alys ride today, or not? And were hounds with them? She could see white flickering things running between the mounts' legs, like scraps of misty fire.

The shambling thing had vanished into a blackthorn brake. Luna could no longer see it. The hunt was fanning out and to her horror she saw it turn, start wheeling up the slope. She ducked back into the doorway but it was too late: the huntsman in the lead had seen her. He shouted, a crow's harsh yaw, and pointed with the staff he carried. Luna did not wait. She left the hut, hastening around the side of the building and up the slope where the trees gathered more closely. Inside the hut, the ewes were bleating with terror. Luna hated to think of them packed in the shelter, unable to escape, but they must belong to someone, must have been put there in the first place, so perhaps the hunt would leave them alone...

Something crashed past her. She saw the dappled side of a deer, leaping a thicket of bramble, and glimpsed its rider's face. It was long and pale, a narrow, jutting chin, whiteless black eyes. It was human and yet not. Luna was getting used to that. She caught her foot in a wire of bramble and fell, sprawling into the snow. The lead huntsman had caught up with her now, he hauled the horse's head up and it half-reared back. Luna scrambled to her feet. There were dogs with him: huge and pale, she could see them more clearly now but then, panicking, she looked again and the nearest hound was not a dog at all but a man, naked, crouching in the snow with his hands over his head. His mouth was open in a silent scream and his hair was fire, flames like winter sunset, then blood red then gone and it was a dog once more who stood stock still, staring at her from cold crimson eyes.

The oval end of the hunter's staff was a pine cone, intricately carved, and deep within there was a glimmer, a hot-coal glow. He swung it at Luna. She ducked, shielding her head with her arm, but the staff connected. An electric jolt ran up Luna's arm. She cried out. The world whirled around and Luna found herself suddenly at the bottom of the slope, face down, staring into the unmoving ice. A shadow passed over her: another of the mounts, leaping across her prone form. Then a hand caught her by the collar of her coat, lifted her up, almost strangling her, and she was thrown gasping over the pommel of a saddle. She struggled, thinking of the child inside her.

A voice said, "Hang on. I'm trying to save your life!" Male, English, upper class.

Beneath her, Luna saw a chestnut flank and a boot in the stirrup. He kicked the horse's sides and it sprang away, leaping the brook and landing amid the rushes on the opposite bank in a flurry of snow as the bulrush heads discharged their cargo. Beyond, at the woodland's edge, she heard a voice cry, "Hob! Quickly!"

Luna struggled to see. Aln ran out from between the trees, barefoot and sprinting through the snow.

"Hob!"

Then Luna saw the otter-faced creature. Aln was running towards it. It held out its hands. Aln's lips were moving and she thrust her hand beneath her shawl. She threw something onto the ice: a handful of sparks. From further up the hillside there sounded a roar of fury.

"Shit!" said Luna's rescuer. He turned the horse so abruptly that Luna was swung around and nearly fell. The snowy bank of the stream was melting, slipping. The horse's hind hooves went out from under it and they were suddenly half into a rushing stream. A spark whisked past them on the current: a burning leaf which grew and grew. The bank disappeared. The horse was now swimming; splashing Luna's face with icy water. She spluttered.

"What a fucking mess." Her rescuer grasped her arm and lifted her up. "Sorry! Off you go! Good luck!"

He pushed her backwards off the saddle and Luna fell into the boat. The world was full of dark water, a current which span the boat around and around. There was a sharp pang deep within her.

"Luna!" Aln's green face bent over her. "Are you hurt?"

"I don't know!" She sat up. "Ow!" She clutched her stomach. The hillside was very far away now and it had become an island: she could see the field shelter in the fading light with the hunt clustered around it, pacing. But the valley was gone, become a black and churning river.

The boat was carried along at a furious pace. Behind, she could see the man on the horse, swimming strongly against the current towards a hump of land. He wore a Barbour jacket: nothing otherworldly about him. But in the bottom of the boat lay a figure, covered in a sheepskin.

"Hob!" Aln said. "Luna's hurt. Help her!"

The figure sat up, revealing its otter-face. Its cloak was a patchwork of skins but underneath Luna could see not a body, but a knotted, knitted tangle of withies, bound together with leafless ivy and wild clematis vine; roughly the shape of a man, but only vaguely. Had it not been for its face she would have thought it to be no more than a framework figure, made of willow and bent switches of hazel. It reached out a twig-like finger and Luna tried not to flinch, remembering the thing that had broken the window pane.

"It's not the same one," Aln said. She must have read Luna's expression. "That was another. A bad one."

The twig touched Luna's hand and she felt the pain ebb away, vanishing into the water swirl. She caught a glimpse of the thing's thoughts: an image of an egg, secure in its nest. Safe within. Luna took a breath.

"Thank you!" She checked herself over. Nothing broken. Even the bronze wren that Serena had given her at Christmas was still around her neck. She was glad she had not lost it.

The creature nodded, and lay back down like a puppet with its strings cut.

"You speak English!" Luna said to Aln.

"What? What's Aenglish? Is that what you speak? I speak our own tongue, the tongue of the green world."

Behind them, the horse scrambled up onto the hump of land, kicked its heels and was away with its rider. There was a distant shout from the hunt, but they were lost now in the rising spray. There was a flash of light, perhaps the cone on the huntsman's staff. Luna's arm still bore the trace of a burn but it was fading. Then they were gone and the boat spun away down the river.

Aln did not say anything more. She crouched in the bottom of the little round boat as the river took the coracle up and carried it along. When she closed her eyes Luna seized her moment and twitched the sheepskin aside. The otter-faced thing lay curled in the coracle. Its eyes were open and stared at nothing. The claw-tipped twigs of its fingers occasionally twitched, as if the thing dreamed, as a dog dreams.

Luna replaced the sheepskin and sat back, her hand to her stomach. She felt shaken and yet strong. There were no more pains within. And the urge to wee all the time had gone, thank God. She thought, without knowing where the thought had come from: *it's going to be all right.* The voice was strong, too, sounding quite sure, and it was her own. Perhaps she had sent herself a message, from some future time? At least the motion wasn't making her sick. She looked over the side of the coracle, into the black swirl. The current was fast and choppy: creamy brown froth splattered the little waves. There was no moon and no visible source of light, and yet Luna found that she was able to see. The water took them past islands, a low mound with some kind of building on it, a ruined tower and fallen stones. Then, over the water, she saw an island with an actual house on it: a mansion of some kind. All the windows were lit up and there were people moving within. She could almost hear the laughter and chatter of a house party and glimpsed a woman in a gown of golden silk. Luna opened her mouth to call out, vain though it would have been against the rush of water, but Aln's eyes suddenly snapped open and she caught Luna's wrist in a hand like a vice.

"Don't."

Luna subsided into the coracle. When she looked back the house was dark, overgrown and with the roof half-fallen in.

She must have dozed after that, aware that Aln was alert and watching. She did not dream. When she once more woke, it was to find that a silver wash of light illuminated the waves. No islands were visible, only a distant line of grey shore. Ahead, lay the open sea.

BEE

Bee was in the kitchen, tidying up, when there was a knock on the door. She dusted her hands on a nearby tea towel and went to open it. For a moment, she did not recognise the man who stood on the step.

"Oh! It's Nick, isn't it? Mr Wratchall-Haynes."

"Yes, we've met in the pub a couple of times, haven't we? I'm a friend of Caro and Richard's. Can I come in." It wasn't a question. Automatic assumption of privilege, thought Bee, but it amused her rather than offended.

"Of course. Would you like some tea? Sherry? Glass of wine? We've got lots of the Christmas spirit."

He laughed and his grey-blue eyes crinkled. "It's the time of year, isn't it? I'm not driving but I did bring my horse. I can get away with a glass of wine, if you don't mind. That's very kind."

"Great! Will it find its way home if you drink lots?"

"I'm not planning to! But yes, slumped in the saddle, like some eighteenth century squire, stopping at every hostelry." He followed her into the kitchen. He smelled faintly of cigars, and horse. Bee found some wine and handed him a glass.

"Here you go. Merry Christmas!"

"To you, too."

"My sister said she saw you this morning – at the meet? I hope you've had a good day out."

"A curate's egg." He sat down at the table. He was a tall man, Bee thought, and wiry. The kind of frame which was fit through riding and farming, not from working out in a gym. A classic English face, one that did not give much away.

He said, "I spoke to your sister. One of them, anyway. I know your family by sight – she was in the pub on Christmas Eve. Girl with light brown hair. Rather trendy."

"Yes. Stella."

"Do they still use that word these days? Trendy? I use it, anyway."

"She's a DJ," Bee said.

"I hope I didn't – upset her." He took a sip of the wine. "Thank you, this is nice. I've actually come about your other sister. The young woman. Long red hair."

183

"Luna." Bee fought down a rising dismay. Luna had anti-hunt sympathies, too. "Is she all right?"

He looked at her directly. "She is all right. She is in good hands. Just don't expect her home quite yet."

"Oh God. Where is she?"

"In a," he stopped. He looked into his glass, as though it might hold answers. "It's a lane."

"A *lane?*"

"Your mother will know what I mean. There are other places. But they don't all join up."

"I do know what you mean, actually."

"There are – areas, which join them up to some extent."

"Like a wildlife corridor?" Bee asked. "Hedgerows, wild places left to do their own thing? Between all the managed farming land, joining fields."

"Yes. That's it! You've put it very well." He looked at her approvingly.

Bee had a faint urge to curtsey. *Why thank you, my lord.*

"What happened to my sister? And what part do you play in all this, Mr Wratchall-Haynes?" She gave him a mischievous smile. "Is it Mr, by the way, or do you have a title?"

"It's doctor, in fact. But call me Nick, please. She – fell into a dangerous place. I don't know why."

"She just went out for a walk! Mind you," Bee said, "that's never stopped any of this before and none of us went looking for trouble. Going for a gentle breath of fresh air seems to be the most hazardous thing you can do."

"I got her out of it." He was still looking into the depths of his wine. "I am a Master of Foxhounds. You know that. But there are other hunts. And sometimes we ride at the same time."

"But not over the same land?"

"Sometimes. Your sister is not out of danger but she is with someone who knows the territory. The girl with green skin."

"Aln?" Then Bee thought that perhaps she ought not have told him Aln's name.

"Is that what she's called?"

"I think so. I found her in the churchyard and she stayed here until just before Christmas. Then she disappeared. I'm afraid I thought that

184

she had probably gone back to where she came from. Wherever that is."

"She did. She will look after your sister, I am pretty sure of that. I don't know much about her people but they are gentle, mainly, and they know the deep woodlands, the far forests."

"Who are her people? She's not human, is she?"

"She's human enough." He looked up. "Someone's coming."

The kitchen door opened and Alys stepped through. She looked as though she had just woken from a nap. Her hair was loose and she wore her blue and white kimono, patterned like a china cup. It was only when you got close to her, Bee thought, that you could see the lines in her face.

"Oh, I'm sorry, turning up in my nightie. I didn't realise we had company." Alys sounded completely unapologetic.

"Quite all right," Nick Wratchall-Haynes said. "I was on my way. Popped in to have a quick chat about a horse."

"Are we buying one?"

"No, one of yours got out. Rounded him up in the lane. Need to get your bottom hedge mended."

"I'll have a word with Sam," said Bee. With perfect truth, after all.

She showed Nick out. Once he was through the door, he turned to her and said, "Try not to worry. I'm sure all will be well."

"Thank you for everything you've done," Bee said. She wished she knew him well enough to read his face, inexpressive though he was. But she thought that he did not trust Alys, and Bee did not know if this made him enemy or friend, or somewhere in between. But she now urgently needed to speak to Sam.

She found him in the stable, sweeping up some of the loose hay.

"Who was that?" he asked. "I heard hooves."

"It was the new MFH. Nick Wratchall-Haynes. Dr Wratchall-Haynes, in fact."

"And what did *he* want?"

Bee told him. Sam sank onto a hay bale.

"She's been – very loose, recently. Luna. I mean, loosely tied to the world. I think she's been slipping in and out. My nan once said it happens sometimes, with pregnancy."

"It's not a normal part of the process, Sam! Otherwise pre-natal classes would be a lot more interesting than they apparently are."

"For those like us, I mean."

"Whatever we are... I'll ask Serena. Anyway, Wratchall-Haynes thinks she's safe enough. She's with Aln."

"I'm inclined to think that's a good thing. Which doesn't mean I'm not worried sick, mind you."

"So am I." Then Bee thought, a similar thing had happened to her: through a gate in a hedge and suddenly hundreds of years in the past, running down to meet her ghostly lover's ship without a care for anyone back home. It had shamed her then and it shamed her now. A bit, anyway. But it had not been her fault and it was not Luna's, either.

"We'll just have to wait," Sam said.

She nodded. "And wait we will. But Sam, I don't really want Mum to know about this." She lowered her voice. "She was with this hunt, after all."

"If it was the same one. And she did pull Luna to safety. She knows a lot more than she's telling, though, your ma."

"If she is indeed our ma."

"I know. But I don't know how to prove otherwise."

"I can say Luna met up with a friend in Glastonbury, gone to stay overnight. A girlie evening."

"Yes, good idea. She does in fact do that sometimes, doesn't she? Hopefully she'll show up before we need to explain to Alys why she's not here. Ward and Serena will need to be going back to London soon, too, and Stella. I'm not quite sure when. But they've got work commitments."

"I'll make some enquiries of my own," Sam said.

"Do you mean, with your family?"

"Mainly. I don't know a lot about all this, you know. Nan does but she works on a bit of a need to know basis."

Bee surprised herself by laughing, despite her worry. "Like spies."

"It's not so far removed from that, seems to me. Though I have a hard time thinking of my nan as a Bond girl, I must say."

"Maybe in her younger days?"

"She must have been a looker, actually. I've seen photos. Only a couple, mind. We don't have much in the way of family albums." He stood. "I'd better check the horses. I'll keep an eye out. I don't like it, but we haven't got much of a choice."

Bee reached up and squeezed his hand. "I know."

Back in the kitchen, she found that Alys had gone and this was a relief. Bee was not confident of hiding her worry from her mother. If she had trusted Alys more – Alys had rescued Luna, after all. But too much of Alys' behaviour still lay in the shadows.

Stella and Ward were in the pub again. It was the day after Boxing Day, and quiet after the Christmas crush. Serena had elected to stay behind at the house, have a bath and pack for the return to London, and Bella wanted to watch something, so Stella and Ward had taken themselves down to the Hornmoon Arms after dinner to plot. As far as that might be possible. It was only after that they had sat down in one of the tucked-away areas at the back of the main bar that they discovered they had been joined by Dark.

"Christ!" Ward snatched at his almost spilled drink. "Sorry. Wasn't expecting to see you, Ned."

"No, I am sorry. To come here so unexpectedly, I mean. I can go away again."

"No, stay. We'd like that. I see you have a drink."

For a pewter tankard, remarkably solid, sat on the table before the ghost.

"I did not buy it at the bar," Ned Dark said, with a smile.

"You surprise me. I don't suppose they take groats."

His smile broadened. "Ha'pennies and farthings, if you were me. They used to, in here. You will go back to the city, soon?"

"Yeah, tomorrow. We think we ought to check in with whatever's happening in London but I don't really want to," Stella said. "Because of Luna."

"I understand. But there is little you can do."

"Do you know where she might be?"

"No." He took a sip of his drink, whatever it was. Ale? Stella had a vague idea that this was what they drank in Elizabethan times. Unless it was a pint of wine. Still, it wouldn't do Dark much harm, given that he was dead anyway. He said, "Beatrice does not want your mother to know that your sister is missing."

"Do you think Alys… is Alys, still?"

The ghost's dark eyes remained fixed on a point beyond the table, until Stella grew uncomfortable and stirred, restlessly. At last Dark said,

"I do not know." The pearl which hung from his ear gleamed softly in the firelight.

"Bee doesn't think she's to be trusted," Ward said.

"Neither do I. How is your cousin faring?"

"Caro? Basically having a nervous breakdown."

Stella thought she might have to explain this to the ghost but he seemed to understand it. He nodded. "She cannot be blamed."

"I don't really get how a lot of this works," Ward said.

"Nor more do I. Death does not confer wisdom, or even knowledge. Scraps and fragments, that's all. Like life. I have spoken with your grandfather and he is at as much a loss as I."

"So," Stella asked, since this had been bothering her, "When you talk to grand-dad, do you – see him? As he was in life? As we see you? Or as a little blue spark?"

"No, not a spark. He is a man in his prime."

"Not old, then?"

"A man of perhaps forty years of age?"

"That's so cool." On the table, her phone buzzed. "Hello?" It was not a number she recognised. But she did recognise the voice. "Stella? It's Ace. Phoning from the boozer. Think you might want to consider getting back to town."

New Year's Eve was a little while away but apart from Luna's absence Stella considered it to be high time that they were on the road again. Christmas was over and she was looking towards the future. She thought Serena felt the same. Bee had promised to let them know if there was any word from Luna.

"Do you want us to stay?" Serena had asked.

"I'd love you to stay as long as you want but in regard to Luna, there's nothing you can do. We can't go looking for her, after all. Sam's tried and he hasn't got anywhere, so he and I will hold the fort. Try not to worry."

They were in the car now, heading back down the road to the city. Somerset was gone and Stonehenge lay behind them in a last blaze of winter sunlight. Then the long sweep of the plain itself fell away as they pulled onto the M3. The aircraft were the first clue: planes tilting low over the hills, indicating that Heathrow was not far distant. Soon, Stella thought, they would be able to smell the city: that stifling metallic tang on the air after the freshness of the countryside. Then the bland tree-lined sides of the motorway began to change and soon they were up onto an overpass, with high buildings rising up, then onto the Great Western Road and into Ladbroke Grove. Serena pulled the car into a reserved space and Stella heard her breathe out.

"Well done!"

"The parking goddess has been kind."

"I'll help you get the stuff into the house, Mum," Bella said.

"We'll all help." Ward opened Stella's door for her, letting in a blast of wet wintry air after the warmth of the car. "It won't take long. Are you seeing Ace tonight, Stella?"

"I said I'd go down to Southwark. You want to come?"

He nodded. "I think so."

"Do you want something to eat before you go?" Serena asked. "We could get a takeaway. Although I do have a care package from Bee."

"Let's get Chinese. I've had a lot of leftovers."

"At least you're not a carnivore," Ward said. "Goose sandwiches from here until Twelfth Night. Not that I'm complaining."

"I've got a menu for the Golden House. I'll give them a ring. If I do it now you can be out by six."

"Can you get me that fake Peking Duck? I like that. And some rice. I'll give you some money."

While Serena arranged this, Stella took her things upstairs to a spare room, which was hers whenever she stayed in London. She undid her case, threw all the clothes onto the bed, and rescued her wash bag, which she took into the bathroom down the landing. Then she returned to the bedroom, turned off the light, and sat down in the chair by the window.

Dusk had already fallen, in this darkest part of the year, and the pane was rain-streaked. Occasionally the sash rattled, as a gust of wind caught it. It was no night to be heading out, but Stella felt restless, as though the world was on the move once more. She herself had plans, with the gig on New Year's Eve fast approaching. But Stella was prepared, having spoken again to Dejone and sorted out a playlist before leaving London. She knew what she was going to give them, some new stuff, some nostalgia. She wanted it to be great – something for people who didn't want to be celebrating in their own living rooms with a bottle of Prosecco and Jules Holland. Not that Stella had anything against old Jules; he was a great pianist, in her opinion. But if you really wanted to kick off a new year in style, you had to be out and about.

The doorbell rang. Stella heard her niece's footsteps as she ran down to answer it and when Stella looked out of the window, she could see a moped outside and a young man leaping back onto it. Supper had arrived. Suddenly hungry, she went down to investigate the fake duck.

"Did you want a glass of wine?" Serena asked, serving up from tinfoil cartons. "I'm having one."

"No, I'll wait, if we're going out. I'd like to be on the ball. Also Ace is quite the drinker. Gotta keep up."

Serena smiled. "Give him my love."

"Yeah, will do."

"Are we meeting him in the same place?" Ward asked. "Southwark Tavern?"

"That's the one."

But before Stella and Ward headed off into the night, everyone went to the studio.

Stella could see that Serena was cautious in opening the door. Who could blame her? But when she deactivated the alarm and turned on the light, it was clear that the studio had remained untouched over Christmas. The big nest of shredded fabric had been removed before the holidays: Stella and Ward had helped a tight-lipped Serena and Charlie bundle it into bin bags and take it to the nearest recycling centre. Now the studio had the air of a place which had been empty for some time, a kind of psychic quietude, and nothing sat upon the mantelpiece. Below, the fireplace was dusty and dark.

"Okay," Serena said aloud. "That's that, then."

"For now."

"I'll settle for 'for now.'"

Having been reassured that nothing visibly nasty was lurking in the metaphorical woodshed, Stella felt that she and Ward could get on with their evening mission. They caught the same bus, in reverse, that Ace had made them take from Southwark, but now Stella looked at the city with a new eye, a post-Christmas eye that made her long for the festive decorations to be gone, for the city to be filled with its own sparkling darkness, with the newness of the year. As they crossed the Thames, with the tower of Southwark Cathedral outlined against the borough and the slice of the Shard glittering high above, she was aware of a sense of keen anticipation, a hunting feeling, as you might feel when the game is finally afoot. She felt like Sherlock Holmes. Or maybe Dr Watson, more realistically. Maybe Ace was Holmes, a bit gone to seed and frayed around the edges, but still capable of handling a three pipe problem. Hopefully not shooting up cocaine, though. She felt determined to get some answers.

Ace sat in the same corner of the Southwark Tavern, looking as though he hadn't moved since Stella had first met him there.

"Want a drink?" Ward asked him.

Ace nodded towards the bar. "Being got one, cheers all the same."

To Stella's stifled joy, Anione was perched on a bar stool. She had dispensed with the kimono and was wearing a second hand fake leopardskin coat, along with fingerless lace mittens and high heeled patent boots. This time, her hair was a dark blue-red, the colour of rotten meat, and her fingernails had been painted a bright and unlikely gold. With amusement, Stella watched Ward's expressive eyebrows rise.

"A friend of yours?"

"One of my old muckers," said Ace.

"That's Anione," Stella said. "I'll give her a hand."

Rather to her surprise, Anione greeted her with apparently genuine pleasure.

"Oh, *hello*, love. How nice to see you again. He said you might be along at some point. Had a good Christmas?"

"Lovely, thanks. Well, sort of. Afterwards was a bit... You?"

"We don't really do Christmas as such," Anione said, gathering up a pint and a large glass of something that was almost the colour of her hair; Stella thought it might be port. "But we've had a bit of a rest and that's what counts, isn't it. Who's your friend? Is he that one off the television?"

"He's an actor, yes."

"I do love the theatre," Anione said, slightly overcome. Her voice wobbled. "Ever since I was a girl. Very important, the theatre. I shall tell him so."

She tottered off the bar stool and bestowed Ace with his pint, while Stella got drinks for Ward and herself. Now that she thought about it, Anione did have a somewhat raddled thespian air and when she got back to the table, she could see that a Ward-related charm offensive was well underway, while Ace watched sardonically, though with no discernible trace of annoyance.

"And how's your sister?" Ace said. "Bearing up?"

"Better for the break, but worried about Luna." Stella had told him about that on the phone. "But she seemed okay about coming back to town. She's got a business deal in the offing."

"She mentioned that." Ace sat a little straighter in his seat. "But it might not be a good thing. I've been making some enquiries."

"About Caspar – "

Ace reached over the table and put a finger to Stella's lips. She was so startled that she let him.

"Sorry, that was out of order. But I don't think it's a good idea to be bandying names about."

"If that had been anyone else, I'd have bit," Stella said. Anione gave a caw of raucous laughter.

"You tell him! But he doesn't mean any harm."

"I don't think we should talk about it here. Back at the gaff. When you've finished your drinks."

After a damp walk around the corner, Ace's house was as Stella remembered it. She thought she heard Ward give a faint sigh at the sight of multiple saucers of partially dried cat food, perched at intervals across the kitchen. He appeared more impressed by the parlour, in which they were briefly left while their hostess disappeared to 'take my boots off' and Ace went in search of drinks. Since there had been no mention of tea, Stella was pleased she had exercised restraint in the matter of alcohol earlier in the evening.

Ward leaned over to her. "Jesus. This place."

"What do you think of Anione?"

"I think she's a right old card. And she reminds me of someone. In fact, she reminds me of several people."

"All old troopers?"

"I wouldn't be surprised if she's trodden the boards. Possibly in vaudeville. During the Boer War."

"I don't know anything about her. But I told you what I saw." Stella glanced rather uneasily at the statues on either side of the fireplace. She wouldn't put it past them to report back.

Ward nodded. "I haven't actually seen any cats. I presume he does have some?"

"Yeah, they're not pretend cats. At least, I heard one come through the cat flap. I'm assuming it was a cat."

"Ace mentioned Cas – Serena's new business interest."

"Yes. I don't like that. That Ace knows about him."

"Neither do I." At this point the fire, which must have been smouldering in the grate, flared up with an intense blue-green flame, more like a gas than coal, and Ace came into the room with a tray.

"I thought since it is still the festive season, so to speak, we could have a sherry."

Ward laughed. "How civilised! It's the time of year when one does, isn't it?" Then he took a sip and his eyes widened. "My God, this is fantastic."

Stella tried to see the label on the bottle but it was too old and dusty. She saw what Ward meant, however. The sherry was raisinous and resinous, as rich and thick as distilled gold. She smelled sage and spice, glimpsed a sudden sunlit dazzle, was warmed to the core.

"That's one *hell* of a sherry, Ace."

He looked almost pleased. "Can't see that going down too well at the average vicarage do. Although it's hard to tell. Maybe it would."

"Where did you get it?"

"I got it a long time ago. Mate who was a wine merchant. Closed now. I laid it down." He frowned. "I don't even know if you're supposed to do that with sherry. I don't know a lot about wine and that."

"Well, it hasn't hurt it," said Stella.

Ace twirled his glass between his fingers and said, "I mentioned the man who approached your sister. I'm not going to say his name, even in here."

"He's dodgy, isn't he?"

"He's more than dodgy. He's dangerous. But the thing is, I don't know why. I've made some very discreet enquiries among people I trust and all they will say is, don't deal with him. If you don't deal with him, you'll probably walk away. And don't sign anything."

"Who is he – the Devil?"

Ace laughed. "No, I don't think anyone would go that far. I don't know what he is."

Ward eyed him askance. "Do you mean, he's not human?"

"I don't know. I did look into his background a bit and he comes from the Midlands. Warwickshire. Shakespeare country – well, you'd know that, being an actor."

"I have done some work with the RSC, in fact."

"Well, then."

"Warwickshire is not somewhere I associate with criminals, necessarily," Stella said.

"He's got a mum and a dad and everything but that sometimes doesn't mean a lot."

"It doesn't?"

"Nah, because babies can come from all over the place. You've met a couple."

"A changeling?"

"As I say, I don't know. Also people can create – backgrounds – for themselves which don't quite bear up when you look more closely. There's something off about him but no one seems to know quite what. All most mysterious. He's a player, though. He's got a lot of dosh and it's not quite clear from where, but then that goes for a lot of actual human people as well."

"Maybe he's a Russian oligarch," Ward said. "From Warwickshire."

"I ought to have asked Serena to ask Sydney Hannon," Stella said. "That's his ex."

"I did think of that," Ward said, "and she dropped her a line before Christmas, but Syd hasn't emailed back. But then, Christmas. She's probably taking a digital break or something."

"When she does get back to her, can you let me know?"

"Of course."

"Oh, and this is frankly a bit embarrassing, I think I know who sent the demon, by the way."

"Really?"

"Who?" said Ward and Stella in unison.

"It was actually a friend of mine. I wish he'd said something, but he didn't know I was connected with you. He knows now, though. Sent it to look after Serena."

"Does he know Serena, then?"

"No."

"So who is he?"

Ace sighed. "This is where it gets a bit tricky. I think I might take you to meet him, Stella, sometime soon. He's – well, better you meet him than I tell you. But your magpie friend is also one of his people."

"Is this some kind of, what, supernatural kingpin?" Ward asked with suspicion.

Ace laughed. "You could put it that way. He's limited in what he can do personally so he relies on outside help. He's not some sinister criminal mastermind, though: he says he's in the dark as well, doesn't know everything that's going on, though I think he knows more than I do and more than he's telling me, too. It's just a bit difficult to explain. If I tell you his name, you'll be calling for the men in white coats."

"It's not Boris Johnson, is it?"

Stella was gratified to note that this made Ace choke on his sherry.

At this point Anione returned, minus the leopardskin coat and the boots. She had changed into a crimson kimono and her hair was once more black, thus definitively settling the wig question for Stella.

"Sorry I was so long. Had to give someone their dinner. I see he's been hospitable? Ace, are you all right, love?"

Ace, still spluttering, handed her a glass.

"I thought we could try a little something. Clear the glass, as it were. These days between Christmas and the New Year, they're a nice dead time, I always think. All sorts go quiet for a bit and without that static in the background, it's easier to see."

Stella could tell that Ward was on the verge of asking what she was on about, but he chose not to speak. The woman went to a sideboard at the end of the room and took out something wrapped in a black brocade cloth.

"Had this for years. Never lets me down."

It was a glass circle, as dense and lightless as a captive black hole.

"Who wants first go?"

"Er…" said Ward.

"I'll do it." Stella was determined not to let the side down. Anione gave her a look that, Stella thought, might have contained a trace of approval.

"Well done, love. Used one of these before?"

"No. What is it?"

"A scrying mirror."

"There's one in the British Museum," Ward said. "Didn't it belong to John Dee?"

"Indeed it did. And what do you know about Dee?"

"Not a great deal. Wasn't he Elizabeth's court magician? Or astrologer, or something like that?"

"He was both," Anione said, "as men were back then. All manner of things. And this is the twin to Dee's mirror: it comes from the same place. From Mexico and the Aztec Empire. It's obsidian."

"Is that a sort of volcanic glass?"

"Yes, it is. And it swallows light. Look." She raised a commanding hand to the fire and the green flickering flame streamed out, filling the room like the Northern Lights, cool and caressing on Stella's skin, then sucked into the black mirror with an emerald flash. It made Stella jump and blink. When she took her hand away from her eyes she was still sitting in the chair, but the room had gone away. Stella was facing blackness, framed in grassy fire.

Images began to march across it, tiny, but very sharp and clear as though she was watching them through the wrong end of a telescope. First she saw a black-sailed ship, driven before the wind. She could almost feel the spray and hear the shouts of the sailors. It reminded her of the Golden Hind, Drake's own brave little ship, but this was bigger, blacker, blockier, and the sea below was like tar. The sails, too, were the colour of jet. Then she saw a wharf looming out of the spray and the ship was roped in. Men dressed in tunics leaped to the dockside and Stella saw a huge crate, bound with iron bands, being lowered onto the flat stones of the dock. But the crate continued to shudder and shake. The deckhands were afraid; she could see them avoiding the big crate.

Then suddenly, sunlight. Wintry and cold, just like the sun that they had left behind them going down over Salisbury Plain. Stella was looking into a thorn thicket and in the thicket scrambled a tiny brown shape, a scrap of feathers and will with a bright apple-pip eye. A sparrow – no, because she saw the little perked up tail and knew it for a wren.

Then this, too, was gone. Next came a mansion on an island, or perhaps it was not an island, but a flood: a racing torrent of water which roared over lawns and swamped the bulrushes at their edge. She saw a small boat, round like a coracle, snatched from its moorings and torn away down the water race. She thought she heard church bells, tolling the hour, and all the windows of the mansion were ablaze with light, but it did not look like candles or electricity, but the flat searing brightness of the light of sunset, catching the glass from far away.

And then black.

Stella found herself with her head on her knees.

"Here," Anione said. "Have a top up."

Stella took the glass of sherry and had a big swig, which made her splutter in turn.

"Steady on," the woman said. "Bit strong, perhaps."

"I saw a load of stuff," Stella said with triumph.

"Did you? Good girl! Tell me what you saw."

Stella did not think to disobey. She related everything to Anione and the woman listened with a still, abstracted face.

At last she said, "Hmmm. Well. I don't know, love. What it all means. But we need to remember it, so that when it happens, we can tie it all together. And maybe we can make sense of it then."

"So what do we do now?" Ward asked.

"Sit tight," Ace told them. "You've said you don't think you can help Luna. Get on with your stuff – you're rehearsing a play, aren't you?"

"Yes. Midsummer Night's Dream."

"And Stella, what are you up to?"

"I'm doing a New Year's gig."

"All good stuff. Just get on with it, I suggest, and if anything happens, you know where to find me, and in the meantime, I will continue to make enquiries. By the way, I've not come across any trace of your cousin, but don't give up. I'm very resourceful."

"I'd noticed," Ward said.

SERENA

The city was black and wet but Serena did not mind that. She needed to get out of the house and it felt good to be doing something normal, mundane and productive. Although the last couple of days had not been wasted: she had got on with sketching, housework, the accounts. It had been good to get back into the swing of things, even though she had spoken to Bee and Luna had still not come home. The worry nagged at her like a twinging tooth but Serena tried to thrust it to one side.

She had even remembered to bring a bag as well as a shopping list, rather than leaving both in the house, and that made her a little pleased with herself as she headed onto the main road. The supermarket was not far away: she could see its scarlet neon sign through the rain. Head down, boots on, Serena marched down the middle of the pavement and passed briskly through the pale, bright aisles of Tesco, selecting milk and crumpets and cheese and loo paper. She did not overstock, mindful of having to carry it back again. Ward had offered to help, but Serena told him that she felt like a walk and there was no point in both of them getting wet. She paid at the checkout, making sure it was staffed by an actual person and not a machine, smiled and nodded and exchanged banalities about the weather. Then she walked back. The downpour had become stronger while she was in the supermarket and contained a stinging touch of sleet.

Serena left the main road and headed into the maze of mews. Usually she enjoyed this walk, taking time to admire the divergent facades of the little houses, with their bay trees and swags of wisteria, their geraniums and the occasional climbing rose. But that was a walk for the spring and summer, not this lamplit darkness. She walked quickly, wanting to get home now before she was soaked through, and always mindful of who else might be about.

When the footsteps rang out behind her, Serena was not immediately alarmed. She glanced over her shoulder, expecting the usual: a passer-by heading past her. If a woman, the person often spoke: *it's all right.* Because other women knew what it was like to hear a step behind you on a winter night. But when Serena glanced, she realised that the person was almost on top of her. She saw a cap, a startling bright red in the lamplight, and a white blank face. He raised his hand but Serena was already running. She was in flat soled boots and she knew the way. She did not expect to be rugby-tackled, however, and the breath went out of her as they hit the floor. He was breathing hard, almost grunting, and Serena smelled something odd and strong: a country smell of dung, like a cowshed, or the fields after the muckspreader had been over them. She rolled over, kicking, trying to dislodge him, but the man grabbed her wrists and pulled her onto her face with her arms trapped behind her back. His hands felt oddly hard, as though encased in some kind of sheath.

Serena struggled and the alleyway was suddenly filled with light. The man gasped, a harsh grunt like a dog choking, and her wrists were free. She pushed herself onto hands and knees. He said something in a language she did not recognise and that countryside stink, so familiar to Serena but so alien to London, intensified. But the pale light grew. She looked up, conscious that the man was up and running, footsteps beating away along the cobbles of the mews and around the corner. A figure stood in front of Serena. She saw a long draped gown, above ridged white boots that ended in a cloven foot, rather like Japanese *obi*, but smaller and higher. Then she realised that they were not boots, but legs. She looked up, gaping. The gown did not cover the thing's breast, which was ridged, the ribcage visible but filled with bone. Above, its mouth was closer to a beak and filled with big square teeth; it had no eyes, only a fan of bone which covered its forehead. Serena tried to scream but only a squeak emerged. Her face was brushed with something huge and immensely soft, a feathery fringe in which she glimpsed a dark and liquid eye. It blinked in a flash of gold. The thing raised a hand, two thick clawed fingers and a thumb, and with a loud harsh caw something came to rest on its wrist, a homing hawk.

Not a hawk, though, but the demon. It looked down at Serena and grinned its semi-circle grin. But Serena no longer felt afraid. The touch of the thing's feathers had drained the fear out of her. Even the demon's little quicksilver eyes seemed familiar and reassuring. The figure bowed its head once, then it turned and strode away in a rustling hiss of wings. She had one last glimpse of myriad eyes staring at her with remote gentleness and then it was gone through some invisible door, leaving her alone in the mews. Quite calmly, Serena rescued the shopping: even a packet of eggs which had, with equal miraculousness, remained unbroken. Then, a little shakily, she went on her way.

Ward was horrified.

"What? You were mugged?"

"He wasn't after my bag," Serena said. She sat huddled on the bed, nursing a cup of tea.

"What was he after, then? Rape?"

"I don't know. He smelled. Like a cow shed."

Ward passed a hand over his face. "If this had happened in Somerset..."

"Oh, come on. It's not like Somerset is full of cow-herding rapists."

"I wouldn't be at all surprised."

"But that was definitely the smell. I mean, I've smelled it all my life, especially when they do the slurrying in spring."

"So have I. It's one reason I moved to Kensington at the first opportunity."

Serena had to laugh. "But you know, Ward, at one time, not so long ago, where we're sitting would have been nothing but fields."

"It's not now, though, is it? This is what I like about Ladbroke Grove. A distinct lack of cow. But *why* did he smell like that? It's not exactly a classic West London profession these days."

"I don't know. And I don't know what saved me, either."

But as it turned out when they told him about the incident later, Ace did.

"An angel. Definitely. I saw one of those myself once, long ago. I think it's one of the seraphim but I'm never quite sure, to be honest. I'm better on the demonic hierarchies. Basically because those will sometimes speak to me whereas the hosts of heaven can be a bit sniffy, to be honest."

"Well, talking of demons," Serena said. She told him about the pterodactyl. Ace stirred from the depths of the armchair and the light of interest appeared in his eyes.

"Oh, really? And it came to sit on its wrist? Interesting. That's really interesting."

"Surely," Ward said, "Demons don't hang out with angels."

"Well, no. Except yeah. They're not supposed to but they do. Happens all the time. Because it's been a long time since the Fall, whatever that really was, and they're basically the same kind of entity. Celestial beings. They all come from the same realm. Things that come from the same place tend to hang out together. The thing is, if your little demonic pal is chumming up to an angel, this tells us a lot. I must speak to – well. I told you about my friend."

"So the demon isn't evil?"

"No. Or, of course, that the angel isn't all nicey-nicey either but then they're not, we know that. All that stuff in the Bible about shepherds and that, *and then they were filled with awe and fell to their knees.* Well, they fell to their knees because they were frigging wetting themselves."

"It should have been scary," Serena said. "And it was for a bit, but then I stopped being scared. I think it helped me."

Ace looked at her, suddenly rather misty eyed. "It would. That's because you're a rather lovely person, Serena."

"Thank you! Aw!"

"Don't worry," Ace said to Ward, whose eyebrows were somewhat elevated. "I've not got *designs.*"

"Didn't think so for a minute. Obviously I agree with you."

"Overall, I think this is a positive development. But it does raise some further questions."

BEE

The house seemed very quiet after Stella and the others had left for London. Alys was upstairs and Sam was out with the horses. Holding the fort, he said, making sure that everything was tight for when Luna came home. When, not if. Bee could tell that he was worried: he had said as much to Dark, a man-to-man talk in the stables, apparently. Well, man-to-ghost. But he was holding up well enough, despite the unease that had become a part of the landscape of his face, a flicker behind his eyes. Following his lead, Bee cleaned the kitchen, taking the opportunity to remove the old blanket from the dog basket and wash it. She found that she missed Aln; she had grown used to the girl's silent presence. The spaniels missed her, too. They drooped.

"You're both very spoiled," Bee said to them, aloud. Their tails thumped against the flags as they looked up, pleadingly. She gave them both a biscuit. Then she emptied the dishwasher and filled it again, took a pile of laundry out of the dryer and set it at the foot of the stairs, and ran the vacuum over the ground floor. After this, she felt better, telling herself that things were getting back to normal, Luna would come home and all would soon be straight again. She had never minded this liminal time between Christmas and New Year, and then the extra days until Twelfth Night which also seemed part of the holidays, even if many people were back at work from the second of January. The nagging awareness of Luna's absence, of Aln's absence, that Ben Amberley was still missing – all these losses were with her and very present. But for this evening, she could perhaps pretend.

The Christmas tree still sparkled in the corner of the dining room. It would not come down until the day before Twelfth Night. Bee went in to admire it in the soft light from the standard lamp. She could hear footsteps upstairs: Alys moving about. There was a sudden rattle of rain against the French windows and Bee was glad to be inside but then something moved, out in the garden. Bee froze. There was someone there, on the other side of the glass, a figure in silhouette. Bee felt her hands clench. She went quickly to the window and switched on the table lamp. Dark stood there, in the rainy dusk.

She did not need to fumble for the window catch. He stepped through the glass, leaving a moment of milky shimmer behind him. He wore a greatcoat, although she knew that he did not feel the cold of the world. He said,

"That huntsman's coming."

"Who, Nick Wratchall-Haynes?"

Dark nodded. "I saw him before. A big chestnut. He's riding hard up the lane."

"Why hasn't he come by car?" Bee asked. But she soon found out.

She was not the first to reach the back door, in response to the knock. Alys had come down the stairs and was already opening it.

"Good evening. Are we expecting you?" She wore an embroidered Indian top, a long skirt with fragments of mirror.

"Good evening. And no, I don't think you are, Mrs Fallow."

Alys gave her sidelong, wry smile. "Miss."

"Miss! Sorry, I just assumed…"

"I suppose I ought to use 'Ms' but I never like the way it sounds – like a wasp, buzzing. Won't you come in?"

"Yes. Thank you."

Wratchall-Haynes wore a thick tweed jacket with a great many pockets, and riding boots: very expensive ones. His hair was wet. She knew that Dark stood behind her but she did not think that Wratchall-Haynes could see him; the huntsman's gaze flickered past her, unlingering and away.

"Is something wrong?" Bee asked. Wratchall-Haynes' face was pale. She could sense his nervous tension. Then the phone rang. "Hang on a moment." She picked it up.

"Alys, is that you?" It was Richard Amberley's familiar voice.

"No, it's Bee. Alys is here. Do you want me to put her on?"

"No, it doesn't matter which of you I speak to. Caro's gone."

"Oh!" Bee said, feeling as if she had been punched. "Gone where?" Well, *that* was a stupid question, she thought. Under the circumstances.

"I hoped she might be over at Mooncote."

"No, we haven't seen her. I'm sorry, Richard. How long has she been missing?"

"She left the house shortly after three o'clock, I think. She didn't leave a note. She didn't take the car. Or her phone. One of the stable girls saw her heading across the field. She said Caro wasn't wearing a coat. The girl shouted but Caro didn't hear her and then apparently she vanished. The girl's new: she doesn't really know what's been going on."

"Have you phoned the Hornmoon Arms? Maybe she popped in for a drink?"

"I rang them, and the vicarage, and several other people who live close by, and now you."

"What do you want us to do, Richard?" Bee tried to sound as firm and calm as possible.

"I don't know. Keep an eye out. I can't expect people to start searching the landscape as yet – she might just have gone for a long walk."

Bee glanced at the clock. It was now a quarter past six. She knew, from bitter experience, that it was much too early to phone the police: you needed to leave it for at least twenty four hours. She said this to Richard, followed by whatever assurances she could, conscious that the police were already involved over Ben's disappearance. Then, casually, she said, "Have you spoken to Nick Wratchall-Haynes?"

"I spoke to his housekeeper. She said he'd gone out. Some meeting or other although you'd think they'd leave it till after the New Year. Still, committees and all that."

All the while Bee was conscious of the hunt master's cold grey-blue gaze upon her. She could not tell what the man was thinking, only that wire-like singing tenseness. He said nothing.

"I'm going to speak to Danielle Compton over at Marshlake," Richard said. "She might have gone over there to talk horse or something."

"I really hope she shows up soon," Bee said. "And of course we'll do all we can. Don't hesitate to call if you need us."

She hung up. Her mother's face, and that of the hunt master, bore a similar expression: sharp and predatory. Hunting faces.

"What?" said Bee.

"I've seen her," Wratchall-Haynes said. "That's why I've come."

SERENA

After the Christmas break, and the attack in the street, Serena braced herself for more things to happen, but the following day dawned with a light pearly glaze over the rainwashed city and after breakfast the sun came out. Ward had a meeting at the theatre, so Serena tidied up the kitchen, let Mrs James the cleaner in, and took herself into the studio for the morning, to tidy that up as well.

"I'm glad it's all over to be perfectly honest," Mrs James said. "I shall take my decs down at the weekend and then we shall be back to normal."

"Are you doing anything for New Year's, Mrs James?"

"I shall stay at home with my daughter and the gin," her cleaner said. "I expect there will be something on the box."

"Very sensible!"

"And you?"

"I don't know, yet. Ward got invited to some big showbiz party but he's not sure if he really wants to go. So we might stay home, too."

"I recommend it to the house," said Mrs James. "No point in traipsing all over the place and the BBC says it might be wet."

"Not more rain!"

"It's climate change, they say. Or perhaps it's just England being English."

They agreed that this was likely to be the case.

The studio was grey and quiet, with a steely light coming through the glass panels of the ceiling. There was no demon, nor any sign of things amiss. Serena wondered about this friend of Ace's, the person who had sent the demon, and perhaps the angel, too. It felt strange, to think of someone whom she did not even know looking out for her, some fairy godfather. Although perhaps 'fairy' was the wrong word, she thought with a shiver. She got the vacuum out and cleaned the floor, then set about her desk until everything was in its rightful place. This did not take long, since she had done the same thing before going away: nothing worse than coming home to a mess, and there had been quite enough of that already. She tidied the desk drawers a little bit more, all the same, and stood back to admire her efforts. She was just thinking of making mid-morning coffee when her phone rang.

"Serena, it's me. Caspar. I hope you've had a good break? I wasn't sure if you were back."

"Yes, we got back yesterday. We had a nice time." Well, mostly. She had no intention of mentioning Luna. "It was very Christmassy."

Pharoah laughed. "Sounds fantastic. I got some sort of bug. I was laid up over the whole week – couldn't face food. Lost my sense of taste. Probably saved a fortune."

"Oh no! You poor thing!"

"Well, I don't really do the whole Christmas thing so it wasn't too bad. I watched a lot of films and read a lot of books."

"That sounds all right, actually." She thought of Mrs James and the gin. "I hope you had plenty of booze."

"Yes, I did manage to force down the odd whisky and lemon even if I couldn't taste it. I called to confirm our meeting and speaking of which, what are you and Ward doing for New Year's Eve? I expect you've got something glamorous planned?"

Serena told him the same thing that she had told Mrs James.

"Oh," Caspar Pharoah said. "Then maybe you'd like to come to a celebration? I'm having one, you see."

Serena hesitated for only a second. It was true that she and Ward had no firm plans. It might be good for business, for the association between them and after hearing what Ace had to say about the subject, she wasn't sure if it was the kind of invitation that it would be wise to turn down. She had discussed this with Ward and Stella and they had agreed that trying to extricate herself now might cause more difficulties than it solved.

"I could just walk away," Serena said.

"But you've already attracted someone's interest, not just Pharoah's. Go to the meeting and see what he says," Stella had advised.

So she said,

"Thank you so much! Actually, that would be lovely."

"Great. It's at my place out near Shepperton." From the way he said it, Serena got the impression that it was only one of his 'places'. "I'll text you the address and the details."

"That's so kind," Serena said. Her phone pinged a moment after he had hung up. The address appeared on the screen and she wasted no time in looking it up. What she saw made her stare.

"This," said Ward, that evening in the kitchen, "is pure house porn."

"Isn't it, though?"

"The thing is, when I see all that glass, I just think what it must cost to heat. Who would have thought that I, such an aesthetically-minded boy, would grow up to have such a prosaic soul."

"You couldn't walk around in the buff, either."

"Oh, I expect he has Alexa-controlled curtains. Or no neighbours."

"No, I googled it. Passing boats."

"Perhaps he doesn't care," Ward said.

"Anyway, he probably doesn't walk around starkers because it's too cold, because of all the glass."

"This is why I bought top floor Georgian."

"Your roof garden is pretty epic, though, Ward."

"I am aware that you only go out with me for my roof garden."

"That is not true!" Serena refilled his glass. "If that was true, I'd ditch you around Hallowe'en, then go out with a man with a woodburning stove and a cosy basement, and hitch back up with you at the end of February."

"You really are a mercenary baggage, aren't you?"

"Actually," Serena said, "I'm wondering if I really am, given the speed with which I calculated that accepting Cas Pharaoh's party invite might earn me Brownie points."

"Oh, I have no problem with it per se, it's just the doubts Ace cast on the whole association. It will get me out of Jude Ostler's bash in the Shard, to which he has invited Miranda, even though he knew I'd said I might be there. He's probably invited some hack from the Sun to take notes when she hurls my shoes from the top of the building."

"She'd have to wrench them off your feet first."

"After that episode with the Loakes I wouldn't put anything past her. And you've had quite enough to put up with so no, let's head upriver not down. It's not like I don't know Shepperton. I've been for a lot of walks along that stretch of the river during lulls in filming. Fresh air beats sitting in a trailer playing Pong."

"Shouldn't you be reading improving literature in your trailer? Or writing poetry?"

"Also, there are some really quite decent pubs along that bit of the water," Ward said, warming to his theme. "So if the party's shit, we can go to one of those."

"They'll be crammed. And you'll need tickets for New Year's."

"I shall say "Don't you know who I am? And they will let me in, because I have been on the TV. I'll pretend I'm a policeman."

"Then we have a Plan B," Serena said, smiling.

Then Serena threw herself into work. This felt like a good time to make a start, in these dark days before the New Year while much of the working world still slept. After the shock of the destruction, she found that her mind was racing and spinning with new ideas, almost a little manic and needing to be nailed down, in case they flew away, sparkling into the winter light and disappearing. So she drew and drew, since Bella had packed a bag and flitted across London to spend New Year's with her dad and her little half-siblings. Ward was either out and about or learning lines on Serena's sofa. And Stella was preparing for various gigs. Occasionally Serena heard music, much of which she did not recognise or understand, and cackles of laughter coming from the spare room. Stella was having fun, it seemed.

She spoke to Bee every day and each day she hoped that Luna had made it home, but each day brought no news, although Bee had hinted at something happening with Caro. *I'll tell you when I see you. I'll try and come up to town once New Year's out of the way.*

It felt as though they were all waiting for something. One morning, Serena had a visit from the crime support officer about the episode in the studio, but the police had no new information and Serena did not expect them to.

Then she woke and it was New Year's Eve. Ward said that he had written the day off – no meetings, no learning lines, and would she like to go down the Lion and Unicorn for lunch? Stella had set off for work, with a rather bad grace: she still did not know where the New Year's Eve gig was.

"Most mysterious. Then how will you get there?"

"A friend of Dejone's, whom I know and who is a top man, absolutely reliable, is picking me up and the organisers are texting him the details. It's apparently a private party but it sounds more like a rave. I'm taking Ace with me: he says he's never been to a rave, and would I mind. So I told Dej's mate to pick me up and then we'll nip down to

Southwark and pick up Ace. It will be fine. I hope we don't end up getting busted."

"This has happened to you before?" Ward said.

"Yeah. Several times. Nothing bad has ever happened, but it's still a pain. I hope it's not in the middle of a field, at this time of year." She picked up her bag. "Anyway. See you next year!"

"Don't get arrested!"

"I'll try not to!" Then she was gone.

"You don't have to drink," Ward said. "At the pub."

"I won't be! Not if we're going to a party later. I'll be saving myself for champagne."

And they had a pleasant, slightly celebratory lunch with a smoked salmon platter.

STELLA

"The thing is," Dejone's friend Gil said, "I really liked that thing they put out on Spotify last year, but I don't like any of their other stuff."

"I liked *Alarmalong*."

"See, I didn't. It just didn't do it for me. It should have done, but it didn't. Because I had that with *Lovelution*, which was a massive hit and everyone liked that except me."

"I know exactly what you mean."

"Could I just say," Ace remarked, "that I have no idea what you're talking about."

"Oh, sorry. Musical stuff."

"At least you didn't say, *you're too old.*"

"So how old are you, Ace?" Stella said. She and Ward and Serena had had a discussion about this and reached no firm conclusions beyond fifty to seventy five.

"Too old," Ace said, darkly.

Stella peered out of the window. They had come through Docklands now and the skyscrapers were falling behind. She could see the little red eye at the top of the Gherkin, winking in warning for low flying aircraft. She had thought, initially, that they were heading to Docklands itself, but Gil had said not.

"I'm to take you right down the river and then we're catching a boat."

"A *boat?* Where are we going? Holland?"

"I don't actually know," Gil admitted. "I don't think it's Holland."

"Hope not, because I didn't bring my passport. But we will be wherever we're going in time for the gig, yes?"

"I'd think so. Wouldn't you?"

"But there's nothing in the mouth of the Thames, is there? No islands?"

"There are several of the coast of Essex," Ace said. "Actually about thirty of them, if I recall rightly. Mersea. Osea. Foulness."

"Essex. Jesus. I'm starting my new year in *Essex.*"

"Don't knock Essex. My sister used to live in Goodmayes. Mind you, some of those Medway towns can be shitholes, I grant you."

"Not dissing your sister," Stella said.

"There's more to the place than people give it credit for, is all I'm saying. There's some ancient ways in Essex."

Stella, faintly reproved, shut up. The miles rolled by. Stella glimpsed a road sign to East Tilbury. The car swung down a long stretch of road, sporadically lit by streetlights. It looked deserted. They came out onto a wharf. A hulk rode at anchor on the dark water of the Thames.

"It's not on *that*, is it?"

"I dunno." But Gil did not look exactly thrilled at the prospect and neither did Ace.

"Hi! Are you Stella?"

A woman was striding along the wharf. Stella noted Doc Martens, a long flounced skirt like a Flamenco dancer's, a tight bodice and a sweep of white and blue dreadlocks, bright as naptha in the rain, caught up onto the top of her head.

"Yes!"

"I'm Evie. You made it." She gripped Stella's hand. Her makeup was Kabuki goth, blue and white, surprisingly cheerful. Stella was reminded of a galleon in full sail. She thought of those women in Versailles, sporting model ships above their powdered coiffure.

"This is my friend Ace," Stella said. "I think you know Gil?"

Evie and Gil high fived one another with whoops.

"Looks like they do," Ace said.

"The boat's waiting," Evie said. "Hope you've got your waterproofs. If not, I've got some for you."

"We're not sailing in that, I hope," Ace said, looking askance at the hulk. "It looks like it's on the verge of sinking."

"No, she can be sailed, actually, but we're not doing it here. We're going in a rib."

"In a what?"

"A Rigid Inflatable Boat," Stella said, who had been in them before. "Have you not seen 'Rib Rides' advertised along the Thames?"

"If I have I probably thought they were something else."

"It's gonna be a quick and dirty ride," Evie said. "You're probably not far wrong." She gave a ribald laugh. "In you get."

With Ace, Stella clambered gingerly into the boat, which was rocking on the light-splintered water. Gil was, it seemed, remaining behind to await their return, saying that he did not do New Year's so no worries. Stella could see something across the estuary, presumably a town. Gravesend? She was not certain of her geography this far down the river. Otherwise the rivermouth stretched bleak and black to the eastern horizon. Suddenly, she wished that the comet was still visible. But autumn's visitor had streaked away on his journey past the sun. Over and out.

She was issued with a life jacket and once everyone was seated and given brief instructions (mainly *don't fall in*, thought Stella) Evie's companion, whom, it turned out, was called Jake, took the inflatable out into the river. Stella would not have admitted it, but she felt nervous. It was this vast wet dark, especially so close to the capital. As the boat turned she could see the orange glow of London staining the sky. They passed huge cranes, angled against the sky, and there was something coming upriver: a great barge in from the North Sea. No wonder, Stella thought, that the word 'Baltic' had become slang for 'freezing.' The wind was icy and stung her face. She had brought a woolly hat which she pulled as far down as she could over her face.

By her side, Ace huddled against the side of the boat. He said something but the wind and the roar of the boat snatched the words. She thought they might have been 'it's bloody cold'.

Jake was handling the inflatable with confidence, keeping well out of the way of the oncoming barge and shooting down the line of the shore. Ace then began to take an interest and pointed out various places as they passed.

"Southend. You can see the pier. Ever been?"

"No."

"Don't bother. On your right, the Isle of Grain. And the Isle of Sheppey."

"Where are we going?" Stella shouted above the noise of the boat. Evie just pointed a gloved hand, due east. "Christ, it *is* Holland." They were clearly heading out to sea. She could see the coastline picked out in lights and all of it was falling behind. Those were starting to be proper waves, too: big rolling swells over which the inflatable bounced and juddered.

"Oh, *I* know where we're going now," Ace said. "Yeah, that makes sense." He looked grimly pleased.

"Where, then?"

"Hang on," Ace said. He lifted himself up and peered into the murk. "See those lights?"

"Oh, I see," said Stella. "It's a boat."
It wasn't.

The searchlights began to blaze after they had been travelling for another ten minutes or so. Stella could not tell where they were coming from. They lanced across the sky, sending fractured reflections across the waves. There was a strong salty smell, the kind of smell that Stella had always thought of as ozone, even though it apparently wasn't. Then, in the powerful beam of a searchlight, she could see directly ahead.

"What the fuck is that?"

"Have you not seen them before?" Ace asked.

"What *are* they? They look like something out of Star Wars."

The structures were rising out of the waves. Huge boxes, on spindly legs. Stella could not get past the Star Wars comparison: the things looked like the mobile forts on the winter world, marching across the landscape. Beyond, she could see the tall spires of a windfarm.

"Where are they from? Alpha Centauri?"

"Red Sands," Ace said. "The Maunsell Forts."

"The what?"

Evie turned. The boat was coming quite close now, slowing down considerably, and the things were looming over them. Stella heard the creak of metal. She could smell seaweed.

"They were built by a man named Guy Maunsell," Evie shouted. "They date from the Second World War. They're watchtowers, set to guard the mouth of the Thames. They used to be armed. They shot down a lot of German bombers."

"Pirate radio set up on one of these in the sixties," Ace said. "If I remember rightly. Unless that was one of the others. There are more, further out," he informed Stella.

"That's right. Radio Invicta. And Radio Eve broadcast from Sealand, which is just beyond British waters. My mum was involved with that – she named me after it. They took the ladders off most of these so people couldn't climb up but the one we're going to –" she pointed, directly upwards, "This one, still has a landing gantry. Mind your footing. It's very slippery."

She got out first and Ace, rather to Stella's surprise, followed. The gantry was narrow and wet with spray. Ace took Stella's hand firmly and hauled her onto the landing. He did not let go and Stella, despite this slight manifestation of male dominance, was glad enough to have something to hang onto. Jake roped the inflatable to a rail.

"Up we go," Evie said.

BEE

Bee was used to getting wet. You had to, if you lived in the countryside and walked dogs on a regular basis. She usually wore a waterproof of some sort in this kind of weather, Wellingtons, hiking boots, thick socks, an unlovely hat. But sometimes you came across rain that just wasn't going to go off and rain on the plain in Spain or wherever: persistent driving rain that found its way into the cracks and seams of your clothing, penetrating even the stoutest macintosh until it reached your skin.

This was that kind of rain. Bee stumbled along the hedgerow, trying to find the gate and feel her way out of the field. Wratchall-Haynes said he had seen Caro up in the woods at the back of Amberley, towards the summit of the hill, but then he had lost her. He had not said what he had been doing, up there on the hill in the wet, and Bee had not asked. A silent alliance seemed to have formed. She would go back with him, Bee said, and help search.

"But don't tell her husband. For the moment. Just in case."

He did not have to explain further. But sooner or later, Bee thought, someone would have to talk to Richard about, well, the supernatural. Whether he liked it or not. It would take a concerted effort, she thought, involving herself, Alys, and Ward at the least, and possibly others: Nick Wratchall-Haynes himself, and perhaps even Dark. You couldn't refuse to believe in spirits when one was standing in front of you. Could you? In the meantime, they had to find Caro.

Wratchall-Haynes had disappeared, spurring his big hunter along the lane. They had a plan: meet back at the church in a couple of hours, but Bee thought she might not last that long. They had segmented the Amberley fields, heading along the hedge in case Caro might have fallen and be lying, hurt, in one of the ditches or, God forbid, the long rhyne that ran along the northern edge of the property and separated the hedgerow from the road. Wratchall-Haynes had said that he would take that side of it, sending Bee up towards the copse on the hill.

Her one comfort was that Dark was with her. Wratchall-Haynes did not know that. Or perhaps he did? The hunt master seemed to have a lot of hidden depths, as many layers as Alys herself. Bee's mother had

215

gone to the western side of Amberley, ignoring Wratchall-Haynes' suggestion that she go to the house and help Richard. It was entirely possible that she had some errand of her own, some mysterious agenda, but Bee could not worry about that now.

"No sign of her?" she said now, to Dark.

"No. No trace. But it is hard to see footsteps in this weather. The horses have churned up the mud."

Bee nodded. She turned, stood straight, and looked down the valley. The copse, a scrub of bramble and young ash, was directly behind her. She could see the lights of the houses, the village, blurred by rain. Everything looked like a watercolour over which a jam jar had been overturned, swamped and running. When the clouds parted briefly and let the moon peep through, Bee saw the silvery glint of standing water across too many fields.

"It's flooding up," she said. "That wasn't there yesterday."

"We'll go to the copse, yes?" Dark said. "And then back. You are very wet."

Bee smiled. "Not you, though." Dark wore his usual clothes, and his black hair was glossily dry.

"The weather does not touch me," Dark said.

"Well, you're lucky!" She wiped the water out of her eyes and headed up the hill. Then something loomed out of the rain and Bee gasped at the big pale shape before she recognised it as one of the Amberley's horses. But surely those thoroughbred hurdlers shouldn't be out in this like common livestock?

"That's Cloud Chaser, surely – why isn't she in her stable?"

Dark was staring. "I don't know."

"God! What a nightmare – Caro missing and now one of the horses has got out." But when she looked again she could not see the horse.

"She's gone through the gap in the hedge," Dark said. "She'll be all right."

Bee was not so sure. She reached for her phone. "I'll text Richard. As if he doesn't have enough to worry about."

The signal, however, cut out. Bee tutted and replaced the phone. Dark was already striding up the hillside towards the copse and she followed. They made a thorough search of the little patch of woodland, stumbling over the long whips of brambles and the sudden prickle of holly. This must be, Bee thought, where Caro got the red-berried skeins that in past years had decorated the Amberley mantelpiece at Christmas. The festivities seemed an age ago now, drowned out by rain and worry.

There was no one in the copse. Bee and Dark conferred briefly then started walking back down the slope. When they reached the stile that led into the field, with the footpath sign pointing down and away, Bee hopped up onto the step and over. There was someone standing on the other side of the stile. Bee almost cannoned into them and she gave a little shriek. So did the person.

"Oh my God!"

"*Laura!*"

"Bee, I'm so sorry!" Caro's daughter exclaimed. "I didn't know you were there!"

Bee leaned back against the stile. Dark was not in evidence but she thought he had stayed on the other side of the hedge.

"You gave me a start, that's all. Laura, one of the horses is out – I think it was Cloud Chaser."

Laura nodded. "Yes, it was Cloudy. She's such a baggage – she undid the bolt with her teeth."

"She's a clever girl. But a bad girl!"

"I collared her up at the top of the field and took her back down. I've been looking for Mum, too." Laura's face was tight with worry.

"So have w– so have I," said Bee. She glanced at her phone. "I'd better get down to the church. I told Nick that we'd meet back there. He's helping to look."

Laura nodded. "I'd better get back to Dad, too. And you're soaking! Thank you so much for helping – I really appreciate it. Poor Mum. It's been such an awful Christmas."

"Laura, you've no idea where your brother might be?"

"No. Not at all. But our lives have been so different – when we were younger we were really close. I've said this to you before. We keep in touch but – well, that doesn't mean I'm not worried sick. And now Mum…" Her voice trailed away.

"Of course," Bee said. "And I know what *that's* like."

They headed down the slope. Bee was conscious of Dark, walking just behind her shoulder, but Laura showed no sign of noticing anything untoward. She strode along, head down, and when they came to the path that led to the house she said good night and went swiftly in

217

to her father. Bee kept going. Just as they reached the hedge and the gate to the road, however, something happened which caused her to halt. It was a little hole in the air, about eye level. It reminded her of the knot in the glass of the church window and through it she could see a summer woodland, and two people, deep in conversation in a shaft of greeny sunlight. One was tall, wrapped in a white skin cloak. She could just see the stumpy edges where the legs of the creature had been. They wore a deer's skull over their face, the horns jutting forwards. The other person was Alys.

SERENA

At six, Ward stood waiting for the taxi. He looked elegant and thespian, Serena thought, but not too theatrical, although he was wearing a dark cravat rather than a bow tie. He had agonised over this until Serena talked him into it.

"You'll look like the Master in Dr Who."

"Without the facial hair. Or the widow's peak. Nor am I black haired. Or do you mean the one who was a woman?"

"You'll look distinguished, is what I mean. A bit sinister."

"Sinister will do nicely."

Serena herself had chosen a pale chalky blue, one of her own creations, to match the earrings Ward had given her at Christmas, and it was spangled and sparked with sequins. You needed a bit of bling for New Year, Serena thought, and the colour reminded her of a spring sky. You needed that reminder, too, in the winter dark.

"The cab's here."

Even from West London, it was a long run out of town: just short of an hour, without traffic. Serena and Ward sat in silence, watching the city roll by. Serena sent Stella a text.

Are u ok?

A short while later, a reply came back.

Fine. All sorted. Ace sends <3

So her mind was put at rest a little, but still there was Luna… Serena clenched her fist, trying to avoid biting her nails. She had painted them silver blue and they caught the streetlights like stars.

"I can't believe I'm voluntarily going to spend New Year's Eve in *Surrey*. How unspeakably middle class."

"It's not all stockbroker's Tudor."

"Well, Pharaoh's house certainly isn't."

"I hope he has fireworks."

"Think of his neighbour's cat."

"You don't know that his neighbour has a cat."

"I don't know that he has a neighbour. Although he must have some. If not on the same island." Ward studied the passing suburbs. "Did he say how we were to *get* to this island?"

"We have to swim."

"No, we do not! You are lying to me!"

"He sent me an email saying that we are to wait on the dock – dock 'E' apparently, it is clearly marked – and someone, I'm hoping for an actual butler, will come in a rowing boat and ferry us across."

"That's rather romantic. If chilly."

"I don't think it's very far."

Once they had disembarked from the cab, Serena could see that she was right. The road had taken them down a leafy lane – they were definitely out of London now – and around a corner to where a sizeable Edwardian pub, heaving with New Year revellers, stood opposite Dock E. Ward paid the driver, confirmed the pick up at half midnight, and they went down to the end of the dock. A small rowing boat was, indeed, making its way across the black and choppy water of the Thames.

"Told you!" she said.

Ward rolled his eyes. "You actually told me we'd have to swim. I would expect that's the house? Through those trees?"

Serena could see a blaze of lights. From the photos on the net, the whole front of the place was glass, hence their conversation about heating. But from here, standing on the dock in the rainy dark, the glow was inviting.

"Good evening! Guests of Mr Pharoah?" The boatman was tall, wrapped up in a muffler.

"I've got proof," Serena said, waving a printout of Caspar's email. But the man seemed to be expecting them.

"Mr Garner? I recognise you, in fact. Watched your program. And Miss Fallow?"

"That's right."

"Step into the boat, please." He had a faint accent, which Serena could not quite place. Geordie? Perhaps. It sounded slightly northern. "Mind your footing. We'll soon have you across."

And he did, just as another gust of rain spattered against Serena's waterproof wrap. She hoped there was a proper path, fearing for her heels. In fact, the walk to the house was short and the path was concrete and flat. The boatman stayed behind, setting off again on the brief voyage across the river.

"Wow," said Ward, as they approached the house. "How the other half live, eh?"

"Technically you are part of the 'other half.'"

"I'm not this rich," he replied. "Look at that painting! Who's that by, do you think?"

Through the glass they could see a huge room, in which guests were already circulating, champagne flutes in hand. On the wall nearest the window was an enormous canvas, painted in swirls of indigo and azure and green, which seemed almost to move. Serena blinked. It was a compelling optical illusion.

"It's like it's moving," Ward said.

"I was just thinking the same."

"I wouldn't want to look at it for too long. Make you dizzy. My aunt moved into a cottage once which had this kind of dayglo wallpaper, probably dated from the sixties, and it was a real migraine inducer. She had to have it removed."

"It sounds ghastly. But that painting is actually really beautiful. Just a bit disorienting."

The front door slid into the wall as they came close to the house. No one was behind it.

"Like Tesco," said Ward.

"Don't make me giggle! This is nothing like Tesco."

She hoped their host hadn't heard, as he now stepped to greet them at the door.

"Happy New Year!" Pharoah shook Ward's hand and air kissed Serena's cheek. He wore dark blue: designer jeans and a mao-collared navy shirt with a faint tinge of silver weave. It suited his lean frame, Serena had to admit. "You look lovely, Serena. Come in out of the rain. Marcus will take your coats."

"We have met, Caspar, but it was a while ago. In LA. You probably don't remember."

"I remember very well. At a party at Chateau Marmont."

"That's it. I was with Miranda Dean."

Serena thought that Ward was sparing Caspar Pharoah the embarrassment of mentioning this, but he said only, "It's so good to see you again. Let's find you some champagne."

Gratefully, Serena accepted a pale, fizzing glass. She was not an expert on wine, but Ward knew quite a bit about it.

"Vintage," he said now, taking a sip. "Very good."

"I won't drink too much. It's a while till midnight."

Ward laughed. "You never do drink too much, Serena. You're a cheap date!"

"I'll take that as a compliment. Do you know anyone here?"

"Not that I can see. Good looking crowd, though."

Serena agreed. She saw people of all ages, all ethnic backgrounds. The clothes were wonderful and her professional eye surveyed them with pleasure. Evidently Cas Pharoah had got the heating bill sorted out, for the big open plan room was as warm as toast, pleasant after the chilly night outside, and many of the guests wore filmy, flimsy gowns. Serena had admired an Asian woman in a short dress like a scrap of rainbow, and a blonde girl in a sequined halter which made her look like an Amazon warrior. She noticed that Ward was appreciating the throng, too.

Serena had the impression that most of these people knew one another, but so far, they had not met anyone familiar. The guests were friendly, however, and welcoming: Ward was chatting about the theatre to an animated young man with a lively, laughing face and Serena had been complimented on her own attire. She had been asked for business cards, which she had forgotten to bring, but she had given details to several of the women and had been assured that she would see them again once the year had got underway.

She glanced at Ward. The young man had drifted away but Ward's gaze was fixed on the opposite doorway and Serena froze at his expression. He looked quite simply horrified.

"Ward? What —"

He gave a little nod. Serena turned. Standing in the doorway, wearing a chilly smile and a dress that could be accurately described as almost frontless, was none other than Ward's ex-girlfriend: the shoe-hurling, scene-throwing Miranda Dean.

STELLA

Fortunately, Stella had opted for Converse rather than anything fancier. This made it a little easier to climb the slippery metal ladder into the box of the old fortress.

"Want a hand?" Ace had gone up ahead of her.

"Cheers!" She reached up and he pulled her in.

"You okay?" Evie was waiting.

"Yeah, I think so. When you said 'a gig', I kind of assumed that there would be an audience! Good job I didn't dress up. Not that it's that kind of job anyway."

Evie laughed.

"Oh, you'll have an audience. Just not one you can see. We're reviving the pirate radio thing. That's why we couldn't tell anyone where it was."

"Are you not legal out here, then?" said Ace.

"Well, it's a grey area, so to speak."

Stella was now energised. "Fantastic! This is so old school."

"We do have proper equipment – you won't have to crank any handles or anything."

"Let me at it."

Inside, the fort was far from empty. Boxes lined the walls, but there was no indication of what was in them. A full music deck linked to what appeared to be an impressive DVS – a Digital Vinyl System – stood at the end of the room, beneath a curving wall. It was not warm and the room smelled strongly of the sea. Stella was reminded of a submarine, fathoms deep, encased in a metal shell. It felt secure and unsafe at the same time: not a bad way to feel on New Year's Eve, Stella thought.

"Wasn't there a plan to turn these into a luxury hotel complex at one point?" Ace asked.

"Yeah. Apparently."

"That would take a fortune!" Stella said.

"More dosh than sense, if you ask me. It keeps being rumoured but it never comes to anything. I mean, would you? By the way, I can make you something hot to drink after the ride, if you'd like."

"Yeah, coffee. If you've got it."

Evie produced a large thermos, apparently out of thin air.

"Certainly have. Would madam care for milk?"

"Madam drinks it black and strong. Just like her heart."

Ace guffawed at this. "Nice one, Stella."

"I nicked it from someone else, but don't tell anyone."

Stella sipped her coffee and took a look at her phone. No signal, but she was searching for the time.

"We need to think about getting started."

Evie nodded. "Come over here. I'll be your producer, basically. You just worry about the music."

"Suits me," Stella said, as the clock ticked down and the year began to slip away. She put her headphones on, adjusted the mike, and the celebrations began.

A couple of hours later, Stella became aware that Evie was mouthing something at her.

"Do you want a break?"

Good plan. Stella nodded.

"We're gonna leave you with a couple of tracks…"

She introduced them, then rose, somewhat stiffly.

"You're super focused," Evie said.

"Tell him that!"

Across the room, on an ancient sofa, Ace was engrossed in an old copy of the Guardian.

"What? I don't understand all this modern music."

"Oh come on! You must have been in your heyday when punk was around!"

Ace smiled. "I remember it, yeah. Still, I can tell you know your stuff, Stella."

"Is there a loo?"

"Yes. Well, sort of. It's a bit ancient. But functional. It's through that door and along the corridor. On the left."

"Okay." Stella followed Evie's instructions and found the lavatory. It was indeed old but in somewhat better shape than the facilities at Ace's house, so Stella felt that this was a plus. The tracks she'd left playing were long ones: cigarette length. She was supposed to be giving up, but then, that was a constant. Stella's relationship with nicotine was a stormy one. Serena had recently given up, with apparent success, and this made Stella feel even more conflicted. She fished one out of her pocket and experimentally, opened a door: more of a hatch, really. The wind whipped in, nearly snatching the cigarette from her mouth.

"Hey!" said Stella, as though the wind was a living thing. She pushed the hatch shut behind her and found herself on a small platform, overlooking the black sea. It felt safe enough, although she did not think it was wise to go too close to the wire mesh which fenced the platform in. She leaned back against the bulk of the fort and squinted upriver. From here, when they had arrived, the distant glow of London had been visible, but now it was not: Stella looked into an endless dark. The flare of her lighter was a welcome spark. She took a drag of the cigarette, feeling suddenly shaky, and noticed that the wind had died. She stood in a still pause of space; even the churn of the water below seemed to slow.

The quiet did not last. A vast sound blared out across the sea, making Stella gasp. She tore the cigarette from her mouth and threw it over the metal side of the fort. There was a rising blare of sound, thin at first, then filling the air. It rose and fell like a rollercoaster. Stella was too young to have heard it in her lifetime, but she knew what it was: an air raid siren. And from the coast a disc of light flared up, sending a beam into the skies, then another and another. The strange searchlights were back, twitching across the heavens, bringing the heavy clouds into sudden relief and illuminating the water. Stella stood frozen. She had wondered what they were when the rib came in, but Ace and Evie had said nothing so she had assumed vaguely that it was a normal thing in the estuary, to do with the docks, perhaps. Now, she wondered if the others had even seen the lights.

She could hear a plane, somewhere out to sea. The high whine came closer and closer, and more were coming to meet it from the black land beyond the searchlights. Stella knew nothing about aircraft. Presumably they were bombers, but they did not sound like modern planes. Her mind cast up images of old war movies: her grandfather, who had after all fought in the war, had been a fan and there had always been one or two on at Christmas: most inappropriate, Alys had said. *The Dambusters*, that was one. Stella had a montage of impressions, but no real knowledge, and she stood now, staring up, as the little planes chased across the sky, stitching it with gunfire, and the searchlights seemed to march endlessly onwards and the huge siren's wail filled the mouth of the river.

Then the sound of the planes diminished. One by one the big arc lights switched off and the siren's voice began to fade. Movement caught her eye. Stella turned and saw a magpie see-sawing on the railing of the fort.

"Mags? That has got to be you."

The magpie gave a harsh cry. She crouched, then launched, shooting low over the waves. Stella glimpsed a last flash of white and the bird was gone.

Cold and shaking, Stella groped for the handle of the hatch and made her way back to the makeshift studio.

Inside, no one appeared to have noticed anything. Ace was still engrossed in the newspaper and Evie was repairing her eye makeup.

"Hey, well timed. Track's just finishing."

But Stella knew that she had been out on the platform for much longer than the few minutes taken up by the music. She did not say anything, however: she would leave that till later, when she could speak to Ace privately. For now, she sat back down at the deck and resolutely put her thoughts into midnight.

They left the fort around one in the morning. Stella nerved herself for what they might find outside, but all was as before. Far away, the city was still undergoing sporadic outbreaks of fireworks: chrysanthemum bursts erupted in the western sky, eclipsing the handful of stars. Shivering, Stella and Ace descended the metal ladder into the boat, which rocked against the leg of the fort.

"This has been a – an experience," Stella said to Evie. "Thank you for everything."

"Cool. And thank *you*. I've had a lot of fun. Great texts from listeners. Not everyone's living it up in Trafalgar Square." She began to untie the rope. "I've paid you, by the way. Did it online when you were on your break. You can check your phone."

"I'm cool. Haven't got a signal, anyway." She took her seat. Evie handed her a life jacket, and one to Ace. Then she cast off and Jake sent the rib flying over the sea. Stella looked back as the forts receded into squat shapes against the eastern skyline. The clouds had lifted and although it was still far from dawn, she could see the shimmer of a single star. She felt her shoulders sink a little, the further they drew away from the fort, but she pulled her hood more closely about her face. It felt very cold, out on the water, that deep small-hours cold. No wonder people tended to die at this time, so they said, more than any other.

But she was pulled out of her isolation by voices. They were suddenly all around the boat, shouting, crying out. Stella could not distinguish individual words but their alarm was palpable. She sat bolt upright and gave a yelp of her own. The voices were gone, as abruptly as they had come.

"Stella? You okay?" Ace was gazing at her in concern.

"No – yes, sorry," Stella lied, remembering the presence of Evie and Jake. "Nodded off a bit. Must have been dreaming."

"You must be knackered, Stella," Jake said over his shoulder. No one else displayed any signs that they had heard anything amiss. And indeed the journey back to the docks passed swiftly from then on, with nothing untoward.

"Want to come back to mine for a nightcap?" Evie said.

"If our driver's okay with it. Ace, you up for that?" Stella should have been tired, but she'd been resting for most of the day: she was always wired after a gig, too nervy to sleep and this had been some gig…

Ace shrugged. "Why not? I don't often turn down a drink."

"Cool. It's not far. It's over there, in fact. I'll go and get your driver."

Stella looked. The black hulk rode at anchor, rocking gently on the night tide.

"You live in that?"

"Converted Thames barge. She's called the *Nitrogen*. There aren't so many of them left these days, but they used to be a regular site on the river – you ever seen one before?"

"I don't think so."

"I have," Ace said. "Big red sails. Shallow draft, to cope with the depth of the water."

"That's right!" Evie beamed at him, as at a particularly promising pupil. "'*Laden deep with sugar, with barley, sand or coke, spitties keep on sailin', they were built of English oak.*' It's an old poem, don't know who wrote it. My grandfather always claimed it was his dad but I think he was having us on. They stopped using them round about the 1950s – too old fashioned. But there's a real community here, Gravesend, Maldon, who restore them."

She helped Stella onto the walkway. "So how did you end up with one?" Stella asked.

"My family were bargees and lighter men. I grew up on the river. I bought *Nitrogen* a few years ago and did her up."

They were now on the deck, feet ringing on the boards. A hatchway led below.

"Does she sail?"

"Yeah, I get her sails up sometimes – they show them on the river for the tourists. Mainly in summer. She's river-worthy, like I said earlier."

"Don't you need a crew?"

"Not for these – the rigging's made so they're a two-person job. Jake gives me a hand. Women and the kids were able to sail them if the men were busy. Easy peasy, really."

Stella doubted this but she liked Evie's confidence. And it was snug below, with a glow from a woodburning stove taking away the river chill. A large ginger cat was curled on a chair next to it; Ace immediately went over.

"Oh, he likes *you*," Evie said, impressed. "He can be a right old sod with some people."

"I get cats," said Ace, making a fuss of the ginger.

"I can do tea. Or a gin. I have a nice apple and pear gin. Jake and I got it in for the New Year. Or we can get you a coffee."

"Gin," said Stella and Ace.

"Fucking hell," Stella added. "Hark at us. The gin twins."

But it was very good gin and Stella had two before they finally decided to call it a night. She could easily have stayed here, she thought, curled up like the cat. But Gil the driver needed to get home and it wasn't fair.

"So how did you, you know, find me? As a DJ? I'm not one of the better-known names, even though I've got my following."

Evie looked across at Stella and there was a sudden light, a flicker behind her eyes. Stella saw it but it was nothing nasty, just an odd complicity.

"A friend of my cousin mentioned you, to my cousin. He knows you. The friend, not my cousin."

"He does?"

"He's going out with your sister. His name's Sam."

As they walked to the car, Ace said, "Stell, do you want your man to take you home first? You're welcome to crash with me."

She hesitated. "Yes, I think I would like that, Ace. Cheers."

He nodded. "Anione will make you up a bed."

Quite how the phoneless Ace intended to make this request known, Stella never asked, but when the car had dropped them into Southwark and they made their way up Ace's untidy privet-beset garden path, Anione was waiting at the front door.

"What a night, eh? Oh and Happy New Year." She once more wore a kimono and, reaching into its pocket, she took out a pack of cigarettes and handed one to Stella. "You look like you need one, love. Cup of tea's waiting in the kitchen."

Stella could not seem to get warm, though the car had been fully heated, but the tea helped. Over it, she told Ace and Anione what she had seen and heard, out at the fort.

"I'm really sorry, I probably should have said something at the time, but –"

"Nah. Not in front of civilians. Don't want to spend the new year in a straightjacket, do we? I saw the searchlights when we went out but I wasn't sure where they were coming from. Although Evie's not quite straight, I'll tell you that, and I don't mean in a sexual sense or whatever they say these days. Something was off but I don't think in a bad way. Don't know what, though."

"If she's connected to Luna's Sam, then they'll be pretty weird. Not like, um, normal people."

Ace cocked her a look. "Oh really? Like what, then?"

"You haven't met Sam and I don't think I've mentioned much about him, but he's a traveller. Not a New Age sort and he says he's not Romany, either. Something else. He's a really lovely bloke and he has this old nan who's a bit mysterious, apparently."

Anione cackled. "I like her already."

Ace said, "If he's connected to Evie and her family were bargees – there's a lot of enigmatic stuff about those people. They've been here a long time."

"In London?"

229

"In England. I don't come from that sort of background but I've come across them from time to time and they're – yeah, connected. To things that are old and strange."

"But they seem okay. I like Sam. I liked Evie. And I've met plenty of old strange things that I didn't like."

"So have I. Bloody hell." Ace snorted at whatever memory this conjured up.

"It was an odd gig," Stella said.

"The sirens and the voices – it's obviously all war stuff. I've heard a couple of things from out that way. Mate of mine spent a night on a Thames barge, once, long time ago, and he mentioned something similar. Scared the beejazus out of him, he said. It's a warning, I know that. But I didn't hear anything and you did."

"But he never knew what it was?" Stella started as the catflap rattled. Something ran in, very quickly, and scuttled under the sink.

"No. Never found out. I think you were hired for that gig to do a bit more than pirate radio, somehow."

"To pick up the warning?"

"Yeah, maybe. Or perhaps something else. The combination of the things you played – I don't get modern stuff but when you're sitting behind a music desk, Stella, something happens."

"Like what?"

"Something magical, perhaps. Stella, we need to get going on all this again, now that the year's in. I get the feeling things are hotting up."

"I agree. And I saw Mags. The magpie I told you about. I'm sure it was her."

"Funny place to find a magpie if it wasn't – they're not seabirds. I think we should ask Ward if he's up for a trip to Norfolk. And there's someone I'd like you to meet, before we do that. The one who sent the demon."

"Okay." Then Stella yawned. She couldn't help it.

"Bed, young lady." Anione was brisk. Stella felt as though she had been placed in the hands of two very weird parents. "I've made one up on the couch for you."

The room was, if possible, even more dishevelled than before, and the blankets were rough. Stella did not care. She took off her Converse, wrapped herself in a cocoon, and slept.

LUNA

When Luna woke, the world was full of light. She sat up. The coracle was drifting past a grove of alder: she could see the small green-brown catkins hanging stubby from the twigs. But beyond, there was nothing but water.

"Aln?"

"Luna, you are awake." Aln was pale beneath the green, but her face was peaceful. A collection of sticks now lay in the bottom of the coracle.

"The – he ..."

"Hob is sleeping. Don't be afraid."

Luna nodded dumbly. She did not feel quite up to dealing with this right now, but she thought she ought to, so she said,

"What – what is he? I have never met anyone like him before."

"He is – was – my brother. Now he is a wose."

Luna thought for a moment, because the word was familiar. "A woodwose? Is that a thing?"

Aln frowned. "Maybe. I'm not sure. I know it differently. A person of the woods, who is part of the wood itself."

"Yes, that's the one, I think. I thought –" Luna hesitated. She had been about to say "I thought they were a myth." *Well, look at you now, Luna!* It would have been a very silly thing to say and she felt herself blushing. "I've heard of them, sort of. But you said – he *was* your brother? Isn't he now?"

"He was like me," Aln said. "Though of course he was a boy. But then something happened, and he – changed. Sometimes the wose are not kind. Hob is still a good person, though."

"You are human, though, Aln? Are you?"

"I don't really know what that means," the girl said, blinking. "I have two arms and two legs. At the moment, anyway."

Luna stared at her. "Do you change into other things?"

"Yes, sometimes. But most people do."

Luna thought of her eldest sister, becoming a swarm of bees, and Serena, dropping from a window and landing as a hare.

"Maybe they do." The thought that she herself might become something else, some animal form, was wild and exciting. What would she be? She had already been another person and she had dreamed that she had become a wren. That had just been a dream, though, hadn't it?

"Bee turns into bees, sometimes," she said. "My sister."

"Your sister was very kind to me," Aln said. "I think she saved my life. She didn't have to do that."

"Aln – where are you from?"

"Why, from the green world," Aln said. "It's not so far from yours, or from White Horse Country."

"I don't know where the green world is," said Luna.

"You can get there through the world of the wood, but it's very dangerous. The huntsmen, you know, and others. But sometimes people from the green world find themselves in Angaelland – that is what your home is called, isn't it? – through other gateways. But you think us strange, because we're green."

Perhaps she was part plant, Luna thought. But she was afraid that it might sound rude to say so.

"And the wose? Do they come from the green world, too? Or from the place of the wood?"

"Both," Aln said. She gave Luna an approving smile, as though at an apt pupil. "We are on the borders of the world of the wood now, the great forest, that and another place. And be careful if you meet the wose. Not all of them are good. Remember the one who broke the window?" Luna remembered the long finger, that had become a twig of ash, with a shudder."

"Those islands. There seemed to be houses on them."

"Yes, but it's too dangerous to land there. The borderlands are very dangerous, even more so than the deeper places. I was glad when the water took us past, but running water will cancel some kinds of magic. We crossed an arm of the sea and then through these inlets. Soon we will be back in your world, if my map reading is right." She pointed to a line of sparks along the curved wall of the coracle, which briefly caught the light. "It's very hard to map these lands. But we should be in the estuary now."

"Do you mean the Severn Sea?" Luna said.

"I think that is its name, yes. Ah, you are waking."

This last was addressed to the bundle of withies on the floor. It stirred, the sticks rattling as if caught by a breeze, and then the wose sat up. The dark golden eyes, which gazed out at Luna from a mass of withies.

"The girl is still with us," he said, in a breath like the wind through the branches.

"Yes, and we are all safe enough, Hob," Aln patted the thing's twig fingers. "Well away from the hunt. Don't worry. No one's going to use you for kindling now." She fished in a pack on the floor. "And we can have breakfast."

Aln did not seem to be steering the coracle in any way, but letting the water take the small boat where it liked. Luna thought that this was probably a good idea and that she should trust the girl from the green world to know what was best. They had eaten bread, even the wose, although Luna could not see how. Afterwards, the creature had looked less stick like and rather bulkier, the withies filling out into smoother branches.

The river seemed much wider than the Severn estuary in Luna's own time. The air tasted of salt, fresh and sharp, but the shore was soon lost in a pearlescent rising mist. It enveloped the coracle and around the little boat, the water seemed quite still. Yet the coracle continued to move, seized on the hand of the river's current. The mist lifted for a moment, revealing the distant bulk of an island, a green cap in the stream.

"That's Flatholm!" Luna said.

"Yes."

"But we're going up the Severn. If we're caught by the current, shouldn't we be going downstream? No, wait, is it the tide? The estuary is tidal here, isn't it?"

"It is not the current that has caught us," said Aln. "Look."

Luna peered over the side of the coracle and saw a swell, a ripple on the water's skin that was propelling them upstream. They were riding the Bore, only a little one, but enough to catch the light craft in its pull and carry it up the river.

They were definitely travelling north. Luna had glimpses of the Welsh shore, and she could not see the white glitter of Cardiff and the docks; that did not seem to be there now. But the Beacons rose beyond the shoreline, familiar, crowned with snow. She could see the conical shape of the Sugarloaf. Then she blinked and the hills were soft and summer-blue.

"Aln?"

"Time's always shifting," the green girl said. "Or maybe people like us aren't tied too tightly to it."

"Has it always been like this for you?" Luna asked.

"Sort of. I grew up as you did, in one place. Then the Hunt came to the Green World and there was a bad spell cast and Hob changed and we had to run. I don't know how long ago, even. Hob and I have been running ever since. The Hunt chase his kind, steal their powers."

"What for?"

"It gives them greater freedom in the forests. Some of the wose have sided with the Hunt, too. Trees speak to you, don't they?"

"Yes."

"That sort of power," Aln said. "Except the Hunt will force a tree to speak, to tell them what it knows."

"Is that why the Hunt is interested in my family?" Luna asked.

"Maybe. I think perhaps your mother has made some sort of bargain." She nodded towards the shore. "Look. The wave is bringing us closer in."

SERENA

Serena froze, but not for long. She shot a glance at Ward, who had made no actorly attempt to school his features and who was looking simply horrified. Miranda's elegant face (she looked like a 1940s aristocrat, with her dark arched eyebrows, Serena thought) was spiteful.

"Miranda!" he said. It was nearly, but not quite, a squeak.

Serena summoned her most gracious smile and said, "Miranda. How lovely to see you. And what a lovely dress." *That you are almost wearing.*

"Ward. And Stella – no, wait, that's your sister, isn't it? I'm so sorry. I find it so hard to remember some people's names." Miranda, famously from both screen and stage, had an annoyingly lovely voice: rather deep and thrillingly resonant for a woman. As an actress, it had proved invaluable.

"I totally understand. Nominal asphasia must be *such* a difficult condition to live with. Especially in your profession. I do think you're awfully brave."

Ward's eyes widened. Miranda gave a rather sickly smile, obviously unable to work out what Serena had actually said.

"And your dress, too. Is it one of your – creations?"

"Yes. One I made earlier." *And who dressed you, Miranda? A fetish catalogue?* Serena did not make the mistake of taking Ward's arm and she had noticed that the fingers which gripped Miranda's champagne flute were white with tension.

"Darling, you wanted to have a word with Cas, didn't you?"

"What? Oh. Yes, yes I did!" Ward seized Serena and marched her into the kitchen, leaving his ex staring after them.

"Fuck! Also," Ward said accusingly, "'*Nominal asphasia*'?"

"I read an article about it at the weekend. Came in handy. It's an inability to remember people's names."

"Everything all right?" Caspar Pharoah straightened up from his wine fridge, which was floor to ceiling. "Just selecting a bottle for someone."

"Miranda Dean, my ex, just showed up."

Caspar put the wine on a work surface and turned to face Ward fully.

"*What?* She certainly wasn't invited. I can't stand the woman – I knew her through Sydney, whom I used to go out with, you know – lovely person, didn't work, different continents, long distance, very sad – and Syd hated her. She was an absolute bitch."

"She was supposed to be at some bash at the Shard."

Serena was terrified for a second that Ward might add 'so that's why we came here', but he had got a grip on himself by this time and did not do so.

"I'm awfully sorry – these things are so awkward. Would you like me to get rid of her? She really isn't terribly welcome."

"Please don't do so on our account," Serena said. "These things happen. She possibly came because she knew we'd be here, wanting to cause a scene. I can assure you she won't get one. I shall be perfectly lovely to her."

Caspar gazed at her with respect. "You're a very special person, Serena."

"I don't know about that! I was brought up to behave in a civilised manner."

"However, I think I shall have Miss Dean escorted to the shore on my own account. Since this is my house and tonight, only people whom I really want to be here, are here." He smiled, picked up the bottle of wine, and disappeared.

"Ward, who knew that we were coming here tonight?"

"I didn't tell anyone. Stella knows, obviously. But it was all a bit vague and last minute. I texted Jude Ostler to say I was staying at home and working on my New Year's Day hangover. Who did *you* tell?"

"I didn't tell anyone – didn't have time, like you, even if I wanted to. So how did Miranda know we were going to be here? Assuming it's not just coincidence."

"It's not a coincidence. Trust me. She has a sixth sense for shit-stirring."

"Well," Serena said. "Anyway, Cas is going to get rid of her."

But as it turned out, Cas had done no such thing, because Miranda could not be found.

Later, Serena found it hard to say how she had spent the remainder of the night. She had not realised that the island on which Caspar Pharoah's house stood was so large, either. The river was not wide at this point, a meandering series of channels winding around the small islands in its stream, and when they had arrived the lights blazing from nearby residences on the shore and on neighbouring islets had been clearly visible. But when Serena walked with Ward down to the dock for a breath of fresh air, the river was dark and silent.

Serena turned to Ward to comment on this but he was no longer there. She did not find this remotely worrying, something that later struck her as very peculiar, especially given some of the episodes over Christmas. She thought, vaguely, that he might have gone in search of Miranda, but the notion brought no anxiety or distress. She stood on the dock, watching the silvery ripples in the water, almost as though a shoal of fish was passing beneath, and sipping champagne. The crystal flute seemed limitless but Serena did not feel remotely drunk, just dreamy. She turned to go back to the house and found that it was summer. Bees hummed among the lavender and the sky was a twilight glow. The warmth of the day was just beginning to fade. Serena strolled across the lawn, but before she did this she reached down and took her heels off, dangling the shoes from one hand. The grass was clipped and cool beneath her feet.

But the sky darkened quickly: ocean into indigo, then black. It had been so clear, but Serena could see no stars although she searched for them, peering anxiously into the heavens. She could still see the garden; there were shadows, silver moonlit paths between, though there was no moon, as if the trees themselves cast their own light. Serena wandered, feeling colder.

At the end of one of these paths she could see a building. The house itself was no longer visible and she should surely have come to the riverbank by now, but this little structure rose out of a grove of bushes. It was a temple, a Classical folly, and its white walls glimmered. A statue stood in front of it, a nymph, minus her arms – there was a name for those but Serena could not remember what it was – and there was a pond, too, starred with water lilies.

Slowly, Serena approached the temple. A small flight of steps led up between two columns. Inside, the floor was marble, the veins gleaming gold, and when Serena stepped forward she found it to be wet. The marble flushed red and the white walls of the temple were charnel red, too, raw meat and bone, and there was the stink of dung again and blood. Something was coming out of the shadows of the temple, something enormous, its great head swinging from side to side and she could smell blood on its breath – and then her shoulders were seized and she was pulled backwards from the temple.

Serena collapsed onto the sunlit grass.

"Serena, are you all right?"

And amazingly she was. The dark memory was draining from her, a stain on the grass, then gone. Caspar Pharoah knelt beside her, her hand in his. Bees hummed again in the lavender and the little temple looked cool and inviting. Pharoah wore pale linen trousers and a silk shirt, apple-blossom pink. It did not look remotely effeminate.

"Yes. Yes, I think so." She could barely remember it now. Pharoah pulled her close. The silk shirt was water cool, but she could feel his skin beneath it.

"Just a bad dream, Serena. They happen."

"Just a dream," Serena echoed. Her head was on his shoulder.

"Here's your glass, I think. You must have dropped it, but it didn't break. How lucky. Are you having a good time?"

"It's so lovely here," Serena said. She gazed out at the wide expanse of water that now lay past the little temple, turning a slatey blue in the dusk. There were fireflies far out over the river, dancing specks of light. For a moment, she thought she saw a little boat whirl by, but it must just have been a log, or fallen leaves.

"I really am terribly lucky to have this house," Cas said, rather apologetically. "But the garden's quite superb, too. Have you seen the roses?"

"No. I love roses." Wasn't it winter? No, it couldn't have been, for there were no roses then.

"Well, we have some old varieties here. Look," – and he plucked a five-petalled blossom, like a wild hedge rose, the colour of sunrise, and held it out to Serena. "This comes from Germany, originally, and it's supposed to be a thousand year old rose – the oldest in the world. I obtained a cutting from a friendly gardener. Quite illicitly, I'm sure, but… And this is a Canterbury rose, much more modern. I don't really know that much about them – just what my gardener tells me."

"It's beautiful," Serena said. She could not stop staring at the rose and its sweet scene filled the air, almost visible as a haze, and when Caspar Pharoah gently took her chin in his hand and kissed her, she was not remotely surprised.

"Your fur's so soft." He laughed, as if pleased.

She reached out and her fingers brushed against the roses. There was the sharp prick of a thorn, Serena jerked away, and it was winter cold once more. Pharoah was nowhere to be seen. A tiny bead of blood was visible on her ring finger, in the lights from the house. She could see Ward, standing in the window of the living room and looking out. He was alone. She ran to join him.

"Serena, are you all right? You've taken your shoes off."

"My feet hurt." But they hadn't, not really. She had been out there for hours, wandering, but a glance at the living room clock told her that it was not yet midnight. A few minutes to go, perhaps. She felt cold with shock now and her glass was empty. Ward took it and put it on a tray held by one of the serving people, a girl with startling golden eyes. Contact lenses were very good these days, Serena told herself.

"Here, have another glass. You can't toast the new year in air."

"Thanks!" She took his arm. "Ward, this is a very odd party."

He gave her a slanted glance. "You're telling me."

"Why, what happened to you?" Miranda was nowhere to be seen.

"I'm not really sure."

There was an electric moment. The year hung on the balance; Serena could see the guests holding their breath. Then a great bell began to sound, ringing in midnight and the hour, and Serena felt time stretch and grow. In those moments, she glimpsed several things reflected in the big windows of the room: the little boat, once more, whisking into a sea of mist, and a man standing anxious on a harbour wall, his cloak the shade of blood, then a white pointed face that seemed made of malice, and then the spirit of the naked child, dancing with gleeful spite in a whirlwind of scraps of cloth, as the demon shrieked in fury and out of sight something hissed and spat. Finally there was a great shadow turning, thundercloud dark, and Serena screamed but no one seemed to hear her, no one was moving at all and then the bell rang out midnight and the new year began.

BEE

Bee had begun to get seriously irritated with Dark. She was even wetter than she had been, and he was not. It was totally unfair to feel so cross and even worse to say so, thus Bee struggled on. They had abandoned the lane and were heading to the church across the fields, just in case Caro might be lying out there, hurt. This had been Bee's own idea and it made her even crosser. Then they came to a stile and realised that Bee, at least, would be unable to go on.

The field beyond glimmered with water. The rhyne which banked it had overspilled its banks and Bee could not even see the corn stubble, which normally poked up through the standing water like the struts of a wreck. She was in Wellingtons but she did not know how deep it might be. Even in this sedate part of the English countryside it was possible to be swept away in the floods. A woman had died that way earlier in the week, up north.

"Ned," she said. "I think you ought to go on. I'll go back and down the lane."

"I don't think I should leave you. Bee, if your friend is in that field, and we cannot see her, then she will already have drowned."

Bee took a breath. He was probably right.

"And daylight is a better time to find a body."

"Yes, all right. Ned, can you – see anyone?"

"Another spirit, you mean? There was an old man by the gate, not from my time. A shepherd, I think. I've seen him before. He greeted me."

Bee had seen no one. But she felt that if Caro had, God forbid, gone under the water, then, if her shade was still here, Ned should be able to see it. She asked him this. The sight of the flooded field filled her with a kind of horror which she did not understand.

"I – don't know. I didn't think of that. But usually, yes, if someone has died, I will see them. They are very bright, you see, at first." He sounded apologetic. "So she is not here."

Bee was grateful to be persuaded to return.

"Anyway," Dark said. "You agreed to meet the huntsman."

"Yes, I did. I don't want him sending out a search party for *me*."

Back at the lane she was glad to be standing on firmer ground. They set off in the direction of the church but when they had gone no more than half a mile, Bee found herself walking on a kind of spine of land, with the flooded fields stretching away to either side.

"Ned, surely we haven't had *that* much rain. I know we've had a lot recently, but these higher fields don't normally flood up." Living where she did, Bee was used to flooding: where it did and where it didn't. She had few qualms about driving through an active ford, was accustomed to planning winter journeys around where the roads were passable and where not. Some years were worse than others and some of it depended on where the Environment Agency had been dredging. But this year, though wet, should not have resulted in this suddenly drowned land.

"The Summer Country," Ned said softly, echoing Bee's own thoughts.

"Yes. Country only when it's summer, otherwise an inland sea."

"In my day, people lived only on the eyes."

He meant, Bee knew, the eyes or islets of higher ground, rising above the water meadows. In Dark's day, much of Somerset would have been underwater in winter, the great abbeys such as Muchelney and Glastonbury rising above the flood. Mooncote stood on higher ground, too, as did Amberley: water sometimes reached the bottom of the drive, but never further in Bee's lifetime. Alys had said that the orchard had once flooded, after days of torrential rain…

"Bee!"

Her head jerked up to see Alys herself, coming towards her down the road as though the thought had summoned her up.

"Mum! Any luck?"

"No. I've asked around," Alys said. She brushed a wet strand of hair out of her eyes. "No one's seen her. Anywhere."

Bee decided on a direct attack.

"She's not with the Hunt?"

"No. She's not with the Hunt." Alys met her gaze squarely. She did not ask Bee why she had asked.

"Might she have been?"

Alys sighed. "It's possible but unlikely. When are we supposed to meet Nick?"

"A few minutes ago," Bee said, rather pointedly.

241

But when they reached the church, the huntsmaster was not there.

"I'll go in," Bee said. "Just in case he's inside. I hope no one sees us..."

"Well, if they do," Alys said, "We'll tell them the truth. We're looking for Caro."

"I wonder if anyone's looked in the bloody church already. We should have gone there first..."

But the little church was empty of all but shadows. Bee stood for a moment, listening and remembering the carol service. There was no Christmas music now. The church felt oddly anticipatory, as though waiting for something. Bee had the curious impression that its ears were pricked. She went back outside to where Alys and Dark waited in the porch, locking the door behind her.

"I can hear something," Dark said.

He was right. From across the fields at the back of the church rode Nick Wratchall-Haynes. And across the saddle before him lay something drenched and white.

STELLA

Stella woke to sunlight. She had thought the curtains were closed but now they were open and the light was streaming in, showing the dinginess of the room to maximum effect. But the blankets, if somewhat oddly smelling, had been warm and so was the room. Stella knew where the bathroom and kitchen were by now and utilised both. It was ten o'clock in the morning, not too early, not too late, and her phone was full of Happy New Year messages, although there was not one from Luna. Shit. But Stella herself felt clear headed and light, in spite of last night's exertions and alarms, not to mention the gin.

An interesting way to begin your year.

Neither of her hosts were visible but as Stella sipped a second cup of tea, Ace appeared. He was in the clothes of the night before and unshaven.

"How are you?" Stella said.

"About as well as I usually feel first thing in the morning." He grimaced. "Anione's still crashed out. Said she had an 'eventful evening', whatever that means. I hope to find out later, could mean anything. I'll take her some tea."

"There's some in the pot."

"Outstanding."

A few minutes later he returned and sat down at the kitchen table.

"Right. You'll be wanting to go home and change, I expect. Do you have plans for the day?"

"Not really. New Year's Eve is the biggie and after that I usually have a couple of days off, like everyone else."

"That's good, because I want you to meet someone."

"You mentioned that. Your demon-summoning mate."

"I did. I have actually been in touch with him and the plan is to go over this afternoon."

"Where does he live?"

"Lambeth."

"Not far, then. I might as well hang on here if you can put up with me, rather than go all the way back to Portobello. Don't tell anyone, because I have a reputation as a scatty free spirit to keep up, but I always carry a spare pair of knickers with me."

Ace went rather pink. "Jesus, Stella, I don't need to be privy to your underwear schedule. Women's mysteries!"

"Well, now you are, so, you know, be honoured."

"Anione could probably lend you something, anyway."

It was Stella's turn to be shocked. "Women don't borrow other women's undies, Ace. Not in my experience unless dire, dire emergency. Or perhaps they do. I don't know. My sisters never have, neither have my mates. But it won't be necessary!"

Anione, when she surfaced, concurred with Stella.

"He hasn't a clue, love. But if you give me your knicks, I can wash them out with the rest of the laundry now, bung them through the mangle and put them in front of the oven. They'll be dry by the time you set off for Lambeth."

Stella gaped at her. "You have a *mangle?*"

"All mod cons here."

"Anione, you're a domestic goddess."

The woman smiled. "If only you knew."

The Southwark Tavern was open for a couple of hours over lunchtime, so Stella and her hosts made full advantage of this and had cheesy chips. Afterwards, Ace said,

"It's about a mile and a half to my mate's. Bus goes nearly door to door so I've got it all worked out, you see."

"Fine." The sunlight of the morning had faded by now, and a wintery drizzle had set in. It was not weather for walking and Stella felt as though she had already had a workout, not an unfamiliar sensation after a gig even though she had not really done anything physical except sit in a boat and behind a mixing desk. So she was happy to follow Ace, lamb-like, onto the bus. It dropped them off outside Lambeth North station and Ace pointed to an adjacent road.

"Down there."

"Hercules Road," said Stella, reading the name. "Is your mate a hero, then?"

Ace laughed. "Yeah, totally."

At the entrance to the road stood a tall building, wedge shaped, with a pub sign on its side proclaiming it to be the Pineapple.

"That," Ace said, "is a very decent boozer and I recommend it to the house. I sometimes meet Bill – that's my mate – in there, but we thought, New Year's Day, it might be a bit crowded with people having a hair of the dog so home it is."

"Whatever." They passed the Pineapple by and hastened on.

Ace's friend's house was Georgian, fronted with London brick and, like its neighbours, rather shabby. Ace gave the front door a push and let them through into a hall.

"He leaves his front door open?" Stella said. "Jesus, that's trusting round here."

"He knows I'm coming," said Ace. "And they all know him, anyway, in this road."

Was it actually someone's home? Stella wondered. The front room, glimpsed through a half open door, seemed to be full of picture frames and the air smelled of paint. More like a workplace. But the hallway ended in a kitchen, which to Stella's surprise had none of the usual accoutrements apart from a large, white enamel sink, a table set squarely on the tiled floor, and an open fireplace. It was airy and light, though, with big sash windows.

"Blimey, this is unusual in London these days. Won't he get copped for air pollution?"

"No idea."

There was a note on the scrubbed pine table, which said in a sprawling copperplate hand: *we are in the garden. B.*

Ace and Stella went through the back door. There were a number of flowering shrubs – very early, Stella thought, but it must be quite sheltered. Even the air seemed warmer. Half the garden had been turned over to neat rows of vegetables and surely those shouldn't be growing quite so well at this time of year, either. Perhaps Ace's friend practiced biodynamics or whatever that thing was called. Or perhaps it had been done with the aid of dark forces? A winding path, through overgrown hazel, led to the end of the long garden and a summer house covered with a vine.

"He'll be in there," Ace said.

He was. Ace's friend Bill was sitting in a chair, with a china tea set on a table between himself and a woman. She was in late middle age, with a coil of white hair, and Bill, too, Stella estimated to be around sixty, with fluffy grey locks and the slightly protuberant eyes suggestive of a thyroid condition. Both of them beamed up at Stella. Both of them were also stark naked.

245

"Um!" said Stella.

"My wife, Catherine." Bill indicated the woman, who shyly ducked her head.

"They're naturists," Ace said.

"Yes, I'd guessed!"

"Sorry, probably should have mentioned it but he's not usually in the buff when I pop round to see him so it slipped my mind."

"It's not a problem. It's not like I'm not used to it on festival sites."

"The principles of Swedenborg, you see," Bill said. He had a strong baritone voice, which combined with the rather staring eyes produced a slightly hypnotic effect: you would listen to this man, Stella thought, naked or not. "You see us as Adam and Eve, freed from the troublesome disguises of the age."

"Fair play," Stella said. "I've no issue with nudity. I'd rather not strip off myself, thought, if that's all right with you, as it's still a bit parky at this time of year. Although I must say that your garden's lovely and warm."

"There is no requirement to do so. Would you care for some tea?"

"Tea would be great!"

Ace found a couple of extra chairs.

"So, getting down to it, Bill, we've got a problem." He outlined the situation: Serena's missing ex and now missing sister, the slips in time and place, Serena's meeting with an angel, and Stella had to admit that he did this surprisingly concisely.

"So." Bill stared into his tea cup. "You come at an interesting time, an interesting day. The year has spun on. We are in a different age."

Stella leaned forwards. "Ace says you sent a demon to look after my sister. It's been hanging around and as he just said, she met it again in the company of an angel. Ace tells me you sent it."

"I did."

"Do you know Serena, then?"

"I have not met your sister but she is under the protection of a star, as are you, as are your family. It was the star who first spoke to me. You see, their powers are great but not in this sphere, in this realm. They are like me, you see. I am confined to this part of the city; I cannot move freely throughout, and must rely on those who assist me."

"Would one of those be a magpie, by any chance?"

"She is young, but enthusiastic."

"She told me that she remembered Peckham when it was just fields," Stella said. Bill bent upon her a look of amused benevolence.

"As I said, she is young. The Behenian stars must also act in an oblique way although they are strongest in this world when they are close to your house, in the West Country, I understand."

"There's an old box," Stella said. "It holds some gems: I think they're connected to the star spirits. They're linked to my family and we think one of them might be an actual ancestor. A great great grandmother."

"Star blood?" Ace said, intrigued. "I like that. Hey, Stella, you're an alien!"

"It wouldn't half explain a lot. So the star asked you to – what? Keep an eye on Serena?"

"Yes, and I sent a spirit to watch over her. But it was too late. The damage had already been done. There's a great deal going on. The underland of London has heard rumours, but they are sparse."

"Yeah? Of what?" Ace asked.

"Of a golden man, who charms all that he touches. Who has gained an inheritance, but the nature of this is not clear, except that there is talk of a toll to be paid."

"A toll? I don't like the sound of that. What does that mean?"

"I do not know. But it has been disruptive. Things have been coming to the surface of the world, to the attention of the ordinary human world, and this is unusual. You'll know that. Voices crying out in the night. Things half seen and glimpsed, particularly along the river, the artery of this city, its main beating vein."

"Well, I certainly did," Stella said. "Last night."

"The river is the key. Those who work there say that something is wrong, something is imminent. Last night, Stella, I think that was a warning that something will come by way of the river."

"But no mention of what?"

"No. No one seems to know."

"This 'golden man'," Bill. Do we know who he is?"

"Ah," said the naturist. "That we do know, as I said to my friend here. His name is Caspar Pharoah."

Stella walked back to Portobello after taking leave of Bill and Ace. The latter had more or less dispatched her ("off you trot, Stella. You've had a long day"). Except she hadn't, really, although it had been a long night. But it was clear that Ace wanted to talk to Bill alone and so Catherine had shown Stella back through the house, placidly and unselfconsciously unclad as she was. She had said very little and when she did, Stella found her accent unfamiliar: it was a London accent, and yet not. When she found herself out in the street, she blinked, and had to collect herself for a moment. The drizzling rain had stopped, leaving grey skies in its wake. She walked back to the big pub called the Pineapple and looked back. The dingy Georgian terrace had gone; instead, a block of sixties flats stood in its place. Stella stared at this for several minutes. Somehow, she was not surprised.

She made her way across the river and into Westminster. Big Ben towered above the buildings, reminding her of New Year's Eve and the tolling of the hour. She strolled along Birdcage Walk and up through St James, then Hyde Park. The trees were all bare now, except for a few furry globes high in the plane trees, but the shrieking green parakeets – first escapees, then natives – still flocked and fought among the branches. In summer, their presence and that of ornamental foreign trees imported to Kensington Gardens often made Stella feel that she was somewhere other than England.

She came out onto the very unexotic Bayswater Road and thus eventually home. She let herself in to find Stella and Ward opening a bottle of champagne in the kitchen.

"Happy New Year!"

"Happy New Year to you, too. Thanks for your text. I got it this morning."

"Good timing," Ward said. He poured her a glass.

"Cheers! How was your New Year's Eve?"

"Peculiar," said Ward. "How was yours?"

"Yeah. That. Sorry I've only just got back. I've been at Ace's. And his friend Bill's." She related the story of her day and they listened in silence. When Stella delivered the punchline of Caspar Pharoah's name, Serena spluttered into her champagne.

"And this man, Bill – a star told him to look out for me? I expect that was Capella. A demon, though… Well, Stella, wait till you hear about *our* night."

It was Stella's turn to listen.

"There's some weird shit going down, for sure," she said at last. "You know, I do trust Ace even if he is quite dodgy, and his friend Bill – there was something about him."

"A lack of clothes?"

"Well, yes, that, but also he seemed – he had integrity, I'd say. We chatted a bit after he'd told us about Pharoah and he seemed straight down the line."

"But you said his house had disappeared."

"Can I have some more of that champagne? Thanks. I didn't get pissed last night because I was working so I think I might save it up for tonight... I think there is another London, alongside the London we know, and it's like White Horse Country and the Elizabethan world that Bee and I slipped into, Dark's world, the past, and they're all mixed up like Bee said to me at Christmas, like patchwork. The Secret Commonwealth, she called it. Bits and scraps of other places and times. I tell you what, hanging out with Ace is like being around Dr Bloody Who."

"Wasn't one of the assistants called Ace?" said Ward.

"I can't remember. Not in the new series, I don't think."

"Showing my age," Ward said gloomily.

"Oh come on, you're not that ancient. Yet. But I think Ace might be. Older than he looks, anyway. He's let slip that he remembers things – like the Thames barges – which haven't been around for quite a while."

"And you said this woman who had you on her radio show, Evie – she's Sam's *cousin?*"

"No, Sam's a friend of *her* cousin. So a phone call to Sam is called for, I think." But that was not to happen that evening, for Sam was not answering his phone and Bee, who sounded somewhat distracted, said that he had gone to see his nan. And still no sign of Luna.

No one got drunk, although they did finish the champagne and then a bottle of wine. Serena had made a vegetable lasagne and the evening was, for a change, peaceful. Ace had said he would be in touch and Stella had primed Ward for a trip to Norfolk.

"When do you start rehearsals again?"

"Not till next week. So it had better be a quick trip. Although I feel moderately confident about this play, I must say."

"When you left Pharoah's party last night," Stella said, "Did you see Miranda the Malevolent again?"

"No, Pharoah said she'd left of her own accord and thank God she did, is all I can say."

"Would you in fact have gone full-on cat fight?"

"Only if she'd started it," Serena said. "I wonder if we can persuade the little demon to transfer its affections?"

"Oh God, please don't take up conjuration," Ward said. "Although it's no more than she deserves. I haven't forgiven her for the shoe episode. Plus much else."

"Did you find out why she came to Pharoah's party in the first place?"

"No. I didn't tell anyone we were going. Serena says she didn't, either."

"But one person did know you were going," Stella said. "Caspar Pharoah."

"He hates Miranda, though."

"He *says* he does."

There was a short silence, then Stella added, "And given what Bill said about him…"

"I don't know what I should do," Serena said. "I'm supposed to be having this business meeting with him in a day or so. It's at his office, not a bar like last time."

"I think you should go. Check it out. String him along. Where is his office?"

"Down near Temple somewhere. He said it was new, the building's been undergoing renovation."

"If you go, maybe someone should go with you and wait in the foyer or something," Ward said. "Excuse me a minute. Champagne's having its effect." He disappeared upstairs in the direction of the bathroom. When his footsteps had faded, Serena leaned over the kitchen table and hissed,

"He kissed me!"

"Who? Caspar?"

"Yes. That bit where it went weird and he showed me the roses – he kissed me then. I didn't tell Ward because we were in the man's house at his party and things had become very strange, Stella – I wasn't even sure it really happened."

"Maybe it didn't. What's he like, anyway? Is he attractive?"

"Yes, very. In a different way to Ward. There's something charismatic about him. He's glamorous."

"Oh dear."

"I know." At this point Ward came back.

"So what's the plan with Ace, then, Stella?"

"He's going to let me know tomorrow. Serena, if we do need to go up to Norfolk, can I borrow your car? I'm assuming you're not coming?"

"I've got Bella back soon. And I've got to concentrate on getting some stuff together for Cas – for Pharoah. If you think it's a good idea still that I go to this meeting."

"I think it's an idea," Stella said. "Whether it's a good one remains to be seen."

LUNA

The sun had come up, dispelling the river mist. They were closer to the shore now and although the Severn had changed – the two big suspension bridges were not there, and neither were the ports and docks along the river – Luna could recognise the terrain, from the rolling Welsh hills on one side and the long neck of land that was Brean Down on the other. The current was taking them closer to the Welsh shore.

"We'll reach the dock soon," Aln said.

"Aln, where are we going? Is it Lydney?" But the girl, frowning, did not seem to know that name, so Luna amplified, "Where the Romans were?"

Aln's face cleared. "You know it? The dreaming place?"

"Yes, I've been there."

"We are all meeting there."

"All?"

"Those who stand against the Hunt, and others."

"And," Luna said carefully, "who are those people, then?"

"Many and different." She smiled. "You might meet some whom you know."

Alys? Luna wondered. She did not want to broach the subject of her mother; her mind skittered away from that subject. *Denial,* Luna told herself, *you're in denial. You don't want to face the fact that Mum might be on the wrong side.*

Aln pointed. "Look, there's the dock."

Luna could see a small wooden structure reaching out into the river. Two boats were already tied up alongside it, their sails furled. She knew little about boats but they did not look modern. An eye had been painted on the prow of one, like the protective eye found on boats in Turkey and other places around the Mediterranean, but it was not the same eye. It looked more Egyptian, but what would an Egyptian boat be doing here? She thought of the dark ship in her dream and shuddered.

"I will say now, Luna – I am glad we are here, at last. This is a place of safety. I had begun to wonder if we would reach it."

"I'm not surprised!"

A man was waiting at the end of the dock: Aln threw him a line and he caught it. He was stocky, middle aged, unremarkable except for the tunic and sandals that he wore, along with a brown cloak. He said nothing but reached out a hand to Luna and pulled her onto the boards of the dock, then did the same for Aln. The wose scrambled woodily onto the dock; the man showed no surprise at its presence.

From the dock, a path led up the hillside. It was still winter here, Luna noticed: bare withies of hazel stands and, later, the convoluted arterial map of oak. Her feet crunched on acorns. Soon, the temple itself came into view: startlingly Italianate in the English countryside, more out of place than it had seemed when she had visited it that night. Luna saw a cluster of white-plastered buildings, with the ridged russet tiles that she associated more closely with the Continent. But the Romans had brought their architecture with them to their furthest outpost, of course.

Inside the largest building was a long oblong hall, Luna again recognised the setting of her dream. The statue of the god was here, too – and there was Victorinus! She felt as though she had run into an old friend. But in her dream she had been a boy.

It did not seem to matter. Victorinus' face lit up when he saw her.

"Why, it's young Felix! As was. Who are you now?"

"My name is Luna," she said, shyly. "You – know who I am, then?"

"Of course, of course. We never forget a visitor. I'm glad you are here, and safe."

"I came with a girl called Aln, and Hob."

"Yes, we know them well. I knew their grandfather."

"But don't they come from – well. Somewhere else?"

Victorinus laughed. "So does everyone here. There is water and food in the next room, if you need it."

Luna realised that she was, in fact, very hungry. She followed his directions and found jugs of water, earthenware cups and plates of bread and cheese, plus bitter dark greens, young dandelion leaves, and onions. She stood with a platter, eating slowly and looking around her. Aln was nowhere to be seen but Luna glimpsed the wose and then someone else that she recognised with a shock, talking to Victorinus. The huntsmaster, the man she had last glimpsed when he had thrown her into the boat. Except that now he wore clothes that looked like something from an old hunting print, a black frock coat and high boots. Not so different from contemporary hunting clothes, Luna thought, but maybe Georgian? Victorian? She did not know enough about costume to be sure. She reflected that her own clothes – the layered skirts and woolen jumper – probably just made her look like a peasant, though perhaps a relatively well-off one. Would a peasant be lucky enough to wear stout boots, though? No, maybe not.

Luna finished her meal and, restored, went exploring. The huntsman had disappeared but there were many people here and she saw all manner of costumes, from an old woman in an impressive crinoline to a tunic-clad boy with the yellow eyes of a cat. He had a furtive air, as though he should not really be there, but Victorinus spoke to him kindly if gruffly and his face cleared with relief. Luna, knowing so few people, had no clue as to the dynamics that were going on and she didn't really understand the situation anyway, so although curious, she was content simply to observe.

A woman whom she had never seen before, in a fir green, sleeveless dress and amber beads, said, "Ah, Luna. The meeting will be soon. You won't know what to expect, I should think. Don't worry. I have a task for you now. And I am Hafren."

She was in her forties, perhaps, with a dark, beautiful face. She reminded Luna a little of the Behenian stars: there was a similar intensity in her gaze, and her black hair was dressed with green beads. But she carried no herb, unlike the star spirits.

"Pleased to meet you, Hafren. What is my task?"

"It's simple. You know where the dock is? There's a boat coming in. I need you to meet it."

"Okay," Luna said. "Is that all? I might not be very good at helping tie it up but I'll do my best. I'm not really much of a sailor."

Hafren laughed. "No, that's all right. The skipper will know what to do, don't you worry!"

"All right," Luna said, and she made her way out of the hall and past the shrine, and down along the side of a large herb garden, tidily raked for winter sleep. But she could still smell the scent of box, sharp in the chilly air. The sun was sinking now, behind the ridge of the Forest of Dean, and Luna could also smell the strong weed-salt odour of the river. Coming down the hill, she could see the banks plunging down towards the water and there, indeed, was a little boat coming upstream. Its brown sail was up and the evening wind, a south easterly, was driving it fast. Luna hurried up: at this rate the boat would be there before she was.

Just as she stepped out onto the dock, the boat was indeed coming in. She could see two people in it, one tall, with his back to the dock as he did something to the sails, and a smaller, hunched figure. Then the boat was gliding alongside and the tall figure turned but before he did so Luna would still have known him anywhere.

"Sam! Oh, Sam!"

His face crumpled. She had never seen that before. The smaller figure stood up and said, briskly, "Well, dear, I must say I thought we'd *never* get here, what with one thing and another, and we were hoping so much that you'd be here. Hello, Luna." And Sam's nan, Ver March, stepped out onto the dock, holding her skirts and ignoring Luna's glad outstretched hand.

BEE

Sam had gone in search of his grandmother. Luna and Aln were who knew where. Stella and Serena and Ward had gone back to London. The house felt very empty.

Alys was still there, but… Bee, currently engaged in cleaning the kitchen, would have almost preferred that she were not. A Trojan horse? Who knew? At least, thank God, Dark was around and Grandfather's spirit, if not greatly in evidence over Christmas (perhaps he was busy elsewhere?) could still be found in the churchyard.

But beyond the immediate family, Bee's main worry was Caro Amberley. Since Nick Wratchall-Haynes had brought her back over the saddle of his hunter, Caro had been confined to bed. Bee had only just recovered from the shock of thinking that Caro had died, that it was her corpse that the huntsman had been bearing on the back of the big chestnut. She still remembered her mother's gasp and the huntsman's quick response.

"It's all right. She's alive, but only just. I've called an ambulance."

After that the situation had devolved into phone calls to Richard and Laura, flashing blue lights and distant sirens. Alys had gone with Caro in the ambulance, while Bee had gone to get the car and follow them to Yeovil. Wratchall-Haynes had ridden home.

Bee and her mother waited, while Caro was wired up to tubes and a heart monitor. When Richard and Laura arrived, not long after that, Bee asked if they wanted her to stay.

"No. You've both done wonders. Thank you."

"Well, Nick Wratchall-Haynes was the one who actually found her. I don't know where she was." For the huntsmaster had forborne to say. "They're doing a lot of diagnostic tests, Richard, while she's in here. They may well find out what's wrong."

But Bee did not think that they would, somehow. A day or so later, Caro was discharged, with no conclusive diagnosis. Richard proved a strict gatekeeper, telling people that she was too unwell to see people, that it had been a combination of shock and a bad chill. The hospital had been concerned about pneumonia. But Bee and Alys both thought that this was untrue.

"He won't want her telling people what she's seen," Alys had said at the time, sitting at the kitchen table with her chair turned to face the Aga. Her long legs, jeans clad, were stretched out to the warmth. She nursed a glass of whisky in her hand and her downcast face had been inscrutable.

"And what might that have been, Mum?"

"I don't know."

"I think you do." Ooh, gloves off, thought Bee.

"I've told you. I don't know everything, or even a lot. Just scraps and patches. I don't think there's anyone alive – in any time or place – who has mapped the whole thing, who knows the full story. We each have our own little stories. You do, after all."

"Yes."

"Bee – one's instinct as a mother is to protect your children. And sometimes knowledge can be dangerous."

"Is that why you're not telling us everything you know?"

"Some of it. But some – I just don't feel I know enough to talk about it yet. I think maybe I should have gone to see Ver March again, with Sam."

"Are you planning on – heading out, again? Soon."

Alys looked her daughter directly in the face. "Do you want me to?"

"No. This is your home. I'm simply asking."

"No, Bee, I'm not, because I am so very worried about Caro. I'm worried about Ben, too, but I don't know where he is and it's possible that he has just met some girl and gone off to the Riviera or wherever – do people still do that these days?"

"Probably."

"I suspect not, though. I think he might be in real trouble. But Caro is here and findable and she is my immediate concern."

That conversation was still fresh in Bee's memory and she was running over it again when the kitchen door swung open and Alys came in.

"Bee, I just drove past Richard Amberley's Jag: he was heading up onto the A39 going north. Laura was with him. I know he had to go up to Bath for something or other soon, some business thing – he mentioned it the other night."

Sometimes, although Bee felt that communication had been sorely lacking between herself and her mother in recent months, they did not need to speak.

"I'll get back in the car," Alys said.

"I'll find my shoes."

The windscreen wipers lashed the oncoming rain from side to side, but Alys had put them on full. The fields were still badly flooded and the main road out of Hornmoon was at one point under water; Alys was taking another route to avoid it, she said. She drove faster than Bee was comfortable with, if expertly, slowing once into what was almost a skid down one of the narrow lanes, as a tractor suddenly appeared around a bend.

"Steady on, Stirling Moss," Bee said, clutching the door.

"Sorry," her mother murmured, taking the Land Rover over a series of humps. The road here, built on top of shifting peat, was like a small roller coaster: terrible on the suspension of all but the most robust vehicle. Bee, accustomed to it, was nevertheless relieved when they pulled back out onto the main road opposite Amberley.

"There's a light on in the top of the house – look."

"Do you think Richard and Laura saw you?"

"I don't know. They obviously saw the car but it's covered in mud and I had a hat on and my scarf, so I'm hoping they didn't realise it was me. His Jaguar's not here, though, and Laura's is, that little Renault."

"Well, we shouldn't need to be so furtive!" Bee said, feeling defensive. "After all, we're old friends."

"I'm hoping it's just that Richard's being all male and over protective."

"Yes, that." Bee hopped out of the car and into the squelching yard. Although it had been swept, wisps of hay had blown in and were now sodden. They made their way to the back door, no one in the country ever going round the front, and found that it was unlocked.

"God, I feel like a burglar."

"You're really not cut out for a life of crime, are you, Bee?"

"I'd be off work from stress if it was my day job."

They made their way through the silent house. Amberley was almost as familiar to them as Mooncote, Bee reflected, though not so much the upper storey except for the room where, last year, she had organised a deceased relative's library.

"Which is Caro and Richard's room? Is it that big one on the end?"

"It's down the end of the corridor, yes. I've visited her when she had the flu, this is no different," Alys said, firmly.

As they drew near, the boards creaked beneath their feet. A voice quavered, "Richard, is that you?"

"No, it's Alys and Bee!"

"Alys! Oh, Alys!"

Bee pushed the bedroom door open. Caro lay huddled in the big bed, looking as small as a child.

"Caro," Alys said. "What in the world is wrong with you?"

Bee, who had been shocked before at Caro's appearance, was now shocked all over again. Caro, who had been, like Alys a tall and willowy woman, seemed to have shrunk further. She looked ancient, almost mummified. A bony, tiny hand groped out towards Alys.

"Don't leave me, Alys. Please."

"Sweetheart, I'm not going to. Are we, Bee?"

"Of course not, not if you need us," Bee said, wrenched with pity. "Caro, we came before but Richard –"

"He wouldn't let you in, I know. He doesn't understand. It's too hard for him. He thinks I'm dying."

"And are you?"

"Mum!"

"We have to try and find out what's going on, Bee."

"I don't know," Caro whispered. "This shouldn't be me it's happening to. It's Richard's family who – who are whatever they are."

"What's that, Caro?"

"Witches. Magical – I don't know. Richard won't talk about it, pretends it's not real. Ward knows, though. I'm not sure how much, not very much, I think, but he remembers things from when he was a child."

"Such as?"

"Richard and Ward's grandmother – there were rumours in Hornmoon that she could change her shape, turn into other things. Not just animals, but other kinds of things. And that she could alter people's fate. I tried talking to Richard about it when we first got married and he said it was all superstitious rubbish. She'd died years

259

before, I barely knew her. She seemed perfectly normal to me. But then in the autumn, Ward – Ward said something to me, about your disappearance, Alys."

"Weird shit happens, Caro. Apparently."

"It all seemed so – it scared me. Not because I thought it was real but because people I'd always seen as quite rational and reasonable started behaving so strangely. Like some sort of collective madness... But then I started hearing things. I told your daughters, Alys, I saw them in the church at Christmas and I said then."

"I know what you told them," Bee said. Alys arched an eyebrow at her.

"Oh, do you? You didn't tell me."

"There was a lot going on at Christmas," Bee said feebly, but she thought Alys must have realised that it was really a lack of trust. Briefly, she explained.

"Since then, it's got worse," Caro went on. "I see it all the time. The thing, whatever it is. It never seems to sleep, it just paces, endlessly, to and fro. It's as though it's trapped."

"Do you know what it is?"

"No. It's big. And the smell is always there, I can't seem to get rid of it. It's driving me mad. And there's Ben."

"What, Ben is – with this thing?"

"No, but it's something to do with him, I think. I suddenly *knew*... I knew he was alive. I could feel him, and I couldn't before. I felt as though he was standing in front of the house and calling for help and he couldn't come in... so I went out to look for him. Only I got lost and then... I don't remember. There was a man on a horse."

"Yes, Nick Wratchall-Haynes. You know him. He found you. He brought you back," said Bee.

"I didn't recognise him."

"I'm going to try something, Caro," Alys said. "Don't be afraid."

She passed a hand over her face and when she drew it away, something came with it. It was filmy and translucent, barely visible, like a veil which retained an impression of Alys' own features.

Like a mask.

But beneath, Alys looked unchanged.

"Mum," Bee said, sharply, "What *is* that?"

"A way of seeing. Caro, look through this."

She held it close to Caro's wizened face but the woman's eyes widened. "No, no! Take it away!"

"All right," Alys said. "I won't be able to see anything through this except – what I see already. Bee, could you try?"

Bee did not want to do any such thing, but she thought she ought to be brave if it might furnish some answers. She allowed Alys to hold the thing – really, it was almost like a kind of skin, with faint lights in it – up to her face, and bent as close to it as she could, so that she could see through the holes of its eyes.

She did not know what to expect. At first, there was darkness. She was dimly aware of the bedroom around her, still visible in her peripheral vision. But then she felt herself standing up. Bee looked down. Instead of her own well-padded form, in its jumper and jeans, she found long legs, sandal-clad, and a tunic belted around a waist that was a lot slimmer than Bee's own. She put her hands to her face, noting the long fingers: on one, there was a small golden ring. But her mass of curls felt the same, her face felt the same. Perhaps she only looked different. She touched the belt at her waist and felt something hard and bulky digging into her hip. When she investigated, it turned out to be a scabbard. Bee took the hilt of the thing it contained and half pulled it out: a short bronze sword, in the elegant shape of a leaf.

At least she was armed. Whoever she was.

She was standing in a tunnel. The floor was tiled in red and the walls, curving to an arched ceiling, were plastered in a rough pink wash. Conscious of a fluttering anticipation in her stomach, Bee tiptoed forwards, knowing that she needed to be as quiet as possible. She kept one hand on the sword at her hip. The smell that Caro had mentioned, shit and blood, was growing stronger and she could see stains on the floor and walls. It was an unhealthy, stifling place, very hot, as though Bee walked into a furnace.

She paused. She could hear something breathing, almost snorting. It was coming from up ahead and, very cautiously, Bee peered around the bend. There was a chamber, quite big, with piles of dung scattered across the floor. She could see a huge ring set into the opposite wall, with a heavy chain dangling from it, but there was nothing attached to the other end of the chain. Very slowly, feeling that the pounding of her heart must surely be audible, Bee drew the sword.

She could hear something large moving about, and that breathing... But she could not see anything. Then, suddenly, the entrance was blocked by an enormous shape and Bee's ears rang with a bellow of misery and pain. She gasped and stumbled back. The thing rushed towards her but before it could trample her, the mask was torn from her face, where it had started to cling, and Alys was crying sharply,

"Bee! Come back, come back. Open your eyes."

She had not known that they were closed. The bedroom looked so ordinary after the tunnel that Bee nearly shut her eyes again in relief. She looked down at herself. All normal.

"God," Bee whispered. Alys reached out and gripped her wrist, too hard.

"What did you see?" she hissed.

Bee told her. It was the expression on her mother's face, almost avid, envious, that made Bee detach Alys' hand from her wrist, quite firmly.

"I don't know what the thing was. It was upright. But it was bigger than a man. A lot bigger."

"And that's all you saw?"

"That's all I saw." Perhaps Alys didn't quite trust Bee, either.

"It's what I see," Caro murmured from the bed.

"If you're seeing that all the time, I'm not surprised you're going downhill," Bee said.

"Neither am I," responded her mother. "The thing is, how are we going to stop it?"

They left before Richard returned. Caro had promised not to tell. Bee did not like this; there were too many secrets. Many of those concerned her mother. She looked at Alys sidelong as they bumped home in the Land Rover: Alys's face looked unchanged. What had happened to the mask? And what was it, anyway? Bee had a lot of questions and one of these concerned the bone flute, an ancient thing belonging to the family, that Alys had taken away with her when she had left again in the autumn. What had become of the flute? Bee asked her mother this directly, as they pulled back onto the main road.

"It's in a safe place."

"Here, in this world?"

"No, not in this one."

"Then can I ask, Mum, how you *know* it's safe?"

She expected Alys to be defensive but instead her mother sighed.

"I don't know, one hundred percent, darling. You can never be absolutely sure with anything – in other worlds or in this one. I hope it's safe and I trust the people who are looking after it."

That, Bee thought, might be as good as she'd get. Time for another question.

"And this patchwork of – of places and times. Is there anything resembling a map? Of entry and exit points, for example?"

"What an intelligent question, Bee." Her mother spoke approvingly, not patronising. Bee stopped bristling as soon as she realised this. "In a way, that's my new job. Mapping. And other people are doing the same. An informal network of otherworldly cartographers. I can show you my plans of the Gipsy Switch, if you like. That's my main beat. I have one other partial map of some of the other entry points in London. But it's very incomplete and possibly not reliable. I – paid for that one."

"With money?"

"No, not with money." Alys' mouth tightened. "It's a very recent acquisition and I got it because I thought the girls ought to have it."

"I'd like to see it and I think Serena and Stella should definitely have a copy."

She had expected prevarication but instead Alys said, "Yes. We can take a photo and email or Whatsapp it. Do they have – plans? In London?"

"I don't know. Possibly." Again, Bee felt that reluctance to bring her mother fully into the picture. Perhaps she ought to get over that, though? It was as though there was an invisible wall of mistrust between them: things unsaid, things unsayable. If only she could be sure that Alys was on the right side, but which side *was* that? And was it really Alys herself anyway? She thought of the Hunt and her doubts flooded back.

Rather to her surprise, Alys fetched the map at once, on their return to the house. It was on a single sheet of A4, not ancient parchment: Bee felt vaguely disappointed. She studied it: the map was based on a small plan of the city and some points were hard to see.

"It's only points along the river. You see what I meant when I said it was incomplete."

"This paper's modern. Do you know who compiled it?"

"It's someone in London. I don't know who he is – I only met him once. I contacted him a few days ago and he copied his original plan for me. I think he might be an academic; he reminded me of Abraham."

"That's good to know. Reassuring, somehow." She picked up the map. "I'm going to scan this with my phone and send it to Stella."

Alys nodded. "Let's hope it might be useful."

PART THREE:
WHEN EVERYTHING
MUST COME DOWN

SERENA

Serena stood at the base of the building, looking up. It was not as tall as the Shard, but it reminded her of the Southwark building all the same: a high, sky-piercing spire. Unlike the cloud-reflecting Shard, however, this was steel and black, tinted windows shutting out the sun. Not that there was much of that today. Eleven o'clock in the morning and the raindrops were already pattering onto the fabric of Serena's umbrella. She had dressed warmly today, with the little silver hare that Luna had given her for Christmas at her throat for luck. She had chosen pale pink cashmere and a wrap skirt in a deeper shade and it was only when she had left the house and was sitting on the Tube that she wondered why she had selected these rosy colours today. Then she began to worry that Caspar might think it was deliberate, a delicate allusion to the party. And maybe it was. *Oh, Serena*, she thought to herself. *Why do you do these things?* All these family stories, about the inability of Fallow women to be tied to one man... But the current generation weren't doing so badly. Except for herself. Stella didn't count: she had said to Serena that she wasn't interested at the moment and wasn't looking. One could hardly regard Ace as a love interest.

She did not like to think of herself as fickle, though perhaps it was the truth: *you moved on quickly enough from Ben, didn't you? Even though you really loved him.* But it wasn't just that and Serena knew it. Caspar Pharoah frightened her. So amiable, so charming, so sinister. The party had alarmed her and Serena knew that she had felt like a frightened rabbit ever since she'd met him; caught in a web, or in headlights. This was why she was hesitating now, despite the rain splashing down all around her and everyone else scurrying to their destinations. This meeting was yet another trap. But if she didn't go inside, she would never know what he had in mind. And Stella and Ward would be waiting close by, in the coffee shop down the road, next door to Temple Tube: Stella had texted her once they arrived, having been on an errand for the trip, apparently. Once she had emerged safely from her meeting with Pharoah, they were going to pick up Ace and head up to Norfolk, to Hex Heath. And Serena would be safe at home, with Bella, who was returning from her dad's that afternoon in time for school when term started a few days later.

"If you don't come out of that building – we'll come looking for you. Don't worry," Stella had said.

Stella made her mind up. Furl the umbrella – unlucky to take an unrolled umbrella indoors, family superstition had always said – and march inside. She knew she looked smart and her reflection in the mirrored doorway of the atrium confirmed this. Inside, she found herself in a marble palace: stone floors and high ceiling, with a modern kind of abstract chandelier hanging from it. An enormous black desk ran along one side, glossy as the bottom of a well. No less than three receptionists sat at intervals behind it. Serena chose the least intimidating one.

"Good morning, madam," the receptionist said brightly. "Have you come to see the museum?"

"No, I didn't know there was one. I'm Serena Fallow. I have an appointment with Caspar Pharoah, up in Everlight Holdings, at eleven fifteen…"

"Of course. I'll let him know you're here. Please take a seat."

Serena did so and noticed some leaflets strewn on the table in front of her. She picked one up, noticing that it featured the name of the building she was in, and what looked like columns. Roman remains? There was a sign along the atrium, saying MUSEUM and pointing downwards. Serena was about to read the leaflet but the receptionist motioned to her.

"He'll see you now, Ms Fallow. It's on the twelfth floor. It's the whole suite but Mr Pharoah's door is marked and it's on the left."

"Thank you so much," Serena murmured. The lift whisked her upwards, swiftly and silently, and she stepped out into a thick-carpeted corporate space, the kind that seems to swallow sound, with a plaque on the opposite wall that stated the name of the company: *Everlight Holdings,* in an elegant script. The colours were rich and muted: deep bronze and browns. She turned left and found Caspar's office immediately. Serena knocked.

"Come in!"

He was on his mobile, but gestured towards a seat. The office was oak panelled and book lined; it looked as though someone had taken a Georgian gentleman's library and spirited it up into the heights. Serena looked past Pharoah to the ever-fascinating view of London: church spires and domes, the sweep of the Thames, and the wheel of the

London Eye beyond. She picked out the brutalist slabs of the National Theatre. Pharoah shoved the phone into a drawer; he had said nothing, not even a farewell.

"Serena, good morning. It's quite a view, isn't it?"

"I love these high up offices. No wonder your desk's facing away from the window. If I was in here I'd spend all my time gawking out."

Pharoah laughed. "It's exactly why the desk's where it is. I'm the same. So how are you today?"

"Good, thank you. It was a lovely party."

"I got your very sweet thank you note courtesy of the Royal Mail. So lovely to see that some people still actually *write.*"

"I sometimes think it's a bit pretentious, but we were brought up in a rather old fashioned way, so…"

"And I must apologise again for the incident with Miss Dean. I'm so sorry."

"It was okay in the end. She just seemed to disappear."

"Yes, I was intending to ask her to leave, but I couldn't find her. I suppose she threw her bomb and ran away."

The image made Serena laugh. "Like an anarchist in one of those cartoons from the nineteen hundreds."

"Yes, with a bomb that says BOMB on it."

"I shouldn't laugh, sorry…"

"It's by far the best response. I gather you handled it very well. Now, can I get you some coffee? Yes? Milk? All right. And then let's forget the tiresome Miranda and get down to business…"

An hour and a half later Serena, rather dizzy with figures, was ushered to the lift.

"I won't come down with you – I'm so sorry not to see you out but someone's due to be coming straight up, back to back meetings, I'm afraid, as everyone gets over Christmas…"

"The businessman's lot," said Serena. "Thank you so much for seeing me."

"I feel this is all really positive. I'm very excited about it"

"So am I." And she really was. "I'll get you everything by the end of the week."

"That would be splendid."

A firmly professional handshake and Serena was in the lift again, this time being sent downwards at speed. She gave a small gasp of relief. But when the lift doors hushed open, she did not find herself in reception.

STELLA

"She's later than she said she'd be." Stella took an anxious sip of her latte.

"What was it, quarter past eleven to quarter past twelve?"

"Yeah. I wonder why the quarter past the hour? You'd think business meetings ran hourly."

"Maybe Pharoah wanted elevenses?"

"He's not eight years old." Stella glanced at Ward, who was staring through the big windows of the coffee shop. "What?"

"For a minute I thought I saw fucking Miranda. But I don't think it was."

"Where?" Stella stood up.

"In the crimson mac."

"Right. I've never met her. Although I've seen her on screen."

"You've been spared. I expect I'm just paranoid. Seeing things. I thought I glimpsed her yesterday in Tesco Express but it was a totally different woman. Anyway, Miranda wouldn't be seen dead in anywhere less than Waitrose."

"Probably just paranoid," echoed Stella. "Anyway, she's going in the wrong direction."

"What time is it now?"

"Twenty to one. That ciabatta was a good idea, Ward – we can make sure Serena's safe and then get straight on the road without worrying about lunch."

"Such was my thought."

"When is Bella coming back?"

"Later on this afternoon. She said she'd text Serena but it was likely to be about four. She's a reliable kid."

"Yeah, she's a lot more punctual than I ever was at that age. Or indeed, now." She looked at Ward. "Calm down. You're starting to twitch."

"Sorry."

"People will think I'm your carer."

"Stella!"

"Made you laugh, though." She turned to the coffee shop, which in that section was mainly empty, and said in a loud voice, "He's doing very well, now that the drugs have started working."

"Stella, shut up!" But he was smiling. Good, thought Stella. She was a lot more nervous about this meeting with Pharoah than she was letting on, given what Serena had told her. But she could not let Ward know that. A secret was a secret, especially between sisters. She took a surreptitious look at her phone. Quarter to one, and still nothing.

"I told Ace we'd be down there at half one. By the way I printed off that scan Bee sent me – you know, the gateways on the river – and I've given it to Ace. He said he'd look into it."

"Does he know about them already?"

"He said what Mum told Bee was right: no one knows all the ins and outs, if you see what I mean. He knew some of the ones along the river on Mum's little map and I got the impression that he knows others. Well, he obviously does – he's taken me to some of them. He said Bill knows a lot of them, too."

"It's not that far off half past now. I know Ace's place is only just over the river but given the speed of the traffic…"

"He'll wait, Ward. Oh – there she is!"

Serena, looking pale but composed, was pushing open the coffee shop door.

"Hey! How did it go?"

"It was fine. No problems." She kissed Ward on the cheek. "Hello, sweetie. Sorry I was so long. A lot of business to get through but it was a really professional meeting."

Ward took her hand. "You're really cold!"

"It's a chilly day. "

"Are you going straight back home?" Stella said. "We need to belt down to Southwark."

"I'll be fine."

"Look after yourself." Ward kissed her in return. "We'll keep you posted and see you soon."

Serena nodded. "I might have a quick cappuccino now I'm here. And something to eat."

"I recommend the ciabattas."

"Sounds great."

They left her sitting, composed, with a copy of the Guardian and a coffee on the way, and headed for the car park where Stella had left Serena's little car.

"You're very quiet," said Stella, as they searched for change for the parking meter.

"Serena's never called me 'sweetie' in her life."

"No, come to think of it, I don't think I've heard her say that either. Why do these things always spit one of the coins out?"

But eventually she got the machine to work and in a few minutes, they were pulling out into the city traffic, windscreen wipers on full. Stella forgot about Ward's comment, but later, much later, in the night on the North Sea, she thought of it when she was drifting to sleep and it brought a memory with it, one which she could not grasp and which whisked away from her into dreaming.

Now, she took them over Waterloo Bridge, crawling behind a double-decker, but it gave her time to look at the imposing columned side of Somerset House, and then upriver. The Thames was gunmetal and choppy today, churned by rain. She thought of the forts and found that it was not a memory from which she flinched. She had been part of something that night. She just didn't know what.

Once across the bridge, she threaded her way through the streets to Southwark.

"And no sat nav, either!" Ward said in admiration. "You should do the Knowledge."

"It takes longer than a university degree."

"I know a couple of actors who did it. Black cab driving being a bit more reliable and lucrative than the theatre."

"I know a DJ who did it. I don't think it's me, though. Anyway, here we are."

And a good thing that Ace's house, unlike that belonging to the mysterious Bill, appeared to have stayed put. Ace himself emerged out of the front door as Stella pulled up, carrying a couple of carrier bags.

"I hope that's not cat food," Ward said, opening the boot.

"None of your lip. One of these is my overnight bag. The other contains some essential materials which I hope I won't need."

The bag clanked as he put it into the boot. Stella had resolved not to ask any questions. But Ace had some of his own.

"Which way are you planning to go, Stella?"

"Greenwich and then the Dartford Tunnel and up onto the A12. Chelmsford, basically. There's a roadmap on the back seat, Ace. Either hang onto it or give it to Ward. We might need it."

"God, I never thought I'd have to go to Chelmsford." Ward was appalled.

"We're not going *into* Chelmsford. We're shooting past it."

"Thank Christ."

"I'm really getting to know this end of the river," Stella said.

"I wouldn't get too excited. It's the end with Southend in it, after all."

"We're not going there, either. Although I shot past it the other night."

"Where are we actually staying tonight? I take it we're not planning on making it back to town. It's what, three hours' drive?"

"About that and no, we're not going back tonight. I have booked us three rooms in a Travel Lodge outside Lowestoft. Sorry, Ward, I know this is not exactly the Riviera, but needs must!"

"Little did I think," Ward said, closing his eyes briefly, "that I would be spending the start of the year in a Travel Lodge in Lowestoft."

"Think of it as being on the boards," Ace said. "Have you done any rep?"

"Oh yes. I have even been to Lowestoft, which has no less than three theatres, in a production of *The Importance of Being Earnest*. I was twenty. It rained a lot."

"No change there then."

"There were some not-bad pubs though. I was hopelessly in love with the girl who played Cecily Cardew, who was engaged in a torrid affair with one of the set builders."

"Oh dear. There weren't fisticuffs, I hope."

"No, and she would probably have won if there had been. Cecily was a slip of a thing but the set builder woman was built like a rugby forward. And she was actually very nice. It was just one of those things."

From the back seat, Ace snorted. "I know the kind of situation."

"So is Anione your partner or what? Sorry to be nosy."

Stella was glad Ward had asked that question.

"No, it's all right. Sort of. On and off. She's a bit of a law unto herself, frankly, but that's all right with me. She does as she pleases. But she's around a lot, which is also all right with me."

"Fair enough. Is that the Dartford Tunnel coming up? Do you need any change?"

"I think I can pay by contactless," Stella said and this proved to be the case. The dreary suburbs slid by and in another hour they were well out into the countryside. Chelmsford slid by, then Colchester, then Ipswich, and they drew closer to the North Sea coast.

"Very flat, round here," Ward observed. "Sorry to be Captain Obvious."

"I like it. Rolling ploughed fields and copses. There was a big snaky river mouth back there, too."

"I think that was the Orwell. I don't know this end of the country so well," Ace said. "Kind of interesting, to see it. You want to stick on the A12, Stella, and then the A47 towards Great Yarmouth, but that's after Lowestoft."

"What's the actual plan, guys? It's going to be dark when we get there. So I'm assuming we want to hit Hex Heath in daylight? What do you think, Ace? Check into the Travel Lodge and find a pub for dinner? Or go to the house instead?"

Ace was quiet for a minute or two, then he said, "Part of me thinks it would be interesting to check Hex Heath out at night, but it might be a bit *busy*, if you get what I'm saying. So maybe checking into the Travel Lodge and supper, and then an early night, or alternatively a hard drinking session until closing time, depending on democratic vote, and getting up there around dawn. When anything really nasty ought to be heading for its bed and we can at least bloody see."

"It's a plan," Stella told him, and Ward nodded.

"I reckon it's about half an hour's drive from Lowestoft, so if we get up early and head out, as you say..."

"Okay, let's do that," said Ace, as they headed onto the Lowestoft road. It was by now close to dark, but Stella could still see the North Sea, opening out to the eastern horizon, a relentless expanse of grey. It reminded her of the forts. She wondered what they might hear, there in the night, and she was suddenly grateful that she had chosen a Travel Lodge, that blandest and most banal of hotel accommodation. Surely, nothing eldritch could beset you in so mundane a place.

LUNA

"Sam!" Luna hauled the boat as close as she could alongside the dock and tied it up. By this time, Ver March had already clambered onto the dock itself.

"No, I don't need a hand, thank you, lovey. I think I can manage. Mind you, I've said that before now and – no. It's nice to see you again, Luna. How's the baby coming along?"

Luna felt herself close to tears. She swallowed and said, "It's all right. I thought it might, you know, not be, a couple of times. What with everything."

"I told Sam he should never have let you go off alone but I don't suppose anyone could help it, could they? These things tend to take you by surprise."

"I only went to feed the horses," Luna said.

Sam, Luna saw, was a bit damp eyed himself. He said, hugging her, "Are you all right? We were really worried. Everyone's been worried. *Moth* was worried – I left him behind at the house, by the way."

"I know. I just had to – go with things. I didn't have a choice. You know where we are, Sam? It's Lydney."

"Yes, Gran found you. She had word from someone."

"I must say, it's rather pretty round here, isn't it? I know Gloucestershire a little bit but I expect it's changed. Look at this lovely red soil. I should think you could grow plenty in that." Ver March beamed approval.

"Everyone's up at the – the dreaming place. The temple. It's Roman. But there are a lot of different people here."

"Yes," Ver said. "There would be."

"Aln is here! And the hunt master from Hornmoon. I asked. Nick Wratchall-Haynes."

"What?" Sam looked genuinely astonished. Then he laughed. "I didn't think you'd ever end up hanging out with a MFH, Luna. You'll be sipping a stirrup cup next."

"Glad to hear it," said Ver. "Good old fashioned part of country life."

Sam sighed. "Oh, Gran. Along with snaring bunnies and poaching badgers and rook pie, I suppose."

"What's wrong with that?"

"I totally disapprove of him," Luna said. "But I think he's all right. I hate to say. I think he saved my life."

"Well, he must be if he's here. This is a very safe place, you see, Luna. One of the few."

"Good to know! It feels all right. And I had a dream…"

Up at the temple, she told them. Ver March listened, with her eyes bright and her lips pursed.

"I don't hold with all this past life stuff, you know. I don't think it really works like that. I think it's more that time doesn't behave like we think it does and why should it? When you think about it. It's nothing to do with us, really."

"Do *you* know people here, Gran?" Sam said. "A lot of them seem to know you." For Ver March had been greeted with smiles of recognition and knowing looks. A woman in an indigo dress, draped over one arm, her hair a complex head-dress of tight curls, had laughed when she saw the old lady and said, "I might have known *you'd* show up, Vervain." Though not in a nasty way.

"Portia, lovely to see you again, dear."

She had insisted on bowls of soup. "You might have just had lunch, Luna, but you've a baby on the way and you never know when you might get the chance to eat again. Ah, this must be your friend Aln. I knew someone like you, once, lovely. With the green skin and all."

Aln smiled. She sat down at the table with them.

"Hello. I know who you are, too. One of the tribes."

"That's right. And you are from the Green Land. You've come a long way. They say the sun's very small from where you are."

Aln looked a little sad, Luna thought. She said, "A long way and I don't know if I'll ever see it again."

Ver squeezed her hand. "I'm sure you will. Everyone makes it home one day."

"But not today." Aln returned the squeeze. "We have work to do."

Luna, later, found it hard to remember what took place next in the big main hall. Someone addressed them, walking through the assembled ranks of people, but she found it hard to look at them directly. She did not know if they were male or female. She tried to see out of the corner of her eye but they seemed to change and she was conscious that she was transgressing. They were very beautiful, she knew that, and for the first time in her life she was conscious of an emotion that she realised, eventually, was not fear, but awe. She felt a little as she did when in the presence of the Behenian stars, but the star spirits were familiar and therefore not so – unsettling.

But she had met a god, before: Nodens, the bright river's son. In her mind there was laughter at his name and a voice, very faint, "only a little god, you see." So perhaps this person was something greater.

She asked Ver March, when it was over, but Sam's gran only gave her a beady look and said, "Who, dear? I'm not sure which one you mean." Luna thought she knew very well. She trusted Ver, though, and if Ver did not want to tell her, there had to be a reason. The younger Luna would have balked at this assumption of authority and become cross and defiant, but now she simply found herself nodding.

"So," Ver said. "We will be heading south, with Aln, and we need to check in with your hunting chap, when he comes back from wherever he's got to. I think he's speaking to someone. That's the plan. We have something to do."

"What about the wose?"

"Hob is going to the wood," said Aln. "Into the Forest."

"Best place for him if you ask me – it's where he belongs, not these haunts of men."

"Where are we going?" Luna asked. There had been a name, but she could not remember it now.

"Ystraigyl. The river bend."

"I don't know where that is."

"You do, actually," Sam said. "It's the old name for Chepstow."

"Oh! Where the castle is. Was. Will be."

"Talking of which," Ver March said, "we need to keep an eye on the time. Because it's slipping and sliding all over the place at the moment. And we have a date to meet."

That night, Luna woke. It was the opposite of the dream, in which she had drifted into this world; now she was wide awake and clear headed. Sam slept beside her in the hard narrow bed, across the room Ver was bundled into an alcove, while Aln lay curled on a rush mat on the floor. None of them stirred and it occurred to Luna that they might not have done so had she shouted out loud.

She went to the door and gently opened it: it led out onto a long terrace that ran the length of the building. The courtyards and verandahs of the south still pertained. There was even a vine, curling up one of the struts and heavy with small green grapes, no bigger than peas and glistening in the moonlight. Luna looked up. The moon soared overhead, full and familiar. There was plenty of light by which to see.

A safe place, Ver had said. Luna felt this, too. She stepped down from the verandah, still bundled up in her clothes, and made her way down to the dock. There was something she needed to do, a very strong feeling, but she did not know what it was. There were shadows in the moonlight but the dreaming place felt safe indeed. Nothing disturbed Luna on her way down the path, into the cool scent of the rivershore. When she got there, however, she found that things had changed once more.

There was no sign of the dock. Instead the river stretched away, huge as a sea. She could no longer see the opposite shore, close to where Bristol began in her own day, with the big bridges arching across the Severn. The water sparkled in the morning sunlight, mist rising up from the river and coiling away. There was the family again, down on the shore. They were human but she could see their wren-forms, too, superimposed upon the scene, the tiny birds scurrying like mice over the mud. The woman had a stick and was digging. With an exclamation, she brought up a muddy shell, held it up, waved. Then she put it into a rough woven basket slung around her neck. The man was playing with the children, a game of chase along the foreshore. They looked dirty and happy. Luna smiled and then she remembered the wave, the Bore, like the Bore which had carried them up the river to Lydney and the temple. The wave which might sweep this family away.

But there was no wave now. The river remained calm and untroubled, except for a small breeze which ruffled its surface. The distant shouts of the ancient children and the yearning cries of the gulls were all that was audible. The little girl ran down the foreshore, feet splashing in the wet mud, and she left a line of silver footprints, dancing down the shore. They did not fade but the child did: gradually, the hawthorn scrub along the bank became visible through her body until she was as insubstantial as the mist. Then she was gone. Luna stood alone, under starlight.

"Your mum," said Ver March, over the early breakfast: crusty bread and honey and milk. "I've been meaning to say something but it's not my place. I wanted to speak to you alone, without Sam or Aln, because it's not really their business, although it might become so."

Luna found herself alert, almost trembling. "What is it, Ver?"

"Well. I've only met your mum the once. In White Horse Country, that time. But I'm not sure that's right, you see. I think I might have met her before, but I'm not sure."

"Okay."

"And I talk to people, you know that, and word filters back. Now, I don't want to speak out of turn about your mother –" She lowered her voice, "I won't use her name – but she's been running with a dangerous crowd."

Luna, very inappropriately, burst out laughing. "Sorry! Oh Ver. I really am sorry and I am taking this seriously, obviously. But it's like we're talking about a teenager."

Ver laughed as well. "No, I know what you mean. And your mum's only a bit younger than me although I have to say, she doesn't look it – she's a lovely lady, could have been a model."

"She was, when she was younger. In a sort of amateur way. But she was in Vogue and all sorts. Lord Snowdon took her picture once."

"Did he really? Well, I can't say I blame him. It's the bone structure, you see."

Luna nodded. She had not inherited Alys' fine bones, although Serena and Stella had. Luna was round faced and rosy cheeked, like Bee. But Luna didn't really care about such things.

"And talking about bones… Your mum has made friends in the Hunt."

"I've seen the Hunt. They scared me."

"They scare everyone. It's what they're for."

"When we were in White Horse Country, some – men, sort of, came after us. On the lych path."

"Yes. Those were not the Hunt. I think of them as the undertakers – they take you under, you see, and you don't come back up again. But that's just my fancy, it's not what they're really called. They keep their real name secret, most people do. The Hunt's the same, but everyone calls them the Hunt, for ages now. I asked young Aln about it last night and she calls them the Gefliemen, and he who runs the pack the *hǽðstapa*, the Heath-Stalker, I think I'm saying that right, might not be, but some call him the Helwyr. I don't like saying these names, mind. I don't even like thinking about them."

"There were big white dogs," Luna said. "But they were also men."

"I know. Some of them can't help it – they're bound, you see. But they, and the undertakers, and some of the others, like a brother and sister you met once – they're not kin but sometimes they form alliances."

"What do they want, though?"

"They don't want what we want, that's for sure. Money or sex, 'scuse me for mentioning it. Or even power. Or world domination." She laughed. "Isn't that what the villain always wants in those films Sam likes? Superhero stuff or those spy ones. And the baddie always wants to rule the world. Well, in my experience, which in all modesty I may say is considerable by now, they don't want that. They don't want the bother, I expect. They want other things. Souls. Certain things, like a scrap of bone or an old flute you can whistle through. They want things to happen, which make or change a pattern. Some pieces of territory, which is a bit more understandable, I suppose."

"And you said Mum is involved? We thought she might be. Actually we were sure she was."

"None of you girls are stupid, from what Sam says, and you've all got eyes in your heads. Your mum might be keeping things from you or she might not. You know, you think you know people and then they turn against you, and they might not do so for things which you think are big things – like a pot of gold or a crown on their heads. They might turn on you for a frond of a fern or a lapwing's feather. All sorts of things. So if you ask me what your mum is after, or what game she thinks she's playing, I couldn't tell you. But it must be a big thing for her, else she'd be at home looking after her daughters, in my opinion. I'm not against this women's lib, far from it, but nothing should come between mother and child. As you'll find out."

"All we really know is –"

Ver nodded. "Running with the wrong crowd."

SERENA

Serena took a step from the lift and as soon as she did so, the doors slid shut, trapping her in the basement. She swore under her breath. Where were the stairs? And was this, perhaps, the 'museum' to which the signs had pointed? She pressed the button to summon the lift and waited, but there was no answering rattle up in the shaft and the doors remained firmly shut. After a moment, the illuminated green button grew flat and black.

Shit. She had arranged to join Ward and Stella after the meeting, but it had gone on longer than anticipated and she was now late. She pulled out her phone, which she had turned off ahead of the meeting with Pharoah, but there was no signal, possibly because she was now down in the basement. Typical! Sighing, Serena replaced the phone in her bag. They would be worried and moreover she was holding them up: Stella had said it was a long drive to Lowestoft and they did not want to be on the road too late.

She would just have to find the stairs.

The place was dimly lit, not fully dark: Serena could see a high ceiling and, across from the entrance to the lift, a glimmering pool. She went over to have a closer look. The pool – a water feature, in fact – was retained by a low wall and lit from within, and it shimmered golden-black. Behind it, water cascaded down a gilded curtain. It was perhaps twenty feet in length and rather beautiful. Serena walked along it, listening to the calm rush of water. She could hear something else, a rhythmic sound, like a giant hammer, far away. She paused to listen, but the water had the edge, drowning it out. Construction? Something down in the London underground? There was definitely something, a rumbling noise. Must be the Tube.

She came to a pair of frosted glass doors and hesitated. Then she pushed them, gently. They swung open with ease and Serena stepped into a golden hall, like an amphitheatre. Semi-circular rows of seats ringed the place in which she stood, and there was perhaps room for three hundred people. The wall behind was blank but presumably a screen could be set up. That's all it was, Serena thought: a lecture theatre, either for the companies above or perhaps some other organisation. The place smelled of money, somehow, with the lavish but muted fittings and the quietness. Except for that drum-like sound, which Serena could still hear, but very faintly now.

She trotted across the lecture theatre to the doors at the other end and opened them. Then she gasped, because someone was standing right behind the doors, inches from Serena herself: a woman in a long metallic gown, with her red hair unbound and flaming down her back. Her unblinking gaze was as blue as the Mediterranean sky, falling hot on Serena's skin and making her flush. She tried to close the door but the woman's hand shot out and closed around Serena's wrist, tight as a blood-pressure cuff.

"Oh no," said the woman, mockingly. "You're not going anywhere, love. Or you might be *late.*"

STELLA

The Travel Lodge, perched high on the outskirts of Lowestoft, had plenty of parking. It was also wonderfully quiet and the rooms had a kettle. Great, thought Stella. She sat on the perfectly ordinary grey and mauve duvet and texted Serena.

Arrived. All OK. Hope things good w u.

Her main duty for the night accomplished, Stella put the phone into her bag and went in search of what delights a small English coastal town in early January might have to offer. She found Ace and Ward sitting in the rudimentary foyer, looking at tourist brochures.

"Here's one. The Green Dragon, bit out of town. Sounds all right. It's got five stars. Although what that actually means, I don't know. This is not the Michelin Guide. Excuse me, love," this last to the receptionist. "Do you know a boozer round here called the Green Dragon?"

The receptionist looked up from her screen. "Yes. It's quite nice if you like that sort of thing. It's really old."

"Sounds tremendous," said Ward. "Do they do food?"

"I believe so. Would you like me to give them a ring?"

"That would be most kind."

Having established that the Green Dragon was indeed serving food, and that they would be happy, possibly delighted, to reserve a table for three for seven o'clock, and that a taxi could easily be summoned to transport people to it, Stella and Ace and Ward sat waiting for the cab to arrive.

"I don't think she's recognised you," Ace said to Ward, sotto voce, once the receptionist was off the phone.

"Thank God! Is that the cab? That was quick."

"We might be his only customer."

The Green Dragon claimed to date from 1630. It was oak beamed, had many small rooms and an open fire in the bar. The Christmas decorations were still up, just this side of Twelfth Night. Stella was by now tired, hungry and contemplating Wine o'Clock. Ace offered to pay for the first round and had ordered a large Sauvignon for her.

"I will have," Ward considered his options, "A pint of the Trawlerman, please. Is it local?"

283

"From just down the road."

"I'll have the same," Ace said.

"It's like you're a couple of old salts," said Stella.

"I feel a need to fit in. I imagine people looking at me, and thinking, he's a city boy if ever I saw one. Unlike men round here, who are men. And do things like fishing from trawlers."

"A Southern ponce," said Ace.

"Yes, exactly. I should have worn a cableknit sweater."

"We're not exactly in the north, though, are we," said Stella. "We're in the east and that's different. Anyway, the barman is Polish."

"How do you know that?"

"Because he was speaking Polish when we came in, to that waitress."

"Half the people in the dining room probably have second homes here and come from Islington."

"Norfolk's very hip now."

"You surprise me, Stella. Really?" Ward greeted the arrival of his pint with approval.

"Well, Aldeburgh and that."

"Oh yes, I suppose. Opera and literary festivals. And the aristocracy. Don't they call them the 'turnip toffs', round here? I should probably keep my voice down."

"I feel like Sherlock Holmes," said Ace. "He would always find an inn. And question the staff in a penetrating yet subtle manner."

"I think that sort of thing might get you flung out with a flea in your ear. Holmes had the advantage of being a genius detective, as well as being fictional."

"And a gentleman. Although it might surprise you to know that my own origins are not in fact especially common."

Ward laughed. "I noticed your accent shifts a bit."

"I don't think we should ask about Hex – you know," said Stella. "I don't want to rattle anyone's cage. You never know who knows who in small country districts. I think I shall have the halloumi burger."

"I shall have scampi. We are on the coast and it's seafood, allegedly, and I've never got over the impression that it's sophisticated. Blame a childhood being taken to Berni Inns."

"I remember Berni," said Ace.

"I don't!"

"You're too young, Stella. They were taken over by Beefeater. And possibly Brewer's Fayre."

"I thought your family were a bit too posh for Brewer's Fayre. And certainly for Hungry Horse."

"No, we never set foot in one of those. Were they around then? We were quite posh, I suppose – just not always very rich."

Just as they were finishing dinner, a young woman nervously approached the table. She wore a very short skirt, leggings and a parka and her hair was shaved up both sides of her head, displaying many-ringed earlobes.

"Excuse me, I'm so sorry, I know you're eating, but... I thought I recognised you."

"I'm on television rather a lot," said Ward, apologetically.

She glanced at him without comprehension. "No, I meant, aren't you Stella Fallow? Only I follow you on You Tube and I went to Aestival last year and it was so amazing, and when I saw you walk in tonight, I thought, oh my God, I've just got to say something, you're totally awesome, I love your work, thank you so so much for your music, bye."

And she was gone, before Stella could thank her in turn.

Ace said to Ward, "I'd just plant your face right there in your scampi, mate. If I were you."

Stella woke, blinking, at the sudden shriek of the clock. There was no light visible around the curtains. 5 a.m. All right! Game on, thought Stella. She jumped out of bed, had a quick hot shower, dressed in a lot of layers and went down to the empty foyer, where she got a can of an energy drink out of the vending machine. Ace and Ward were a little later and a little slower, but it was still dark when they went out to the car.

"Right. Ace, get in the front. With the map. I googled this and I printed out a map of Hex Heath itself. Here it is."

"I'm surprised it showed up on Google."

"The village did. This might or might not be the house. This square here."

"All right," said Ace. "Let's see how much sense it makes when we get there."

285

This must be one of the first places in the country from which you could see the dawn, Stella thought. It wasn't here yet; the North Sea was visible almost by absence, a wall of black at the edge of the world as they pulled up the cold coast road. There were few cars at this time of the morning but at least it wasn't wet: a relief to Stella after the slog through rainswept A roads yesterday. Ward had offered to drive and she had refused, feeling too twitchy, but she thought she might let him drive back. If they survived.

Soon enough, they reached Meopham, the village which Stella estimated to be nearest to the hall. It had a perfectly ordinary sign attached to a post, black and white, proclaiming the name. Stella parked on a back road, as far as they could manage from the place where the hall was supposed to be. It was remote, which she did not care for. There had been early morning lights in some bedroom windows, the last sparkle of Christmas decorations, but out here, there was nothing.

"Do you suppose this is it?" Ward was out of the car and looking at a high stone wall. "Goes on for miles – typical for some of these big estates."

Yew trees fringed it, which Stella associated more with churchyards. Weren't they supposed to ward off bad luck, hence their clerical adoption? Not doing a very good job here, then. And then one of the trees spoke to her, its fringed branches dipping as it did so, revealing the little waxy scarlet cups.

"*Go back.*"

"I don't think so," Stella said, aloud, but low. "We've come a long way, you see."

"Who are you – oh, it's the tree," Ace said. "Letting you handle this, Stella."

"No, you must go back." It had a whispering, hissing voice, like a wind in the boughs.

"Are you warning me or threatening?"

"I seek to save you."

"Well, you don't need to worry. We're quite capable."

"I have to try," the yew tree said and it sounded unhappy. It muttered, the small voice trailing away into nothing.

"So," Ace said, "I only got half of that. One of these one sided telephone call type things!"

"It told us to go back. It was warning not threatening."

286

"Reassuring," said Ward. "Do trees often talk to you, Stella?"

"Well, as a matter of fact…"

Ace nudged him. "Bet you wish you hadn't asked. It runs in families."

"Anyway, I'm not giving up now." She marched along the wall, followed by the others, until she came to a pair of high gates. A pair of stone dogs crowned the gateposts, mildewed with lichen and missing their ears, and in one case, a paw.

The gates themselves had once been imposing, but were now rusted and askew, hanging from their hinges. Someone had made the effort to secure them, as there was a large and ancient padlock and a notice: KEEP OUT. It looked as though it had been written in biro, by a child. There was plenty of room to squeeze under the padlock and through.

"That's one of the least imposing *keep out* notices I've ever seen," Ward said.

"Yes, it's pretty crap, isn't it. And a touch trap-like for my liking."

"If you fancy scrambling over that wall and hoofing it through the undergrowth…" said Stella.

"Nah. Too early in the morning. We'll walk up the front drive. Like men. Well, maybe not men. Like warriors."

"Like the warriors that we are," said Stella. She ducked under the padlock and with a little effort, was through.

The drive was uneven and pocked with potholes, as though it had suffered a plague. *Wouldn't fancy driving up here in a coach and four,* Stella thought; your chances of being flung out into the nettles were high. Young trees had flocked to what had once been a verge, mainly blackthorn, iron-spined and hard-boughed, with a few pale fragile stars of blossom. It was very early, a blackthorn winter – although that was supposed to be later, she had thought, the last late cold spell when the blackthorn flowers. But when she looked again, the blossom was gone and only the thorns pricked the morning air, and then again, turning, she saw that the trees were fully out, flower before the leaf, frothing onto the damaged stone.

The drive was not long, but it had a bend in it. When they came to the end, they found their way blocked, also with blackthorn and a mesh of spindle, still with some of its startling pink berries. Stella walked up and held out her hand.

"Won't you let us go by?"

And obligingly, the branches did so, shrinking aside to let her pass.

"Well," said Ward, "if we have to rescue any sleeping princesses, I'll let you go first."

"Happy to help the odd damsel."

She was keen to see what might lie beyond. But when she stepped through the withdrawn boughs, brushing them aside, there was not much to see.

"That's what it looked like in one version of that photo," Ward said.

"Basically it's a hovel."

"It's not even a hovel," said Ace. "I've known peasants who lived in classier accommodation."

"It's partially collapsed – look, you can see where the roof's come in."

"You'd think the trees would have taken over. This looks like it's been deserted for decades."

"Maybe they don't want to get too close," Stella said. But she knew this was Hex Heath, would have known even without the aid of the photo in Ben's flat. It felt wrong, it felt like the Stares, that jarring sense of oddness. *I can smell you now*, thought Stella. *I will know, if I meet your kind again. I will smell you out.*

"Christ!" Ward said. Stella turned. The shack was changing. In the blink of an eye, a mansion stood before them. Light glinted behind handsome, well-proportioned windows.

"Someone's at home," said Ace.

"Someone or something."

The front door was ajar just as the gates had been.

"It wants us to go in. And that worries me, Stella."

Ace was carrying one of his plastic bags, she saw now. She had not noticed it before.

"That's your equipment, isn't it, Ace, not your pjyamas?"

"I bloody hope not – getting up at this hour of the morning, I wouldn't be surprised if I'd grabbed the wrong bag." He peered inside. "Oh good."

"Right one?"

"Yes. So, are we going to give this a go? I don't think we should split up. One for all and all for one, the three musketeers and all that."

"We've come this far," said Stella, although she felt like running, running and not looking back. "We might as well go inside."

Cautiously, they approached the hall. It appeared sturdy and enduring, as though it had always stood there. Perhaps it had, Stella thought, its glamour concealed behind a hovel's mask. The house looked Georgian but the Stares, she was willing to bet, went back a lot further than that. Perhaps the hovel was the real hall after all, prehistoric and beyond.

Stella went first, and pushed the front door. It swung open easily, with barely a creak. She stepped into a dim hallway, the floor lined with once-polished boards. The panelling had started to come apart and the untidy spikes of a bird's nest poked through the splintered oak. A dresser stood at the end of the hall and a vase filled with dead flowers, no more than withered stems, stood on it. Stella was getting the hang of it now and she looked away, glanced from the corner of her eye. Roses spilled in profusion over the polished mahogany, cream and pink and white, summer in a vase. She could smell their sweet faint scent. Sunlight spilled in through the window and she heard voices laughing outside. Croquet, perhaps, or tennis. But then the dilapidated hallway was back.

"What do you want to do?" Ward asked. "Take each room in turn?"

"Yeah, you know I said we weren't going to split up? Well, now we are. You and Stella stick together and check out the ground floor. I'm going to try and secure the perimeter, as they say in the army."

Ward and Stella looked at one another.

"I'm game if you are," Stella said.

"All right."

The first room into which they ventured had been a dining room. The table was not laid, though silver candlesticks still stood along its dusty length. Stella, standing at the end of the room by the French windows, tried the sidelong trick again and saw a dinner party: beautiful women with jewels in their hair, garnet and emerald green, sapphire fire and indigo black. Then she looked again and thought she saw birds: a peacock perched on a candlestick and screamed, tail feathers shimmering in candlelight, and there was no one sitting at the table.

Perhaps she wouldn't try that again.

"What is it?" Ward said. The room was empty and quiet, Havishamed in dusty aspic.

"Nothing. Let's try the rest."

A parlour, the kitchens. There was no sign of life. Ward and Stella went upstairs. Ace stood, perfectly still, in the centre of the hallway, staring out of the front door. He did not acknowledge them as they went by. He held a small white stick in one hand, like a fingerbone.

"I'm leaving him to it!" Ward said.

"So am I." Perhaps it was not wise, either, to trust Ace so much, and yet she did. They came out onto a narrow landing. The light through the windows was faintly grey.

"I wonder what will happen when the sun comes up."

"I think I want to be out of here by then. I'm really looking forward to the Travel Lodge's full English."

"That's a bloody good idea," said Ward. "With sausages."

"They do a veggie one but I am so having two eggs."

As methodically as possible, they made a search of the bedrooms. These were similar, abandoned, smelling of age and mould. Four poster canopies were rotting away, drooping onto the floor.

"Hey, Stella. Look at this."

Ward held up a photo, of Tam and Dana Stare. He had a Cure hairstyle and shoelace tie, she wore black eyeliner as thick as a stripe of paint and a feral smile.

"It says 1983 on the back."

"They didn't look like they had even been *born* in 1983," Stella said. "But they were, weren't they? They were very old."

"Old and not human but still they posed as teenagers and had Polaroids taken."

"Playing dress up," Stella said. 'In human suits."

She went to a window and looked out.

"Ward."

Outside it was winter now, the snow deep and covering the world to a patch of far yew trees. From here, they could see a Christmas card scene: a formal garden, the beds covered in snow, almost concealed, and far away at the garden's end was a little ornamental bridge and a pond. Two people were skating on its frozen surface, tiny as dolls, a girl in a red coat and a boy in a cap. Their clothes did not look modern.

"I don't think we should look out of these windows," Ward said.

"No, I don't either." Abruptly she turned away.

The last room was at the end of the mansion and it was empty of furniture, except a big wooden chest. Ward looked at Stella.

"You want to give it a try?"

"Seriously, I can't see a box without wanting to know what's in it. It's like a compulsion."

"Let's give it a go, then."

The lid was heavy but not locked. Together, Ward and Stella hauled it open.

"What is that thing?"

"I don't know." She reached down and touched the tangle of leather and bronze. "Ow! That bloody hurt."

Ward glanced at her in alarm.

"Are you all right?"

"Yes, I think so – it *stung*. Like nettles."

Ward went to the window and ripped off a rotting section of the curtains.

"Let me try." He wrapped a hand in a makeshift mitten and reached into the chest. He poked the tangle cautiously. "Seems okay."

"It looks like a bridle. But it's bigger than they usually are. Must be a massive horse."

"Shire, maybe. Let's take this. Then we'll go and see what Ace is up to. I don't want to spend longer in here than I have to."

They went back downstairs but there was no sign of Ace. Ward and Stella looked at one another askance.

"God, where's he gone?" Ward said. "I don't fancy going into that dining room again."

"We'd better look. So much for not splitting up…"

There was a passage which led to the back of the house, past what was evidently a kitchen. It was deserted, covered in dust and with greasy pans still standing on the stove. The smell was unpleasant; Stella hastily withdrew.

"Reminds me of Ben's place," Ward said.

"Yes, you're right, it does. That mouldy odour."

They continued down the passage, but Stella was finding it difficult to breathe. She stopped and rubbed her nose.

"Are you all right?"

"It's like moving through treacle."

"I know." Ward had become rather pale. He said, "Do you think we should go back?"

"Ace might be in trouble."

"If he's even here."

But Stella was not prepared to give up so easily.

"I'm not being beaten by a bloody house." She forged past Ward into the singing tension at the end of the passage and stumbled out into what had been an orangery. The floor was a mess of cobwebs, mud and glass from the broken panels of the ceiling. Dead vines veiled the windows and there stood Ace. As Stella stepped towards him something, perhaps an ex lemon, exploded with a mouldy puff of air.

Ace was holding the little white wand out before him.

"Hang on, Stella. This could get nasty."

Outside, through the dirty windows of the orangery, Stella could see scratches in the air. The garden beyond looked like a torn stage backdrop, all in tatters.

"What's doing that, Ace?"

"Don't know. Walk forwards, keep pace with me. Ward, you with us?"

"More or less."

Again from the corner of her eye, Stella could see a ring of frost blue flame, surrounding the old orangery, surrounding Ace. It moved with them as they walked. Ace's lips were moving, but she could not hear him speak. The white wand quivered; she thought he was having difficulty holding it steady. For a second the air quivered and she saw the orangery in its heyday; the curling stems of the vines green against the garden, water plashing from an ornamental urn into a pond. Now the pond was no more than a rim around thick dust and the air stagnant and stale.

As they went towards the door of the orangery the atmosphere continued to feel thick. She heard Ward gasp. It was like trying to breathe through a sponge. The air pressed against her face and Stella coughed, but she couldn't breathe and – she saw the white wand in Ace's hand flare into fire and ash. The orangery exploded, cascading noiselessly into great shards of glass that were whisked up into the air, catching the distant lights, and then the air was filled with the sudden sound of breaking glass and with a curse Ace snatched his hand back. But Stella could breathe again.

The garden lay before them, grey in the rainy dawn. They ran outside and Stella whipped round to see. The orangery and the house had gone and so had the hovel; all that stood there was a twisted mass of bramble and thistle. Ward clutched the bridle firmly, still wrapped in the curtains.

"Out of here, now," Ace said, and they went.

"I'm thinking of having a second breakfast. Like a hobbit."

From the windows of the Travel Lodge, hitherto only seen in the dark, the dawn was coming up over the North Sea. The drizzle had blown out as they drove back down the coast road and now the sun was visible, a red rind.

"Stella, you are a pig. I don't know why you are so skinny."

"Metabolism. Nervous energy." Outside she could hear gulls screaming over the sea and a blackbird's sharp warning cry. "They've got croissants."

"Is that *included* in your £9.99, though? Are you allowed to?"

"What are they going to do, wrestle them off me?" But she settled for more coffee, instead.

The bridle, if such it was, sat at Ward's feet, still bundled in the length of curtain and Ace's carrier bag.

"I'm pissed off about that wand. I made that myself."

"What was it, Ace? It looked like a bone." The wand had reminded her of the bone flute that Alys had taken away with her in the autumn.

"No, it was mistletoe. From some old Christmas decorations. You strip the bark off but it's not easy, there's not much on mistletoe."

"Very Druidic," Ward said.

"Yeah, well. I like these sausages. Quite reasonably priced, their breakfasts in here. For these days. What time do we have to check out?"

"Ten, but it's only half eight now."

"I think I want to be out of here as soon as possible, to be honest. I don't like the thought of hanging around."

"Neither do I." Ward's phone pinged. "Oh, it's Serena. *'Everything okay hope you are all right lots of love'.*"

"Great. I was a bit worried about her." Stella finished the last of the coffee and stood up. "I need some fresh air. See you at the car. Don't forget *that.*" She pointed to the plastic bag.

"No worries," said Ace.

Stella walked out into the car park, where the little vehicle awaited their return to London, and stood for a moment looking out to sea.

Then she climbed down a long flight of steps, strode across the road and onto the beach. It was a long stretch of sand, weed-marked and shingle pocked. The sun had gone up into a bank of cloud and everything was steel and grey and shadow and light. Stella stood with her hands in her pockets against the morning cold, staring out across the North Sea. She realised with a slight shock that today was Twelfth Night. She felt something hard and round in one of the pockets, and brought out a spindle seed, slightly withered now from its sojourn in her jacket, but still fiery bright. It sat in her hand like a coal.

It must have fallen into her pocket when she pushed through the undergrowth at Hex Heath. She wondered what would happen if she planted it. Perhaps let's not. But instead of casting it into the sea, she put it back in her pocket, all the same.

Then her phone sounded again and Stella's heart leaped within her when she saw the name. Luna!

I'm OK. <3

Stella called her at once, but got the answerphone. Never mind, contact had been established. She sent an answering text and went back to the Travel Lodge.

The rain held off for most of the morning. Ward drove and Stella had a chance to see the countryside roll by, unfamiliar and therefore interesting. Towards noon the outskirts of London started to make their presence felt and soon they were crawling back through the Dartford Tunnel.

"So what's the plan now, Ace?" Ward asked over his shoulder. "Shall we take you home?"

"Yes, might as well. Come in for a cuppa if you want. I think you should leave the thing that you found at mine, if it's all the same to you."

"I don't want it at Serena's," Stella said. "She's had enough supernatural visitations as it is, even if some of them do come from Bill."

"And I don't want it at mine," said Ward. "Best you have it if you don't mind, Ace. I feel that your house is a sort of containment unit."

Ace gave a snort of laughter. "Mainly of cats."

"Did you take a good look at it?"

"It's some kind of halter, or bridle. But you were right, Stella, at breakfast. It is big. I don't know a lot about horses, city boy me, but it strikes me it's too wide."

They reached Southwark shortly after this and parked. To Stella's surprise, Anione had made soup and it was surprisingly good, although it was a little hard to tell what was in it. Ace told Stella to keep in touch and that he would be in the pub later if she needed to ring, and then Ward drove Stella back over the bridge to Portobello.

"Are you coming straight to Serena's?" Stella asked.

"I – yes. I have to pick up some stuff from mine but I'll pop round there later."

"You're spending a lot of time at my sister's. Any plans?"

"To move in? We haven't discussed it. Shit!" Ward stamped on the brake. "Why don't you use your *fucking* indicator, you halfwit." After a moment, he said, "I think she wants her own space. I don't mind, actually. But we're keeping both places for now."

Stella grinned. "Two lots of council tax, though."

"You mercenary, you."

The house was quiet when they walked in, echoing. It smelled, as always, of the candles Serena burned, lemon and rose, and lavender and beeswax polish. A civilised, grown-up smell. Stella couldn't help thinking of Ace's house.

As they closed the front door there was a clatter of footsteps on the stairs and Bella ran down them. She threw herself at Stella.

"Stella! I'm so glad you're back! I've got to tell you."

"Why, what's wrong, sweetheart?"

"It's Mum. She isn't my mum. She just looks like her."

BEE

"I can't believe it's raining *again.*" Bee stood at the landing window, looking out at the streaming world. It was late in the afternoon and Bee had been busy taking the Christmas decorations down: unlucky, it was said, to leave them up past Twelfth Night. She had left them to their last day, then stripped the tree with her mother's help, and despite the faint sadness that was always present at this time of year for her, Christmas over and done with for another twelve months, not to mention this year's worry over a great many things, for a little while it was as it had been between Alys and Bee. Like childhood again, and Bee could forgive and forget.

"We haven't always had the tree in the dining room," Alys said.

"No. We used to have it in the sitting room – do you remember the year the cat got up it and it fell on Grandfather?"

Alys laughed. "Yes, that was Marco. A feline fiend from hell. Dad didn't swear much usually…"

"I learned words I'd never heard before."

"How old were you then?"

"About twenty-three."

"I knew some people once who found an owl in their Christmas tree."

"What, a real owl?"

"Yes, a Little Owl. Three days after they brought it inside. It was hungry and sleepy and rather cross. They had to phone the RSPB."

"Wow."

Together, they packed the ornaments carefully away in bubble wrap and boxes, and took the big box ceremoniously up to the attic. Then Bee made lunch and now, later, they were standing upstairs watching the rain. Not long ago, there had been a text from Stella, saying that they had come back from Norfolk and there had been 'developments'.

Bee did not mention this to her mother. Truce over.

Alys disappeared into her room and Bee went back downstairs. This was an angsty, twitchy time, these days around Twelfth Night, and she was always glad when they were over and the world went back to work.

This year, doubly so. And the rain was fast bringing the afternoon to a close: a darkening of the day.

When she went into the dining room, Ned Dark was there, staring at the tree.

"It is very bare."

"Yes. I hate seeing it without all of its glitter and tinsel and baubles. Never mind, though, it's always nice to see them again in due course and we probably wouldn't appreciate it if they were up all the time."

Dark smiled. "I wish they were. I am like a child, you see. Sparkle and gaud."

"We need it. Even when we are grown, Ned. Look at it out there, at that rain."

His head went up and all of an instant, Dark was gone. Someone was hammering at the door. Bee ran to answer, her head full of Luna, Sam, Aln. But it was Caro Amberley who stood there on the step.

Perhaps 'stood' was the wrong word, however. Caro was clutching the doorframe and when Bee tugged the door open, she sagged, her knees folding beneath her.

"Oh God!" Bee caught her under the arms and half carried, half dragged her inside. Then she shouted for Alys. Together, they managed to carry Caro up the stairs. She was very light, although Bee had experience of people becoming suddenly extremely heavy when unconscious. But Caro felt as light as a bundle of sticks.

"Take her into my room," Alys said. "I've just changed the sheets."

"Great. I think she's coming round." For Caro's lips were moving. She moaned.

"I'll call Richard," Bee said.

"No…" Caro's eyes were still shut, but she reached out and gripped Bee's hand with a painful clasp; surprising that she had so much strength. "Not Richard. Not Laura."

"We really ought to let your family know, Caro."

"Ben."

"*Ben?*"

"Darling, Ben's still missing," Alys said with firmness.

"But I can *see* him. I have to find him!"

"Where is he, Caro?" Bee asked. "Do you know?"

"He's here," Caro whispered. "He's back. I can hear him calling. Like before but he's closer now."

"What?" Bee glanced around her.

"I think she might mean he's back in our world, Bee."

Caro was trembling.

"Go and get her a tot of brandy."

"And some tea?"

Alys sighed. "Why not?"

"I know it's the British response to a crisis but it might actually do her some good."

Bee ran down the stairs, boiled the kettle, and put tea and brandy on a tray.

As she carried this back up the stairs, she found Dark standing by the landing window.

"The water's rising," he said.

Bee looked out. It was dusk now and a rising gibbous moon was caught in the ash trees, sending a silvery path out across the fields. She could see a glimmer of wet at the end of the drive.

"You're right. God, all we need now is a flood. What if it reaches the house?"

"Bee? What's wrong?" Alys had appeared at the bedroom door.

"Mum, the lane's flooding right up. It's at the end of the drive and I can see it at the back of the orchard. Mooncote's going to be an island in a bit if this goes on."

"I know. The Hunt has sent the floods."

"Shit! Can you stop it?"

Alys looked furtive, almost guilty.

"They're not sending it to drown us, Bee. They're sending it for protection."

"What do you mean?"

"Protection for me. Because whoever has Caro's son may not be happy at the thought of crossing running water."

STELLA

Stella and her niece sat with Ward in the Lion and Unicorn. Stella had marched Bella straight out of the house, in case of being overheard. The girl was not prone to hysterics, or fantasy, and the nagging sense of wrongness that Stella had felt for a day or so now was back, volume dialled right up.

Bella's long thin hands, so like her mother's, cradled a latte. She stared down into the cup, as though addressing the coffee.

"She had her business meeting, she said, and she was there when I came back yesterday, from Dad's, but she wasn't herself – she seemed, I don't know, off, somehow. Funny. We had pizza and usually she complains a bit, like we should eat more healthy stuff, although we do eat a lot of healthy stuff, actually. And we always have pizza when I come back from being away because it's my favourite. But this time she didn't say anything. I went to the loo and when I came back I could see her in the mirror, except she was really – blurred. Her reflection was there but it wasn't right. Not like a vampire, but…"

"Shit!"

"I know! I didn't know what to do. I thought of texting you but you were in Norfolk and I didn't want to drag Dad into this. I thought I'd better handle it myself. I didn't sleep very well last night and I don't think she went to bed at all. When I came downstairs this morning she was just – sitting there, in the same clothes, with the same expression on her face. Like a doll."

"I told you, didn't I, Stella, that she called me 'sweetie.' And she never does that," said Ward.

"Yes, it reminded me of something but I couldn't think what."

"That awful woman, Dana Stare, the one I – the one who went off with Ben, she used to call people 'sweetie' and it was really fake."

"Christ, you're right," said Ward.

"Bella, where is Serena now?"

"She went out, around lunchtime, really quickly. Without her coat or her bag, she said she was just popping down the road. I called after her – she'd shouted up the stairs, but when I came down she'd gone. And that *thing* was in the living room, on the mantelpiece."

"What, the demon?"

"Yes, it seemed really angry. It kept muttering and shuffling about. Like a cross parrot. And it was scary so I shut the door and ran upstairs and locked the door. I haven't had any lunch, by the way."

Ward produced a ten pound note. "Go and get something to eat! I don't care what. Chips, if you like."

Bella managed a smile. "I don't think I should have chips, Ward." She returned with a salad baguette.

"I'm beginning to think *she's* a changeling," Stella said to Ward. "Given the difference in our eating habits, we may not even be from the same family."

"She likes pizza, though."

"It was only £4.99. Here's your change."

"No, keep it. Get something later. Is there food in the house?"

"Oh yes, Mum stocked the fridge. Real Mum, not weird fake Mum."

Ward said, "You are an exceptionally level headed chi – young woman, Bella. I want you to know that."

"Thanks!"

"We'd better get in touch with Ace."

"Do you know," said Ward to Bella, keeping his voice low, "if the demon is still in the house?"

"I didn't look. I was too scared."

"Charlie isn't there, I'm assuming?"

"No, she's not back at work yet. She's supposed to be coming in on Monday."

"All right. We'll go back, see what's happening, and ring the Southwark Tavern."

The demon was indeed still upon the mantelpiece. Stella had an impression of ruffled feathers.

"Hi," said Ward, warily.

The demon shut its eyes tightly and clucked like a hen.

"Will you talk to me?" Ward said. Stella thought that he was trying to create an Ace-like impression, and he wasn't doing a bad job. She did not expect the thing to reply but to her surprise the mercurial ball-bearing eyes opened and the demon said triumphantly,

"I shall!"

"The woman who was here earlier. What was she?"

"You noticed." The demon shook its diamond-shaped head from side to side, quite violently, so fast that it, too, appeared blurred. The big mirror behind the mantel, Stella noticed, bore no trace of a reflection. "Not a person, just the form. A fetch, a glamour."

"Thank you! That's very helpful. Where is Serena now?"

"Where I do not want her to be. I have tried to stop this. I came here for this, for my master, but I found her gone."

"Where do you come from, demon?" said Stella. "I don't mean, from Bill. And what do you mean, where you do not want her to be?"

"I come from a place that you might call hell, but your sister is in a worse place than that and there is not much time. Today is the day."

"Today is Twelfth Night," Stella said, taking a guess. "That's what you mean, isn't it?"

"When everything must come down. Today is the day," the demon repeated. "She is in the place where she should not be."

"The man we brought here, to meet you that first time. Your master's friend. Will you come with us, to him?"

"The magician? Yes."

They had to put the demon in a laundry bag, plastic and tartan. It was the only thing big enough to hold him.

"He's bloody heavy," Stella complained, as he hopped into it. The demon said nothing but the bag at once became light, as if empty. "Cheers!"

Ward flagged down a cab on the main road.

"Oh," said the cabby, in a jovial manner. "Present for me?"

"It's a stuffed toy. For my sister's kid." She put the bag hastily into the back footwell.

"Not me," Bella said.

"A younger kid. Look, could you swing by Kentish Town first? We're dropping this young lady off at her dad's." For it had been decided that Bella should go there and wait; she had not greeted this without protest, but Ward had overruled her.

It was not a quick run. By the time they headed south, the day had begun to darken and the southern shore of the Thames was starting to become murky, despite the Shard. The smaller tower of Southwark Cathedral was not yet lit. Stella worried about Serena, but felt glad to be on the move again. As long as you're on the move, you can cope; you're in control. She hoped.

In the more shadowy reaches of the Southwark Tavern, Ace peered into the bag.

"I see," was all that he said. "What we need to do now is get this little bugger to explain where your sister is."

"I remember what you said about their – obliqueness. As in, he might think he's told us already."

"I think he's gone to sleep," said Ace. "It's not quite dark yet out there, is it? Not quite lighting up time."

"Getting there, though."

"We need to wait for official dusk." He glanced at the clock behind the bar. "Civil twilight, nautical twilight, and the one we need – astronomical twilight."

"I didn't know we had different ones!"

"You do now, Ward old son, you do now. Astronomical twilight is soon but not yet. Twelfth Night starts then. Time for another pint. Ward, I recommend the Tiny Rebel, but it is a pale ale. Stella, I'll get you a wine, you paid for breakfast."

"What about him?" Ward looked at the laundry bag.

"I don't think he drinks. By the way, you'll note I have the ubiquitous placcy bag with me. I'm keeping the thing we, ah, liberated in my close personal possession. Anione thought it best."

"I am," Ward said, "Exceedingly worried about my girlfriend. Do you know what's going on?"

"No. But I'll tell you what's on my mind. I don't think Serena actually came out of Pharoah Towers. I think Caspar Pharoah is not a human being, and I think he sent something out of his office in Serena's shape, to ensure we shot off to Hex Heath without having to worry about her. Which begs a massive question, obviously, about where she is now and what's happened to her. I also think we might have been followed, although I didn't see anything. What we met early this morning – Christ, was it only this morning? It was, wasn't it – was either what Pharoah must have sent after us if he has any sense, or Hex Heath's own defences. Also, Anione's been doing some digging, on my instructions, and unearthed *this*."

He handed Stella an oblong leaflet. "Read that."

"Museum," Stella read aloud. "London Mithraeum. *Everlight Holdings returns the Roman Temple of Mithras to the location of its discovery in the heart of the City. Situated on the site of Everlight's new European headquarters, this anticipated new cultural hub showcases the ancient temple, a selection of the remarkable Roman artefacts found during the recent excavation, and a series of contemporary art commissions responding to one of the UK's most significant archaeological sites."*

"You know what a Mithraeum is?"

"A temple to Mithras? Who was a – what? A soldier's god?"

"Well done, Ward. Yes, correct, but also a bull cult. I knew about this but I didn't make the connection. I should have made the bloody connection, because I saw a thing about the temple in the news a while back, but I didn't make it because its actual address was listed in a different street, at the back of the offices not the front. And I've not been in the Mithraeum. Serena told me she saw a ship, in one of these glitches between past and present – a Roman ship coming up the Thames estuary. There was something big on board, something in a crate, which freaked out the crew. And Stella was giving a warning at the mouth of the Thames, of something coming by river. I think Pharoah has brought a bull into the country, from the past, for his Mithraeum."

At this point the laundry bag stirred and the demon's sweet honeyed voice said, "It is not a bull."

"Hang on!" But Ace was staring towards the door.

The drinkers and revellers of the Southwark Tavern were suddenly still, frozen in the act of lifting their pints to their lips, laughing, turning to the door. A man stood with his hand on the latch but the door was open and in the entrance stood a girl in a white shift, crowned with stars. Her hair was feathers, her face was pale as death. She smiled when she saw Ace looking at her.

"The geese have come," said Ace. "Must be twilight." There was a rattle from the carrier bag and the demon shot like an arrow towards the door. Then it was gone. "Come on!" Ace said.

SERENA

Serena rolled over and fell. She hit a hard floor with a thud, thinking, *Oh, how stupid! I've fallen out of bed.* But she was not in her own peaceful bedroom and she did not remember falling asleep. Bright images flickered before her mind's eye like a silent picture show: a golden waterfall, a silent amphitheatre, a woman with hair like fire and blue eyes.

"Oh!" said Serena aloud, but no one answered. It was pitch-dark: she could not see her hand in front of her face, but when she looked up there was a daylight flash from an opening, high in the ceiling. Then it was gone but she had seen the little window. She groped out and touched the hard metal edge of a bed, covered with a rough blanket that felt more like horsehair than anything softer. There was a lumpy, badly-kneaded-bread sort of pillow at one end. The air smelled musty, unlike the careful non-smell of the plush atrium through which she had come. Who had that woman been, then? Something about her reminded Serena of the star spirits, but the accent had been more London estuary.

She had to think. As methodically as possible, Serena felt her way around her prison. The walls were rough and slightly damp, perhaps plaster, and curving. The floor was unevenly tiled; she could feel the edges of each tile. It reminded her of something and then she had it: the tunnel through which she had gone underneath the church of All Hallows, close to the Tower. She remembered the chill smell of the river and the swinging crate being lowered from the boat, the shouts of the men, the crate shuddering, and then the fear came back. Serena pressed her hands to her mouth and sank against the wall. She could hear the drumbeat again, the thump and thud of something's heart.

There came a dazzling flash at the opening up the wall. Serena was struck by something small but very heavy. She collapsed against the bed and the metal frame hit her in the back of the knees. She sat down hard.

"It is I," said a sweet thin voice. She recognised it at once.

"Demon!"

Serena had never thought, a month or so ago, that she would be pleased to encounter the thing again. She put out a hand and touched its hard ridge of a head. It ducked away.

"Sorry."

"Help is on the way," the demon said. "Our friends do come. But you must be brave. There is a thing you must do."

"What sort of thing?" Serena quavered.

"You must face a monster."

"Oh, my God! Can you help me?"

"Why, I can but try," the demon said, and it began to sing, in a small high voice, in a language that she did not know. It was the song that a star might sing, or a flame, but then it stopped abruptly. The wall of the cell began to open.

LUNA

Ver March looked fit for walking. There were stout, mudstained boots visible beneath her long brown skirt and she carried a cleft thumbstick. She smiled when she saw Luna and Aln.

"All set for a wander, my lovelies? Sam's gone down to make sure the boat's secure. Although we might not need it again, but you never know, do you? And even so, it's the principle of the thing."

"Sam likes to make sure that things are done properly," Luna said.

"He does and that's a good thing. Oh, there he is. It's not far," Ver said. "But I'd like to get going."

"About ten miles? When we drove down from Rowan's place, it didn't take long."

"But now we're on foot. I was having a chat to one of the gentlemen in the temple and he says, too, that it's not as it is in our day. There's no main road. A track through the forest, at best."

Aln looked uneasy. "And there are things in forests."

"Your kinsman, though? Hob. Might he assist?"

"I don't know. He is fearful. He's been very brave but he's – well. We've seen terrible things happen."

"Haven't we all, lovey," said Ver March, gently. "Haven't we all."

At first, the winter woods were quiet. The path led down through stands of oak, which Luna thought must be very old, from their gnarled grey appearance. Acorn mast crunched underfoot and she was again reminded of Rowan's cottage. The path narrowed, becoming in places more akin to a badger track, and by tacit consent Ver March led the way, with Aln close behind. It was overgrown with briar and occasional skeins of wild clematis, traveller's joy, the old man's beard that they had gathered from the hedgerows at Christmas, to set on the mantelpiece along with the holly and ivy and bay. Ivy marched up the trunks of the oaks and beyond the path, the woodland was dense. Luna was uncertain what she felt about this: on the one hand, it would be difficult to ride through the tangle, but on the other, difficult also to escape pursuit. She said so to Sam.

"I think Gran might have a trick or two up her sleeve. I hope."

"I think Aln might, too."

"Are you doing okay, Luna? You've been through a lot. I think you've been brilliant." He squeezed her hand.

"Cheers, Sam! I'm doing all right. I'm a bit worried about the baby, obviously. I was so happy when you and Ver came up the river, though."

"I couldn't tell Bee where we were going because I didn't know. I was setting off to go and see her when Ver herself turned up in a taxi, of all things."

"She never did!"

"She said she'd come down on the train and got a cab from the station. Then she took me down to the stream, didn't have a chance to speak to Bee, and the boat was waiting. She said there was no time to waste."

"I sort of expect your gran to have, I don't know, more unusual forms of transport."

"She says she believes in conserving her energies. This was a few days ago."

"Do you know how long I've been gone? In our world?"

"It's not the same length of time so I don't know, really. Days not weeks, though. But you know, Luna, we've just been back in Roman times. So who knows?"

"I keep thinking of those fairytales in which someone spends a year in fairyland and they come home and everything's changed and it's three hundred years later."

"They usually crumble into a pile of ash shortly afterwards, though."

"Thanks, Sam, that's really reassuring."

"I've never known it happen to someone I know."

"Even more reassuring! How many people do you know who have actually travelled in time? Apart from my family and probably yours?"

Sam admitted that the list was not extensive. At this point Ver stopped, so suddenly that Luna almost cannoned into Aln.

"Shhhh!"

Luna froze. Ver was listening, head cocked on one side like a blackbird. Then Luna could hear it, too, a distant crashing and shouts.

"Quickly!" Ver abandoned the path, ignoring the brambles tearing at her skirts. Sam took Luna's hand and followed, behind one of the bigger oaks. The undergrowth was so thick that they had to climb up onto the exposed roots but Luna liked being so close to the old tree. It felt safe. She looked up and for a moment the canopy stretched above them in spring's green-gold. But the branches were swiftly bare again.

By now, she had seen and heard enough of the Hunt to recognise it when it appeared. She could not hear the horses, but in the thick of the forest even a supernatural horse or deer might have trouble running. She could hear people coming through the undergrowth, however, and it was more than this: a kind of electricity in the air, bringing fear with it. Luna's knees started to buckle and she gripped the old oak more tightly, pressing her face against it. Sam was behind her, and that was good, too.

From the corner of her eye, she could see movement in the soil. She watched it, to take her mind off what was coming. A mole? The earth stirred. A white tendril emerged, groping in the air, and for a moment Luna felt disgust — but it was a shoot, not a worm. It flushed pale green, then a tiny leaf sprouted. More followed it, springing up from the acorn mast around the tree. They grew faster and faster until Luna and her companions were surrounded by a wall of oak saplings. Through a gap Luna looked into the face of the woodwose, sad and wizened. It raised a hand, as if in farewell. Then it was gone, fading into a bundle of upright twigs.

Ver reached out and touched Luna's hand.

"Stay still."

Luna nodded. Through the gap in the saplings she could see a white shape, taller than a man. It was one of the Hunt. He wore a cloak of scraps of skin but beneath it he was naked: his skin looked as hairless and hard as marble, with the long blue veins visible. His lantern-jawed face reminded Luna of the comet, who had visited the world in the autumn and now was gone, but the comet's face had been merely unhuman. The hunter's countenance was both unhuman and cruel. There was a silver light in his eyes; his grey tongue flickered across his lips. His hair streamed pale down his back and his teeth were sharp. A big white hound stood briefly in his place, ears pricked. Then the hunter was back but as he shifted position Luna could see that there was a collar around his throat, with a ring attached. He raised his head and bayed like a dog. An answering call came from within the forest.

He was smelling the air, Luna realised. She could hear the panting rhythm of his breath. Sam pressed her closer to the tree: when they came though this, Luna thought with resolution, *when*, she would have the creases of the bark marked into her cheek, like the folds of a sheet, on waking. But this was not a dream.

The sapling shield held. She saw the white form stalk away. Then a horn sounded, an urgent note, and the hunter dropped to all fours. A hound tore through the briars, leaving a bloody spray, and then it was gone.

They remained by the tree until the sound of the hunt had died away. Then Ver and Aln struggled past the saplings, which were beginning to wither now, the leaves drying into frail russet. Aln ran to the wose, fighting her way through the briars and nearly falling. But the bundle of twigs did not move.

Ver followed her, more slowly.

"Will he come back, love?"

"I don't know. Maybe. Sometimes they just –" Her head drooped. Ver put a hand on her shoulder.

"I'm so sorry."

"We should get on," Aln said, gathering herself. "I will come back later, when I can. The day's growing old."

"All right. Up to you."

Luna had by now lost track of the time. They did not stop to eat, but gnawed bread from the temple as they walked. It was slow going, but at last the path widened a little and they came out onto the top of a high red cliff. The river stretched grey beyond, with the opposite bank hazy in the dying light.

"If we stop here, p'raps," Ver said. "I don't want to be travelling when it's dark."

"Fine by me. But no fire, Gran."

"No. No fire."

Luna did not think she would sleep but exhaustion overtook her. She woke to grey light and assumed it was still evening, but when she sat up she realised it was dawn.

"We didn't wake you, lovey," said Ver. "Thought you and the baby needed the rest. So we've taken it in turns to keep watch."

"Was there – did anything happen?"

"No, all quiet, mostly. Something was crying out across the river. A voice."

"Could you hear what it said?"

Ver shook her head.

"Ver, I didn't ask you yesterday, but those – that hunter. I've seen them before. We spoke about them and you said she, Aln, called them the Gefliemen. That was one, wasn't it?"

"Yes. But they have another name, which I didn't tell you. Some call them the Lily White Boys."

"That's from a song, isn't it? Green grow the rushes o."

"I'm glad to see Sam's with a young lady who's so educated," Ver said primly. She inched closer and into Luna's ear she whispered,

"I'll sing you one, O
Green grow the rushes, O
What is your one, O?
One is one, and all alone,
And ever more shall be so.

I'll sing you two, O
Green grow the rushes, O
What are your two, O?
Two, two lily-white boys
Clothed all in green, O
One is one, and all alone,
And ever more shall be so.

And there's a lot more verses, too. I would sing it because if I say so myself, I haven't got a bad voice. Well, I did when I was younger, anyway. But I don't want to sing it out loud in case something hears me and takes notice." She clambered to her feet. "We should make Chepstow by noon at the latest. I think this might be a very interesting day."

They started early, without much discussion or fuss. Sam and Luna walked side by side: the path was wide enough now, following the river cliffs. Without the big suspension bridges the river looked oddly naked, though once Luna thought she glimpsed the towers of the crossing through the morning mist. There was something up ahead, the path disappearing now and bringing them out onto a high expanse of meadow.

"We're here. I've just seen the castle," Sam said.

"Did you? I haven't seen anything."

310

"How could you miss a whopping great Norman keep?"

And Luna could see it then, rising brown as an owl above the river.

"Hang on," said Sam. "There are cars on that road."

"So there are!" Ver shaded her eyes with her hand. Luna was more thankful than she cared to admit to see the twenty-first century. Her knees felt weak and she gripped Sam's hand tightly.

"They'll think we're all hippies," Sam said.

"They're probably not wrong."

They made their way down into the town. They must have looked an odd little band, Luna thought, but they met no one as they walked through the quiet suburbs, though an elderly man walking a dog gave them an initially old-fashioned look. Aln ducked her face away and he stared at her for a moment, but not with horror or fear. Then he chuckled. Ver wished him good morning, brightly.

"Gave me a shock when I saw her all green and that, but then I remembered. You'll be here for the Marys, of course. Have you come from the campsite?" the man asked.

"That's right. Are you going yourself?"

"No, no, the pub's got the rugby on later." He had a South Welsh accent. "Otherwise I might. Brings a lot of people into the town. Enjoy your day."

"Thanks! You too!"

"What," asked Luna, "are the Marys?"

"Haven't a clue."

They crossed the bridge into the town, skirting the castle, now clearly visible on the river bank. The Wye was winter-muddy and brown: to Luna's relief, they seemed to have arrived back at the same time of the year as they had left. She only hoped it was the same year... She went into a corner shop and bought a carton of milk, taking the opportunity to check the dates on the newspaper rack. January the fifth, and the year – yes! – the right one. Luna felt herself slump with relief. And no piles of ash, either. As she left the shop, her phone pinged.

Luna asked Ver to wait, and sat down on a nearby bench to read her messages. Awful to worry everyone so, but she had not been able to help it... She sent quick texts to Bee, Stella and Serena, then switched the phone off. She did not like to do this, shutting herself off like that, but she could do without the distraction of having to make explanations and reassurances. And from the sound of it, Stella at least had enough on her plate.

Sam said, "Would anyone like to find some breakfast? Since we're here."

There was a café close to the castle wall: it had a small terrace at the back which was too cold to sit on, but the window looked out over the keep and a small orchard.

"I love 'em," Ver March said, staring out over the grey stone wall. "I know they're symbols of the oppression of the working man but you don't think about that, do you, unless you're of that persuasion. But I always think of ladies in those pointy hats and brave knights in shiny armour. Even though I know better."

Aln, who was eating a piece of toast, gazed at her, bemused, but Luna said, "Me too. I always thought castles were exciting. Except when I was little I wanted to be a knight, not a lady. Mum said that was okay. With no historical accuracy, I now realise."

"Well, a girl can dream. And I must say, I've always thought Chepstow was a very *castly* sort of a castle."

Aln said, in a low voice, "Who are those people?"

Luna was only vaguely surprised that she could still understand the green girl here, in the modern age. The indicated people had green faces, too. There were eight of them, men and women, all of a vivid emerald hue like grass after rain. They wore top hats and crows' feathers; ragged stripes and bright, and their legs were bound with bells. They were laughing and happy. None of them looked amiss at Aln and Luna realised why the elderly dog walker had been so unfazed. They were Morris dancers, but in greenface rather than the old black paint, which had become unacceptable these days. Originally it had been soot. Green was better anyway, Luna thought.

Ver said, "Well, don't you lot look fine! Are you here for the Marys?"

"We certainly are!" The man's teeth were very white against the greenness of his skin. "You too? Looking forward to it?"

"Yes, indeed. It's our first time." Luna wondered if that had been the right thing to say. What if it was everyone's first time, had never happened before? But a woman with a gold spiral glittering on her cheek said,

"Oh, you'll love it. We've been going every year since, I don't know, when was it, Dave?"

"It's at least eight years." Dave placed his hand on his heart – a green hand, Luna noticed – and gave a slight bow. "Good sir and ladies, we are the Thorn and Raven Morris side. All the way from Ludlow, and we shall be performing for you today at eleven o'clock and again on the bridge at dusk during the Morris-off."

"A 'Morris-off'?"

"Battle of the bands, as it were. We all do our thing and then the judges choose."

"So where do we go, then? If we want a good view?"

"Oh, you can't miss it. Up in the square. It always starts at the Green Man pub, appropriately enough."

At this point, Dave's breakfast arrived and he bowed again before sitting down.

"I love a good Morris side," Ver said. She was clearly in her element. When they left the café, they saw more people dressed up, this time in Medieval velvets, and as they made their way up the side street to the square, as indicated by Ver's new friends, a woman gave a cry and bolted across the road.

"Luna!"

"Oh, hello, Rowan!"

Rowan's hair was braided into many plaits with bells on the ends, and beaded with the berries of the tree whose name she bore.

"I didn't know you were coming to this! You should have texted me. Moss is in a caff with the kids. I just nipped out to get a programme – the café's run out."

"We didn't really expect to be here," Luna said. "We'd have dressed up a bit."

"Well, your friend has, hasn't she? She looks lovely and green. Is she dancing later on?"

Aln gave a tentative smile. "This is Aln," said Luna.

"What a beautiful name! There's a river called Aln, isn't there? My name is Rowan, I'm a friend of Luna's, too."

"Thank you. Luna, you mustn't be late – they'll be coming out soon." She waved her programme. "I'll just get Moss and the little ones." Then she was gone.

Luna was greatly intrigued but also worried. "Do we have time for this?"

"We're here for a reason, lovely," Ver March said quietly. "Best to see how things plays out."

Luna nodded. She still felt hunted, still felt the urge to run all the way back to Mooncote, but she trusted Sam's nan; so they joined the others and followed the growing crowd up the street.

Chepstow was high above the wind of the Wye, with steep streets still based on Medieval patterns. They came out into a small square, surrounded by shops, and containing a wide flank of steps leading up to a war memorial. Luna caught a glimpse of the river and the H shaped towers of the first Severn bridge. On the far side of the square, a green face grinned from a sign high on a wall. Luna could see a poster on the window, but she could not see what was on it.

Many of the crowd wore costume and carried staffs; many were members of Morris sides and there were Dave and the Thorn and Raven, ready, so Dave cried out, to rock and roll. A man began to bang a rhythmic drum. The crowd was calling out to one another.

"Where are they?"

"Are they ready yet?"

"Nearly, don't worry! Bang on time!"

The church clock struck the hour. Luna counted eleven chimes. The crowd fell silent, with only the rustle of a Morris bell, soon stilled. Luna ducked through the back of the crowd and across the square. Everyone stood statue-still: she wondered for a moment if they had been snatched from time, frozen, but then a girl shifted position. They were simply watching. Luna found herself standing in front of the Green Man. The bottom of the windows was frosted glass, but above that the panes were clear and inside she could see great shadows moving. Luna frowned. What –? The poster was on the window but there was someone in the way, and within a head swung around, huge and pale, then the doors were opening.

"They're coming out!" someone cried.

"Hooray!" And there were cries throughout the square, a frenzy of drumming and whoops from the Morris sides. The green face smiled down at Luna, a thin shaft of winter sunlight fell on the doorway and the first of the Marys came out. She saw the skull of a horse, a tangle of ribbons.

Luna knew at once what it was. A Mari, not a Mary; a Mari Lwyd, the old horse spirit of the Welsh borders, made from a bedsheet and a skull, the toothy jaws clacking from side to side. Once they had gone around the villages on Twelfth Night, door to door, demanding money or cake, with laughter and menaces. Its eyes were empty sockets and it wore ribbons of scarlet and green where its ears had been, but the Mari that followed it out had ping pong balls for eyeballs, the pupils drawn in with marker pen. Underneath the sheet could be seen a pair of jean-clad legs, and trainers.

The Maris came out one by one, a seemingly endless procession. One man carried not a horse but the blind skull of a bull, decked with flowers. Soon, around twenty of the beasts were milling about among the excited crowd, with people trying to identify friends or acquaintances beneath the bedsheets or taking photos with their phones. Luna felt a plucking at her sleeve and looked down into Aln's green face.

"This must be why we're here," she thought she heard Aln say, but then someone took her hand and whirled her around. The Thorn and Raven, black-clad, green-faced, were all around her, dancing, and Luna danced too: they were gentle, as if they knew she was pregnant. The beat of the drum seemed to slow down, stretching. Luna was spun softly about by Dave's wife, her brown eyes sparkling amid the green paint, but then she stumbled, letting go of the dancer's hands. She saw the brown eyes widen with alarm but Luna did not fall, someone had seized her hands and fingers fierce as winter ice gripped her own. She looked up into a cold white face. The collar around his throat was stiff with rusty bloodstains. He smiled, but again it reminded her of the comet's smile, with nothing human in it, only a kind of limitless empty greed. His eyes alone were whiteless, red-black. He held Luna close despite her struggling and his breath smelled of meat and meadowsweet. He wore a battered black hat, with a crow's feather stuck in it as trophy; she could see the fragment of flesh still adhering to the quill.

Luna tried to fight free but the hound was holding her tightly. He swung her around. It was as though she were a toy that he had picked up, as a dog may snatch at a piece of fur. She could feel talons through her thick jumper. He threw her upwards, easily, Luna no longer gravid and grounded but dandelion-light, and she saw the laughing crowd and the silver river beyond. From the direction of the old castle came the heartbeat thump of a drum but all else was silent. Luna hit the ground hard, she felt the jolt. She glanced around, frantic, but she could not see Sam or Aln or Ver anywhere. She opened her mouth to yell and saw someone she recognised.

He was young, dressed in a Morris man's black and tatters. His eyes were kind and the colour of the sun. She had last seen him on a statue's plinth in the temple of Nodens. In his temple. He raised a hand and it shimmered a little. The rags of his garments burst into flame, flickering unburning until he was part dressed in fire, which moved as he moved. Dancing with him was a little girl, dressed in skins: her footprints shone silver on the road. She smiled at Luna and Luna heard the warning chatter of a wren.

The Mari Llwyds turned, moving as one mare, and the young man threw back his head and laughed. He carried a staff with a pine cone on the end – like the one the Hunt leader had carried, thought Luna, was it the same? – and he pointed at the hound.

The hound snarled and dipped his head. Luna saw the glint of teeth but then he was knocked sideways by the blow of a horse's skull. The white eyeless head swung around. The sheet whirled up like the mouth of a bell and she could hear the church bell itself toll again, twelve strokes for noon and midnight. There was a click inside her head and she was tiny and weightless, woman turned to wren. But the space beneath the sheet was vast and starlit. Luna saw a tiny moon, flung up over the world's shoulder, gibbous to the full. Then all was black, with the clacking of the horse's jaws over and away to the left of her. When she looked down, however, she saw a spidery web of lights: flaring up against the dark. It was like a land seen from a plane at night, and after a moment, Luna realised that this is what it was: the leys and tracks and droves and ways between the worlds, with the gateways shining starbright at their crossroads. She could feel the web pulling at her, tugging her east.

She reached out a wing and felt someone touch it. Into her ear Ver March said, "Look at it! All spread out and visible, nice as you please. Just let it take us, lovey. And don't worry about the Hunt."

"But Ver," Luna said, for she could hear the horn sounding out behind them, the summoning call to hounds, "won't they follow us?"

"I think perhaps they're meant to."

STELLA

The Goose led them, running through the back ways of Southwark to the river. It was twilight now, with the lights coming on, but Christmas had been swept away while Stella, Ward and Ace sat in the Southwark Tavern: the city had taken down the local lights for Twelfth Night. But the cathedral still rose beyond the awnings of Borough Market, a soft gold in the winter drizzle, as the Thames churned gunmetal beneath the bridge.

The Goose was a spirit, a ghost; Stella could see the city through her fleetfooted form. She wore a white shift, with a headscarf covering her hair. She looked about thirteen but may have been older. But death was being kinder to her than life ever had. She grinned at Stella over her shoulder, full of excitement. Ward was hurrying to keep up.

"I bet Bill sent her," said Ace, nodding at the Goose. "Probably doesn't get out much."

"That's not very kind!"

"What? I mean it – some people never left their neighbourhoods back then and still don't. Trip north of the river's a big one for some."

"I know people who don't like going north of the river now. Or south, in the other way round," said Ward. "Might as well be a foreign land."

"There you go."

"Anyway, Ward," Stella remarked, "*You* weren't initially that keen."

"No. The National used to be the limit of my territory."

Ace smirked. "Chelsea boy."

"Yeah, I'll cop to that."

Stella paused to stare at Tower Bridge, visible upriver. The two halves of the bridge were rising, to let a ship through.

"That's supposed to be lucky," Ward said. "To see the bridge opening."

"It doesn't look very lucky," Ace told him.

The Goose, too, had stopped to stare. Apprehension was written all over her face and when Stella saw what was coming through the opening bridge, she could not blame the girl. There was a black ship coming down the Thames, its ragged sails cracking in the river wind. It flew dark pennants and it was coming fast, too swiftly for just an old

317

sailing ship. She had seen it before, gliding through a lost bridge as though the bridge had not been there. But now, she somehow knew, it really was coming up the river and this was no vision or dream. Stella looked away. She was standing by the statue of a dragon, rearing up above its red and white shield; its twin stood on the other side of London Bridge, marking the boundary of the City. The iron dragon turned its head and hissed when it saw the ship.

"You don't like it either," Stella said. It looked down at her and winked a crimson eye.

"Get going," Ace said, giving Stella a mild shove in the back. "I don't think we have a lot of time."

"Sorry."

The Goose had resumed her pace. Stella followed her over the bridge, darting between early evening revellers. Twelfth Night might be the traditional end of the Christmas period but Londoners seemed determined to make the most of it: the pubs were already spilling out onto the pavements despite the rain. She checked that Ace and Ward were following, then pursued the Goose off the bridge and down past the tall column of the Monument, gold-crowned testament to the Great Fire. For a moment, Stella thought she could smell burning; flame flickered in her sidelong view. But then they were out into the main thoroughfare.

The Goose turned and shouted something about candles.

"What did she say?" Stella asked Ace.

"Candelewrithstret. Candlewick Street. It's the old name for Cannon Street, she'll know it by that. Even though it didn't have buses running down it then. Hang on, wait a mo."

He paused in front of a thing like a fireplace, set into the outer wall of one of the big buildings.

"It's the London stone," said Stella, to Ward. She had read an article in the Metro about this: the foundation stone of the city, it had said, very ancient indeed, and in the last few years brought back here to Cannon Street.

Ward gave her a withering look.

"I know. Because it's got LONDON STONE carved over it. What's he doing?"

The Goose had crept back to watch. Ace held his hand a short distance from the stone's covering. His lips moved but he remained watchful. After a moment, he said, "All right. Come on."

"What did you do?" Stella asked.

"Just checking. It's awake. Things are happening."

"You don't say!"

Halfway down Cannon Street, the Goose dodged down a side road and Stella saw a large dark glass tower block looming above them.

Ward said, "What if we can't get in? These places are like fucking fortresses. Even if there's someone on reception, they'll have gone home by now."

"I'm counting on Ace and the Goose," Stella said.

"It's a bit late to say *I hope he knows what he's doing*. I certainly don't. I wonder where Anione is? She seems a bit more grounded, somehow."

"I'm wondering where the demon went. Look," Stella said.

The Goose had stopped in front of the black glass front of the building. As Stella watched, she reached out her hand and it rippled through the glass like water. Neatly, the Goose stepped through. Ward and Stella did not wait. They followed.

SERENA/STELLA

The woman in the golden dress stood in the opening of the cell. She was smiling, but it was an empty smile. Her face was mask-like. For a moment, Serena wondered if the woman even realised that she was there. Then the woman said,

"C'mon, love. Out you go."

"Who are you?" Serena asked softly. Wasn't there something about trying to befriend your captors? Making them see you as a person? But somehow she did not think this woman would care.

"It will be," the woman said, "a great and passing show."

"What will?"

"It always is."

From behind, Serena heard a tiny rattling flutter. The demon? It gave her a shred of hope. So she stepped through the opening, with as much dignity as she could muster, before the woman reached in and dragged her out. Serena thought that she would not have much trouble in doing so.

"Take off your coat."

"Why?"

The woman simply looked at her. Serena removed her coat.

"And your boots."

"How about my knickers?"

The woman ignored this. "You will not be able to run, in heels like those. And you will need to run."

This made Serena grow cold but she did as she was told. And the hateful woman was right about her boots. She could walk perfectly well in them, but not sprint. She would not let the woman take them – but the woman stalked ahead, her dress rustling like dry grass. Serena turned to see what was behind her in the passage – if the bitch wanted her to run, then run she would – but there was no tunnel, only a blank terracotta wall, inches from her face. Gritting her teeth, Serena went after the woman.

Around a bend, and Serena noticed that it was becoming very hot. She could smell smoke – oh Christ, please don't let the place be on fire. How would they get out? *You will not be able to run.* Was she about to be burned at the stake? *Witches in England were hanged*, said a voice at the back of Serena's mind.

She turned. The wall was right behind her. Perhaps this was just a nightmare, thought Serena, nothing more, and soon she must wake. With that thought came a rush of anger.

"Fuck you," Serena said, sweetly, to the woman, and strode past her.

"Down the stairs," Ace said. "There's a sign to the museum. Oh, there you are!"

The demon perched on the edge of a large, glossy reception desk, rocking to and fro. When it saw Ace, it stopped rocking and gave a melancholy caw.

"Well," said Ace. "Suggests we've come to the right place."

The demon turned its head to one side; Stella looked straight into its mercury eye. For a moment the world swung and she knew what it was like to have great power. But the demon was in invisible chains; she knew that now. Who had put them there, though? Bill, or someone else?

"You can't help. And you want to, don't you?"

The demon opened its beak and screamed. Stella clapped her hands to her head; it was as though she had entered a bell tower, with all the bells ringing. Then the demon opened its wings and shot away.

Serena found herself standing in the lecture theatre. But it was not a lecture theatre any more, no screen, no smooth pine seats. It was huge, a crescent of stone and there were people in rows, ledges running up into the shadows of the ceiling. She had seen some of them at the party, she thought – only a few days ago but it felt like centuries. Some wore gowns and ruffs and pearls, the great rustling dresses of Elizabeth's day, the men bright-eyed with swords at their sides, and one woman was seated, clad all in shimmering black with her pale face downcast. The man at her side was handsome but he smiled when he saw Serena and his smile was unkind.

And there, by God, was Miranda.

She stared directly at Serena, with malice. She alone wore more modern dress, a sharp tailored suit with a 1940s air. Her lips were red, her eyebrows painted dark arches. Serena gave her a cold look, but somehow Miranda's presence, a tangible enemy, cleared her head.

Everyone else was looking at her, even when Caspar Pharoah walked down the steps between the rows. He wore a gently reproving expression.

"Darling Serena," he said. "I'm so glad you're here."

Serena stared at him for a moment. She turned away. Then, at the end of the row, she saw someone who made her heart lift. Aldebaran, one of the Behenian stars, the Eye of the Bull, stood in the shadows in crimson and garnet. Serena looked quickly away, not wanting her face to betray the star, but when she glanced back, Aldebaran was no longer there. But the next person she saw, standing in torn clothes on the other side of the amphitheatre, was as unexpected as Miranda or the star, and at this sight, Serena gasped.

It was Ben.

"Shit," Ace said. "I can't open this fucking door." They had come downstairs now, into the warren of passages. The doors looked modern, but the tile above them, with its relief of a bull's horned head, was not.

"Can you hear anything in there?"

"No, but I can feel it. Magic. A lot of it."

The Goose clung to Ace's arm and her face was full of fear.

"It's all right," Ace said to her. "You're a dead 'n. Nothing's going to get *you.*"

But Stella wondered if he was right, at that. And behind the door, something roared.

When it charged into the amphitheatre, to a great cheer from the crowd, Serena could not for a moment take it in. It was enormous, surrounded by smoke. She glimpsed its muscled arms, the strong legs ending in a bull's cleft hooves, the over-developed shoulders and massive animal head. Horns gleamed ivory in the torchlight. It opened its mouth and roared. The sound almost brought her to her knees: it seemed to reverberate on many levels, all at the same time. Ben dropped to the floor and covered his ears. The crowd leaned forwards.

Caspar Pharoah whispered into her ear – yet he was several yards away – "They want to see a show, Serena. The old toll, the beautiful youths of a city, against the beast. Will you run or will you fight?"

How stupid, Serena thought. There was nowhere to go and she could not fight a man, let alone this great creature, this minotaur. The thing turned its head from side to side, and saw Ben. The musician's face was filled with horror; he looked years older than the breezy young man Serena had fallen in love with. The bull roared. Ben struggled to his feet. He brandished a sword, she saw, a thing shaped like a bronze leaf.

"Run, Serena!" he shouted. "Run!"

The thing lowered its head and charged. Its footsteps made the ground shake. Ben dodged and turned but the doors were fast shut. The thing slowed, stopped, its head went down, the wicked horns pointing.

"Fight, fight!" The crowd sounded like kids in a playground, Serena thought. She caught a glimpse of the baying audience from the corner of her eye and they were no longer fine ladies and gentlemen, but ragged things, wan-faced with stick-like limbs. Only the sorrowing woman in black remained the same, as did Miranda, who was standing, fists clenched with excitement. Ben rattled the doors to no avail.

"Fight! Fight!"

The thing pulled back its head and went forward in a rush. Ben swung the sword but the thing's huge fist knocked the weapon out of his hand. Ben threw himself to the side but Serena sprinted forwards. She pounded the thing's hairy spine. Its hide felt hard and hot. The audience roared approval.

"No! Serena!" She saw Ben's anguished face as he sprawled on the floor. The thing turned. It snorted in fury. Serena had a moment to be glad that, in fact, she was no longer wearing high heeled boots. She started to back away, shot a glimpse over her shoulder, panic rising inside. Her hand went to her throat, touched cold silver: Luna's hare. As if reminded, she felt herself begin to change. At first it was slow, a tingling in her ears, a shivering across her skin, and all of a sudden a rush. Serena found herself facing the minotaur's ankles, noting with a strange level of attention how human skin met bull's hoof. She was not a woman any longer, but a hare. And only then she ran.

The demon, now circling above them, screamed again.

"Fuck!" The noise level was unbearable, Stella thought, but it had one result: the doors blew open. Ace, followed by Ward, ran through. Stella went after them.

The room beyond, a sort of lecture theatre, was empty. Stella, glancing around, did the corner-of-the-eye trick by accident and saw a large number of people, standing in rows and staring at her with glittering hate.

"Ace!" she yelled.

"Seen 'em! After me!" He ran along the room and she could feel the suffocating weight of magic now, filling the theatre with heat. Ace vanished.

Serena ran the length of the lecture theatre. She could hear heavy footsteps pounding behind, hot breath on her animal neck. Unlike Ariadne, she had no thread to guide her through the labyrinth – and as soon as the word popped into her head, Serena was running through a maze.

The curving red-plastered walls fell away from her. She hastened around the bend, around and around, and then there was a gap, and she went through, zigzag jinking. But the maze led her on and now she could hear something coming fast behind, the beat of hooves on stone, the stormcloud breath and roar. For a moment she hung high above the labyrinth, seeing her hare-self race through the maze and the great man-bull charged behind, and Ben was there, too, with a sword as tiny as a pin, and she knew that this was what the spectators saw and craved, just some cruel old magical game, brought to these shores by the Romans, by soldiers who worshipped a bull-slaying god, who had brought it from the Cretan Greeks, who had brought it from Asia Minor.

But no one could slay the bull for her now.

Serena ran this way and that, still grateful, even in animal form, that she had removed her boots. Who knew where they were, or her coat. She could still find a sliver of indignation about that, in the midst of danger. She could hear someone shouting her name and she thought it must be Ben, but could not be sure. The beat of hooves grew louder and the place stank of blood and dung, just as it had in the street, when she had seen the demon, and the angel. Where was the demon? Where was Aldebaran, the Eye of the constellation of Taurus, the bull?

Serena came out into a circular space and her paws slipped on the floor. It was a byre, and she'd been in plenty of those in her time, if not as filthy. Scrambling, she ran across it but there was only one way in. And now the man-bull filled that entrance, head lowered, bison-huge. Serena held her breath. The horns glinted as the thing's head swayed from side to side. Its bare chest was striped with blood, the marks of a whip. Its wrists were red with the legacy of shackles. Serena felt a twitch inside her head and she stood as a human once more.

And behind it, Ace the magician was suddenly there.

"Get out of my way, Serena!" he shouted.

He threw a tangle of straps and bronze over the minotaur's head. The gleaming leather curled and clung. The minotaur gave a roar of fury and pain. It dropped to its knees, in front of Serena.

"Serena!" Ace cried again.

But Serena was not listening. For the first time since the battle had begun, she looked into the minotaur's eye.

Small, and bewildered, and afraid. An animal, hurt. But beyond that, she sensed something vast and anguished; neither a bull nor a man, but something else, immensely powerful and sorrowing and yoked. A god?

"Oh!" Serena said. Without thinking, she held out her hand. The minotaur took it: his hand was enormous, twice the size of a man's, but it held her own delicately in its hot fingertips. Serena closed her own fingers over them.

To face a monster.

"But you are not the monster, are you?" Serena said, furious. "Pharoah is the monster, but not you."

"Serena!" Stella's voice cried.

But the minotaur gazed up at her, trusting, and Serena heard a great sigh of disappointment from the audience. It caught her hair like a hot dry wind, stirring it, growing in volume until it caught Serena and the minotaur up and carried them whirling away.

"Well, that was interesting," Ace said.

"Where's Serena? *Where is she?*"

"I don't know, Ward. Chill out. I don't think she's in as much danger as she was, if that's any comfort."

"I saw Miranda. Out of the corner of my eye. She was in that audience."

"There's no one here," Stella said. They had made their way back to the amphitheatre, just a lecture theatre again now. The Goose went to the rows of seats, and without speaking, picked something up: a black lace handkerchief. She handed it to Stella. It was sopping wet.

"I don't think I want it, thanks!" But she took it gingerly, all the same.

"Something's there, though," Ace said. Stella heard a groan. With Ace behind her, she ran to the first row of seats and saw a curled body huddled beneath them.

"Shit. Are you all right?"

The figure raised its head. A great red bruise covered one side of its face. Its mouth dropped open.

"*Stella?*"

"Oh my God! Ben!" Then the room started to tremble. From below their feet came a rumble like distant thunder.

Serena sat on a garden seat, made of oak. The minotaur knelt at her feet. Around her, the smell of box and roses scented the air, summer-spice and sweet. Serena remembered another rose garden but this time everything was sharp, her senses not lulled and dulled, now that Caspar Pharoah was not here. She did not think that this place had much to do with Caspar Pharoah. She looked down with wonder at the back of the minotaur's head, the coarse black fur, the scabbed spine.

"I'm so sorry," Serena said. She patted the head, like a large dog. "What have they done to you?"

"You have ruined the game," said a voice. Serena looked up. The woman in the bronze dress stood before her, eyes sparking blue fire. "This is not how it is supposed to go. The toll must be paid!"

"I suppose you wanted a bullfight," Serena said, with contempt. "They're illegal here, you know. Though not yet in Spain. I signed a petition once. Vegetarian. We're often inconvenient."

"Well, it isn't too late!" the woman said. She reached out a hand and Serena felt it touch her heart and squeeze. Her vision swam black-red and the minotaur raised its suffering head and roared again. Serena was suffocating in the scent of roses and blood.

"Stand up, Serena," Caspar Pharoah's voice said.

Serena looked up, struggling for breath. Her vision throbbed but the handsome, debonair business man was gone. Caspar Pharoah's skin showed the yellow-green of leprosy. His eyes burned black and the matted pale mane of his hair spilled over the tattered cloak that covered his shoulders. He did not look remotely human; something wearing a man's skin. "Let's see some fun."

"No," Serena whispered. The minotaur roared, but Pharoah did not flinch.

"Some fun," the fire-haired woman hissed.

But the world thumped like a drum.

"*Enough!*" cried a voice.

The woman gave a gasp of fury but Serena was able to breathe again. Panting, she turned and saw her persecutor's twin, wearing a rather grubby dressing gown and slippers and in the process of removing a cigarette from her mouth. But behind her stood Aldebaran, smiling and rather faint, a star in daylight.

"Dearie me, Niobis. Can't take you anywhere, can't leave you at home."

"Who are you?" Serena cried.

"You're Stella's sister, aren't you? We've not met. My name's Anione. This is *my* little sister. Unfortunately."

Niobis hissed like a cat.

"Look, Serena," the newcomer, Anione, said, "It would be lovely to have a chat and we will, but for the minute, I've got family business to attend to. See you down the pub, maybe."

"The pub?" echoed Serena, but it was too late. The newcomer extended a red-nailed hand. A ball of gold clung to it, and it grew and grew until everything shivered with light and the woman in the bronze dress gave a great cry of rage and despair. Then there was no woman, only a great cat with a speckled coat.

It struck out at Serena, but the minotaur was in the way. Serena snatched at its bridle; it burned her fingers but she clenched her teeth and held it tightly. Anione raised a hand and again it held a golden ball: light fell from it and grew and grew, encompassing the cat. Anione spoke a word that made the light flare up like fire and engulf the screaming cat.

The minotaur jerked its great bull's head and the bridle came free. It clattered to the flagstones as Niobis and Anione disappeared and the bull's head, liberated from its constraints, swung around. Caspar Pharoah lunged for the bridle but he was not quick enough. The bull's horn caught him across the throat. There was a fountain of foul-smelling lemony blood and Pharoah crumpled. Serena watched in horror as his body changed, back to the urbane businessman she had known, then to another form in a mailed tunic, a kind of armour she did not recognise, with a face distorted by hate. There were others. Then these, too, were gone. The form of Pharoah dwindled, shrinking, until only a tiny pallid twig remained on the ground, like a twisted bone. Serena and the minotaur were alone in the knot garden, with Aldebaran by their side.

Bee and Alys and Dark held vigil around Caro Amberley's bedside. Beyond the house, the flood waters glistened in the light of the rising moon. Bee felt as though the house was a ship, riding on a swelling tide, and despite what her mother had said she could not help feeling that the waters might rise further yet and sweep the house away.

Caro herself lay rigid, on her back. She reminded Bee of a crusader's wife on a tomb: her patrician profile was marble pale and she barely breathed. Once, she said, very faintly,

"The star. That's good."

"Which star, Caro?"

But she did not reply. Then, a moment later, her eyes snapped open. She did not look at anyone clustered around the bed; her gaze was turned inwards, as though she watched some internal screen. She gasped.

Slowly, Bee became aware of a smell. It was rusty and foul, seeping into the room from somewhere beyond. Iron and shit, thought Bee: the odour she had encountered during her vision in the bedroom at Amberley. It grew in strength, until she gagged and coughed. Dark's face was troubled and he reached for her hand. Alys' gaze was fixed on Caro's face like a hunting hawk.

Bee's sight began to redden. The bedroom grew dim: it was like seeing everything through a filter, with occasional sparkles of light that reminded her of a visual migraine. All red, everything red, and a great many presences, watching and malign. Then Caro cried out and fell still.

Stella and Ward, dragging Ben between them, and Ace, had made it into the street. The Goose had lingered, for what purpose Stella did not know, but now she was here and they were running.

"Hang on, hang on." Ace bent forwards, wheezing, and gripped his knees. "Christ, I really should pack in the fags."

"I don't think it's actually coming down," said Ward. Stella looked back, to where Caspar Pharoah's black tower was shimmering in the street lights. "Just sounded like it was."

"No, it's doing a Hex Heath," Stella said. "Look."

They watched as the black glass tower began to ripple and change. Like streetlight reflected in water, the tower shivered and shimmered and in a few minutes Everlight Holdings was gone. A little old house stood in its place: Elizabethan, half-timbered and tumbledown, incongruous between the tower blocks.

"Scuse me, love." A young man shouldered Stella out of the way. Then he looked again. "Is your mate all right?"

Stella, still holding up Ben, said, "Bit too much to drink at lunchtime."

The young man laughed. "Been there, done that." Then he went on his way, impervious to the recent changes along the street. Other passers -by, Stella noted, seemed to have noticed nothing.

"That's a shift," Ace said. "Whoever Pharoah is, that wasn't half a big effort, glamour-wise."

"He had a lot of power," Ben croaked. Ace looked at him.

"If ever I saw a man who needed a drink…"

LUNA

There was a star over Luna's shoulder. It hung, fat and yellow as a tallow candle in the heavens, towards the south west. She knew it for Arcturus, and that was her star, her Behenian star. It was good to see her there in the sky, even though Luna was being pulled east. They had been flying for some time now, over the estuary of the Severn and Avon and Wiltshire and beyond, flying from winter into summer. Luna was wren still and Ver March had the soft brown feathers of a female blackbird, and the bright gentle eyes.

"You can smell it down there," Ver said. Luna was very glad she was there. "Meadowsweet and cowslip. The year's turned, won't be so long until spring comes. I think all this rain might stop now."

"The sky's lightening," Luna said, faltering through a thermal. "Are they coming after us?"

"Let's have a look, shall we?" Ver flew down to the top of an oak, perching on the bare twigs. The tree itself was not so high, yet from it Luna and Sam's nan could see the whole south of England: Stonehenge tiny as a child's school project, the rolling downs of White Horse Country, the little hummock of Glastonbury Tor, all the way to the shining seas in south and west. "Yes. They've picked up the scent. Here come the Lily White Boys and not all-alone o, either."

And Luna could see, very far away, the throng of dogs and deer and men and more. The pinecone at the end of the staff held by the pack leader, the Heath-Stalker, Aln had called him, burned bright.

"Why me, though, Ver? They're after me, aren't they? That hound, he looked at me like I was prey," said Luna.

"Why, yes, they are after you. You'd think your mum would've had a word – but that's a conversation for another time. It's now that they hunt the wren, between St Stephen's Day, that's Boxing Day, and Twelfth Night."

"But if they catch me…"

"They won't. It's almost too late. Twelfth Night's nearly passed. But we need to get going. You're about to lead them a merry dance, Luna. I don't know why or what's at the end of it but I feel it in my bones."

But Luna thought she knew. Far ahead, among the stars, a silver hare was dancing. She had given Serena the hare necklace, at Christmas, and Serena had given her the bronze wren. Now the hare was tugging her onwards.

The eastern sky was growing lighter now. Luna could see the city ahead in the distance, the smoke from London fireplaces, and they flew over the bend of a river, quite wide: the Thames.

"Dawn's coming. Look. There's a house down there."

"So is my sister!" For the hare was dancing still and she could feel Serena's presence, down there in the unknown house, and Arcturus was whispering in her ear, telling her to fly down to it. She gave a wren's chattering alarm call.

By the time they reached the house, in no more than a snippet of time, dawn was almost there. The sun rolled up towards the curve of the world; the stars were fading.

"Serena!" Luna cried.

"Luna! Is that you?"

Luna could see her sister shading her eyes with her hand, the banner of pale blonde hair. The tiny figure of the hare winked once at her throat. Then, as she and Ver alighted on the back of a bench, she saw the bull. No, not a bull. A bull's horned head but the body of a man. A minotaur.

Luna shuddered into her human shape and a moment later Ver stood beside her, in her old brown skirt and boots.

"Serena?"

"He won't hurt you," Serena said. She had her hand on the nape of the thing's neck. And from far away, up the hill, Luna heard the sound of a horn.

"Oh no! Serena, it's the Hunt. They've been hunting me. We have to go."

But the bull, the minotaur, had heard the horn as well. His great head turned.

"Come," Aldebaran said. She took Luna and Serena by the hand. Ver March followed. The star drew them under a fall of roses, an archway close to the house, away from the knot garden, just as the sun came up.

So Luna and Serena and Ver were able to see as the hunt swept through, with the white red-eared racing hounds and the antlered man who led them, the motley in their wake and one masked rider whose head, perhaps, turned fractionally in their direction as a big bay horse

331

leaped the low hedges of the knot garden, scattering rose petals in all directions. The minotaur rose to his feet as they came, to stand tall in the centre of the low maze. He did not turn and flee, but waited until the Hunt had flown almost by, the hounds, the horses, the hunters and the deer, and others, too, foot followers. A horned and golden-eyed boy. A running girl who left a trail of white flowers behind her, fading into the grass. Then the minotaur turned and ran with them, faster and free, until the whole pack had passed the garden by and out of sight and taken the man-bull with them.

"Oh," said Serena, after a moment. "I hope he's going to be all right."

Ver March said, "I shouldn't worry, lovey. Wild things like that find their place in the end. And it's not with men. Humans, I should say. Mustn't be discriminatory these days. He'll be all right, I'm sure. They came for one and they found another."

Luna clasped her sister's hand.

"Are *you* all right?"

"I – I think so," Serena said. But she was still staring after the minotaur.

STELLA

"The Star and Garter," Ward said. "That's an old name."

They had found a table in the back of the pub, which was a long building not far from Cannon Street.

"Ben." His cousin clapped him on the shoulder. "What are you drinking?"

Ben Amberley managed a grimace, not quite a smile. "A big bottle of mineral water. Thanks. I haven't had enough water since… And maybe a large brandy. A really enormous brandy, actually, and a coffee as well if that's okay. And can I have some crisps? I haven't got any money."

"No problem." Ward disappeared in the direction of the bar.

Stella looked at Ben. "What the fuck happened to you?"

"I don't know. Not really. After Dana and I split up – did we split up? I can't remember."

"Fairy led," Ace said. "Characteristic case."

"You didn't split up. Dana died. You told everyone that you and Serena split up."

"Did I? Did we?"

"God, this is going to be an uphill struggle."

"Take it easy, Stella. It's not his fault."

"I just can't remember." Ben put his head in his hands and rubbed his forehead. His hair was dusty. He looked like a vagrant. "I went out of the house. I remember locking the door. Someone had rung me, some while ago – before Christmas, I think? Said he wanted to talk to me about a solo gig, up in Norfolk, for a big birthday party. I think I mentioned it to the guys. I don't know… Dana kept saying I ought to do more solo work."

Ace grunted. "Separate him from his mates. That's typical, too."

"It's not unusual for people to hire celebrities, though. Ben, do you remember speaking to your cleaner? Telling her you were taking some time out?"

He looked completely blank. "No – oh my God, what about the cats?"

"The cats are fine, Ben. About this gig?"

"Anyway, yeah, the money was fantastic. I went up there by train and the guy picked me up at the station in this beautiful car, think it was an Aston Martin. He seemed very pleasant. Obviously rich."

"Do you remember his name, Ben? Or the name of the station?"

"Swaffham? The station, that is. Something '-pham,' anyway. The guy's name was Cas. I think I did the gig. It was a really weird party. All these people, very glamorous, but I looked at the inside of the house once and it seemed – I don't know, a bit derelict. The guy said he'd inherited the place from some relatives, said they'd just died and the place needed a bit of work." He took a long swallow of the water that Ward, by now, had procured for him. "He wasn't wrong. When I'd done the gig the bloke, Cas, the one who'd hired me, he was in sort of shimmery golden clothes, gave me this drink. It was really nice stuff, some sort of wine, but it was like honey, too… I don't remember much after that. Just some place, which was all red, and always hot. There was a woman there, too. She –" He gave a convulsive shudder. "I don't – oh, Jesus! It's her!"

He was staring with horror at the entrance to the bar. "Her," he said, in a whisper.

"No, mate, you're all right," Ace told him, kindly. "It's not her. That's my friend Anione."

"Oh," said Ben, as he took in the fact that Anione was wearing a fake leopardskin coat and tight pvc leggings. "Sorry, I'm…"

"Easy mistake to make," Anione said, soothingly. She had evidently heard the last part of the conversation. "That would have been my little sister. Looks a bit like me, but she's not here, and she won't be coming, either."

Ace raised an eyebrow. "That so?"

"Oh yes. She's not best pleased right now, mind you. And your mum's been going spare about you," Anione said reprovingly to Ben, "From what I hear."

"Oh Christ! I ought to call home." His voice was sounding stronger now, probably a result of the brandy, Stella thought. "What's the *date*? How long have I –?"

"It's January the fifth. Sorry, Ben, you've missed Christmas."

"You can use my phone," Ward said. "Go into the street, reception in here's not what it might be."

When Ben, still dazed, had gone outside, Ward added, "So where's Serena, Anione? Do you know?"

"Yes. She's quite safe, don't worry. I came to tell you. She's just sorting out some – things. She's with one of the stars and they're waiting for your sister Luna, the star told me. They'll be back tomorrow morning."

"Thank you!"

Stella said to Ace, "You said: fairy led. Is that what Pharoah was? What Dana and Tam were?"

"In a manner of speaking. I'm not talking twee little winged girlies, though. Or Tolkien-y elves. Old country types used to call them the People, which is a bit ironic, really, because they aren't."

"What, you mean they aren't human?"

"No, I mean they aren't people. Not like you and me. Well, not like me, anyway. They look like us, when they want to, but they don't breed like us and they're – it's like their clothes. You see them in all this designer-type stuff, cloth of gold and velvet and that, but when you look out of the side of your eye they're dressed in rags. They're like that themselves. They're all scraps and patches, bits of greed and lust and envy and spite. And some good things too, sometimes. But not often. They're not supposed to have souls in the old folklore and I think that's actually right. They're hollow and they know it. They're shells and they're constantly trying to fill the lack."

"So, Ace," said Ward. He did not look comfortable. "They're not human, I get that. But there's some weird stuff in my family, too. And Stella's. What does that make us, then?"

"You're both human. So is Ben. But you have a vein of magic running through your ancestry. Someone or something who's given you a bit extra. The spirit of a star, perhaps."

"And you, Ace? What are you?"

"Me? I'm just human. I am a magician, though. I paid for what I have; I didn't inherit it. I didn't come by it naturally." There was no envy in his tone, or bitterness. Perhaps there might have been once, Stella thought, but Ace simply sounded a bit weary.

"What about you?" Ward said to Anione.

"Er, well. Bang to rights, I'm afraid. I was human at one point, though. Long time ago. If that counts."

Ward gave her a long stare. "Right."

"I saw you in your real form once, didn't I?" Stella said. Anione laughed.

"This is my real form, love. But it's probably more accurate to say that it's my real form *as well.*"

"If the lad's back now, safe and sound, where does that leave you?" Ace said to Ward. "I mean, on a personal basis."

"That's up to Serena."

"I see."

"So what about your sister?" Stella was still bursting with questions. Relationships could wait.

Anione said, "That giant cat you saw... I didn't realise she was involved with this until very recently. Otherwise I'd have taken steps."

"Ah."

"She was hanging out with Pharoah, apparently, and I'm assuming she tore up your sister's collection, probably on his instructions, so Serena would be grateful and more willing to get involved with him when Pharoah made her an offer of financial support. If she'd taken the money – well. It all turns to leaves and dust in the end."

"Couldn't he just have *made* her do stuff?"

"Possibly, I don't know. She'll have a bit of magic of her own, you see, and from what you've said, she and her daughter already dispatched one enemy, so perhaps Pharoah was wary. I'm assuming he's kin to the boy and girl you dealt with. Also, if someone's will is freely given it's more powerful. I don't know what Pharoah hoped to gain with his toll, by giving Serena and Ben to the minotaur, but I expect it had to do with some kind of power."

"There are sides, are there?" Ward was frowning. "Enemies and allies?"

"Yes. But it's all very fragmentary. I don't know half of what's going on," Ace said. "Honestly. Some people might be quite friendly with me, but hate each other. The Hunt, now – they're not necessarily mates with anyone. They might help you, or they might hinder, or they might harm, and you won't know which from one day to the next. This is why I have a few very close connections and I keep my cards close to my chest."

At this point Ben returned, looking happier.

"I've phoned my dad. He's obviously very relieved. He says Mum's at Mooncote – your mother and sister are taking care of her. Said she's been ill, but he's going to tell her. I didn't think I was gone for so long… God." He collapsed into a chair. He looked slightly better, Stella thought. "I'm catching the train down there tomorrow. I don't know when I'll be back in town. I phoned the band, as well. I told them I'd been in rehab and the doctor had taken my phone off me."

"And how did they take that?"

"They were a bit pissed off. Not unreasonably. But relieved, as well."

"You look cream crackered, love," Anione said.

"I ought to go home, get some sleep."

"I think," Ward said, very firmly, "that for various reasons, Ben, you ought to sleep at my place tonight."

SERENA

Serena greeted the familiar sight of her own street with a gasp of relief.

"What a lovely place," Ver March said. "I do love these old London mews, you know."

Serena was trying to hang onto the memory of the garden, but it was fading, leaving only a faint impression behind, like a dream at the first light of day. Aldebaran had sent them home, with no more than a word and the motion of her hand. The sky was quite light and the traffic was streaming past on the main road. Serena's phone told her that it was just before eleven in the morning. She ought to ring Bella, and then Ward, and then Bee.

"Luna and Ver are staying here tonight," Serena told her sister. "Luna's just rung Sam, who's on his way back to Somerset from – where was it?"

"Chepstow. It's been a long couple of days, that's for sure." Ver March sank into a kitchen chair.

"Do you want some tea?"

"Yes, thank you, that would be lovely."

"I'll make some, then. And before I pop out I'll make sure there's some food in the fridge. Bella's coming back this afternoon."

"Why, where are you going?"

Serena smiled. "Only to the end of the road. The Lion and Unicorn. It's past eleven now and it's just opened, Ward says. You could join us for lunch, actually?"

"That would be delightful," Ver said, "But you have your moment first. Luna and I will have our tea."

When she opened the door of the pub, Ward was sitting on the nearest table. He jumped up when he saw her and gave her a big, unBritish hug.

"Thank God, Serena. Or maybe not God. I've left Ben in the spare bedroom, crashed out. He'd better be there when I get back, is all I can say. He's catching a train to Somerset this afternoon."

"He nearly died. Caspar Pharoah is dead, I think. I hope. I'm so pleased Ben's all right."

Ward held her at arm's length and looked at her. "How pleased are you?"

"Really pleased. But, not as pleased as I am to see you."

"One council tax's worth of pleased?"

"You could easily rent your flat. It's a superb location."

He nodded. "Easily."

"Although it would mean not having access to that roof garden any more."

"Serena!"

She beamed at him. "I think it's my round."

BEE

Serena had called from London, to say Luna and Ver were there with her and everything was well. Sam was on his way home. And Ben was alive. He had rung his father, who had called Bee and Alys. Bee felt herself washed with relief. All present and, hopefully, correct.

She went upstairs and made her way quietly along the landing. She opened the door to her mother's room, which still lay in curtain-closed shadow, and went inside. The room smelled of perfume and incense, much as it always had. By the light from the open door she could see Caro's face, half turned into the pillow. Caro looked herself again; Bee thought that the dreams had fled from her now, the dread of her son's slaying no longer haunting her, even though Caro had not known what the threat might be. And Ben was coming home today: that would be something wonderful for Caro to wake up to.

Bee left the sleeping woman in peace and went downstairs to let the dogs out. Usually it was the spaniels who went haring off into the distance; the more sensible Moth remaining on the step for a moment. But this time it was the lurcher who raced away, barking in excitement. Bee slid her feet into her trusty Wellingtons, and followed him down the drive.

The flood waters had stopped at the end of the drive. Bee stopped too, with the dogs by her side, and waited until a small round boat appeared, swirling along on the floor, seemingly under its own power. In it sat Sam and Aln.

Sam beamed when he saw Bee and Moth was beside himself. He charged into the water, scattering droplets everywhere.

"No, Moth, no! Not into the boat!"

But Aln was laughing. "Goodbye, Sam! Bee, thank you for all you have done. I'm sure we'll meet again. Goodbye!" She spoke accented English, but it became more difficult to understand, as the words went on.

"Goodbye, Aln!" Bee cried, waving. The girl's skin was flushed a deeper shade of green in the wan dawn light, she thought. "Where are you going?"

"To find... my brother," was what Bee thought she said. She produced an oar as Sam waded to drier ground, then spun the coracle around. Bee watched as the light took her, as the boat faded into mist and so did Aln, back to her own journey and her own story.

"Good luck!" Bee cried, "Good luck!" To Sam, she said, "Luna and your gran are with Serena."

"I know – I've spoken to her."

"Good! I'll ring Serena again in a bit. In the meantime, this is no season for wet feet. There are dry socks on the radiator. I'll put some breakfast on."

"That," said Sam, "would be most acceptable. Although believe it or not, despite everything, I did have a proper supper last night. At a pub in Chepstow. With a bunch of Morris dancers."

"How remarkably ordinary."

Sam sighed. "Long may 'ordinary' last."

STELLA

A week past Twelfth Night, Stella was walking through Southwark, on her way for a drink with Ace. It was mid-afternoon and the sky was leaden and overcast, although it had finally stopped raining. She had been south of the river to speak to someone about a gig, and had got off the tube at the Elephant and Castle. As she came out onto the street, she looked up and there was Mags, perched on the top of a corrugated iron fence, in human form.

"Oh, hello!"

"Hello." Mags slid down to join her. "All sorts of buzz around the town, about what you've been up to. Everyone's excited. Lots of changes going on."

"I bet there has. Your tip about Crossbones was pretty epic, though. I've met all manner of people through you. Or through Bill. I'm assuming he's, like, the mastermind behind a lot of this?"

Mags smiled at her. Her eyes were kind.

"And you met the geese," she said.

"Yes, I met the geese. Though I don't know what part they play."

"The geese try to look after this city," Mags said. "Which is good of them, really, since it didn't do much to look after *them* when they were alive."

"Maybe that's why."

"Yeah, maybe it is." She looked past Stella and smiled. "Oh."

"What?" Stella asked, following her gaze. There was a hoarding opposite the Tube, an advertisement for something at the Cuming Museum. EXHIBITION, it pronounced. A HISTORY OF MYSTICAL ART IN LONDON. Stella stared, then stared some more. She recognised one of the faces in particular: she'd last seen that self-portrait in a friend's house. But this one was a little older, a little rougher: the face stared pugnaciously back at her, wild haired and raddled. Still familiar, though. She stepped closer for a look at the dates: "Austin Osman Spare, 1886-1956. *The works of occult painter AOS are exhibited at the Cuming from...*"

"AOS," Stella mouthed. She'd never heard of him. But it was unmistakable. Another of the faces was familiar, too: she had last seen the firm jaw and slightly protuberant eyes above the rest of him, stark naked in a summer house. On the poster, however, he wore a frock coat and a high stock at the neck. The painting on the poster was very famous indeed: the bearded God, hair streaming, reaching down to the world with his compasses.

"Oh." Stella said, echoing the angel. "Oh." She turned to find Mags at her elbow.

"What's brilliant about this city," the angel said, "is how many people choose to stay on to help."

"But William Blake died – it must have been what, the eighteen hundreds…"

"Well, he might have said he did." Mags gave her little hop. "Nice to meet you again, Stella. See you around!" And she was gone.

She would, Stella thought, have a few things to say to Ace when she saw him in the pub.

343

About the Author

Liz Williams is a science fiction and fantasy writer living in Glastonbury, England, where she is co-director of a witchcraft supply business. She has been published by Bantam Spectra (US) and Tor Macmillan (UK), also Night Shade Press, and appears regularly in *Asimov's* and other magazines. She has been involved with the Milford SF Writers' Workshop for 20 years, and also teaches creative writing at a local college for Further Education.

Her previous novels are:: *The Ghost Sister* (Bantam Spectra), *Empire Of Bones, The Poison Master, Nine Layers Of Sky, Banner Of Souls* (Bantam Spectra – US, Tor Macmillan – UK), *Darkland, Bloodmind* (Tor Macmillan UK), *Snake Agent, The Demon And The City, Precious Dragon, The Shadow Pavilion* (Night Shade Press) *Winterstrike* (Tor Macmillan), *The Iron Khan* (Morrigan Press) and *Worldsoul* (Prime). The Chen series is currently being published by Open Road.

Comet Weather was published by New Con Press in 2020.

A non-fiction book on the history of British paganism, *Miracles Of Our Own Making*, was published by Reaktion Books in 2020.

Her first short story collection *The Banquet Of The Lords Of Night* was also published by Night Shade Press, and her second and third, *A Glass Of Shadow* and *The Light Warden*, are published by New Con Press as is her recent novella, *Phosphorus*.

The *Diaries if a Witchcraft Shop* (volumes 1 and 2) are also published by New Con Press.

Her novel *Banner Of Souls* was shortlisted for the Philip K Dick Memorial Award, as were three previous novels, and the Arthur C Clarke Award.

ALSO FROM NEWCON PRESS

Liz Williams – Comet Weather

A tale of four fey sisters, set in modern day London and rural Somerset, that will rekindle your sense of wonder. The Fallow sisters, scattered like the four winds but now, with the comet due, drawn back together by their desire to find their mother, who disappeared a year ago. They have help, of course, from the star spirits and the no-longer-living, but such advice tends to be cryptic and is hardly the most dependable of guides.

Ken MacLeod – Selkie Summer

Set on the Isle of Skye, Ken MacLeod's *Selkie Summer* is a rich contemporary fantasy steeped in Celtic lore, nuclear submarines and secrets. Seeking to escape Glasgow, student Siobhan Ross takes a holiday job on Skye, only to find herself the focus of unwanted attention, unwittingly embroiled in political intrigue and the shifting landscape of international alliances. At its heart, *Selkie Summer* is a love story: passionate, unconventional, and totally enchanting.

Best of British Fantasy 2019

Editor Jared Shurin has compiled a volume featuring the very best work published by British and British-based authors in 2019, producing as diverse and surprising a set of stories as you are likely to find anywhere. Full of wonder, wit, delight and malevolence. These stories range from traditional to contemporary fantasy, written by a mix of established authors and new voices, combining to provide a veritable potpourri of the fantastical.

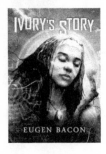

Ivory's Story – Eugen Bacon

In the streets of Sydney a killer stalks the night, slaughtering and mutilating innocents. The victims seem unconnected, yet Investigating Officer Ivory Tembo is convinced the killings are sar from random. The case soon leads Ivory into places she never imagined. In order to stop the killings and save the life of the man she loves, she must reach deep into her past, uncover secrets of her heritage, break a demon's curse, and somehow unify two worlds.

CPSIA information can be obtained
at www.ICGtesting.com
Printed in the USA
LVHW031009190121
676855LV00003B/59

9 781912 950799